The Family Angel

LORETTA GIACOLETTO

Copyright © 2001 Loretta Giacoletto, *Legacy of an Immigrant*
Second Copyright © 2011 Loretta Giacoletto, *The Family Angel*

Cover design by Diane Giacoletto Lambert
Photograph by selimaksan, iStockphoto
All rights reserved.

ISBN-10:1480132268
ISBN-13: 978-1480132269
LCC No: 2012919801

DEDICATION

To Dominic

Works by Loretta Giacoletto
In print or digital

SAGAS
Family Deceptions
The Family Angel
Chicago's Headmistress

CONTEMPORARY
Free Danner
Lethal Play

SHORT STORIES
A Collection of Givers and Takers
Youthanasia

COMING SOON
Fiction
Italy to Die for

Non-Fiction
A Bit of Garlic between Friends

As an added bonus at the end of this novel
Check out the opening chapters of
Chicago's Headmistress

www.lorettagiacoletto.com

TABLE OF CONTENTS

Book One 1
Book Two 137
Book Three ... 205
Book Four ... 248
Added Bonus ... 361

A NOTE FROM THE AUTHOR

My thanks to Joseph Bertot for his recollections on harvesting grapes and making wine; to the late James Stinnett, dedicated miner and storyteller; to John and Eva Dunn regarding life in Mississippi; to the late Stephen E. Ambrose for his account of the Normandy Invasion in *Citizen Soldier*; to Thomas Reese, S.J., author of *Inside the Vatican: The Politics and Organization of the Catholic Church*; to Melvin G. Holli and Peter d'A. Jones, editors of *Ethnic Chicago: A Multicultural Portrait;* to The National Coal Museum in West Frankfort, Illinois and its underground mine tour that has since closed; to the Chicago History Museum for information on Chicago during the Prohibition Era; to beta reader Steven Giacoletto who envisioned WOC, the fictional Western Orthodox Catholic Church; to beta reader Paul Giacoletto for his input on the devious Milo Frederico; to Bonnie Turner for her proofreading and editorial suggestions; to beta reader, proofreader, and marketing consultant Diane Giacoletto Lambert; and to my husband Dominic Giacoletto for his recollections on farm life and harvesting grapes plus his continuing patience and unwavering support.

BOOK ONE

Chapter 1
Chicago 1925

"Another day, another dollar," the young Italian with precision sideburns mumbled to himself. "Another day ... another lesson." Or not, depending on his mood and if he felt like going to Night School after supper.

What Carlo Baggio needed now was a drink—his kind, not the illegal beer he'd been loading into crates all day at Becker's Brewery. Or the near beer the brewery produced as a front for its more lucrative ventures. After flipping the last of his cigarillo into the gutter, Carlo ran one hand through his dark, slicked-back hair and stepped into a Southside saloon geared to immigrants and native Chicagoans who came for the cheap liquor and decent food. He exchanged nods with two regulars, slid onto a barstool, and raised his forefinger to Vincenzo Valenza, a man cursed with a large hooked nose and the scars of adolescent acne.

"Ah-h, *paesano, uno momento!*" the bartender and co-proprietor of Fabiola's called out. While Vincenzo drew five beers and poured as many grappas, Carlo drummed his fingers and sucked in the hazy air thick with tobacco smoke married to the aromas of beer, wine, tomato sauce, salami, garlic, and cheeses. When Vincenzo finally got around to Carlo, he wiped a wet ring from the golden oak bar, filled a teacup with wine, and served it with an unctuous smile. "*Vino rosa,* paesano, from my private stock."

Carlo laid down thirty-five cents. Holding the cup to his nose, he took in the full-bodied bouquet to conjure up memories of Pont Canavese, his village in the foothills of the Italian Alps. Only after this savoring ritual did he allow himself to pleasure the wine, even before water his drink of choice. He spoke in halting English that had improved considerably since his two years in America. "So, about this sister you got back in Locana."

"Ah-h, you mean *bella Luigia.*" Vincenzo cupped a handful of fingertips to his puckered lips and smacked a kiss. "As God is my witness, she has the temperament of an angel."

Carlo took more wine and waited for the next words to roll from Vincenzo's tongue.

"Look, Carlo, you want an Italian bride, a quiet one who will give you many sons? This, I can do for you."

"But can she cook?"

"Wait 'til you taste her rabbit and polenta," Vincenzo said as he started back down the bar.

Polenta, sweet Mother of Jesus. Carlo salivated at the mention of peasant food fit for kings. In Carlo's Italy, life had moved slower, on less money. But after his parents died, Carlo and his younger brother wanted a different life, one that didn't require never-ending work just to survive. While still in their teens they sold the family home to finance a new beginning in America.

Vincenzo had only covered half the bar length before he came back to Carlo. He leaned across the glistening wood and spoke through breath reeking of garlic. "Listen, paesano, with my sister the Baggio name will live on, long after you have turned to dust. Our ma bore seven sons, four who lived and three under the ground, and only one girl, the lastborn. Louisa took care of Ma 'til the day she died."

"A nursemaid I don't need."

"Maybe not today but think about *domani.*"

Carlo checked his pocket watch. He drained the last of the wine from his glass.

Vincenzo poured more and held up his palm when Carlo attempted to pay. "You know, Carlo, bringing relation over ain't so easy. Not like before the Great War."

"Me and Giacomo made it here."

"Consider yourselves lucky. There are those who say America has too many Italians."

"So who's counting?"

"Immigration." Vincenzo smiled like a dog with a fresh bone. "All you have to pay is my sister's passage plus a little extra." He rolled his eyes, opened his palms to the ceiling. "Paesano, for our trouble, be reasonable. Massimo and me, we make all the arrangements."

Inwardly, Carlo bristled at Vincenzo's reference to Massimo, the older brother and saloon partner, a hard-nosed *padrone* known for exploiting Italian immigrants in need of employment and housing.

Carlo felt a pointy elbow jabbing his ribcage. Without looking to his right, he returned the gesture.

"Ah-h, another Baggio blesses our humble saloon with his presence," Vincenzo said, pouring a second teacup, also his best, for Carlo's brother, Giacomo.

Both young men were slight in stature, with chiseled profiles and dark hair; but Carlo's was poker straight, his eyes as round as chocolate malt balls. Cowlicks ruled Giacomo's wavy hair; amber drops floated in slate eyes too vain for glasses. The brothers wore their clothes with the confidence of window mannequins although a trained eye could distinguish the hand tailoring of Carlo's suit from Giacomo's off-the-rack version.

Giacomo waited until the bartender left before he spoke. "Vincenzo still pushing to bring the sister over?"

Carlo shrugged. "I hear she cooks pretty good."

Giacomo shifted his eyes in Vincenzo's direction. "But does she take after the two *brutes*?"

"Only if God played a cruel joke on their mama."

"Just remember: with the Valenzas you pay and then you pay some more, whether the deal works out or gets flushed down the drain. Same goes for a wife, so pick one who's already here. In the long run she'll be a helluva lot cheaper. And if you're lucky, less trouble."

"Sh-h," Carlo mumbled, "not so loud."

"People are gonna find out—from the Valenzas 'cause that's the way they are. Let the ugly bastards pay to bring their own sister over, just like everybody else. Knowing them, they'll probably want you to kick in extra just for marrying into their family."

Carlo's discussion with Giacomo came to a quick end with the arrival of Hildie Kramer. The brewmeister's daughter slipped her arm through Giacomo's in a way that Giacomo ignored and Carlo resented.

"You know I can't sit here, Honey Bun, not on a stool like some common barfly." Hildie pursed her lips into a pout. "Besides, I am positively starving."

"You two go ahead and eat," Carlo said. "I'm not that hungry."

Hildie exchanged the pout for a smile. "Well, if you insist—"

"No way," his brother said. "We'll eat together, just like we do every night."

After getting their teacups refilled, and a root beer for Hildie, the threesome decided on a table near the blackboard menu and sat down. Giacomo moved his chair closer to Hildie's. He rubbed his leg against hers and squeezed her plump thigh. Hildie's blonde bob bounced with the lift of her head. She bunny wiggled her nose and cut through the air with the wave of her pudgy hand.

"Goodness gracious," she said, "how can you tolerate this putrid smell?"

"It sure as hell beats that of cabbage," Carlo said.

She shifted her round face to Giacomo. "Chicago has plenty of good eating establishments. Decent ones, if you know what I mean. Even better, how about some old-fashioned home cooking for a change? I could fix you some wonderful potato pancakes and sausages, just like my *mutter* taught me."

Carlo's nostrils flared. He kicked Giacomo under the table. Hildie's previous cooking efforts had produced gaseous eruptions and heartburn that kept both of them awake all night.

This time Giacomo squared his shoulders but avoided Hildie's eyes when he said, "We're staying here."

"Whatever you say, Sweetie." She kissed his cheek and pushed her chair back. "Now if you'll excuse me, I have to dust my knees."

"Now, when we're just about ready to order?"

"As if I didn't already know what you like. I'll have the same."

While Hildie sashayed to the powder room, Carlo reviewed the evening fare with Giacomo. They vetoed meatballs and spaghetti as only fit for the Southern Italians their papa called *Mezzogiorno*, as in hot sun and hot tempers. Chicken and risotto tempted the brothers but the rice often came undercooked or too dry, either way, unacceptable. Beef could be tough unless simmered slowly in its juices. Veal spelled disaster if overcooked. In the end they ordered their usual Wednesday special—ravioli with a side of the *insalata mista*.

Two tables over a skinny flapper decked out in a burgundy chemise twirled a half-eaten grissini between her teeth, and exchanged sultry expressions with Giacomo.

"Better not let Miss Hoity-toity catch you," Carlo said.

"Looking ain't a crime and Hildie ain't my keeper."

"Neither is Papa Gus but we still salute him every time he signs our payroll sheets."

"*Basta*, enough, okay? Here she comes."

Hildie cozied up to Giacomo. She slipped her hand into the front pocket of his trousers. And to the burgundy flapper, she puckered her lips. Hildie's competition responded with a flash of pink tongue and returned to the conversation at her own table.

"You know, Sweetie, I've been thinking," Hildie said, directing her words to Giacomo but her eyes to Carlo. "Maybe you should change your name to something not so foreign. According to Papa, all the Southern Italians at the brewery are switching to names that sound more … well, American."

"As if me and Giacomo care what those damn *Terroni* are doing."

"Yeah, yeah, I know." She lifted her chin, lowered her lashes. "You and Giacomo are *Piemontese* Italians. Papa says the Terroni call your kind *Mangiapolenta*."

"Better to be called polenta eaters than clumsy yokels. At least, we keep ain't ashamed of our own names."

Giacomo leaned over the table. "Hold on, Carlo. Maybe Hildie's right, I mean about the name 'cause I been thinking the same thing."

Hildie rubbed her leg against Giacomo's. "Yeah, Honey. You could switch from Giacomo to Jake. Hmm, maybe something like Jake Rhodes."

"Jake … yeah, I like Jake. Reminds me of Big Jake Garrity from the Fourth Ward. 'Course, in America Giacomo means Jim," he mused. "But, I ain't going with Rhodes." He nudged Carlo. "So, what do you think, brother? What about Jake?"

Carlo didn't answer.

"Come on, say something."

"Just like that," Carlo said with a snap of his fingers, "You wanna go from Giacomo to Jake?"

"To fit in, be more American. What the hell."

"Like those damn Terroni?"

"They ain't the only ones, Carlo. Some things should stay in the

Old Country."

"Jake—Jim—Giacomo." Carlo shrugged. "Take your pick. Just don't turn your back on Baggio. Without the family name, we are ..." He blew his next word away from the fingertips of one hand. "... *niente.*"

"Then Jake Baggio it is." Giacomo held up his cup to meet Hildie's root beer.

Carlo followed with a toast that lacked any enthusiasm. "To Giacomo's new name."

"*Salute!*," the trio said with a click of their vessels.

Hildie sniffed a few times to show her soft side.

While she searched her cluttered pocketbook for a hankie, Carlo leaned over to his brother and whispered in Piemontese. "Tonight she got you to change your first name. Tomorrow, she'll get you to change her last name."

"Do I look like I just got off of the boat? I'm—"

"Hey, you two, that's not fair," Hildie said. "When you're with me, either talk like Americans or keep quiet."

"Well I ain't about to keep quiet." The immigrant with a new name stood. He stepped from his chair to the top of the table and spread his arms like a Chicago politician. "Listen up, everybody!"

Hildie clattered a spoon against her glass and the room went quiet.

Giacomo tapped his fingertips to his chest. "You all know me as Giacomo Baggio. Well, tonight you're looking at a new man. From this day on I am Jake ... Jake Baggio."

The patrons of Fabio's applauded as Jake lifted his arms and moved to the music of a nearby ocarina. And in an uncharacteristic display of generosity, Vincenzo Valenza banged the side of his fist on the bar before yelling out, "A round of drinks, in honor of Giacomo's rebirth as Jake."

Carlo did the right thing. He bought the next round and his brother the one after that. After the hoopla died down, he watched Jake shake every extended hand and then leave with Hildie, just as he did every Wednesday evening.

*****

After strolling twenty minutes or so through sidewalks crowded with pedestrians, Jake and Hildie entered a brick tenement on Taylor Street. As they climbed the open well of creaking stairs, Hildie was giddy with excitement, all the while oblivious to air thick with the stench of fermenting mash and bootleg brew seeping through the apartment walls. When they reached the second level, Jake slid his hand down Hildie's back and stopped at the crease of her round buttocks, prompting a seesaw of giggles and protests from her. On the third level they stopped at the door of a furnished studio Jake shared with Carlo. While Jake fumbled with the key, Hildie unbuttoned the fly of his trousers. Clinging to each other, they moved inside and Jake kicked the door shut. Neither spoke as they flung off their clothes and tumbled onto the lumpy horsehair mattress.

"Oh Jake, do what you did to me the last time."

What? He tried a couple places before finding one that made her purr like a kitten.

"Jake, Jake. I just love the sound of your new name. See, I have good ideas every so often, don't I?"

Jake didn't answer. He was too busy concentrating on the small of her back.

"Wherever did you learn all those wonderful moves? Ooh-h, Jake, you and me are so good for each other. Jake and Hildie, Hildie and Jake. Such sweet music to my ears."

Within minutes a simpler melody played from the worn spiral bedsprings. In the next apartment their aged Russian neighbor took her cue and joined in the mating ritual, using her cane to bang out a rhythmic accompaniment on the thin wall separating her bed from theirs. Jake pictured a gummy grin erupting to expose the lone eyetooth left in the woman's mouth. Her own sexual escapades, some sixty years earlier, were legendary and usually involved more than two people. At least, that's what she'd told him more than once.

Jake waited for Miss Clarissa Spencer, one floor below. She worked in the notions department at Woolworth's Five and Dime, and was always complaining to him about her overhead light rattling and loose plaster spraying her face. A broom handle to the ceiling usually got his attention and tonight was no exception.

"Quiet!" he heard Miss Spencer scream.

More plaster fell.

"Filthy, disgusting Eye-talian!" This time her voice cracked.

Maybe if she gargled with salt water....

Jake forged ahead with a swell of perspiration and did the right thing, making Hildie squeal before he yelled. Afterwards they lay side-by-side, half-listening to the Chicago night, its screeching taxis and irritating police sirens competing with wailing infants and drunken revelers.

Hildie cleared her throat. "Not that I'm in any hurry, you understand, but I have been giving serious thought to my ... our future, you and me in a long-term arrangement. You know, as in marriage."

He shifted, causing the bed to let out a groan. As did Jake, but his didn't reach Hildie's ears. "Uh, right now I can't afford marriage."

"I'll talk to Papa about promoting you. That is, as soon as something comes up."

He pushed her determined hand away. "Not yet, I need time to recoup." He stretched his arms overhead, folded them to cushion his head. "It's different with Carlo. He's a year older than me and still thinks in Italian."

"Well, don't you be thinking about buying yourself an Italian bride, Jake Baggio. 'Cause if you do, you'd better leave Chicago before I find out. Why, if it wasn't for Papa hiring you and Carlo, you couldn't even afford this dump." Hildie screwed up her face, tried to squeeze tears from her dry eyes. Having failed, she heaved a few audible sighs instead.

Jake knew what was expected of him; he reached for her snatch. "Yeah, Hildie, we owe all our success to the Kramer family."

This time she pushed him away. "Well, you can forget about that special dessert I promised. It's reserved for engaged couples."

With that, their evening ended. Hildie wiggled into her wrinkled clothes and slammed the door on her way out. She stomped down the stairs, and before her patent leather pumps hit the honeycombed tiles of the entryway, Jake was already sawing logs.

Chapter 2
Night School

After assuring Vincenzo he would consider the arranged courtship, Carlo moved on to Pané, a twenty-four-hour bakery that catered to a steady stream of customers. Flipping a quarter on the linoleum countertop, he requested the specialty.

"*Foccacio*," Patsy replied. But instead of a round flatbread, the clerk selected a five-cent loaf of crusty bread from the case and did not return any change. "So Carlo, you want I should keep the pané 'til later?"

"*Grazie*, Patsy. Me and Giacomo will eat it for breakfast." *Giacomo*. Would Carlo ever get used to him as Jake.

"Your brother still dating that little Kraut?" Patsy asked.

"For now but not forever."

"Si, better he should stick with his own kind."

Carlo circled his thumb and forefinger. He went outside, to the side entrance of the three-story brick building where he knocked twice. A little door within the larger one slid open. "Foccacio," he said, the password gaining him access to an inner sanctum.

Two well-heeled couples staggered through a set of swinging doors that led to The Playground, Chicago's most glamorous speakeasy. For the right price flowed the best liquors: Canadian whiskey, French and Italian wines, imported and real domestic beers. Direct from New Orleans a quartet of black musicians played sweet jazz on piano, drums, trumpet, and clarinet. Revolving lights created a hyperkinetic distortion of tuxedos and flappers, their fingers splayed across knees scissoring in and out, in and out. Arms went up, heels jutted outward as they gave their all to the Charleston, a dance Carlo had never attempted.

He stayed long enough to acknowledge one of the bartenders and two waiters from Italy's Piemonte region before returning to the stairs, taking two at a time to the next level. On the landing stood a somber man whose bulging eyes lacked any visible lashes.

"*Bona sera*, Frog," Carlo said. "She's expecting me?"

Ugo Sapone responded with a single nod from a thick neck partially retracted into his round stooped body. With some men words weren't necessary, just mutual respect.

Carlo strode down the hall to a door marked private. One knock clicked it open to the office of Night School's headmistress, sitting behind a gold-inlaid desk cluttered with stacks of paperwork. Giulietta Bracca looked up with a smile. She positioned a cigarette into her rhinestone holder and slipped it between ruby lips that sang to Carlo. After giving her a light, he sank into the plush sofa, crossed an ankle over his knee, and let his eyes caress her fine features. Henna spit curls circled her rouge-painted face, and pencil-thin eyebrows arched over thick false lashes framed her emerald eyes in perpetual wonderment.

"Why so quiet, my pet?" Giulietta asked.

"It's my brother, again."

"Sweet Giacomo?" She closed her eyes for a moment and blew out more smoke. "How I miss our weekly sessions. What has he done this time?"

"Changed his name, just like that." Carlo snapped his fingers. "To Jake of all things."

"To please the little Kraut, no doubt."

"Not according to him."

"Don't be so hard on … Jake, is it? He's all you have besides me."

"Maybe that's not enough. I'm thinking about getting married."

"At twenty-one? You're barely out of knickers."

"I was man enough for you."

Giulietta cocked her head to study him through half-lowered lashes. "Surely you're not considering one of my teachers."

"Chicago's best don't make the best wives."

"Ah-h, my very words. I taught you well." Dragging from a rhinestone cigarette holder, she deliberated before speaking through puffs of exhaled smoke. "So who's the lucky girl?"

"Someone from the Old Country, someone like my mama."

"How quaint. In other words, someone you have yet to meet."

She walked over to the sofa and sat beside him. He leaned over to nestle his head against her breast, felt it rise and fall with a gentle rhythm.

"Of course I wish you well, my pet," she said, playing with his hair. "But this bride, must she come from the mountains?"

"More like the foothills."

"Oh, you Piemontese and your Alps."

"And you Genovese and your Ligurian Sea."

"Piss on Genoa and the childhood I never had. This idyllic life you imagine may not survive the reality of Chicago."

"I'll take my chances," he murmured, his forefinger tracing the outline of her slender hip. "I want a woman who thinks like me. One who cooks good food and will give me a houseful of bambini."

She lifted his head, pressed her lips to his, and opened his mouth, her tongue making its familiar journey before gently exiting. Soft laughter bespoke their former intimacy. "Feels like old times, doesn't it?"

"Did you have to graduate me?"

"You left me no choice."

"Says you, I had no say-so in the matter."

"And now you talk of food and babies. First, look for a woman who will share your passions. The rest will either happen or no longer be important." She left the plump cushion and returned to the chair behind her desk. With a wave of enameled nails, she dismissed him. "Now go. You know how my teachers abhor tardiness."

*****

Down another hallway and in the doorway of the Anatomy Classroom waited the honey blond Miss Molly, her arms folded and foot tapping. She wore a pink and white gingham pinafore with ruffles circling her shoulders and knee-length skirt baring her backside. "Naughty boy, you're late again. Whatever shall I do with you?"

Carlo hung his head, held back the smile he could barely contain. "I'm sorry, Teacher."

"Apology accepted. Just don't let it happen again. Now let's put our heads together and decide on what would be an appropriate lesson for this evening."

Miss Molly often said her classroom was designed to fulfill a schoolboy's fantasy, but none Carlo could've imagined in Italy. Erotic chalk drawings, those artistic expressions by the more talented students, decorated three blackboard walls. On the fourth wall, green shades covered tall windows. An imposing well-padded desk occupied the center area, along with an upholstered chair. Big enough for two, it swiveled and rolled on heavy casters suitable for navigating the length of the room, or to a low stool and wooden paddle in the corner designated Playful Punishments.

"I just love our sessions," Miss Molly said, "but already you know so much. Perhaps we should concentrate on honing some of your basic skills."

"Honing?"

"As in practice makes perfect."

Carlo rested his chin on his knuckles, as if to consider her suggestion. "Maybe this time I could examine you."

"Oh-h! Playing doctor sounds like the perfect test." She turned around and looked over her shoulder. "Could you help me untie this silly bow?"

Fifteen minutes later they were conjoined on the desk, oblivious to a hallway commotion until two uniforms and a vice squad detective barged into their room.

"Enough with the copulating, this teacher's heading for the pokey," snorted a pudgy cop while jabbing his nightstick in Carlo's ribs. "Extinguish the smoking pecker, dago boy. Night School's no place for the likes of a greaser such as yourself."

The insult brought a rush of blood to Carlo's face but he knew better than to trade insults with Chicago's finest. Instead, he rolled off Miss Molly and picked up his trail of scattered clothes.

"Oh, dear," Miss Molly said, transforming her lips into a soulful pout. She covered her luscious breasts with one hand, her manicured fluff with the other. "I've never been arrested before. Whatever will my friends think?"

"If your friends work here, they oughta be thinking about a good lawyer," replied the detective. "Come on, Leroy," he said to the older cop. "Connor can handle this."

Carlo recognized the rookie patrolman whose freckles were competing with his blush but said nothing when Connor handed the naked teacher her costume, and said, "Here, ma'am, you'd better put this on before you get a chill."

"Thank you, Johnny-Boy," Miss Molly replied with a wink and a curtsy before tossing aside the pinafore he'd handed her. "I've missed our corner chats." She twisted her hair into a schoolmarm knot, turned her backside to Connor, and bent over to retrieve her lace panties.

Carlo was already dressed when he walked into the hallway that formed a square around Night School. It was there he witnessed the scene of naked or nearly naked men of all ages, shapes, and sizes scramble from classrooms labeled Literature, Music, Mythology, Painting, and Sculpture. Slowest to vacate was Physical Education since its extensive workouts accommodated groups instead of individuals. Unlike Giulietta's teachers, her students were considered victims of enticement. The police ordered them to dress and get the hell out.

Carlo left first but after crossing the street he stopped to linger in the shadows. He lit a cigarillo, leaned against the wall, and watched the mucky mucks of Chicago politics, business, and high society exit the brick building. They disappeared into the night. But what about the hoodlums, those high rollers who wore spats and bowlers, and weren't afraid to flash their money rolls around Night School. Not one of them in sight. They must've got wind of the raid and went elsewhere. Next came the vice squad, herding Giulietta's teachers. Carlo knew them all, especially Bonnie Bodacious, Fanny Bright, Medusa, Twins 1 and 2, Sister Mary Agatha, and, of course, Miss Molly. One by one the teachers lifted their skirts and climbed into the waiting paddy wagons. Last to board was Night School's headmistress. Not wanting Giulietta to see him, Carlo moved further into the shadows and waited until the wagons turned the corner before he left. The evening was still young, but with any luck, by the time he made it home, the sheets on his side of the bed would've cooled off.

*****

At the police station Giulietta and her teachers were booked and moved to a holding cell. Within the hour her lawyer Bernie Shoeman arranged bail for everyone and a fleet of cabs for transportation back to Night School. Leading the caravan was a green Pierce Arrow, Giulietta's prized vehicle. Ugo Sapone had positioned his bulky body behind the wheel while Giulietta and Bernie sat like Chicago royalty in the back seat.

Bernie held his gold lighter to her cigarette, and then lit his own. He cracked the window before he spoke. "Giuli, Giuli, talk to me. I've represented you in civil matters for the past seventeen years. Advanced you the money to buy your own building. Watched you grow Night School into Chicago's most innovative venture. Advised you on collecting a share of profits from the bakery and speakeasy, even though you're no more than their landlady. But until tonight, I have never crawled out of my bed to bail you out of jail."

"Would you believe, the precinct captain and I go back a long way," Giulietta said. "Last year he brought his son to me, a delightful young man I taught with the utmost sensitivity. At a fifty percent discount, I might add. Good will creates more business and I'm all about business."

"Just give it to me straight, Giuli. What the hell is going on?"

She leaned back, peeled off her false eyelashes, and after cracking the window, sent them into the night. "I suspect a payback from Mr. Capone."

"The Big Fellow? Hells fire, I don't have to tell you how brutal the man can be. Johnny Torrio he most definitely is not."

"There was a time when Johnny had a thing for me."

"Well, Johnny's out of the picture now and Capone thinks of no one but Capone."

"His bagman accused me of skimming the gross profits."

"Holy shit, you mean Fingers Bellini, who once blinded a poor schmuck he accused of cheating?"

"Please, don't remind me. He came in on Monday, flipped through the c-notes in Capone's envelope, and claimed the take was short. I told him business was slow, that I personally recorded every transaction."

"Giuli, Giuli."

"You know my word's good as gold, Bernie. For that, I sacrificed tonight's profits. Capone has put a stain on my reputation."

"Will you please heed my advice one more time: do not mess with The Big Fellow. Call me a self-serving bastard but I'd rather represent the flesh-and-blood Giulietta Bracca than whatever's left of her estate."

Chapter 3
Night Run

Monday on Becker's docks started out as grueling as every other summer day with Carlo alongside Jake, both stripped down to their undershirts and trousers while unloading crates. Then the crew chief showed up, which could've meant anything from a lay-off to unexpected overtime. This day it was, "Gus wants to see you boys in his office."

"Now?" Carlo said, wiping sweat from his brow.

"You got it. Right away, pronto. Or whatever 'hurry up' means in your lingo."

"What'd we do wrong?" Jake asked, stretching his arms overhead.

"As far as I know, nothing," the crew chief said. "But I ain't the brewmeister."

"And we don't mix the beer," Carlo muttered as the crew chief walked away.

"I guess we oughta put on our shirts," Jake said, tossing Carlo his.

"Yeah, show Heidi's papa some respect."

After making themselves presentable, they took the freight elevator up one floor and circled through a maze of bubbling vats before reaching Gus Kramer's office. He met them in the doorway, this stocky man with a pipe clenched between clunky false teeth and pale hair receding from a pink forehead. He pointed to two chairs but Carlo and Jake didn't sit until Gus had settled into his behind the desk.

"So, boys, for you Chicago's finest brewery is going well?"

Jake looked at Carlo, as if waiting for his okay before they both nodded.

"Good, good." Gus sucked on the pipe, sending a sliver of spit out the corner of his mouth. "My Hildie this morning got up early and made coffee." He cleared his throat. "Better she should leave that to her mother. With me she wanted to talk about the name change."

Jake gulped, Carlo figured to calm the bobbing adam's apple so he nudged him with his foot.

The old man spoke between puffs. "Jake she said I should now call you, right?"

Jake nodded. With Gus, the less said the better.

"Maybe a new last name you'd like. Something easy, as in B-r-o-w-n—Jake Brown."

"No," Carlo answered for his brother. "A man without—"

"Thanks, Gus, but I'm sticking with Baggio. Just like Carlo."

For a long moment beady eyes flickered behind Gus's bifocals. "To me it makes no never mind," he said, "but for my Hildie ... well, another story that is, for another time. Anyways, that's not why I invited you boys into my office. Can you handle an outside job? It pays good."

Carlo leaned forward. "How good?"

"One night, just one." Gus held up a stubby finger, as if they couldn't count. "Twenty-five bucks each."

Lifting his brow, Carlo turned to Jake. Jake blinked once. "That depends," Carlo said. "We ain't into killing or beatings."

"And no setting fires, scaring old ladies or little kids," Jake added.

"Don't forget, you're talking to Gustav Kramer. A man of violence I'm not." He stood, went into the hall, and bellowed, "Harold! Come!"

Merda! Carlo slumped in his chair. Not Hildie's brother, anybody but that *stupido*. He whispered to Jake. "It's not too late to back out."

"Like hell. Gus will say, 'no problem.' For him, that is, to lay us off. I'm talking forever."

They stood up when he came back with Harold. The son could've passed for a young Gus, but with more hair covering a thicker head and duller brain.

"Harold, meet your Friday night team." Gus moved back to his chair, but was the only one who sat down. "Hildie's beau you already know but now he goes by Jake."

"Yeah, so I hear." Harold cocked his head toward Carlo. "I know the brother too. So, here's the deal, I'm in charge. Either one of you drive? I didn't think so."

"This I already explained, Harold. Another driver the man don't need."

The man, did Gus mean Capone? Damn, another Siciliano he and Jake could do without.

"Now out of my office with the details," Gus said. "Five minutes I give. Then back to work, all of you."

Harold went first, stumbling across the threshold as he spoke from over his shoulder. "You two're still grunting on the dock, right. That's what I figured. Well, I need privacy to conduct business."

They followed Harold into the toilet facility where he checked the stalls to make sure no one else was there. At the long urinal Carlo stood to one side of him and Jake, the other. An unspoken pissing contest began, with Harold no match for brothers who'd been out-pissing each other for years.

Harold stepped back and made a show of tucking in his balls before buttoning his fly. "Friday night, ten o'clock, meet at the dock to quick load some beer. We'll be running the barrels to Michigan in exchange for some prime Canadian liquor."

"I don't know," Carlo said, crossing streams with Jake. "Loading illegal beer from a dock is one thing, but rumrunners we ain't."

"Me either." Harold wiped his hands on the seat of his trousers. "I'm doing somebody a favor. Just like Pop did Hildie a favor by giving you dagos this chance."

Dagos, some nerve coming from a clumsy Kraut, even if he was Hildie's brother. Carlo wanted to bust him. Instead he tried easing out. "Maybe you should get somebody else."

"And disappoint Pop and Hildie—no way. So what's it gonna take to please them?"

Before Carlo could answer, Jake jumped in with, "Fifty bucks for me and fifty for my brother. Okay, Carlo?"

*****

The next day after putting in ten hours on Becker's dock, Carlo returned with Jack to load more beer for the night run. While they moved barrel after barrel into one panel truck and then another, Harold and a burly man called Otis watched from the comfort of folding chairs, all the while sipping beer and growing a pile of cigarette butts around their feet.

At midnight two groaning trucks rumbled onto the street, with Harold taking the lead and Jake at his side. Otis followed with Carlo riding shotgun, not that he carried one but that's what Otis had called the passenger side. At least Carlo didn't have to put up with Harold. Poor Jake, that's what he got for putting up with Hildie.

Otis didn't have much to say but he knew how to belt a song. His robust baritone voice kept both of them awake, along with endless miles of streetlights and sporadic strings of neon signs illuminating their way. As they drove further east, the lights grew dimmer and eventually faded into night along with the city boundaries. Carlo felt his eyelids dropping, only to snap them open whenever the truck rolled over a bump or deep rut. At some point he realized the singing had stopped. Then Otis yawned. Once, twice, three times.

"You all right, Otis?"

"Sure, but if you're chomping to take the wheel, I might consider it." He spoke his next words through another yawn. "You do drive, don't you?"

"Not so good."

"Hey, I was just kidding." Otis took a deep breath. "We got a long ways to go before Michigan and it's all about making time 'cause making time is making money. Hold on, I feel another song about to spring from my throat."

He belted out an aria from a familiar Italian opera, which prompted Carlo to sit back and relax the muscles tightening across his shoulders. Soon the taillights from Harold's truck started bouncing and weaving from side to side. Were they supposed to do that? Day or night, this over- the-road-trip was a first for Carlo. Jake too, since whatever they did, they did together. Except for the women ... and even that when the occasion demanded. Their jobs at Becker's may've been on the shady side but the brothers earned every dime, alongside other immigrants struggling for a fresh start, young and old men trying to feed their families, here or in the Old Country. This one-time job from Gus paid better but came with a greater risk. Rumrunners, that's what they were tonight, regardless of the cargo—beer, whiskey, or rum.

Somewhere along the deserted Indiana route the welcomed baritone serenading stopped again and Harold's taillights grew bigger as Otis moved their truck closer. Carlo looked over to see the driver's head bobbing on his chest.

"Dammit, Otis, wake up!" Carlo jabbed his finger into the man's meaty ribs.

Otis snorted, rustled his head like a staggering bull. But when the truck up ahead swerved to the left, Otis forged theirs straight ahead. Carlo yelled for him to slow down. Too late, they rolled into a gaping hole. Merda! The only word Carlo could manage when the nose of the truck plunged forward, throwing him and Otis against the windshield. From behind came the sound of clashing barrels, followed by an expected sloshing of the best illegal beer money could buy. At least that's what Harold had called the cargo as he tugged open the driver's door. Carlo looked through blurred eyes, expecting to see Harold yank Otis out. Instead, the singer rammed his fist into Harold's face. Otis's next words were music to Carlo's ears.

"Shut your trap, cabbage head."

Harold reeled, fell to the ground, and let out a groan. Otis stepped out of the truck, reached down for Harold's hand, and pulled him upright. "This here's your fault, Harold. Blinding me with them damn taillights just 'cause you couldn't drive a straight line."

"But you wrecked the truck, not me."

"Tell that to The Man and I'll make sure you never drive so much as a tricycle."

They were still exchanging words when Carlo heard tapping on the passenger window. He pushed open the door, climbed out, and stumbled into Jake's open arms.

"You two, over here," Otis yelled. "There's a mess that needs cleaning up."

"You think he means Harold too?" Jake asked.

"Nah, no such luck. Besides we're better off without that turd."

A bent axle and steam hissing from the radiator had crippled the truck but some of the barrels had managed to survive. This time Otis sat alone on a tree stump, surprising Carlo when he sent Harold to grunt alongside him and Jake as they transferred salvaged beer into the other truck.

"Not one word of this to my pop or Hildie. Understand, dagos?"

"Sure thing, Harold. Me and Carlo ain't telling a soul."

Carlo poked Jake to keep him from snickering. Under the light of a quarter-moon the three men worked in silence, finishing thirty minutes later with a slam of the panel doors. The brothers leaned against the truck, waiting for Harold to catch his breath.

"Hey, you rummies, rest on your own time," Otis said. "I want that bum truck pushed to the side of the road. Nosy cops asking questions we don't need."

At that moment Harold developed a convenient coughing spell, so jarring it doubled him over, which left Otis to take over the wheel.

"Damn, this better not give me a hernia," Carlo grumbled to Jake as they pushed from behind.

After they moved the truck off the road, Otis hopped out and slipped Carlo two twenties. "For you and Jake, my friend," Otis said. "In case anybody should ask, it was an unavoidable accident."

"You bet. That's the way we saw it," Carlo said. "Now, about the broken truck...."

"Damn." Otis peeled five more twenties from his money roll. "*You*, I'm leaving here to take care of the damn thing, but don't spend all of this unless you have to." He pointed to an open field stretching into the black of night. "About a quarter mile off this road, there's a farmer with a team of horses."

"You know this for sure?"

"The yokel helped me out before. What's more, his son's a decent mechanic. I swear, between the two of them, they must be digging these potholes in the road."

"We better get a move on," Harold said, tapping the watch he'd taken from its pocket.

"Yeah, but with me doing the driving," Otis said. "Jake, you climb in the cab with us. We'll stop for your brother on our way back."

"You gonna be okay," Jake asked with a look that told Carlo he didn't want to leave without him.

"Yeah, sure. Now get out of here."

Carlo watched the swaying taillights disappear before he started up the lonely dirt road. The quarter mile Otis had described soon quadrupled into a twenty-minute walk, complemented by a serenade of hooting owls and chirping crickets that reminded him of nightly strolls over the foothills of his youth. Three mutts came from nowhere, barking and baring their teeth as they escorted him to their master's domain. A light flickered outside the house.

As he approached the porch, a silhouetted man held up his kerosene lamp and called out, "Who goes there?"

"Carlo's my name. My truck broke down on the hard road. I was hoping to get it towed."

"Before dawn, no doubt, I ain't no mule. You from Chicago?" The voice teemed with suspicion. The man still hadn't shown himself.

"Just passing through. I'll help with the horses, whatever it takes."

"Damn right you will. But it's still going to cost you. I suppose you'll need a mechanic too."

"He's good and fast?"

"Amen, but he don't come cheap."

"I'll need a place to lay my head too. Forty bucks, that's all I have so don't make me beg, okay?"

Twelve hours later Carlo marked time on the farmhouse porch as his stomach wrestled the ham hocks and beans he'd eaten at noon to please the farmer's wife. And to fill his empty stomach since he had no other choice. Living in Chicago had blurred his vision for the country life, an America not unlike rural Italy and one he could adjust to again. If he had to, that is. He'd been watching the distant hard road, at last felt relief on spotting a cloud of dust building in the wake of the rumrunner's truck that eventually barreled into the dirt yard. A flurry of chickens scattered in all directions. With the mutts yipping at his heels, he strolled out to meet his cohorts, not expecting to find Otis and Harold as passengers and behind the wheel Jake, a grin crossing his whiskered face that reminded Carlo of his own stubble.

Jake climbed out of the cab and they traded punches instead of the usual hugging. Looking over Jake's shoulder, Carlo saw Harold, frowning as he slid over to the window seat Otis had been warming before he stepped out.

"Otis thought I needed some practice driving," Jake said, "just in case the other truck ain't fixed yet."

"According to the farmer, it won't be ready 'til dark."

"That's what I figured," Otis said. "What about the money?"

"I didn't have much choice. The man drove a hard bargain."

Otis curled his lip and spit a wad into the ground. He lifted his thick body into the driver's seat. "I'm leaving Jake behind with you. We still have to deliver our pricey return load, which will arrive in St. Louis on time I might add, thanks to you boys." He shifted into first gear and rattled off, sending the chickens into another uproar.

"How'd it go?" Carlo asked.

"Good, even with Harold pouting which me and Otis ignored. He said you should drive part way back, in case he needs us again."

Chapter 4
Negotiating

On Tuesday evening the overhead lights at Fabiola's had already dimmed, urging the last of their customers to leave with no hard feelings. Outside, Carlo leaned against the building with Jake at his side, both smoking cigarillos that exceeded their daily allotment.

"You really want to go through with this?" Jake asked.

"I'm here, ain't I?"

"That's what scares me. A Chicago bride would be a helluva lot cheaper."

"And a know-it-all, need I say more?"

"If you mean Hildie, we ain't tying the knot."

"Says you, she has other ideas."

"Look, this ain't about me. You got hit with a bad week. First the Night School raid, then our trip into the countryside."

"For which Harold reneged on the fifty bucks Gus promised. What a *bastardo*, giving us each a lousy twenty-five."

"Otis pitched in some extra, even though he didn't know it."

"That extra shrunk when the farmer's wife took her share."

"Yeah, thanks for covering my supper. There's only so much liquor one man can put in an empty stomach."

Carlo peered through the window. The saloon appeared empty so he opened the door and motioned Jake inside.

Jake moved but stopped short of stepping over the threshold. "Did I tell you there ain't enough reasons in hell for marrying somebody you don't even know, a not-so-perfect stranger?"

"So we get acquainted first," Carlo said. "Right now, I just need to know you're with me."

"All the way, brother." He put his hand on Carlo's shoulder. "Just go slow with these Valenza bastards. I keep thinking how we paid Massimo for those apprentice jobs."

"Come on, Jake. Was it Massimo's fault the bricklayers went on strike a week later."

"What about the job with Sieben's. We paid Massimo for that one too. Then a midnight raid closed the brewery."

Carlo shook himself loose and pulled Jake inside with him. "Just for tonight, forget Johnny Torrio and all that shit."

"*Basta, basta*, I've said enough. Look at Massimo, waving us over like we're—"

"Remember, Jake, no wine tonight."

"Right, to keep our heads clear."

Carlo watched Massimo tug at a waistcoat challenging his expanding girth. He had three years on Vincenzo's thirty-seven, and an extra thirty pounds. Still, the Valenza brothers couldn't deny their resemblance: same hooked beak, same pitted skin, same unctuous smile.

"Ah, *paesani*," Massimo called out. "Come, we sit."

While Vincenzo locked the door and pulled the shades, Massimo offered wine from a carafe. Carlo and Jake said no with their fingers. Sitting around a table, the four men exchanged pleasantries in their Piemontese dialect before Massimo eased into the negotiations.

"So Carlo, Vincenzo tells me you desire to meet our Louisa, a woman whose beauty erupts from the very depths of her soul."

"You have a photograph?" Jake asked.

Vincenzo shrugged. "Only as a child."

"Let me assure you, she takes after our ma's side," Massimo said. "Now about the arrangements—"

"Perhaps we should wait," Carlo said in response to Jake's nudge.

"For what, another year to pass?" Vincenzo asked. "As we speak our sister grows older."

"How old?" Jake asked. It was a question Carlo hadn't thought to bring up.

"Paesani ... please." Massimo tapped two hands of fingers to his chest. "What my brother meant was time lost, pleasure lost."

"Maybe we should come back later."

"Of course, but I must caution you: waiting could result in disappointment," Vincenzo said. "A widower from our village is pursuing Louisa. He possesses land, a big empty house."

"And no children to carry his name." Massimo leaned forward. "Perhaps Louisa should stay put. Italy needs more sons; so many perished in The War to End All Wars. The Old Country, it's not like America with its damn immigration quotas."

Carlo leaned even closer. He knew what he wanted and had played the game long enough. "How much did you say?"

"One hundred dollars for Louisa's travel expenses, another hundred for me and Vincenzo."

Jake snorted. He pushed his chair back.

"That's pretty steep," Carlo said.

Massimo shrugged. "It depends on how long you want to wait. We're not just talking the cost of boat and train fares. There's paper work, the usual greasing of palms. It's the Italian way, in case you've forgotten."

Carlo could never forget.

"New clothes for our sister," Vincenzo added. "Naturally, you'll want to show her off for the courtship."

"So what if she and Carlo don't connect?" Jake asked. "Who pays her return passage?"

"Carlo, of course," Massimo replied.

"And if she refuses to go back?" Carlo asked, although he couldn't imagine this happening.

Evidently, neither could Massimo. "Paesani … please, an unlikely situation such if ever there was." Narrowing his beady eyes, he stuck his nose inches from Carlo's, and spoke with a breath of wine and garlic. "But should this happen, trust my words: it would be a matter for Vincenzo and me to resolve. After all, we Valenzas consider ourselves to be men of honor."

Chapter 5
Monte Piano, Italy

Louisa Valenza had read Massimo's words so many times she knew them by heart. After shoving his letter into her apron pocket, she threw a shawl over her shoulders and went outside, closing the door on the home of her birth, a small apartment squeezed between those of her brothers, Aldo and Matteo. They were already working in the field, along with their wives, each with a baby strapped to her back and two more in school. Louisa hurried along the outer balcony, down the open stairs, and away from the stone building her Valenza ancestors had erected during the fifteenth century, four hundred years before Vittorio Emanuele would unite the disgruntled provinces of Italy into the country it now was. She walked with her head lifted to the alpine clouds and light steps to navigate a rocky road that would carry her to the valley three miles below. A forest of chestnuts lined the winding route, with crests and curves providing a distant view of red tiled-roof villages and an abandoned castle basking under the protection of its ancient stonewall.

 Forty-five minutes later and with her arms laden with wildflowers she'd picked along the way, Louisa arrived at the cemetery in Locana. She strolled through rows of concrete walls holding the bones of earlier generations, those precious remains that had been moved from the ground to make room for the newly deceased. At the end of one wall, she stopped and arranged a handful of flowers in an attached vase. She made the sign of the cross, kissed the fingertips of both hands, and held them to marble-encased photographs of the white-haired Fabiola and Massimo Valenza.

"*Buon giorno, Nonna … buon giorno, Nonno,*" Louisa said to the photographs. "This is not my weekly visit but I could not pass by without stopping to say hello."

But this morning belonged to Anna Valenza, at peace in the ground next to her husband Vincenzo. New grass sprouted from the adjoining plot of dirt disturbed six weeks before. Louisa honored the graves with her remaining flowers. She crossed herself again, and applied finger kisses to images of a man and woman in their prime, before the ravages of old age and illness had changed their appearance.

Louisa stepped back and took a deep breath.

"Yesterday this letter came, Ma." She waved the single page at her parents' stone. "Massimo wrote it but he speaks for Vincenzo too. They want me in America, after all these years and all their promises. Of course, I never would have left you, even if you had insisted, which you never did nor did I expect you to, although it would've made my staying easier. Anyway, it seems a paesano has fallen in love with my picture—that horrible photograph I begged you not to send. I'm thinking maybe I should go. Matteo and Aldo, they have their own lives. They need the extra space your apartment would provide more than a sister who may never find a worthy husband. It's not that I'm complaining, you understand. But the best ones got away while I was … never mind.

"This paesano—his name is Carlo Baggio—comes from Pont Canavese. He has money, how much I don't know, but enough to pay my passage and court me in a proper manner. If we do marry, I might give him one baby … maybe two, just in case the evil eye decides to put a curse on our meager family. About America, they say it's the land of opportunity. I'm thinking about starting a business there—that is, if I go. Maybe a nice trattoria, because in America anything is possible, isn't that what has kept Massimo and Vincenzo there?

"So, I'm here for your approval, a sign telling me to accept this offer for a new life. It's not that I expect the earth to shake, or lightening to split a chestnut tree down the middle. I just need to know I'm making the right decision. Amen."

Louisa closed her eyes and waited. And waited some more.

When nothing happened, she trudged back to the stone house in Monte Piano, a ninety-minute upward trek requiring twice the effort than that of her downward walk. During the next week she returned to the cemetery every other day, each time leaving without satisfaction. At the end of her fourth visit, she was closing the cemetery gate when a middle-aged woman came by in a mule-drawn cart and stopped across the road.

"Louisa Valenza," the woman called out, waving a crumpled letter similar to the way Massimo's now looked. She climbed down from her cart and hobbled over, her face gripped with pain. "My daughter writes that you might go to America."

Louisa answered with a crooked smile.

"Don't you remember me, Vita Grasso from Salle? Your mama—God rest her soul, the woman was a saint—I will never forget her kindness." Signora Grasso grabbed Louisa's hand, covered it with kisses. She looked up, teary-eyed and lip quivering. "Ten years ago my daughter got herself in the worse kind of trouble. Surely, you remember ... the shame my Tillie and that simpering padre brought our family."

"Yes ... of course," Louisa said, unable to recall the incident or either woman.

"It was your mama who contacted her sons in America. They arranged for Tillie's passage, helped her find a job, but not a husband ... scandalous news travels the world, not that I blame your brothers. To this day she rents a nice apartment from them."

"*Bene, bene*, Ma would've expected no less from Massimo and Vincenzo."

"My Tillie works in a factory and sends me what little she can."

"So everything worked out for the best."

"At first, but now I am growing old." She lifted her skirt to reveal thick legs, bruised and ulcerated. "When you get to America, tell my daughter I need her back home. You'll do that, won't you? To honor the memory of Anna Valenza, grazie, already I can see the answer in your eyes."

Thank you, Ma.

Louisa went straight to the post office, and mailed the letter she'd written to Massimo the week before.

*****

Bring only what you need, Massimo wrote back when he sent the money and instructions for Louisa's journey. She packed her clothes and personal items in a tapestry valise. The storage area behind the kitchen produced two trunks suitable for traveling. Louisa had already filled one trunk with what every respectable Italian bride brings to marriage, her linens. *Dodici di tutto*, twelve of everything carefully preserved in tissue paper: white sheets and embroidered pillowcases of the finest Belgium linen, damask napkins and table clothes in assorted sizes, the largest accommodating a table for twelve. Embroidered and lace trimmed linen nightgowns, exquisite in their simplicity.

From the time she turned eleven, Louisa had spent her leisure hours preparing the trousseau with her ma. And when Anna could no longer hold a needle, Louisa finished what her ma had started. The linens represented Louisa's worth as a wife and homemaker. More importantly, they held the memories of those years when mother and daughter had sewed together.

For the second trunk, Louisa decided on a more practical approach. She walked around *la cucina Anna*, her ma's kitchen, caressing items that stirred fond memories, choking back tears over others. Twice she went out to the balcony. With hands on the rail, she burned into her brain an outdoor scene of livestock and jutting rocks scattered over the rolling green meadow. When she returned to her mother's kitchen, the choice still proved too difficult. She settled for the essentials of every Italian cook: large and small sauté pans, stock pot, polenta pot, enamel roaster, cast iron skillet, food mill, cheese grater, wooden spoons, slotted spoons, carbon steel knives and *mezzaluna*, sharpener, ravioli cutter, rolling pin, coffee grinder, espresso pot, mortar and pestle.

*****

Five days later aboard the *Dante Alighieri*, Louisa stood on deck while the ship sailed away from Genoa's bustling harbor. When the ship moved into open seas, Louisa went below and partook of her first meal, a miserable experience of food rendered indigestible when combined with the *Dante's* relentless swaying. That night she woke up suffering from sickness of the water, and for the next week saw little more than her cabin and the nearest toilet. But when the ship docked in New York, Louisa somehow managed to join the first wave of disembarking passengers.

After clearing customs, she noticed her name displayed on a sign held up by a massive woman dressed in black. Nina, the escort Massimo hired to meet her. She greeted Louisa with hugs and spoke in formal Italian. "First we transfer your trunks to the railroad station;

then we go shopping."

"Shopping?" For what, Louis had everything.

"For a New York hat," Nina said, "to impress your betrothed."

They walked for blocks to a millinery shop where all the clerks acknowledged Nina as their best customer. Sitting before a mirror and with stomach rumbling and eyes begging for closure, Louisa allowed Nina control of the selection, a lengthy process that resulted in a black straw creation, its large brim drenched in an abundance of flowers and feathers. The perfect mask to hide behind, Louisa thought, dropping her old hat in a wastebasket as they walked out the door.

"What a shame," Nina said, clucking her tongue. "If only you had arrived earlier, we could've had more time to make you look American."

Louisa didn't care. Given her short time in New York, she'd already singled out the American women. Their short hair, their knees shamelessly exposed.

*****

After two days traveling on the New York Central, Louisa was slumped in her seat, staring out the window and fidgeting with an embroidered handkerchief. Somewhere in Ohio her excitement had worn off and now the fertile farmlands were dissolving into the gray shadows of factories and mile after mile of soot-covered buildings. As for the train conductor, she'd grown to despise him. That horrible man with white hair and a pink face, strutting down the aisle like a proud barnyard rooster.

"Give him a uniform and he becomes a pompous dictator," a passenger grumbled.

"How much further to Chicago?" another one asked.

Whatever answer the rooster blurted out, Louisa couldn't understand. Neither could anyone else. This time some of the Americans took turns asking him questions, just to get his dander up and turn his face from pink to red. After the rooster sauntered away, Louisa tried concentrating on the new life awaiting her, anything to block out the nearby racket of weary mothers soothing colicky babies and whiny toddlers demanding their fair share of attention. Had Louisa felt better, she might've offered to hold a crying baby or entertain a restless child. Nurturing was what she did best, but not this day. Not with a mouth still dry from her earlier fever. Not with lips cracked and parched, eyelids fighting to stay open. She still couldn't hold food, not that she cared about eating. Not after tasting what the Americans gobbled down like half-starved animals.

Anna's last breath had breathed new life into Louisa, and now her first sip of freedom would surpass that of a fine Barola. She'd put her destiny in the hands of others, crossed an entire ocean and half a country on faith alone. Surely, this Carlo Baggio would present himself as a man of honor, one who appreciated the qualities of Piemontese women who carried themselves so proud and graceful.

Thank God she'd bought the New York hat, even though it rode too heavy on her head.

Chapter 6
The Arrival

That same day found Carlo before the bureau mirror in his bedroom. He slipped into a silk shirt and adjusted a blue striped tie, both recent purchases from Marshall Field's Department Store. His hand-tailored suit with waistcoat, a gift from Giulietta the previous year, had earned Carlo the nickname of *Dapper Dago*, a dubious title depending on who said it and the manner in which it was said.

"Ah, Louisa, welcome to America," he said to his reflected image with a smile forced and unsure, as was his heart. No matter how much he practiced, Carlo could not make the words sound natural. Maybe Jake and Giulietta had been right: a bride from Italy with so many beautiful women in Chicago, and at his age—he must be out of his mind. What the hell, he grabbed his fedora, locked the door, and saluted his landlady while hurrying down the stairs.

Five minutes later at Amerigo's Barbershop Carlo leaned back in his customary swivel chair, welcomed the hot towels Amerigo applied to his face, and soon dozed off.

"Bravo," was the next word he heard when Amerigo ripped off the towels. "I commend you for honoring a fading tradition."

Carlo cringed. If Amerigo knew, so did everyone else.

"Hey, no jerking like that when my razor's so near to the throat," Amerigo said. "Now where was I?"

"Something about the Cubs."

"Quit kidding, this is your big day. How well I remember mine, bringing Rosa over from Orvieto. Good thing I did. These American women, they want to be like men." Amerigo deftly moved his razor over Carlo's heavy beard, pausing only to clean shaving cream from the blade. After viewing his work with the eye of an artist, the barber exchanged his razor for scissors and proceeded to clip half an inch from Carlo's hair. "My Rosa, she don't run around, not with six bambini to keep her home. Two hot meals a day she cooks, just as her mama did. And mine."

On a sidewalk bench outside the barbershop sat a row of seven mustachios, carbon copies of the Italy's *mustacci*: old men with drooping mustaches. The American mustachios needed neither shaves nor trims, but like their counterparts they congregated to read the Italian newspapers, argue politics, and reminisce about their inflated sexual exploits. When Carlo came out, to a man they stood and tipped their hats.

As he approached the Dearborn Station, Carlo stopped to buy sweetheart roses from a street vendor. Bending over to select the flowers from her tin bucket, she subjected him to a view of dingy underwear and rag garters holding up her cotton stockings. One of the barbershop mustachios whistled as he passed by and relayed the news of Carlo's intended so the vendor tucked a red carnation in her customer's lapel and patted his cheek. "With my compliments," she said, the good will earning her an extra quarter.

At Clark and Polk, Carlo went into Blackie's Restaurant, sat at the counter, and ordered coffee. "Cream, three sugars," he said as an afterthought. Stirring, blowing, and sipping whiled away another ten minutes before he swiveled off the stool and left. He crossed the street to the railroad station, its stone exterior recalling the sienna-colored structures in Italy. With another hour to kill before the New York Central's scheduled arrival, Carlo decided on a proper buffing for his twenty-five-dollar dress shoes.

Roscoe Johnson introduced himself as a Dearborn resident bootblack going back to the turn of the century. "I'm an immigrant, same as you," he said, applying spit to Carlo's patent high tops. "But I came up from Miss'ippi." He worked with practiced ease, bringing a high gloss to the leather. "You know Mister, I seen thousands of folks pass through this place. Course, since the war, the station ain't been nearly so busy. It's good seeing someone like you again, all jumpy 'bout meeting his woman."

"You know about her?"

"Only from the look on your face. Take it from me, you treat this lady right and she never leave your bed. Respect—that what every woman needs." He finished with a final snap of the rag and opened his palm to the six bits Carlo tossed in the air.

Carlo walked away with a spring in his step but still couldn't shake his private limbo, clinging to the past yet scrambling for the American dream. He squeezed onto one end a crowded bench in the grand lobby and surveyed the elaborate arched ceiling and windows patterned after those in the *palazzos* of Italy. But instead of marking time with the station clock, he closed his eyes to reflect on how his mama had adored his papa. And how they both had died before their time.

*****

Meanwhile on the New York Central its pompous rooster was making his final strut before Louisa. "Chicago Dearborn Station!" he intoned, blustering past her. She straightened up, and swallowed hard. Stiff from sitting and clutching her tapestry satchel, she hobbled down the aisle, bumping into every seat before she finally stepped from the train. The stairs were narrow, her satchel bulky. Someone on the crowded platform blocked her path. A foot caught the hem of her long skirt. She stumbled and lunged forward. Then lunged again.

Louisa's New York hat met the Chicago pavement. Next came the satchel. A sharp twist of the ankle shot an agonizing message up her leg. Her tired eyes went wet with pain. She grabbed a man's outstretched hand, only to have it slip through her fingers. Again she fell as he walked away. Rolling to her knees, Louisa managed to pick herself up. She plopped the misshapen hat over her straggly hair. Standing still eased the pain that trying to walk made worse. Blood from tight, stinging knees oozed through her stockings. She resisted the urge to look down, knowing her skirt hid the shame of her clumsiness. Thank God *he* did not see her fall. But where was he?

Except for Louisa everyone had left the platform. Wait! At the far end lingered a young man, her young man. Just as she imagined he would look. Well, maybe shorter. Not that height mattered. After all, Papa had been shorter than Ma. Ma, if only she could somehow see this handsome suitor, slender as a boy yet dressed as a man of wealth, one who moved as if he'd rather be anywhere but on his way to greet her. He spoke his first words without smiling.

"*Luigia? Luigia Valenza? Io sono Carlo Baggio.*"

His introduction coincided with an awkward thrust of flowers. Caught off guard, she dropped her pocketbook. Immigration papers and passport spilled out; he stooped down to collect them. But when he straightened up, he looked as if he'd swallowed a chunk of cheese that had passed its prime.

"Your pocketbook," he said in English. No Louisa, no signorina, every respectable woman deserved the courtesy of a proper title. Perhaps his rudeness was not intentional. Perhaps he was nervous too.

She pointed to the only luggage remaining on the platform. "My trunks. We must get my trunks!"

*****

Christo! Carlo wanted to bolt, cast this day aside as if it had never existed. From the size of those trunks, he figured the woman had moved her entire household. And now she expected him to transport them to her brothers' apartment. After paying dearly for the delivery service, he picked up the satchel she refused to leave with her other possessions and motioned for her to follow him.

Earlier on the platform he'd stood at a discreet distance, watched every female step from the train and hurry through the exit. When no one except a disheveled woman remained, he knew she had to be Louisa Valenza. His heart sank. Blame it on her backward village, Jake would've said, smaller than theirs and lacking a simple post office. And what about Giulietta; she knew Carlo's expectations had been unrealistic. Such a clumsy woman, when she dropped her pocketbook, he knelt to retrieve its contents. There, on her passport the year of her birth, 1901. Damn: four years older, two inches taller, and plainer than a wooden board.

Carlo headed toward the station exit; she lagged behind. As they passed by the shoeshine stand, Roscoe Johnson waved him over.

"Lawdie, Lawdie," Roscoe half whispered as Louisa kept walking. "Look at them hips move that skirt. That be a woman built for some lucky man."

"Did I ask for your opinion?"

"No but I'm giving it," Roscoe said. "Don't you see her hurting?"

"She's just tired. It's a long way from Italy."

Roscoe shook his gray head. "Damn, damn, damn."

"This way, mister," a taxi driver called out. The same one who'd offered Louisa his hand when she fell, the same one who'd let her fall a second time.

As Carlo followed Louisa into the taxi's back seat, he handed the driver a matchbox advertising Fabiola's. Their taxi merged into heavy traffic and Carlo spent five minutes looking out the window before he finally spoke.

"Your trip, it was good?"

"So-so. The boat ...." She rocked her hand sideways. "The food, the food ...."

"That's nice." He caught the cabby eyeing them through the rearview mirror, and wanted to tell him to mind his own business but let it pass. Why create trouble that could land them on the sidewalk before he delivered this woman to her brothers.

Even now he wasn't sure about her face, although he hadn't detected the Valenza beak, which would've been impossible to miss. He hadn't noticed the color of her eyes, nor her hair. How could he, both hiding under that ridiculous hat sitting crooked on her head. Dear God, he wanted out, now.

The cabbie stopped in front of a narrow brick building, its awning-covered window splashed with the fancy lettering of Fabiola's.

"Oh-h, Fabiola's, in honor of our nonna," Louisa said, wiping her eyes. "She'd have been so proud."

Vincenzo came running out. He and Louisa fell into a frenzy of kissing, hugging, laughing, and crying. Holding her hand, he paraded her through the saloon's entrance. "Look, everybody, my sister from the Old Country. And you all know my good friend, Carlo Baggio. He brought Louisa from the train station."

Good friend, Carlo cringed at the reference. While Fabiola's patrons waved cheery greetings to Louisa, he hung back, not wanting to steal her limelight or call attention to himself.

Since Massimo had stayed behind to mind the cash register, he now repeated Vincenzo's welcome with even greater enthusiasm.

"When did we last hug?" he asked, twirling Louisa off the floor.

"I was seven."

"And look at you now. Bella, bella!"

"Just as I remember Ma," Vincenzo said, pulling out a linen handkerchief, as did Massimo and Louisa. After a mutual purging of noses and patting of eyes, they hugged and kissed again.

"Ma's trunks are coming from the station," Louisa said between tears. "Carlo took care of everything."

"Ah Carlo, our savior," Massimo said. "Vincenzo, get the vino."

Basta, Carlo needed more than a drink. Showing his palm, he stepped back. "*Pardone*, but I must leave now. You and Vincenzo should have this time with your sister."

"But Carlo, you're family now."

"Later!" he called out without so much as a glance in Louisa's direction.

"Please," she whispered in a choked voice. "I am tired."

"But, of course," Vincenzo said. He led the way upstairs, all the while talking nonstop. "We have this big apartment, me and Massimo, and a housekeeper from The Old Country who does the cleaning and the laundry, which means you can take it easy. Just so you know, Louisa, we appreciate everything you did for Ma."

When they reached the landing, he opened the door, motioned Louisa to enter first. There stood a large-boned woman, with henna-dyed hair and coarse features befitting a laborer. She wrapped her sturdy arms around Louisa and kissed both cheeks.

"*Benvenuto, Luigia!*"

"I speak *poco* English," Louisa said, "but not so good."

"The more you speak it the better you speak it," the woman replied, her eyes following Vincenzo as he backed out the door.

"*Scusi*, my customers need their drinks refilled," he said. "Oh, I almost forgot. Louisa, meet Tillie Grasso."

Louisa cocked her head to the housekeeper. "Tillie from Salle?"

"I know, I know. Say no more. Mama wants me back with her but I ain't going."

Tillie was primed to relate the whole story but Louisa didn't feel like talking anymore, not with her ankle throbbing worse than an abscessed tooth. She wanted to lick her wounds in private but when she stumbled and expelled a low moan, Tillie seized the chance to play nurse. Off came the torn, bloody stockings. Abrasions were cleaned and painted with tincture of iodine, a pail soak of hot water and Epson salts guaranteed to reduce the swelling. Later, with bandaged knees and wrapped ankle elevated on a pillow, Louisa sunk into a bed of fresh linens and relived the pain Carlo Baggio had inflicted on her.

Nice, what did he know. He'd said her miserable boat trip was nice. What did he see when they first met? Not her eyes, nor her smile. Certainly not her face, not once did he look at it. In the taxi he sat beside her but not once did he touch her. Instead he hugged the door, no doubt regretting the moment more than she did. But did the humility stop there? No. He shamed her in front of Vincenzo and Massimo. How could they have been so wrong about this man. And how could she have been so trusting. She'd given up her home, the only one she'd ever known. On the day she left Monte Piano, Aldo and Matteo were already knocking out the walls between her apartment and theirs to create more space.

As for her American brothers downstairs they fumed at the bar's quiet end and spoke in voices too low for their customers to hear.

"D'ya see the way that little *bastardo* treated our Louisa?" Vincenzo grumbled. "He barely looked at her. Who the shit does he think he is."

"Patience, brother, all in good time," Massimo said. "Louisa ain't going back. Nor will we allow the Valenza name to be disgraced. She can help out in the kitchen 'til the bastardo comes to his senses."

"And suppose the bastardo don't?"

"Then we knock some into him."

*****

Meanwhile in the restricted area of Night School, Frog Sapone stretched his skinny legs down the hall to a door marked private, and tapped lightly. Not waiting for an answer, he stuck his head inside and spoke with a tongue darting in and out between thin, colorless lips. "Excuse me, Miss Giulietta. I thought you should know: Teacher's Pet has entered the building."

"What about that smarmy taxi driver we sent to the train station?"

"Working out in Physical Ed."

"Well done, Ugo. Leave the door ajar on your way out."

Giulietta disposed of her reading glasses before moving to the sofa. She lowered the neckline of her green satin gown, arranged its monkey fur trim over her knees, and waited for the door to open.

"Ah, Carlo, why so glum, my pet? The Piemontese, was she not what you expected?" Giulietta patted the cushion while projecting her most sympathetic smile. "Come, sit down. Tell me all about your day."

Chapter 7
Rude Awakening

The day after Louisa arrived in Chicago, she inspected the contents of her trunks. Satisfied all the treasures were still intact, she moved them to a back closet for safekeeping until she acquired her own home. During the first week, she cried herself to sleep every night, and after her sprained ankle and broken heart healed, she volunteered her services in the kitchen of Fabiola's. To save face, her brothers announced that for a limited time the granddaughter of Fabiola Valenza would be preparing special Piemontese recipes direct from the Old Country. It was not the life Louise had envisioned for herself but one she accepted without complaint since she didn't expect it to last forever.

"Such *stravaganza*," Louisa told Tillie one morning over coffee. "All these Italian bachelors and *Americani* paying hard-earned money for simple country food so easy and inexpensive to prepare."

"Sure it's easy," Tillie said, "when you got the kitchen, the tools, and the time. You're in the city now. So, think like city people."

"And what about the wine? This great country of America denying the very blood of life to its people, all because of this ... whadayacallit."

"Prohibition."

"Si, Prohibition. My poor brothers, they gotta make a living."

"Not to worry. Vincenzo and Massimo know how to make money." Tillie gestured the enormity with both hands. "Lots of money. They paid my way from Italy, took me in when I had no place to go. Ten years I been here, fixing their breakfast, washing and ironing their clothes. I keep the place clean and sometimes they let me help out downstairs. I never had it so good."

"What about your ma?"

"Like I said, I ain't going back."

"Maybe you could invite her for a visit."

Tillie threw her head back and belted a laugh. "She has three sons and I'm the only daughter. Need I say more."

Louisa smiled. "We're still going shopping today?"

"With Massimo's money, because he thinks you need to look more American."

*****

That afternoon Louisa walked into Fabiola's wearing georgette the color of peaches. A narrow-brimmed cloche with wide satin trim covered hair that a scarf had always protected from the Italian sun. Stylish pumps and silk stockings replaced black oxfords and cotton stockings to reveal her well-turned legs. At first, neither brother recognized her. Then Vincenzo reached for the wine; the cheroot planted in the corner of Massimo's mouth fell to the terrazzo floor. Enthusiastic applause from the customers broke the silence and Louisa responded with a half curtsey. She whipped off the hat and with a laugh sent it down the polished bar to where her brothers were sitting.

"Just wait until that shit hears about this," Vincenzo muttered to Massimo. Neither of them had seen Carlo since the evening he delivered Louisa.

*****

That night after everyone in the Valenza household had gone to bed Louisa awoke from a deep sleep and heard muffled sounds coming from Vincenzo's bedroom. Thinking he was sick, she hurried down the hall and opened the door to his room.

"Sweet Mother of Jesus," she mouthed from behind her hand. Wrapped in a tangle of naked bodies like paintings she'd seen at a Torino museum were Tillie, Massimo, and Vincenzo. In a gallery such displays aroused the curious as well as the educated. Art they called it. Repulsive yet amusing had been her reaction then, but this was now, and her tolerance did not extend to relatives who shared the same parents. "Sweet Mother of Jesus!" she repeated, this time without reservation.

The creaking bed went silent, sagging as its occupants attempted to disengage themselves. On seeing Louisa, Tillie giggled and grabbed the sheet to cover her Rubenesque body. The brothers hung their heads like little boys caught with their hands in the biscotti jar.

"Vincenzo, Massimo! You insult the memory of our parents," Louisa screamed in Piemontese. "You disgrace the name of Valenza. Like filthy pigs you belong in a sty with the garbage. Both of you will burn in hell, along with this ...." Her eyes bore into Tillie's now sullen face. "... this filthy whore of whores. No wonder the good people of Salle ran you out."

Louisa vented until her voice gave out. She turned on her heels and slammed the door behind her, leaving the threesome to resume their activity with more vigor than before.

*****

In the morning when Louisa walked into the kitchen she lifted her nose but not to smell the fresh coffee Tillie had brewed.

"Your brothers went out for breakfast," Tillie said, "something they never do."

Louisa didn't answer. She poured her coffee and started back to her room but Tillie blocked the way. "Please, Louisa. I need to explain. In Piemontese, if you don't mind."

Louise sat down and sipped her coffee while Tillie talked.

"It's like this. In the beginning I traded off between Vincenzo and Massimo, but couldn't accommodate both of them on the same night. After all, I needed some time to sleep, same as I do now. But then one day, Massimo came to me all upset about Alberto Marconi. You remember, the one they called Berto?"

Louisa nodded. "Only by name, he came from our village."

"Si, he was older, and near as I can recall this is what Massimo told me. When Berto first came to Chicago, years before your brothers, he couldn't find work but his luck changed when he met Giovanni Giordini. Johnny Jingles everybody called the shit, because he always kept one hand in the pants pocket, playing sweet music with his ring of keys and grateful balls."

Louis shoved her chair back.

"Wait, hear me out," Tillie said. "For the *Siciliano* to offer a good-paying job to the Piemontese was most unusual. Since Berto had a wife and four bambini, he accepted the offer and wound up working for the Black Hand, a Sicilian secret society known for their evil vendettas and extortion. Berto performed well, a loyal soldier who never refused an assignment. But when the Black Hand no longer held Chicago's immigrants in its greasy palm, the children of those abused immigrants demanded retribution. You know, a matter of family honor."

Family honor Louisa understood, hers had been shattered. She allowed Tillie to pour more coffee.

Tillie continued. "One evening around eleven Vincenzo met up with Berto as he came out of Fabiola's. Vincenzo relayed the events of that evening to me after swearing me to secrecy that extended no further than Massimo and now I tell you, which makes it still a secret, right?"

"I don't have all day, Tillie."

"Sure you do. Anyway, that night a thunderstorm had passed through the neighborhood, leaving it deserted when Vincenzo and Berto started their walk down the street. Berto was in a good mood and said he enjoyed living the simple life again. Maybe he'd go back to the Old Country, but only for a visit. Then a polite voice came from the shadows, asking for a minute from Signore Marconi. Given his past, Berto should've been on guard as he turned to answer. It all happened so fast, according to Lon.

Berto's hands flew to his throat, even before the dark red blood gushed out to spill over his shirt and pants. He tried to speak. No sound came from his mouth. He looked at his hands, at his blood. He looked at Vincenzo in disbelief. At that moment Vincenzo wondered if Berto understood his throat had been slit, his vocal chords severed. Berto was beyond help."

Louisa gasped. She refused more coffee.

Tillie leaned closer. "Horrified, Vincenzo turned and ran and never looked back. The angels were with him that night since he'd not seen the assailant's face. In the morning a foot patrolman found Berto's body, his testicles stuffed in his mouth. This marked the fate of an informer, a role not befitting the man, but a punishment he often meted out to others."

"Basta," Louisa said. "I still don't understand."

"I'm getting to that. Vincenzo pleaded with me. 'Tillie, I need you tonight, even though it's Massimo's turn. How else can I grieve for my friend? We knew each other from Locana. Like an older brother, he was to me.' I would've obliged but Massimo refused to give up his night since Berto was his good friend too, and Massimo wanted to honor his memory. That's when we agreed to our special nights, just the three of us."

"And for this I am supposed to close my eyes, close my ears, silence my tongue. This is what Massimo and Vincenzo expect of me? When I think of Ma …."

"Don't think about her. This is America. What more can I say? Your brothers and me, we get together whenever there's a need, and always when the moon is full."

Chapter 8
Noreen Flaherty

Noreen Flaherty could abide the cleaning, the laundering, the appointment book, but she dearly hated the cooking. The cooking had become her daily cross to bear, her offering for the poor souls in purgatory and those burning for all eternity in hell. Day after day the same routine: prepare, serve, clean up … prepare, serve, clean up … prepare, serve, clean up. Any fool could see the polite compliments for the mediocre fare she turned out were meant to spare her feelings. Feelings be damned; what she needed, what she deserved, was change. In the twenty-five years since coming to America from County Cork, Ireland, her red hair had turned white while she catered to the pastor of St. Sebastian Roman Catholic Church. The occasional covered dish provided by sympathetic parishioners had sustained her and the priests, enabling all of them to persevere a wee bit longer. But employing outside help was a luxury she'd not considered, that is, until one afternoon when an immigrant toting a tapestry satchel appeared at the back door. Noreen invited the young woman into her kitchen.

Louisa Valenza introduced herself and in broken English said, "I'm a good cook, and I need a place to stay. Just until I find my own."

"Hmm," Noreen mused while pouring two cups of tea that even she didn't like. "And what kind of cooking might we expect."

"Only the best. I worked in the family business here and in Italy."

"Ah-h, 'tis a professional … one can only wonder until proven otherwise. Well, nothing but the best for St. Sebastian's. The monsignor is very fussy, and rightfully so. He enjoys entertaining visiting priests, church hierarchy, and influential parishioners."

Louisa shrugged. "And I enjoy cooking."

"Not that St. Sebastian's is highfalutin, you understand. We never turn away a hungry wanderer, or two or three. Of course, they take their meals on the back porch." Noreen waited for some reassurance. Getting none, she narrowed her watery blue eyes and peered into Louisa's. "The monsignor will be wanting to know why it was you left your former employment."

Louisa bristled and blinked away a single tear. "Through no fault of mine."

"Enough said, for now that is. I'll consider you for culinary duties." Noreen could barely contain her enthusiasm. "If the monsignor stomachs your cooking better'n mine, you can count on room and board plus two dollars a week. Now let's get your belongings put away."

"You mean I can start now, just like that?"

"The monsignor runs St. Sebastian's church, Dearie. I run the rectory. Did I not tell you before, he's my brother."

Noreen settled the trial cook in a small room adjacent to the kitchen and then took her grocery shopping. Or was it Louisa who took Noreen shopping. Quick as a wink the young immigrant had put aside her shyness and insisted on visiting the markets she knew from working at Fabiola's, a questionable establishment Noreen had never set foot in. In spite of the wicked aromas, Noreen arranged for charge accounts at a shop specializing in imported olive oils, cheeses, and hams; another at a bakery that produced nothing but loaves of Italian bread and *grissini*, both long and short, fat and thin.

"I hope you know what you're doing, Dearie," Noreen said as they stood at the counter in Pané. "All this hustle and bustle over the daily specialty, 'tis a mystery to me." The bakery had already sold out of its best bread so they settled for Louisa's second choice. Next, the sidewalk produce stands with Louisa shaking her head over what the clerks wanted to bag until they gave in and allowed her to handpick her own fruits and vegetables.

Back in the kitchen Louisa coaxed rich stock from a fat stewing hen. While the broth simmered, she added chopped onions to olive oil and butter heating in a heavy skillet, followed up with garlic cloves crushed under the flat of a big knife. The kitchen took on a pungent aroma while Noreen observed from a distance, not to learn but to fulfill the supervisory duties the monsignor expected her to perform. Louisa swished half a cup of rice through the mixture, alternated more rice and broth with some tomato puree. She turned the heat down low and asked for wine, preferably red.

"You're not a tippler, are you, Dearie?"

Louisa's face went blank. She lifted her shoulders. Still, Noreen allowed her to select a bottle from the monsignor's cellar. Louisa opened the wine, sniffed with approval, and gave a healthy dose to the simmering rice.

"Such a generous blessing—not that I care, mind you, but the monsignor might."

"He won't know it's there." Louisa lowered the gas flame and covered the skillet.

"Then what's the point."

"Without wine the risotto won't taste like my ma's."

"Well, God forbid, we wouldn't want that, now would we?"

Next, the veal chops—pounded flat, breaded lightly, and pan-fried a few minutes on each side. Olive oil, lemon juice, and vinegar dressed the salad greens. After Louisa sliced the bread, plated the meat, and slid the rice into a bowl, she folded her arms and said, "Basta, I gave you my best. Dinner is ready."

"Thank God, Dearie. I for one am exhausted."

Having assigned Louisa to kitchen clean up, Noreen served the meal and cleared the empty dishes. Only when the monsignor and his assistant lean back to partake of their spirits and coffee, did she sit down at the kitchen table to eat with Louisa. Never had food tasted so delicious. After consuming every kernel of the leftover rice, she couldn't help but temper her enthusiasm with a wee suggestion.

"Perhaps a bit less seasoning, Dearie, not that I'm complaining you understand."

Louisa nodded politely, just as had Noreen expected. Her feet ached from grocery shopping. She rubbed one arch along her calf muscles, and then the other, all the while listening to Louisa's reason for coming to St. Sebastian's.

"Oh, 'tis a poor lass you are to have endured such disgrace," Noreen said, "first from your betrothed, then your own flesh and blood." She moved to the edge of her chair, bracing to hear the details; instead, she heard the tinkling of the monsignor's bell. Clucking her tongue, she pushed back her chair, stood, and answered his call.

Monsignor Sean Flaherty bore a strong resemblance to Noreen, five years his senior. Both were round and stooped from age, with a host of freckles fading into pale skin. Other than the archbishop's authority, Noreen's was the only one that Sean Flaherty never questioned. To do so, would've sent all of St. Sebastian's into a turmoil neither of them wanted.

"The new cook, is she still around?" he asked.

"Indeed she is, but don't you be scaring her off."

"And deny you the pleasure, I should say not. Now, if it's not asking too much of you, I'd like to see the unfortunate woman."

Noreen rolled her eyes as if annoyed. She returned with Louisa, who all but genuflected after being introduced.

"Sorry, Padre—I mean Monsignor ... about the bread ...."

"No, no Lass. The meal was good, very good indeed. In fact the meal was ...." He glanced over to Noreen. "I would say quite adequate. It's just that you being our new cook and all, I wanted to meet you, as does my assistant Father Connelly."

The young priest with deep auburn hair stood and extended his hand. "Welcome to St. Sebastian's, Louisa," he said. "I'm sure you'll do everything you can to help Noreen carry out her many duties."

Yes, indeed, Noreen thought. Terrance Connelly could charm the socks off a shoeless beggar. The man exuded such warmth he could've descended from the heavenly angels, which may have accounted for Louisa fumbling through an awkward curtsy and uttering her thanks in Italian. For sure the immigrant would need a guiding hand, whatever it would take to keep lead her away from temptation.

Chapter 9
Terrence Connelly

"There'll be no pointing, Dearie, and none of that mumble jumble either. You'll not be learning proper English by using your hands. Just repeat the words after me until you get them right." Six weeks had passed, with Noreen never letting up. Louisa sat across the kitchen table from her. "Mind what I say and you'll be speaking English as good as me and better'n the likes of certain immigrants who insist on clinging to their native tongue."

"Someday I'll have me a *trattoria*, Noreen."

"A what?"

"You know, a little place that serves good food."

"Café, Dearie. Speak the language of your new country."

With Noreen's persistence Louisa's English had improved, though with a pronounced Irish brogue, decidedly different but to the trained ear easily understood. Noreen broached a different matter with her usual tact, "Now about that no good for—"

"I already forgot his name, just like you said I should. He's out of my head like a bad case of the sniffles."

"Good. Just don't get close enough to let him back in." Noreen glanced at the wall clock. "Glory be, would you look at the time. Now off with you, Dearie. You best not take advantage of the good father's generosity."

*****

Indeed, Terrence Connelly was both good and generous. He was the oldest of seven children, each born a year apart to Irish immigrants in a rough and tumble section of Chicago where having children reach adulthood without landing in jail was lauded as an accomplishment. When Terry turned eleven, he decided on a religious vocation, to become a parish priest like those from St. John's where he worshipped with his family. At thirteen he entered the seminary on a scholarship and lived there year round, only returning to his parents' modest home for visits no longer than two weeks. An exemplary student, Terry never questioned the strict discipline imposed on young seminarians. In fact, he welcomed the rigorous demands and seclusion from worldly temptations that could detract from his calling.

To celebrate his ordination, Terry's parents hosted a small reception at St. John's to celebrate his marriage to the Church. Seamus and Bridgett Connelly stood beside their Son the Priest and basked in his holiness, his religious vocation their direct link to God and hopefully a guarantee of eternal salvation. Terry's six siblings shared those same sentiments. The sextet of blue-eyed auburn-heads had managed to grow up unscathed by their slum environment, a tribute to the devotion of their hardworking parents. The brothers and sisters often joked that God had chosen the best looking of their litter for the religious life. And what a shame they all agreed: Terry's genes would not pass on to another generation.

Father Connelly's first assignment was to St. Sebastian Catholic Church, where young priests got their feet wet under the guidance of Monsignor Sean Flaherty, one of the wisest and most perceptive priests in the Chicago archdiocese. Two years away from the seminary and the assistant pastor still had someone in authority to look out for his soul.

*****

And like Noreen, Terry Connelly had taken Louisa under his wing. By volunteering to teach her the fundamentals of reading and writing in English, he'd also hoped to open her mind and heart to the Holy Mother Church since her Catholicism had been based on superstition and misconception. These afternoon sessions with her had become a highlight of his day, exceeded only by his celebration of the Holy Mass.

"Sorry I'm late, Father," Louisa said as she hurried into the parlor.

"No, no, it was I who came early, to reflect in solitude."

She cocked her head, and smiled. "I don't understand."

"To examine my conscience, Louisa, but enough about me, this time belongs to you."

The room's sliding doors remained recessed in the pocket wall when Father Connelly and his student assumed their usual seats on either side of the library table. They slipped into a comfortable routine that had developed over the past month. As Louisa read from an elementary primer, Father Connelly watched and listened to her master simple words page by page. When she finished one book, he rewarded her with another, a level or two more difficult than the previous. While she continued to read, he took note of her oval face, neither beautiful nor homely, but the classic simplicity of women preserved in old world paintings. Almond-shaped eyes accented by well-defined brows expressed her every emotion, laughter being the most common, but sometimes a flash of anger surfaced in response to a chance reminder of the lost suitor or the voluntary estrangement from her brothers. Although her misfortunes had brought him undeniable pleasure, he'd resisted the temptation of lustful thoughts, a sin that would require his confessing to Monsignor Flaherty who was wiser than Methuselah. No failing, however slight, escaped the monsignor's scrutiny but for now Terry Connelly's innermost secrets belonged to no one but himself.

Chapter 10
Second Thoughts

Although Carlo Baggio still held title to Night School's most popular student, to his disappointment studying with a different teacher each session had lost its luster. True to his traditional upbringing, he avoided the teacher with whips, and the Double Trouble Twins who really weren't related. Sometimes he did nothing more than talk with Giulietta. Other than Jake, she was the closest thing to family. And starting his own family had never left his mind.

One evening found him sitting on the sofa in Giulietta's office, leaning forward, elbows to knees, while she rubbed his neck and shoulders.

"Why so tense, my pet?" she asked.

"It's that damn job at Becker's. They keep pushing me to go on some night runs. The pay's better but—"

"The risk is so much greater, as with all we hold dear. Here, lay down. Let me bring relief to those worrisome muscles!"

He stretched out, closed his eyes, and imagined the down cushions enveloping him like puffy gigantic marshmallows. She knelt on the Oriental rug, removed his shoes and socks, and massaged his arches.

"Once the feet relax the head will follow." She hummed a few bars of "Two for Tea," moved up to his shoulders and neck, and kneaded her fingers into muscles that resisted the temptation to relax.

He'd been on the verge of manhood when he first came to

Giulietta and she'd introduced him to a world he wouldn't have known otherwise. He should've been relishing a romp with her tonight but the Valenza woman kept cluttering his brain.

"Still thinking about the Piemontese?" Giulietta asked. "Perhaps you were a bit hasty in your rejection of the frumpy peasant."

"Did I say she was frumpy?"

"No, but I know you too well. The look on your face said more than any spoken words."

"I made a bad investment so I cut my losses while I could."

"Of course you did the right thing. Given her provincial background, she would have expected ... no, demanded ... a monogamous union. Imagine that: you a lion with no reason to roar."

"I ain't proud of what I did."

"Nor should you be ashamed. You wanted someone like your mother: sweet, safe, an old-fashioned homebody."

"I can't show my face at Fabiola's. I ain't had a decent meal in months."

"Good food feeds the soul and the soul feeds the heart. Perhaps you should give the Piemontese another chance. Compare her to my ladies."

"Maybe you're right." He rolled into a sitting position and was about to get up when Giulietta grabbed his belt loop and pulled him back to her.

"Not so fast, my pet. Let's review some of those special techniques you won't get anywhere but here."

*****

The next morning in the Baggio apartment Carlo sat with his brother at the table, both savoring their steaming latte and coffee served in small bowls with ears. Carlo's lip curled when Jake tore off a chunk of cream bread and played with it in his coffee.

"You gotta do that?" Carlo asked.

"Do what?"

"You know, with the bread. It makes me sick."

"Speaking of sick, I'm sick of eating *cacca* every night," Jake said.

"So pick a place that serves good eats."

"I heard that Valenza woman is working for her brothers, cooking just like the Old Country."

"I guess we could go back," Carlo mumbled with a mouthful of chewy bread.

"Some of the guys say she ain't bad looking."

"Who said that?"

"Hell, I don't remember. Does it matter? Maybe you should talk to her yourself."

Carlo didn't answer. Last night's romp with Giulietta had whetted his sexual appetite but more than ever for a permanent union. Maybe he could have it all, marry the respectable Piemontese and teach her to make love like a whore.

*****

Carlo waited until Saturday before he and Jake returned to Fabiola's. They sauntered up to the bar where Massimo was resting his elbows.

"So, the great Carlo Baggio has decided to court our sister," Massimo said while pouring two cups of wine. "Well, you're too late. She went to St. Sebastian's."

"What, to be a nun ... she just got here."

"No, *testa dura*," Massimo said with a sneer. "You with the hard head and short sight started all this. Louisa's cooking for the rectory. She lives there too."

"Why'd she leave?"

Massimo shrugged. "God only knows, but this much I do know: you got stuck feeding the pockets of priests."

"No way, I ain't been to church since I left Italy."

Jake nodded. "He speaks the truth, unlike some people."

Massimo turned to Carlo and squeezed his arm. "Listen to my words. You paid for a wife and a good cook. You got nothing. Those priests paid nothing and got a good cook. Just 'cause there's no wedding don't mean they won't perform certain services."

Carlo's fingers felt glued to his glass as Massimo moved to the end of the bar where Vincenzo waited on other customers.

"Don't look now," Jake said. "But the Valenza brothers are shooting spit from both sides of their mouths. You think it's safe to eat here?"

"Relax, we're still welcome."

"How can you tell?"

"Massimo, he poured us the good vino. Come on, let's grab that corner table."

"Just don't let the Valenzas sucker you again," Jake said after they sat down. He looked over the chalkboard offering. "Whadaya think, should we try the veal?"

"So, maybe I should drop by St. Sebastian's for a better look."

"What the hell, maybe check her teeth. You ain't buying a horse, Carlo. Just get to know her. She can't be that bad. Hmm ... chicken cacciatore."

"No veal for me."

"You paid plenty to bring her over. Ain't you getting tired of messing with the teachers?" Jake showed his palms. "I know, I know, they're supposed to be clean, but you could get crabs. And I don't mean the kind you fish from the water!"

"You mean clap, not crabs. I'm getting the ravioli."

"Yeah, me too.

Chapter 11
Sunday Dinner

Life couldn't get much better for Noreen, as witnessed by the old Gaelic tune she hummed while setting an extra place at the dining room table. Unless the dinner guests were the archdiocese hierarchy, she never knew in advance who might be coming for Sunday dinner. Not that Sean needed her approval, although, on occasion, she did question the wisdom of his generosity. She'd already checked out the parlor and Sean's choice for today showed a bit of promise, at least in her estimation. Having her own assistant had lightened Noreen's workload, which in turn invigorated her commitment to improving the lot of those less fortunate than herself. She returned to the kitchen with a quick step and found Louisa at the stove, stirring a pot of what Noreen called mush.

"Dearie, you need to take a gander at the young man Father Flaherty has invited to dinner. God willing, this could quite possibly be the one to make you forget the other."

"Not now, or for sure the polenta's gonna burn."

"Take it off the heat, Dearie," Noreen said, pulling the pot aside. "Trust me; this one deserves a look see."

Louisa followed her to the parlor door, looked through the leaded glass insert, and gasped. "Mother of Jesus, that is the other one. That's Carlo Baggio."

*****

Earlier that morning at St. Sebastian's nine o'clock Mass Carlo had knelt in the last pew, a rosary going nowhere in his hand while he scanned the crowd of worshippers, trying to pinpoint a face he hardly remembered. Having had no success, he hung around the front sidewalk after the service and watched the parishioners drift away. At last he made out Louisa, better dressed than that first day and with a fashionable hat covering most of her face. She was head to head with an older woman, laughing as they walked through the back gate of the rectory. At least this Louisa possesses a sense of humor, he thought. In fact, from where he stood, she didn't look half bad.

But how would she react to him? One thing was for sure, Carlo Baggio didn't bow and scrape to any woman—Night School teacher or prima donna. Before he could decide his next move, the white-haired priest from Mass came by. Cheeks flushed from a healthy dose of wine, the old man stuck out his hand, and introduced himself as Monsignor Flaherty.

"Welcome, my son. Now would you be new to St. Sebastian's?"

The hand was warm and soft when Carlo shook it. "Si, Padre, but I been in America for two years." Damn, already he gave away too much about himself. Priests made it their business to know everybody else's. This one must've stood at the altar and picked him out from all the regulars.

"And where did you come from before then? Might that be Italy, judging from your accent?"

"Near the Italian Alps, Padre ... north of Torino, Turin to you. I am Carlo Baggio."

"Well, Carlo Baggio, it seems our new cook is also from that same region. Would you be knowing Louisa Valenza?"

"Not exactly," Carlo said, brushing lint from his lapel. "I brought her over, you know, paid her way but, well ... things didn't work out."

"Hard to fathom, what with Louisa's good heart and work ethic. But not to worry, St. Sebastian's is teeming with bachelors who—"

"It coulda been my fault, the not-working-out part. Maybe I hurt her feelings."

"Since you've come this far, perhaps you're hoping for another chance. Let's see what can be done to put things right again."

*****

Having accepted an invitation to dinner that very day, Carlo returned in the early afternoon and to his surprise was met at the door by Monsignor Flaherty. He followed the old man into the parlor, sat where the old man told him to sit, in a chair near the sunniest window, where he dodged the blinding rays while the old man fired off a barrage of questions, the kind that deserved vague answers. Still, the familiar scent of garlic and herbs filtering from the kitchen kept Carlo grounded. Then a younger priest came bustling into the room, all excited about whatever excites men who wear their collars turned.

"Please excuse my tardiness, Monsignor. A dispute between the ladies of the Altar and Rosary Society—"

Carlo stood and the monsignor introduced him to Father Terry Connelly, who should've been smiling but for some reason wasn't. The old man cut through the silent bullshit with his own malarkey.

"Now Father Connelly, it seems that Carlo here was once the intended of our Louisa? 'Tis a pity they got themselves off to a rocky start but he wants to try again. Maybe we can be of some help."

Too many seconds passed before the priest showed his teeth with a phony smile. "Of course, Monsignor."

Too few words spoke volumes. Responding to an order from the old man, Carlo removed himself from the glaring sunlight to occupy an overstuffed mohair chair reserved for company. He settled back for polite interrogation from one priest, implied indifference from the other.

"Now what is it you do for a living, young man?" asked the monsignor.

"I work for a brewery."

"A brewery, you don't say. Which one?"

"Becker's."

"Hmm. And what is it you do?"

"Many things, not the same from one day to the next."

When they finally sat down to dinner Carlo was determined not to allow the strained conversation to ruin his best meal since coming to America, roast beef resting on a bed of its own gravy and polenta. Making polenta was an acquired skill that neither he nor Jake ever attempted on the hot plate in their room, although they had considered working out kitchen privileges with their landlady. The wine—from a grateful parishioner, Monsignor explained—tasted better than any from Fabiola's because Carlo could swirl it in a goblet instead of a cup.

Coffee laced with Irish whiskey polished off the dinner and only then did Monsignor Flaherty square his shoulders to the chair slats and narrow his eyes to Carlo. "So, lad, just how do you propose to make up for all this hurt you've caused our lovely Louisa?"

THE FAMILY ANGEL

"But, Padre …."

"Now, now, flimsy excuse I cannot abide. First off, you need to admit you were wrong—to yourself, to Our Lord, and to Louisa. And, if you're too proud for a bit of humble pie, you can never be man enough for her. Do you understand what I'm trying to tell you, lad?"

Carlo stifled a sigh. "Si, Padre."

"Now, go home. After you make amends with God, set about planning a proper courtship for this fine young woman. She has free time on Sunday after dinner and Wednesday after supper. Forget today. It's too late for her to drop everything for the likes of a near stranger. 'Course, it's not for me to say, but maybe—just maybe—she might consider a visit from you this forthcoming Wednesday."

The monsignor stood and with a firm hand to Carlo's shoulder, ushered him toward the door. Without moving from where he sat, Father Connelly said his goodbye and when Carlo turned to acknowledge it, he saw the priest pour another whiskey.

*****

Carlo left with the monsignor's blessing, not that he felt he needed such nonsense. Still, a man could never be too cautious in matters of the soul. While crossing the street he made an act of contrition, one that generalized the past two years of lustful pleasures. Then he slipped into a doorway, lit a cigarillo, and waited. Shortly after three o'clock Louisa strolled by, head raised and dressed in the same outfit she'd worn earlier that day.

"Luigia, Luigia Valenza," he called out while approaching her. She neither glanced his way nor slowed her pace. "Could you stop a minute? It's me, Carlo Baggio. I just want to talk."

"So now you want to talk." She stopped and directed her words to a pigeon perched nearby. "You insulted me. You insulted my family. You think I am not good enough."

The woman had spunk, like Giulietta only not so refined. But before Carlo could attempt an apology, she walked away. He fell in step with her. "Look, I'm sorry for … maybe I wasn't ready before but I am now. I want to try again."

"Oh? So you can hurt me again?"

"No, dammit, I never meant to hurt you."

At that moment a ragtag elderly woman came shuffling by. "Sonofabitch, take this," she said, whacking him with her cane, not once but three times. "How does it feel when I hurt you?"

With that Carlo grabbed the raised weapon, hung it from a bus stop sign, and hurried off to match Louisa's stride. "I got mixed up. I mighta been wrong … okay, okay, so I was wrong. But I did bring you half way round the world to be my wife."

Louisa stopped. Words spilled from her mouth like water from a busted dam. "I came to America because of you. Sure, you paid my way but that don't mean you bought me. You wanted a wife. I needed a husband. Then, you didn't want me. So now, I don't want you. Better yet, I don't need you."

"Maybe I need you." He put his hand on hers. "Maybe this was meant to happen, a test to see if we matched up. I'm asking you to forgive me. Maybe give me another chance."

A stingy smile crossed her lips. "There's something on your shoulder?"

He turned his head to where the old lady's cane had left its mark. His ears tingled like a boy caught digging out boogers. "Uh-h, sh-h … it's nothing." He brushed the dirt away with his starched handkerchief. "So, whadaya say?"

"This time you will not shame me. First, we get to know each other."

"You won't be sorry, Louisa." He pressed her hand to his lips, held it there until she pulled away. "How 'bout spending the afternoon with me?"

"Not today, I already got plans. Come by on Wednesday evening, seven o'clock."

Louisa hurried to board a trolley that stopped a few feet away. She took a seat and then sucked in a deep breath. What started as a smile turned into a giggle before developing into full-blown laughter as she recalled turning to see Carlo defend himself from an old lady's anger.

"I knew he'd come back," she said in Piemontese. "And if heaven is full of angels—which I truly believe with all my heart—I know one of them must've matched up me and Carlo Baggio."

From the seat behind Louisa came a tap to her shoulder. She turned to see a stocky young man with hair as stiff as straw.

"You okay, ma'am?"

"Si, grazie. I mean: yes, thank you. And I'm okay now."

Ten minutes later Louisa hopped off the trolley with no idea where she was. She wandered past an imposing stone church at North State and Superior, turned around, and went back to climb the short span of concrete steps. The heavy door of Holy Name Cathedral required her determined tug before it creaked open, jarring the inner silence of a magnificent structure still in its infancy compared to the centuries-old churches of Italy. But like its Italian counterparts, Holy Name Cathedral in the afternoon still drew a few sinners to meditate or kneel with their rosaries. She dipped two fingertips into the holy water, crossed herself, and tiptoed down a side aisle. At the candle station she dropped a coin in the box, lit a candle, and knelt.

"Sweet Virgin Mary and Mother of God, I'm asking you to intercede to Our Holy Father on my behalf. This man who did not want me has now changed his mind. He needs to look into my heart instead of my face. Oh … I guess the same goes for me too. Carlo Baggio could pass for a movie star, but it's his heart that worries me."

Chapter 12
A Proper Courtship

Those next three days didn't pass fast enough for Carlo. He'd told no one about Louisa except Jake, who must've told Hildie because she'd already suggested a foursome at the Green Parrot to which Carlo refused because he didn't consider Louisa the speakeasy type. "She's pretty special, more Madonna than flapper," were Jake's words, sending Hildie into a crying binge that lasted for hours and making Jake wish he could figure out a way to dump her without losing his job, and Carlo's.

Wednesday evening found Carlo sweating on the stoop of St. Sebastian's rectory. He pressed his shaky finger into the buzzer until the door swung open and the scowling housekeeper motioned him to come inside.

"You again," Noreen said as he followed her to the parlor. "Now don't be thinking of bringing any grief to our Louisa. 'Tis a lucky man you are that a lass such as Louisa would even consider you as a potential suitor. She deserves nothing but the best."

Louisa was warming the sofa and invited him to sit beside her. Although he preferred speaking in Piemontese, she insisted on English to which he agreed. Whatever it took to keep the woman happy became his new mantra. Within minutes they started reminiscing about Italy.

"When my brother and I were young, our parents often took us on the bus to Cereserole Reale," Carlo said. "From there we hiked into the *Gran Paradiso*. With so many mountains surrounding us, I thought we were walking to the top of the world."

"I been there, too, many times as a *cita*, I mean little girl. Gran Paradiso is now, how you say, a national park. People come from all over to see it. Maybe we were there at the same time."

"You've been to my village, Pont Canavese?" he asked.

"To settle business affairs, first after *mio padre* died; then, *mia madre*. A beautiful church overlooks the piazza with those tables and chairs. It's where everyone relaxes with a bottle of wine."

Carlo nodded. "I know the place well. Me and my brother spent our last night there."

"And you, have you been to my village Locana? It has the same *vista panoramica*." This produced a broad smile of even teeth that accentuated her olive skin.

Bella, bella, how did Carlo miss the Madonna smile when they first met? Perhaps he'd given her no reason to smile. "I only know Locana from the stories Vincenzo and Massimo told." Louisa dropped her smile; Carlo pressed on. "They opened their home to you, which I hear is pretty nice although I ain't had the pleasure. Why'd you leave?"

She closed her eyes, chewed her lip like a nervous child.

"This is no place for a young woman." He looked around the parlor, shook his head. "Your brothers, they worry about you."

"My brothers need to worry, but not about me."

"Nor about the liquor if that's what's bothering you. Take it from me: Massimo and Vincenzo Valenza are smart enough to make sure every palm gets the right amount of grease. Crooks, cops, and city hall—they don't leave anybody out. It's the Chicago way. And your brothers don't hold back."

"This I know for sure," she said.

"Louisa, we don't know each so good but ... but if you want to talk about ...."

With that she blurted out the antics of her brothers and the sinful woman who'd seduced them, still kept them under her spell. Carlo listened with great interest while Louisa vented her indignation. An amusing cinematic of the roly-poly trio came to mind, similar to the moving pictures Night School featured twice weekly, to stimulate some of the sluggish libidos according to Giulietta. Carlo envisioned Tillie cavorting naked with the brothers, each trying to outdo the other.

"... and so," Louisa continued, "I came to St. Sebastian's. Here I cook. I help Noreen. I learn to speak good English. I learn to read and to write."

Carlo straightened up. "Noreen, she teaches you these things?"

"Oh, no, Father Connelly does." Her eyes brightened, the wayward smile returned. She talked about the Bobbsey Twins books she'd been reading. "They're about two sets of twins, make-believe but what better way to learn about Americans," she said, "at least that's what Father Connelly tells me."

Father Connelly? What the hell, no wonder the priest regarded Carlo like cacca stuck on the sole of his shoe. Louisa's brothers had been right about getting her away from here. He'd start with a simple request. "Louisa, will you walk with me?"

"I know a very nice park not far from here." Sailing out of the room ahead of him, she spoke from over her shoulder. "Come, I will show you."

"Shouldn't you sign out," he said, "or tell someone you're leaving?"

She laughed, without reservation. "Carlo, this is a rectory, not a convent. And I'm a grown woman, not a child. With my free time I do as I please. *Andiamo* ... let's go 'cause I must be back by ten."

*****

Carlo's traditional courtship of Louisa involved a month of Sunday matinees or riverfront excursions followed by music in the park and Wednesday evenings in the Loop, dining and another movie or vaudeville at the LaSalle. At least Noreen hadn't insisted on tagging along although she'd hinted more than once. So far, he'd managed to override her suggestions for attending the street festivals sponsored every weekend by various Catholic churches.

One Wednesday before the movies Louisa insisted on stopping at Murphy's Diner for coffee and sinkers. As they sat in a front booth, Louisa slipped a glazed donut into her coffee. Carlo watched her play with the soggy mixture until crumbs floated to the top. He turned away, focusing his eyes on the window steamed with greasy moisture.

"You're not a dunker?" she asked. When he didn't answer, she burst out laughing. "Okay, from now on I won't do it in front of you. But you must do something for me."

Indeed, Louisa was her brothers' sister. Carlo nodded, anything to please her.

She leaned across the table, pressed her lips against his cheek. "I want to see that famous Neapolitan of the motion pictures," she said. "What's his name? Oh, yeah, Rudolph Valentino. Noreen said he can turn Gloria Swanson into melted butter."

"Not only is he a Mezzogiorno, he is what his paesani call a *finocchio*."

"You and your imagination. Show me a romantic Piemontese and I'll forget Valentino."

"How about Charlie Chaplin in *Gold Rush*?"

"He ain't Piemontese and he's too funny for romance."

"Okay, I'll take you to see Valentino but only if you do something for me."

"I already promised to give up dunking."

"This is more important. Vincenzo and Massimo have been asking for you. They want to make up."

The teasing smile faded from her face. "You ask the impossible, Carlo. For eighteen years I don't see my brothers at all. Then I see way too much."

"Forget what they did and stay out of their bedroom. Grown men have to answer for themselves. So do women."

"And to God. The three of them you shoulda seen. No, forget what I just said. How could you even think of courting me after the shame they brought to the Valenza name."

"They're your only family in America. Massimo and Vincenzo need you. What if something terrible happens to either one of them, or both?"

"Okay, okay. This time you win. Tonight we'll skip the movies and go to Fabiola's instead, but next Sunday belongs to the sheik Valentino."

*****

That evening when Carlo and Louisa strolled into Fabiola's, Vincenzo removed the cheroot clenched between his teeth and called out for Massimo, who took his time strolling over.

The brothers stood shoulder to shoulder, both grinning. "We forgive you for deserting us," Massimo told Louisa. He held his forefinger a millimeter from the adjoining thumb. "In fact we were this close to giving your job away."

Vincenzo nodded. "But not to worry, your apron's still hanging from the hook where you left it."

"I already have a job," she said, "one that I like and they like me."

"Here you are loved." Massimo said. "This job with the priests, it pays you well?"

"Better than the niente I made here."

"So long as you ain't competing against us, it don't matter." Vincenzo came around the bar and administered a volley of hugs and kisses. After turning her over to Massimo, he pulled Carlo aside and shoved a pack of cigarillos in his pocket. "We ain't gonna forget what you did this night, Carlo. Stand tall. You have earned yourself a place at our table."

Soon their celebration matched Louisa's first evening in Chicago, except this time Carlo didn't hold back. At the end of dinner and three bottles of wine they reminisced about life in Italy.

"Remember those biscotti Ma used to make?" Massimo asked. "How we dunked them in wine and sucked like thirsty calves."

Louisa nodded. "Ma taught me how to make biscotti and after she got sick, I always kept the tin full so she'd have something to eat she truly enjoyed."

"Jake and me used to dunk our biscotti in coffee, not wine."

"But Carlo, you're not a dunker," said Louisa.

"Only biscotti and only in coffee," Carlo said, "fast—in and out, in and out." He emptied his cup of the good wine; Vincenzo refilled it.

"I must make biscotti so you can dunk it in wine," said Louisa. "We'll do that on Sunday."

"What about Valentino?"

"Valentino can wait."

Massimo gave Carlo a friendly slap on the back. "For you and Louisa I have just the wine."

He went down to the cellar and brought up a bottle, along with the scent of Chicago's musty earth. After wiping dust from the bottle, he wrapped it in brown paper.

"Massimo, you gave that bottle?" Vincenzo asked after Carlo and Louisa had walked hand-in-hand out the door. "Holy shit, what were you thinking?"

"That those two lovebirds have been fooling around long enough. It's time they married. What's more, I want Louisa away from those priests."

*****

After taking Louisa back to the rectory, Carlo dropped by Night School in response to a message from Giulietta. Dressed in royal blue, she was sitting behind her grand mahogany desk, and spoke in the throaty voice capable of arousing him.

"Ah, my sweet," she said. "How long has it been? Oh yes, not since our last romp on the sofa. Why, Carlo, I do believe you're blushing like a school boy."

He grinned and sat down.

"So tell me," she continued. "How is the romance progressing? Will there be a wedding soon?"

"I think so."

"Then we mustn't waste time talking. You still have much to learn and I have brought over a new teacher."

"Uh-h ... I don't know, Giulietta. Maybe I've gone as far as I can. Louisa would be mad as hell if she found out."

"She won't unless you tell her."

"It's just that ... well, I can't change what's past."

"I certainly hope not. It's been quite the ride."

"But, since I intend to marry Louisa, I'd better stay away from other women."

"Carlo, Carlo. For you I imported a certain signorina from Italy, actually Genoa. She'd have been here sooner, but the paperwork was ... well, you know ... sticky."

"Genoa, you say? Maybe she brought news from the Old Country. Does she speak Piemontese?"

Giulietta laughed. "Not Bettina. But I personally guarantee, she'll teach you a new language."

"Uh, I don't know ...."

"Good people are hard to come by, my pet. First you learn; then you teach." Giulietta pressed the buzzer. She lit a cigarette and leaned back. Within minutes a small, well-proportioned woman appeared. Long brunette hair tumbled down her body, naked to the waist.

Carlo gulped. The barrier he'd been hiding behind crumpled when he allowed Bettina to take his hand. She led him through the door and down to the music room, an area he'd rarely frequented. Speaking in Piemontese, he told her she was pretty and asked for news from Italy. Bettina didn't answer. He repeated his words, this time in formal Italian. Again, she didn't answer. Only then did he realize the lovely lady could not hear nor could she speak. Still, these impairments did little to interfere with her ability to communicate. From a nearby Victrola came the familiar voice of Enrico Caruso.

"What the hell, must I put up with another Southern Italian,"

Carlo grumbled when he first heard the tenor, but that was before Bettina demonstrated her unusual talent for responding to the vibrations of operatic music. Giulietta had been right again; he still had much to learn.

*****

The following evening Carlo and Jake sat around their studio table, about to wrap up a three-hour marathon of gin rummy. Billowy smoke trickled through the air as they puffed on cigarillos imported from Cuba, an occasional indulgence they preferred over the American variety. Carlo leaned back and in a casual manner asked Jake to get lost Sunday afternoon.

"Me and Louisa need a quiet place."

"You're bedding the virgin."

"Watch your mouth. You're talking about the woman I intend to marry."

"So when do I meet her?"

"Real soon."

"You been saying that for a month. How long you need to get acquainted?"

"I know, I know. We just want to make sure."

"If she is the one, it's time to show off your good-looking brother. So-o just to be on the safe side, you got the room all afternoon and evening. I promised Hildie I'd go to some stupid family picnic. Damn, a whole day with the Krauts, their bratwurst and beer."

Chapter 13
Wine and Biscotti

"Bless me, Father, for I have sinned. I confess to Almighty God and to you that I am guilty of the sin of lust. I held in my heart certain thoughts and desires for a woman I can never have."

"You can never have any woman, my son. You made that promise to God and our Holy Mother Church."

"Yes, Father. I know, but I cannot stop thinking about her."

"God does not give us burdens too great to bear, my son. For everything in life there is a reason, even those temptations of the flesh that Satan himself puts before us. You must pray for the strength to overcome these evil thoughts before they overcome you."

"Father, I think I love her."

"You must love everyone, just as Our Lord did. Pray, my son, and I will pray for you too."

*****

With Noreen's permission Louisa spent Saturday afternoon preparing the biscotti she'd promised Carlo. It was a day unseasonably cool; a scorcher predicted for Sunday. She'd finished cutting a sheet of baked almond cookie mixture into diagonal-shaped logs when the kitchen door pushed open.

"Come in, Father … I mean Monsignor," Louisa said from over her shoulder while returning the sheet to the oven for a second baking.

"'Tis a Father I am as well as a Monsignor, lass."

She straightened up and with her customary smile asked if she could fix him a cup of tea.

"Only if you'll have one with me," he said from his perch on a nearby stool.

To compensate for the lack of sustaining spirits, the monsignor added hot milk and two teaspoons of sugar to the brew Louisa had poured.

"And how might things be going between you and that young man?" he asked.

"I'm in love, Father, thanks to you."

"Don't be thanking me, lass."

"But it's true. You asked Carlo to dinner and made him your friend. So did Father Connelly. And because of that we are now having this … a …."

"Proper courtship?"

"Yes, a proper courtship." She took a sip from her cup.

"Then, can we expect a wedding soon?"

"Yes, Father, unless the evil eye …."

"Now, now, there'll be none of that nonsense. Think positive—the sooner the better. And for now, God be with you."

*****

The next day Louisa filled a small wicker basket with a link of salami, two rounds of *tomino* cheese, a loaf of crusty bread, and the biscotti. She had poised her hand on the swinging door and was ready to leave when Father Connelly came by, pushing himself inside along with her.

"What have we here, Louisa? I'd say you're going on a picnic."

"With Carlo, Father. We're gonna eat in the park and then listen to the concert. Nice music, but different." She started fussing over the red and white-checkered cloth covering her basket.

"Do you miss Italy? I mean, do you ever think about returning?"

"I came to America hoping for a good match. I think this one might take."

"Not so fast, marriage is forever."

"Sure, Father, in the eyes of the Church, but nowadays even God plays tricks on us."

"No, it is we who deceive ourselves."

"If you say so, now please excuse me. I hear Carlo." She hurried through the swinging door, her voice carrying over from the other side. "Goodbye, Father."

"God be with you, sweet Louisa."

*****

The young couple walked toward the park with the picnic basket on Carlo's left arm and Louisa on his right. At the end of the first block she suddenly stopped, face in agony as she banged the heel of one palm against her forehead.

"Oh no, Carlo. The wine, you forgot the wine. The biscotti won't be the same without it."

"I didn't forget. How 'bout eating lunch at my place."

"I don't know. Your brother—"

"Jake's gone for the day. We'll have the place to ourselves."

"You sure it's okay?" She searched his eyes.

"The place ain't much but it's clean and respectable."

She waited thirty seconds before speaking. "I should see where you live, maybe meet your brother later."

"Si … yeah, Jake would like that."

As they walked the eight blocks to Carlo's tenement, Louisa explained the finer points of making biscotti, which seemed to interest him although she couldn't be sure. She preferred speaking the new language so Carlo could help her; and since he didn't speak that much better than she did, they agreed to learn from each other.

"Noreen means well and she's a good teacher," Louisa explained. "But she don't always speak right either."

"How do you know that?"

"Because Father Connelly don't talk like Noreen. He was born here. I mean in Chicago."

"That makes him better?"

"Maybe better at English but not everything," Louisa said. "You are my best teacher and much more fun."

The August day was Chicago at its worse, blistering hot and not a cloud interrupting the blue of the sky. Most of the tenement dwellers had escaped to the lakefront or to nearby parks. Instead of the usual commotion of yelling and cursing and kids underfoot, Carlo's building projected an eerie calm that made Louisa uneasy. She climbed the dimly lit stairs alongside him, their only source of natural light coming from large, sooty windows at each landing and naked bulbs suspended from paint-chipped ceilings.

"Watch your step," Carlo said, referring to the stairs cluttered with beat-up toys and empty cardboard cartons. "I'm sorry about the mess."

She raised her brow but made no comment.

Inside the studio Louisa walked around and inquired about every article, every piece of furniture. She picked up the personal items he used daily, held certain ones close as if trying to extract a part of him. "The room, it smells like you," she said. "Maybe Jake too."

"Is that good or bad?"

"You know what I mean, these things of a man: shaving lotion, cologne, cigarillos, shoe polish, starched shirts, coffee, and wine. They're all part of you."

"Me and Jake sleep here," he said. It was a tarnished brass Jenny Lind covered with a white reversible damask spread. "From my parents' bed," he explained about the cover.

Next to the bed a table held one kerosene lamp converted to electricity, two books, and an oval-framed wedding photograph. The groom, wearing a bushy handlebar mustache and tight suit, stood behind his petite bride, corseted into a dark shirtwaist dress and molded into an unyielding chair. Stiff, dark-haired, and wide-eyed—a couple preserved for eternity in faded sepia tones.

"Your parents?"

He nodded.

"They could pass for mine," Louisa said.

Opaque brown paint covered the bureau and frame around a mirror in need of re-silvering. A square oak table and three chairs sat at the only window, one that offered a bleak view of old brick. The makeshift corner kitchen consisted of a single-drain sink with chipped rusting enamel and exposed plumbing, a two-burner gas plate, metal cabinet, and wooden icebox. Louisa peered inside: milk, cream, cheese, salami, and red grapes.

She opened the door to a shallow built-into-the-wall closet. A silk negligee hung from the inside hook.

Carlo shrugged. "Jake's got this lady friend."

Louisa ignored his comment, as well as the dust balls scattered around the floor.

"The room could use a rug or two, but not bad for bachelors," she said, moving on to a bathroom of cracked, black and white hexagon floor tiles, raised toilet seat, and the faint odor of urine. Turning up her nose, she flushed the commode.

"Me and Jake got lucky," Carlo called out from where he sat on the sofa. "Most of the tenants share bathrooms." Their studio with private bath had cost him and Jake a single afternoon with the landlady, a small price for such a luxury. Her husband had been out of town during the threesome but since then he'd watched them like a cat dogging mice. To their relief the landlady had not demanded encore performances.

"I could never marry a man with dirty habits." Louisa leaned over and kissed his cheek. "My compliments to your mama, you passed inspection."

While she covered the table with the checkered cloth, he fiddled with the radio, trying to tune in the Italian station that carried the recorded music of Enrico Caruso.

"I thought you didn't like the Neapolitan," she said.

"Did I say that? I must've been thinking 'bout somebody else. If Caruso comes to Chicago, maybe we'll get tickets."

"Don't count on it. The man's been dead two years."

Having no success with Caruso, he settled for classical music. He opened the window wide to let in still air that refused to move. He poured two glasses of the wine Massimo had given him. She tore off hunks of bread, in the Italian way with her hands. He sliced cheese and salami with the pocketknife he always carried. They sat across the table from each other and picked at their food.

"It's good, yes?"

"Si, the best."

"And the weather, what do you think?"

"Hot. Not like the mountains."

"Neither is the view," she said, referring to the brick wall. With a burst of enthusiasm she jumped up. "Now I show you how we ate our biscotti." She put the uneaten food away and brought out the biscotti. He poured more wine.

"Sit here," she said, patting the table. "Next to me."

He pulled his chair around and sat down. She let the biscotti absorb the wine before putting it in her mouth. She dipped the same biscotti in the wine again, this time giving it to Carlo.

"Don't be afraid," she teased. "Do what I did."

His eyes didn't leave hers as he sucked on the biscotti. "Now, it's my turn."

He dipped the same biscotti in wine, and put it to her mouth. Juice ran down her chin. She laughed and reached for a napkin. He moved her hand away, leaned over, and licked the wine from her chin. Before she could protest, he got up, lifted one leg over her lap, and eased down to straddle her. Taking the glass, he trickled wine down her neck. Using his tongue, he followed the little stream as it rolled between her breasts. While his tongue lingered, he slipped the gauze-like blouse down from her shoulders and buried his face in the warmth of those two lovelies he wanted to savor.

"Louisa, I love you."

"I don't feel so good."

He stood up and took her hand. "Please?"

"The wine. The heat. My head, it's spinning."

"I can make it stop."

"I never done this before."

"That's okay. We'll learn together."

*****

Hours later as dusk settled over Chicago Carlo's bed began shaking to the rhythm of Louisa's sobbing. "What's the matter?" he asked, taking her in his arms.

"I love you but after today I am no longer fit to be your bride."

"You are my bride. In the eyes of God we are one. There's nobody but you and me, right?"

"I want to believe what you say."

"Because I speak the truth," he said, his lips trailing over her shoulders. "We should put on our clothes before my brother comes home."

"Okay, but I've been thinking. Let's wait awhile before we marry in church, just to be sure." She laid her head on his chest, ran her fingers down the length of his body. "One more time, please. Then we get dressed for your brother."

*****

By the time Jake's key rattled the lock to announce his return, Louisa and Carlo had already dressed and were about to leave. Jake's simple grin gave Carlo a rush of blood to his face and ears. He fumbled through an awkward introduction.

"Louisa, this here's my father … I mean my brother. This here's Giacomo, except now he goes by Jake which I keep forgetting. But he's still a Baggio, just like me."

"Ah, Louisa, welcome to America and our humble home." Jake kissed Louisa's cheeks and from over her shoulder, he winked at Carlo. He stood an arm's length from her and let out an appreciative whistle. "Brother, you are one lucky man. So when is the wedding?"

"First, we get to know each other," Louisa said.

"Yeah, there's plenty of time."

"Hell, if you and me wasn't brothers, I could go for Louisa myself."

She blushed and Carlo executed a meaningful jab to Jake's ribcage. "Louisa ain't your type, Jake. Besides, there's Hildie."

*****

When Louisa returned to the rectory, she tiptoed through the dark kitchen until a click of the wall switch illuminated the ceiling light. Noreen stuck her face in Louisa's, peered into her eyes.

"And how did your young man like those cookies you baked especially for him?"

"He loved them. We gotta do that again some time." Louisa stepped back into the shadows.

"I didna see you at the concert, Dearie. Round and round I strolled with the hopes of catching up with the two of you. I finally gave up."

"Uh, we went to a different park, one closer to Carlo's place. Whew, I am so tired. Good night, Noreen."

"Steady, lass." Noreen sent her flowering fan from the mortuary into overdrive. "Don't you be rushing into a lifetime of heartache and too many regrets."

"I won't; I promise." Louisa left the warnings behind when she closed the door to her room. Foregoing her usual cleansing routine, she changed into a linen nightgown, huddled in the chair, and clutched a pillow to her heart. Dismissing all distractions, she rocked back and forth, willing her body to relive every detail of the afternoon.

By midnight not a single light shone in St. Sebastian's rectory and Louisa still hadn't given in to sleep. Her skin was damp from the heat so she moved to the open window, trying to catch the lakefront breeze. A rustle of groundcover disturbed the area below. Her heart leapt and had she been a screamer, this would've been the moment. But before she could react, the familiar whisper of her name drifted upward.

"Holy Mother of God, you scared me."

"I couldn't wait 'til Wednesday," Carlo said in a loud whisper. "Give me a boost."

He stepped onto an overturned bucket, stretched to grab Louisa's determined hand. She pulled him up and then through the window. As soon as his feet hit the floor, they locked in a tight hug, his fingers weaving into her loose hair. He planted a barrage of kisses to her face, neck, ears, and shoulders. Nestling his head in the curve of her neck, he wavered and lost his balance. The resulting tumble onto her bed produced a soft thud followed by their muffled giggles.

"Sh-h, they might hear us," Louisa said. "Better you should go."

"No, no, I'll be quiet, I promise. God, you are so beautiful. When I think of all the time I ... I wasted."

"Sh-h, just think about the now."

They repeated their afternoon performance and then some, each movement, each gesture more exciting than the one before. In the minutes before dawn Carlo slipped into his clothes and kissed Louisa one more time. He left the same way he entered, quietly sliding down the brick wall before landing in a tangle of ivy.

*****

From a window on the rectory's second floor the monsignor watched Carlo scale the iron fence and disappear into the stillness of night. Somewhere in the neighborhood a dog barked to signal the presence of a stranger, a warning that went unheeded. Eons before Sean Flaherty had suffered his own earthly desires in Ireland. During his first parish assignment, he'd fallen for a lovely young woman, not moonstruck infatuation from afar but physical love that joins two as one. Even now he could feel the warmth of her body against his, the scent of her hair brushing against his cheek.

"Sean, I cannot live without you," she'd said through a moan and flood of tears. *"Don't go to America, please. You said you loved me."*

"I do love you, Eileen Fitzpatrick. I will always love you, but I cannot renege on my promise to Our Lord and the Holy Mother Church. Forgive me, Eileen. I didn't mean to hurt you. Forgive me."

"Don't push me away like that, not after all we've been to each other. Damn you, Sean Flaherty, for being so pious, so honorable, so ...."

*****

Throughout the stifling night Terry Connelly had punched his pillow with the resolve of a baker punching a round of bread dough. An innocent woman was distracting him, beguiling him without even knowing it. He couldn't bear the thought of that damn dago putting his lips on hers, leading her into temptations of the flesh. When Terry pushed himself out of bed, his head was pounding worse than the aftermath of an Irish wake. Air, he needed fresh air. He went to the window, looked out, and buckled at the knees. Seeing the damn dago creep across the yard was tantamount to getting punched in the gut. He stumbled to the bathroom, knelt before the porcelain goddess, and wretched until his stomach had nothing left to give. Except a well-deserved case of dry heaves that scrapped the tender lining of his esophagus.

Chapter 14
The Quarrel

"Everything okay between you and Louisa?" asked Massimo, half asleep and face down on his bed of fresh linens.

"Couldn't be better," Tillie Grasso replied with a giggle. Tillie in all her naked glory was straddling Massimo, massaging her fat sausage fingers into the muscles of his neck and shoulders. "Now that Louisa and Carlo are making whoopee, she ain't so shocked about what goes on between you and me and Vincenzo." Tillie bent over and tickled his ear with her wet tongue.

Massimo twitched and jerked and cranked open one bloodshot eye. "You know this for sure, that they are sleeping together?"

"Well, they talk about marriage but they ain't in any hurry to tie the knot. As the saying goes: the bull has sampled the cow's milk and both are now content." She wiggled her tongue in his ear again and slid over to the mattress.

"Loose ends make me nervous. So does Louisa living with those priests. She needs to know it takes more than tail to hold Carlo. Tail he can get at Night School."

"You want me to take care of this, Massimo?"

"Yeah, but first take care of me." He growled and rolled over to fill his hands with the treasures of her bountiful chest.

*****

That evening while Carlo finished his drink at Fabiola's bar, Tillie followed Louisa to a table and asked if there had been a date set for the wedding yet.

"I ain't in any hurry," Louisa replied. "Me and Carlo are still getting acquainted. Besides, I like my job at the rectory. Monsignor Flaherty invites very important people for dinner. He says St. Sebastian's has the best cook in the whole Archdiocese and he wants everyone to know it." She tinkled her little spoon to dissolve sugar in a miniature cup of mud-like coffee. "Ma would've been so proud. Nonna Fabiola too."

"Ah, si. I remember them both from the Old Country. Your ma helped me get to America," Tillie said. "It's just that you and Carlo—"

"I still have lots to learn. Father Connelly helps me every day with my reading and writing." She dredged the last of her espresso. "He's a good teacher, a good priest. And Noreen lets me run the kitchen my way. For now, I am happy."

"Don't be so sure Carlo will always be around. He could grow tired of waiting." Tillie scooted her chair closer to Louisa. "He could go back to his old ways."

"Old ways? What you mean old ways?" Louisa clanked the little spoon in her empty cup. "So what if he courted another woman before I came to America, before he knew me."

Tillie tapped a row of fat sausages to her lips. "Oops, I guess Carlo didn't tell you about Night School."

"Sure he did. He went to night school to learn English and other things from Miss Bracca."

"Louisa, you're so Old Country. Night School is a *bagnio*, you know, a place where men go to buy sex from women, some of them very beautiful." Tillie leaned forward, her fat sausages concealing her mouth from any lip-reading patrons. "Giulietta Bracca runs Night School and Carlo was her pet, leastways 'til you came over."

Louisa folded her arms. She arched her back into a feline hissy. "Not my Carlo. He would never do such a thing."

"Everybody knows about Carlo and Night School where he's called Teacher's Pet. If you don't believe me, ask him yourself. I'm just telling you to marry the man before he returns to his old ways."

"Carlo loves me."

"I ain't saying otherwise. And maybe you don't mind sharing him with Giulietta. You oughta see her, Louisa. She's like a moving picture actress, with shingled hair the color of that brick wall behind you. When she walks down the street, all heads turn. They say she's a vamp.

They say she bewitched Carlo ... that she made him what he is today, good or bad." Tillie patted Louisa's arm. "Take it from one who knows: don't end up like me. No wedding ring. No bambini. A dump of cacca grateful for any crumbs thrown my way."

*****

Later the evening when Carlo walked Louisa back to the rectory, he was feeling his wine and couldn't stop talking. "Look, I've been getting pretty good overtime and your brothers keep asking when we're getting married. So does Jake."

She didn't answer.

"What do you say, Louisa? Let's set the date. You can quit that job and take care of me. And I'll take care of you—every night, all night long."

Still no answer.

"What's the matter?" he asked.

"Nothing."

"Nothing? Don't tell me nothing. It's that damn job, and all that damn studying."

"Just like you and Night School. So, Carlo, tell me: what did you learn there?"

"The usual ... reading, writing." The muscles in his neck tightened like a stretched rubber band when he recalled Louisa and Tillie, head to head at Fabiola's. Damn that Tillie, damn her big mouth.

"Maybe I should get some lessons from this Miss Bracca too. I hear she's a gifted teacher."

With that they stopped under a streetlight near the rectory. Carlo braced his hands against her shoulders. "I can explain, Louisa. When me and Jake came over, we didn't have anybody. Some girl invited us to Night School. We became part of the family."

"Family ... the family?"

"Not real family, but people who made us feel special. Then Jake got sidetracked with Hildie and after a while I found you. Night School's in the past and we're about the future. So what do you say: let's get married right away."

"I need time to think. Come back on Sunday, not before." She leveled her finger at him. "As for tonight, Teacher's Pet, you can forget about any nookie.

Chapter 15
The Breakup

"So what'll it be, honey?" asked the raven-haired Miss Maybelle, the busiest operator in Salon de Beaut on Taylor Avenue. Not waiting for an answer, she removed two mother-of-pearl combs from the chestnut tresses of her customer positioned on a high swivel chair.

Louisa flipped one leg over the other. She wiggled into the cushioned seat. "Make me look more American."

Miss Maybelle's hair epitomized the latest in flapper coiffure: a shingled bob riding high in the back, similar to a man's haircut but with longer sides tapered over her ears. When she moved her head, the precision cut flipped over her prominent cheekbones. Exaggerated spit curls lined her forehead, creating a soft effect on an otherwise severe but chic style.

"You mean something on the order of my hairdo?" Miss Maybelle addressed her question to the reflection in a mirrored wall covering the length of seven hair styling stations. Hers occupied the Number One spot near the door.

Louisa nodded.

"Are you sure that handsome boyfriend of yours will approve? I must say: some of these foreigners prefer their ladies with hair so long they can sit on it."

"Well, my boyfriend ain't the boss of me so cut it off."

"Good for you, honey. That's the way to demonstrate your independence." From inside her mouth came the pop, pop, pop of

Juicy Fruit Gum. "Now before I start my magic, you need to untangle those long legs. We don't want a lopsided haircut, now do we?"

Louisa uncrossed her legs, straightened up, and took a deep breath.

With scissors in hand, Maybelle began her attack on Louisa's thick coarse hair, clipping and snipping while providing a series of anecdotes, mainly on how she'd marched as a suffragette in her younger days. Louisa listened with half an ear, having no interest in how American women gained the right to vote. She was not yet a citizen of America and, like the rest of her family, apathetic to most politics. She dropped her eyelids and shut down her thoughts, oblivious to the shorn hair raining on Salon de Beaut's tiled floor until she heard Miss Maybelle's voice take a new direction.

"Yoo-hoo, honey, I'm all finished. So what's the verdict?" Maybelle shoved a mirror in Louisa's hand and swiveled the chair a slow 360 degrees. "Take a gander, Louisa. You're looking at the same view that boyfriend of yours will see."

Louisa narrowed her eyes to the mirror. She gulped to contain tears welling in her eyes. "Oh-h-h ... Sweet Mother of Jesus."

"Ain't it just the cat's meow?"

"What about the cat? I got no cat."

Maybelle laughed. Pop, pop, pop went her gum. "Cat's meow ... oh, hon, that means something's swell. Take it from one who knows, you look positively gorgeous."

"Like an American, yes?"

"You bet. Goodbye Old Country; hello Chicago. I guarantee Mister Right will think you're a knockout."

*****

Later when Louisa walked into the rectory parlor, Terry Connelly glanced up from his reading and allowed his eyes to linger on her. The stylish hairdo had brought her into the twenties but her classic features remained unchanged. "Ah, Louisa, you've changed your hair. Indeed, it is most becoming."

She reached up to touch hair no longer there. "Thank you, Father. You're the first person to see the new me. I hope Carlo likes it."

"If he truly loves you, the style of your hair won't matter one iota."

She sat down, ready to tackle the Chicago Tribune while he settled into the wingback chair. As far as Terry was concerned, Louisa always looked swell, especially from his bedroom window. He'd watched her sitting on the back porch steps, a damp blouse clinging to her upper body while she dried her tousled hair with a towel, curling the ends around those graceful fingers. After she went inside and out of his sight, he imagined his fingers caressing her smooth flawless skin. A minor sin, venial at best, but one he should probably confess.

Louisa was still concentrating on the Tribune's front page. "A Protestant town north of Chicago called Area has changed its name to Mundelein," she read aloud, enunciating the syllables of each word, "to honor George Cardinal Mundelein. Do I know him, Father?"

"He came to dinner, relished the delicious *ossobuco* you prepared."

"Si, now I remember." She resumed her reading. "The Cardinal recently established St. Mary of the Lake Seminary in their community, bringing with it economic prosperity."

Terry likened Louisa's progress to watching a rosebud open one petal at a time, knowing the beauty of its full bloom would also signal the beginning of its demise.

Louisa finished the article. She sighed, chewed her lower lip, and sighed again. "Father, can I talk about me and Carlo? It's kind of personal."

Did she have to speak the Italian's name, reveal such intimacies Terry didn't want to imagine? The man had done nothing to prove his worthiness. "Of course, Louisa. You can say anything to me."

"I been thinking. Maybe it's time we married."

In his mind the priest bolted upright; in reality he raised a single brow of doubt. "I thought you'd decided to wait until you were sure."

"That was before I found out certain things. You ever heard of a place called Night School, which is not really a school?"

"I ... uh ...."

"Carlo used to go there." She moved her hands in cadence with her words. "I'm afraid he might go back if we don't get married soon."

Terry wanted to quiet those mobile hands, to absorb the passion accelerating their movements. Passion she felt for the wrong man. "Some married men have been known to frequent brothels. What I mean is, those who don't take their vows seriously, which is why it's so important not to make a hasty decision you'll later regret. In the eyes of God and Our Holy Mother Church marriage is forever."

"Just like being a priest, Father. Noreen says you and the monsignor are married to the Church forever. Did you think a long time about becoming a priest?"

"Yes, but thoughts are fleeting. Temptations change our course.

And prayers give us strength. Pray, Louisa, that you won't make a mistake you'll later regret."

"Did you make a mistake, Father?" She stilled her hands, waited for his response.

"Of course not, but life's rewards often come with painful sacrifice. And just because we sometimes question our vocations, whether religious or matrimonial, doesn't mean we've made wrong decisions." He removed his spectacles, wiped them with a linen handkerchief. "I'm sorry to cut today's lesson short, but I must tend to some church affairs with Monsignor Flaherty. Please excuse me."

*****

"Your hair," Carlo yelled on seeing Louisa at the park on Sunday. "What the hell did you do to your hair? You shoulda asked me first."

"You shoulda said you liked it long."

"You shoulda paid more attention. Didn't I take the combs out when we made love? Let your hair rain through my fingers like a summer shower?"

They were sitting on their usual park bench. She shrugged, threw some bread to the doves. "Everybody else likes it."

Like who, he wanted to ask. Not that anyone else should've mattered. He'd been edgy since their quarrel on Wednesday. An impromptu visit to Night School hadn't provided the familiar comfort he once enjoyed even though Giulietta had offered the mute Bettina. He'd refused out of loyalty to Louisa.

"I wanted to look more American," she finally said. "More like that Night School boss."

He stood up to look down on her. "You mean Giulietta Bracca? I want you to look like the mother of the children we're going to have. I want us married so we can have those babies." He sat down again and reached for her jittery hand.

She pulled away. "Maybe I don't want to be stuck in the kitchen with babies hanging on me."

"Isn't that what you do at St. Sebastian's? Spend all day in the kitchen, but without the babies. Maybe you baby that snot-nosed priest." He grabbed her spastic wrist and spoke his next words through clenched teeth. "I ain't stupid, you know. I seen the way he watches you, all moony-eyed."

"That ain't so. Father Connelly's already married to the church."

"Then what about us. I'm tired of waiting for you to decide if I'm the one. Or, if the moon's in its right phase. Or, if the priests will starve if you ain't there to feed them. Let's get married now."

"I ain't ready yet." She pulled away from him, got up, and hurried down the path.

"Keep walking and it's over between us," he called out. "This time I ain't running after you."

*****

Back at the studio apartment Carlo found Jake playing to the bureau mirror, working his fingers of Vaseline into unruly hair that would never stand a chance against Valentino's black helmet that women supposedly swooned over. Carlo kicked the footboard. When he ripped off his necktie and flung it over the back of the chair, Jake stopped his grooming routine. Neither spoke while they watched Carlo's tie slither into a puddle on the floor.

Jake reached for the good wine and poured two glasses. "You and Louisa been fighting again?"

Carlo gulped until he drained the glass, initiating a pounding headache he tried to erase with his fingertips.

"Hold on," Jake said. "Hell, you know you're gonna marry her. You said you was made for each other."

"So I changed my mind."

"She'll come around. And when she does, make sure you stay on top. That way, she'll never forget who's boss. Just remember this, Houdini: once you're locked in the bounds of holy wedlock, escaping ain't so easy."

Carlo plopped down on the bed. With fingers laced behind his head, he tried focusing on a roadmap of cracks intersecting the ceiling plaster.

"So, Carlo, you gonna waste a good afternoon feeling sorry for yourself?"

"I got this headache."

"And I got just the cure. How 'bout coming with me to Hildie's?"

"Hell, don't we see enough of Papa Gus and Brother Harold at the brewery. I ain't spending Sunday with the Kramers. Two visits to that house was two too many." He pictured Elsa Kramer: short, stocky and wielding a tongue sharper than a straight razor, a mishmash of hair faded to dull ashes and knotted behind her thick neck.

"Have a heart," Jake said. "When I go there alone, they turn into a pack of cannibals, waiting for me to make one wrong move so they can serve me up on a platter—like some pig stuffed with that damn cabbage."

"Didn't I warn you about Krauts and their food?"

"I tell you, Carlo, I can't breathe around them."

"It's the cabbage."

"All they do is argue. They're never wrong. When they can't show up each other, they drag me into their fights. Before Louisa, Hildie never gave a damn about marriage. Now she keeps talking about how we should legalize the consummation."

"It'll pass, just like a bad case of gas."

"Remember that moving picture we saw a couple months ago? You know, the little mustachio carrying an iron ball chained to his ankle?"

"Charlie Chaplin, pretending the ball ain't there."

"Well, that's how I feel about Hildie. Somehow she landed on top and now she's squeezing me by the balls. So, whadaya say, Brother?"

Chapter 16
Dinner at the Kramers

As head brewmeister of Becker's Brewery, Gustav Kramer demanded the respect of his underlings. At home he found respect on the screened front porch of his Fremont Street flat, where the Sunday commotion of dinner preparations couldn't disrupt certain routines he held dear. Such noise, such clatter did not belong in his mortgage-free surroundings; nor did those wild antics of those three children out of his daughter Gertrude. Trudy's unruly brats reminded him of the Katzenjammer Kids comic strip; but the paper kids were funnier and after his daily laugh, Gus had the satisfaction of throwing them away.

He pushed tobacco into the bowl of his Bavarian pipe and struck a match against the scuffed leather of his shoe sole. He sunk into the paisley cushions of a well-worn wicker chair and sent up clouds of smoke, a pleasure forbidden in the parlor. His feet aching from fallen arches sought relief atop a matching wicker ottoman. As he puffed and sucked, Gus considered the sorry possibility of his favorite child marrying a damn dago. At twenty-four Hildegard seemed ready for marriage, but to a no-count pup, younger and dumber than her? What the hell did she see in this Giacomo-turned-Jake, this garlic-popping wop trying to pass for an American? If this one ain't the one, she should quit wasting her time before he ruins her for somebody else. On the other hand maybe this dago was the one with feet of clay, and not his Hildie. The bastard better not be messing with her. One thing was for sure: Jake Baggio better not make an ass of his little girl 'cause if he did, there'd be hell to pay. Gus would see to that.

How could any fool not love Hildie. She reminded Gus of Elsa, the Elsa he first met forty years earlier: a sweet, comely blonde, soft as the ears of a pampered kitty-cat. What a shame that marriage and three children had turned her into a washerwoman with the tongue of a tart and a butt bigger than the Goodyear blimp. And what about that damn nose of hers, always sniffing here and there, trying to unearth a tasty morsel. Next to a tasty German meal Elsa enjoyed nothing more than mismatched matchmaking. As soon as she learned Jake was bringing his unattached brother to dinner, she hurried next door and invited the new neighbor, Alice Jean Armstead.

"To even out the table," she told Gus. "What with Jake and Hildie about to tie the knot Carlo will need somebody too."

"Just what we need, another dago."

"Keep it all in the family, or the neighborhood, that's what I say. That way Hildie won't desert us."

"About this Alice Jean, last week did you not say she was too persnickety?"

"Ah-h, so I did. But as my *mutter* used to say, 'For every pot there is a lid.' After all, did I not match up Gertrude with Dietrich Knopelhoff, a solid German with a future to match."

"Too bad he didn't come with some backbone." Too bad for Harold that Elsa had dragged her feet when she should've found the right lid for their only son, before Primula Abernathy found him. Some match—two sour faces for two sour personalities.

*****

As soon as Carlo walked into the Kramer house with Jake, Hildie marched Jake into the dining room and shoved a stack of napkins into his arms. Carlo being no dummy wandered out to the front porch, expecting to hide out there. Too late, Gus had already picked up his scent. The old man ordered him to sit on the glider and then started running off at the mouth about his lofty position at the brewery.

About as important as shit on flypaper, Carlo thought. *'Course he does sign my timesheet. And Hildie claims he knows people who know people. Just don't ask me to do any more night runs. Jake either. I don't care how much they pay.*

"Carlo, come on in for dinner," Elsa Kramer called out while herding her family and guests into the dining room. "For you I saved a place next to Alice Jean from next door."

Carlo offered a heartfelt apology from the glider. "Grazie, Mrs.

Kramer, but I'm not hungry." In response to Gus's penetrating glare, he dropped his eyelids and patted his flat stomach. "Sorry, a bad case of indigestion."

"Nonsense, nobody sits away from the Kramer dinner table," Gus bellowed, loud enough for the upstairs renters to hear. To Carlo, he bent over and growled through breath reeking of tobacco, "Look, bellyacher, take your ass into the dining room before my wife drags you there by the back of your scrawny neck."

Like an obedient pup Carlo followed Gus into the dining room. Elsa directed him to sit next to a young woman, petite with deep blue eyes and dark brown hair curling around a delicate face. She imparted a sweet smile and lowered her eyelashes. After a seesaw grace from Trudy's apple-cheeked daughter, Gus ordered everyone to dig in. One by one bowls of cooked red cabbage, pickled onions and beets, cinnamon applesauce, baked Northern beans, falling-off-the-bone spareribs, and fart-worthy sauerkraut circled the table. Carlo took polite dabs of this and that while Gustav observed with a scowl from his post at the head of the table.

"Trudy, pass Carlo the dumplings," Elsa said, her full mouth competing with the jangle of dishes and serving utensils. "So Carlo, where've you been keeping yourself lately? For months we don't see nothing of you." She waved her fork toward the neighbor. "And look what you've been missing. With her very own fingers Alice Jean turns out such beautiful handiwork."

"Ah-h, so did our mama," Jake said to the blushing Alice Jean. "God rest her soul, Mama could work magic with a needle and thread. Right, Carlo?"

Hildie poked Jake in the ribs. "Ma, Carlo's already betrothed to someone he brought over from Italy. Remember, I told you last month."

"That's right, Ma," Harold said, his first words since coming to the table. "I remember Hildie mentioning an engagement of sorts."

*****

Not that Harold Kramer cared about the weasel wop across the table, squirming like he was about to shit his pants. But Harold did care about Alice Jean Armstead. A young woman of her character deserved better, someone more on the order of himself. After two years of marriage Harold regretted his rush to the altar. At the time he'd been pushing thirty-two, still living at home, and too busy making money to play the romance field. When he brought Primula Abernathy home to meet the family, he introduced her as his fiancée to discourage interference from his mutter. Primula had allowed nothing but kisses during their courtship but promised the works after their wedding, which to Harold meant a dutiful wife submitting to one-sided sex. Two weeks later they eloped, before his formidable ma could mount a decent campaign to change his mind.

Still, Ma considered Primula acceptable. The new bride kept a spotless house, nothing ever out of place, not even a single drinking glass. Every bit of lint got picked up twice daily, morning and evening, with a hand sweeper so it wouldn't settle into the Axminster carpet she'd insisted on buying with his hard-earned money. Not one speck of dust occupied the fringed lampshade or the plastered busts of ancient Romans staring from vacant eyes. Mechanical copulation, the only kind his wife permitted, was performed in a vertical position, over a towel in the bathroom so as not to assault the bed sheets. Primula even insisted Harold kneel when christening the toilet bowl, to keep his piss from spraying her precious floor or walls.

From across the platters of food Harold used his utmost discretion, which consisted of a permanent scowl, to observe Alice Jean. He imagined her syrupy *puderdose* needed the warmth of his powerful *schwanz*. Oh, yah … this was a woman who'd never expect him to screw her in the bathroom. This was a woman who'd get down on her knees—all in good time. For now he wanted to puke, listening to his ma hammer away at the dago wop.

*****

"Is this so, Carlo? To another you're promised? *Booshwa!* If the real thing it was, with your fiancée you'd be today instead of us. Did the two of you quarrel? Well, maybe for you she is not right." With a triumphant smile, Elsa turned to Alice Jean. "So-o, do tell us about the poetry contest you won. You know, Carlo, in a real magazine her poem was published."

"What kind of poems?" Jake asked. "Maybe after dinner you could show us, yes?"

Before Alice Jean could answer, Elsa was wagging her finger at a mischievous grandchild. "Willie, I been eyeing you. Now stop with the beets at Katrinka or your papa will have to paddle. Trudy, for gosh sakes, do something with that boy."

Trudy tweaked Willie's ear and led him away. His sister, tears and snot smeared over her blotchy face, whined and cried while two-year old Oliver mashed bananas into his nose and over the highchair tray. And Dietrich, oblivious to his brood's disturbances, helped himself to seconds before passing the bowls to Harold, who was ignoring Primula who was fanning her face with a napkin. After a momentary silence Alice Jean asked Carlo how long he'd been in America.

"Two years," answered Jake, "same as me."

"My goodness, Jake, your English is quite good … and what do you do for a living? … Oh, both of you work at the brewery with Mr. Kramer."

"*For* me," said Gus.

"But of course," Alice Jean said with a smile. "Mrs. Kramer told me all about your valued position."

Dinner dragged on with Carlo responding only when pressed to do so, and in exaggerated broken English. He draped a napkin over the scattering of food on his plate, all of which Hildie whisked away during a trip to the kitchen.

"Carlo, maybe you and Alice Jean should take in the moving pictures with Hildie and Jake?" Elsa said.

"Mutter!"

"Hildie, did you not tell me the show you were going to see?"

"Well, uh, yeah." Hildie's eyes traveled from Carlo to Jake and back to Carlo. "But, Carlo has other plans. Right, Carlo?"

Jake stood up. He moved behind Carlo and put his hands on Carlo's shoulders. "Charlie Chaplin's playing in the Loop. We can make the next show if we hurry."

"Not without us," Harold said. He jumped up, tore the soiled napkin from his shirt collar, and walked away with the tablecloth he'd been using as a second napkin still tucked in his waistband. Along with the soiled linen came a smorgasbord of leftovers and dinnerware. Food splattered, dishes clattered, Harold sputtered, and Primula shrieked.

"Harold, you idiotic nincompoop," she said. "How can one simpleton manage to create such calamity? Just look at your trousers. You've made a mess of them and ruined my dress. We can't go anywhere but home."

"Damn right, you can't!" yelled Gus. "But not before the two of you clean up this stinking garbage."

*****

That afternoon after taking in a matinee, Louisa spent the remainder of

Sunday secluded in her room, stewing over Carlo while trying to read a novel Father Connelly had recommended. At nine o'clock she went to bed, and soon after a soft knock at the door interrupted her prayerful solitude.

"Can I come in, lass?" Noreen poked her head in and received permission to enter. "The monsignor tells me you've been holed up in your room all evening." She pulled the chair over to Louisa's bed. "Now you just tell Noreen what's been going on with that young man of yours."

Louisa told her about the quarrel with Carlo, but omitted the part about Father Connelly because she didn't want Noreen or Monsignor Flaherty thinking there could ever be anything between her and the young priest. Except for an occasional tsk-tsk and shake of the head, Noreen held her tongue until Louisa had finished.

"Well, Dearie, perhaps that would explain why I saw your Carlo with another woman this evening. Coming out of that new Charlie Chaplin moving picture show, they were. It didna take him long to find another pretty face unless he already had this one while he was playing patty cake with you."

Chapter 17
Bittersweet Goodbye

Several days later Terry Connelly sat across the desk from Monsignor Flaherty, both priests enjoying their morning coffee before tackling the usual administrative duties associated with running an active parish. Lakefront breezes stirred the fine lace curtains but in a few hours the oppressive heat would take over and move nothing but perspiration from the forehead. After adding a jigger of whiskey to his porcelain cup, the monsignor raised his brow, offering the same to Terry who declined with a show of his palm.

"Now, Father Connelly, would you be having any special plans for your annual vacation?"

"Perhaps a retreat after the first of the year."

"Refreshing the body does wonders for the soul, but I have a more immediate respite in mind for you."

"I don't know where I'd go on such short notice." Terry repositioned his gaunt frame. "As you know, my parents live in a small flat and make do on a meager pension. I couldn't impose on them."

"Hmm, of course not, nor would I expect such an imposition," Monsignor said. "However, it seems the Archdiocese has been blessed with a substantial grant that will allow a handful of priests to visit Rome this year. Right in the heart of the city these fortunate few will be staying, in what was once a fine ancient monastery. An August day in Rome can put Chicago to shame, but by mid-September one can count on resort weather."

"By all means, you should go, Monsignor. I'll do my best to look after St. Sebastian's in your absence."

The older priest leaned back. "Ah, 'tis a grand opportunity to experience the Vatican, to live the history of our Holy Mother Church. You'll be pleased to know I've arranged for *you* to be among the chosen few."

"But, Monsignor—"

"Not to worry, my son. I pulled strings and made countless concessions to get your name on the coveted list."

"I don't deserve such an honor."

"Let me be the judge of that, Father Connelly. Repay Our Lord with your loyalty because 'tis favors I'll be returning on your behalf 'til the day I die and then from my final resting place. Already I promised our Louisa's culinary services for an upcoming dinner hosted by the Auxiliary Bishop. Can you believe he heard about her from Cardinal Mundelein?"

"But I ... oops." Terry banged his cup against the desk, spilling tepid coffee over the polished wood. He whipped out a handkerchief and blotted the creeping liquid. "I'm not much of a traveler."

"Yes, but how fortuitous of me to insist on your applying for a passport last year. The matter is settled, my son. You leave in three days." Monsignor Flaherty pushed his chair back and stood. "The Archdiocese will be sending two newly ordained priests to help out. All in all a good experience for them as well, so not to worry about returning too soon." With a firm hand to Terry's slumped shoulder, he ushered him toward the door. "Mark my words: after you see Rome, Chicago and all its warts will become but a distant memory."

*****

That afternoon in the parlor Terry clung to Louisa's every word as she finished the last chapter of Little Women.

"Louisa Mae Alcott is my favorite writer," she said, closing the book with a calm reserve. "Maybe it's because we were blessed with the same first name. What should I read next?"

Rays from the afternoon sun had settled above her head, creating a halo effect. Tendrils of hair refusing to conform to the chic bob softened a face that seemed so vulnerable. He seared that lovely image into his brain.

"Father Connelly, are you okay? I was asking about my next book."

THE FAMILY ANGEL

"I'll make a list."

"Can't you just tell me?"

"That won't be possible, Louisa. You see I'm going away for a while. Actually, to study at Rome and the Vatican."

"Ain't that just the cat's meow. I dreamed of America for years before I finally made it here. Now, you're going to the country I left behind." She pushed the book aside. "I never been to Rome but I read all about its grand churches. They're about as close to God as you can get while still on earth."

"Indeed. To see Rome, the very heart of our Holy Mother Church, is a wonderful opportunity for any priest, or fortunate pilgrim. But remember this: heaven on earth can be as close as the love held deep in your heart."

"My heart will always hold a place for you, Father. Because of you, I can now read the newspaper and write simple letters. And, convert measures from metric to the American way." She cocked her head, flipping hair over her cheekbones. "But, I gotta tell you, when it comes to those measurements the European way still makes more sense."

*****

Terry spent the next two days assuring St. Sebastian's parishioners he'd return with the cherry blossoms. On the eve of his departure he stood in his shirtsleeves at his bedroom window, watching Monsignor Flaherty and Noreen cross the school playground on their way to a St. Vincent de Paul function in the church basement. Terry had already packed, unpacked, and repacked his suitcase. He'd reviewed his list of books for Louisa and made appropriate changes. Given her evening routine, she was probably in the kitchen, making advance preparations for tomorrow's dinner, the first of many he would not be eating. He folded the reading list into quarters before shoving it in his pocket. He knelt before the crucifix and prayed for the strength to overcome temptations preying on his mind and in the depths of his soul. Within minutes he found himself standing at the top of the stairs, one hand crumpling the reading list in his pocket.

Terry lifted his nose to the scent of garlic and herbs. By noon tomorrow Louisa's roast beef would absorb the blended seasonings and balsamic vinegar. Following his instincts, he descended the steps, walked down the hall, and pushed his way through the kitchen door. Louisa didn't see him. She was bent over the stove, peering under a lid when he sputtered some nonsense about his feelings for her. The lid flew out of her hand and clanged to the floor as she twirled around, clutching her left breast.

"Oh, Father, you made my heart jump!"

Indeed, he could see the outline of her breast fluttering like a frightened robin's. "I'm sorry, Louisa. I didn't mean to alarm you. I just wanted you to know how much I'll miss ... your cooking."

She wiped her forehead and smiled. "Don't worry about getting enough to eat in Italy. No matter where you go, the food will be good, or so I've heard. And you could use a few extra pounds, Father. Noreen says you're e ... e ... maciated, which I don't believe for one minute, although you are thinner than when we first met."

He gulped, forcing his Adam's apple to gnaw on his turned collar. "Until I met you, good food and good wine controlled my natural appetite."

Louisa blushed while wiping her hands on the butcher apron. She took off the apron and hung it just so on the wall hook, giving Terry an opportunity to close in on her. When she turned, it was to him blocking her path.

"Whoops! *Mi scusa, Padre.*"

"I just wanted to tell you goodbye, Louisa." His voice cracked with the next words he spoke. "To let you know how very much I will miss you."

"Maybe it won't be forever, Father."

Terry's mouth felt like sawdust. He hesitated for a long moment and when Louisa started to step aside he grabbed her by the shoulders. He kissed her lips, gently at first, then harder, pushing his tongue into her mouth. He'd never kissed a woman in this way, the way a man kisses a woman when he wants to make love. He wrapped his arms around her, felt the beauty of her heart pounding against his. Her hair brushed against his face, tickled his nose to arouse a new sensation. He closed his eyes and pressed his body against hers.

"I love you, Louisa. I have from the first day we met. Just let me hold you." Wanting more, he rushed his lips over her eyes and down to her cheeks where he found both of them wet with tears. "Please don't cry, Louisa. It was not my intention to upset you."

When she didn't answer, he pulled back and saw those almond eyes were bone dry. The tears he'd tasted were his own. He'd laid open his soul, enticed her with a love forbidden. She'd responded with ... dear

God ... indifference. Embarrassment overwhelmed his fading passion. Remorse would follow, later when he was alone with God.

"Louisa ... sweet Louisa, please forgive me. I have no excuse for my deplorable actions."

"There is nothing to forgive, Father. Loneliness I understand."

He sank to his knees, buried his face into her skirt where it covered her thighs. "Just a little longer is all I ask."

And then, miracle of miracles, she was kneeling beside him, cupping his face between her hands, and kissing his flushed cheeks.

"Just this once, Father, and only because you're leaving," Louisa said. "I doubt we will ever see each other again so you take part of me to Rome." She held his hand to her breast. "And I will keep part of you here in my heart."

*****

The next morning after celebrating seven o'clock Mass, Terry Connelly left without saying goodbye to Louisa. Nor did he leave the crumpled list of recommended books. He did not stay for the hot breakfast she always prepared or for the coffee he needed to start each day. An upset stomach from the excitement of the trip, he told Monsignor Flaherty as they shook hands. He'd told half a truth without admitting to the sleepless night he'd spent praying for strength. The solitude of the long train ride to the East Coast would be his comfort.

Louisa's last words to him had been, "Remember me in your prayers, just as I will remember you in mine."

Oh Lord, just a little longer to relive every detail of the last two months. Terry wanted to savor her face, the sound of her voice, her laughter that brought him such undeniable joy, their last precious hour together, first in the rectory kitchen and later to her bed. *Her bed ... her arms, the sweetness of it all.*

Chapter 18
Starting Over

Six weeks passed. Thirty-five miserable days that separated Louisa from everything she held dear. Her one true love had kept his word about not returning; she hadn't seen him since the silly quarrel over her hair. And Father Connelly had left the morning after she'd given him the precious gift of physical love, a gift she now regretted.

She was on her knees in the kitchen, giving up her breakfast to the garbage pail when Noreen found her. Louisa sat back on her heels and buried her face in her hands.

"Oh no, Lass. Not this, anything but this," Noreen lamented. "I don't want to believe what my eyes see even though I should've suspected, given your constant moping." She drew Louisa into her freckled arms and patted her shoulder. "So there was more to your pain than losing that good-for-nothing rounder. He's planted his seed in you and then returned to his old ways."

"I sent Carlo away." She couldn't betray him, the priest, or herself.

"He wasn't good enough for the likes of you. Never mind that my brother was thinking the two of you would be a perfect match. You're better off without—"

"Carlo don't know about the baby, Noreen. I ain't seen him in weeks."

"*Haven't* seen him, Dearie. That being the case, you just leave everything to me."

"No, I don't want you telling a soul. I'm no better than a common whore. Me having a child and no husband will bring a terrible shame to my brothers."

"Those two? After carrying on with that ninny-witted slut ... the very idea."

"Men play by different rules. He ... they might send me back to Italy. I could make up a story about being widowed."

"And raise a child alone, without a proper pot to pee in?"

"God forgive me but there's this woman who can mix a potion, like strong tea they say, and it'll make the baby go away before I even start to show."

Noreen slapped her across the face, hard enough to sting. "Now, you listen to me, Louisa Valenza. There'll be no talk of ridding yourself of this baby. Laying with a no-good scoundrel was a mistake, that's for sure, but that wee one growing inside you is no mistake. If anyone deserves murdering, it's that worthless bum, not some innocent soul." Her voice softened. "Don't you be doing a thing yet, you hear? And promise me you won't go near that witch Hedda."

"You know about Hedda?"

"Does Michael the Archangel know about Lucifer? Very little that goes on within these parish boundaries that I don't hear about. And whatever I know, be assured the monsignor knows even more."

"I don't want you telling the monsignor." Louisa had been avoiding him for weeks.

"Trust me, lass. He's had plenty of experience with young girls who find themselves in a fix. Oh, the stories I could tell you, but I won't. We all have our secrets."

"Some worse than others."

"'Tis a part of navigating through life, Dearie." Noreen tapped a finger to her pale lips. "Mum's the word." She put her arm around Louisa and walked her to the bedroom. "For now, put your feet up, take a nice nap. Just be sure you bring yourself back to the kitchen in time to fix supper."

*****

During Sean Flaherty's early years at St. Sebastian's he'd established a garden retreat behind the garage. A wee substitute for the Irish countryside, he told Louisa when she first started working at the rectory. It became her place of solitude too, where she reveled in the beauty of heirloom roses enjoyed in earlier centuries by admirers long since dead. On Sunday afternoon she'd tried one of Noreen's recommendations, a book of fairy stories by Seamus MacManus. But after reading the same paragraph over and over, Louisa still couldn't understand it. Noreen claimed she knew the author in Ireland, when he was a lad living near her village.

"I always knew he'd amount to something," she told Louisa. "So will your baby."

Louisa knew Noreen meant well, assuming the role of educating her in Father Connelly's absence. But Noreen didn't know about her and the priest. Thank God he wasn't here to share her shame, deserved or otherwise. Dear God, what was she going to do?

"Louisa, can I talk to you?"

The sound of Carlo's voice told Louisa her prayers had been answered. She stood up. Seeing the expression on his face brought tears of joy to hers. She opened her mouth but couldn't release the words before Carlo took her in his arms. He kissed her cheeks, ran his hand over her hair.

"Mother of God, I'm sorry I hurt you again. Why didn't you tell me instead of the old man? I'd have come right away."

"I didn't want it to be like this," she said between sobs.

"I love you, Louisa."

"Me too." She sniffed again.

"We're gonna be a family, you and me and our baby."

"No matter what?"

"Whadaya take me for, asking such a question. There's nothing you can do to make me change my mind. And I'll never make you cry again. This I promise."

Chapter 19
Troubled Triangle

The winter of '26 came early to Chicago, bringing with it unrelenting winds and record-breaking temperatures that eradicated any trace of autumn's late arrival. On a secluded bench in Grant Park a young couple bundled in heavy coats and woolen scarves sat arm's length from each other. Clouds of their warm breath punctuated the air with each word they spoke.

"Jake, I'm just not comfortable with this, not with Hildie living right next door," Alice Jean Armstead said. "Maybe we shouldn't see each other until you decide which one of us you really want."

Jake sniffed the cold air. His nostrils flared and he felt the burn inside his nose. "I'm gonna break off with Hildie as soon as I can. But like I told you before, Gus can be ruthless. Last week he blackballed a bottler who cussed him out. The guy has four kids." Jake moved closer; he took her gloved hand in his. "Come on, Alice Jean. For sure, it'll mean my job, and Carlo's. His baby's due pretty soon."

For months Jake had been working on seeing more of Alice Jean and less of Hildie. But every time he tried to extricate himself from Hildie, she tightened her grip like a vise. Always squeezing for a little more, that was Hildie. To make matters worse Gustav Kramer had given him additional responsibilities at the brewery that put an extra five dollars on his weekly paycheck. And for reasons Jake didn't want to consider, Hildie's brother started acknowledging him at work. Harold hadn't done that before.

"I understand, really I do," Alice Jean said. "That's why I cannot see you any longer." She pulled her hand away and tucked it into her fur-lined pocket. "I will not be a party to Carlo's unemployment situation. Nor to yours."

"A little more time is all I need."

"Please don't call me again until this has been resolved." She leaned over, kissed Jake on the cheek, and left.

Watching Alice Jean walk away brought Jake more relief than pain. His goodbye to the prospect of having the virgin lifted a heavy load from his shoulders. Marry Hildie tomorrow and he'd be set for life, but not the life he wanted. Not with that family, not with that food. He wasn't ready to settle down yet but when that time came, a marriage like that of Carlo and Louisa might work.

It worked for Carlo. Granted, he'd put out some bucks up front but Louisa's tightwad brothers wound up giving more to the newlyweds than Carlo first invested: a new bedroom suite and six month free rent in an apartment building the brothers owned. With impending fatherhood Carlo clearly adored Louisa. Wherever he went, she tagged along, separated only by his job at the brewery and hers at St. Sebastian's. And with the holier-than-thou priest cooling his heels in Rome, Louisa's cooking job no longer riled Carlo.

*****

From another park bench out of Jake's view and too far away for eavesdropping, Harold Kramer peered over the top of his Chicago Tribune. Curious as to how Alice Jean spent her free time, he'd been following her for weeks and was teeming with hostility after learning the identity of her mystery boyfriend. To make matters worse, Pop had given Hildie the okay to marry Jake. That is, if the dago ever proposed. Because of Pop's begrudging approval, Harold felt obliged to lower his own standards by agreeing to accept Jake into the family. He even started speaking to him at the brewery.

Since Harold couldn't detect any sexual hanky panky between Jake and Alice Jean, he took a closer look at Jake and Hildie. One evening after the couple had left Fabiola's, he followed them into Jake's tenement. Harold stumbled on the final stair to the second floor landing, just in time to observe a door on the third floor close behind the laughing couple. His clumsiness created so much commotion that Jake's downstairs neighbor opened her door.

"Excuse me, ma'am," Harold said in his Sunday voice. "Do you happen to know that young couple in the room above yours?"

"Couple my foot." The old gal spat her words out between graying teeth and skimpy lips. "A couple of degenerates, if you ask me. They show no respect for decent folk, what with the racket they make. It's been going on for a year now. What's more, they're not even married." She moved closer to Harold and lowered her voice. "Don't get mixed up with their kind. They're nothing but animals." With that, she slammed the door.

The first-hand account from Miss Clarissa Spencer confirmed what Harold already suspected. What a pleasant dilemma: deciding the best approach to wiping out his enemy. He could tell Hildie about Jake stepping out on her, with Alice Jean no less. But Hildie might insist on marrying the dago right away. He could tell Pop the real lowdown on Jake and Hildie, or just the part about his two-timing her. If the old man knew Jake was fucking Hildie, he might insist Jake make an honest woman of his little girl. But why involve Alice Jean in the Jake mess. Harold had special plans for her.

Marriage to Primula had evolved into Chinese torture: inch-by-inch she rubbed him wrong, like a dull knife grating against his raw nerves. Since he couldn't get any pleasure from his own marriage, why should Hildie nail Jake? Of course, he could just tell the cheating wop what he had on him. Give the shit a chance to disappear. But where would be the fun in letting him off so easy.

*****

Bundled in heavy wool sweaters Elsa had knitted, the Kramer men huddled in chairs on the front porch, Gus with his pipe and Harold, his Lucky Strikes. Storm windows filled the slots formerly occupied by screens, but the outside air still seeped in to chill the enclosure.

"Pop, I gotta talk to you about Hildie and that damn wop she wants to marry."

"What's this, the damn wop we are back to calling him? That don't sound so good, not about the man I gave Hildie permission to go after."

Gus leaned back and puffed. Having swung a promotion for Jake, Gus was pleased with his progress. The little pisser showed himself as a hard worker and appeared to have some common sense. Gus liked that in a man.

"It's bad, Pop ... really bad." Harold dragged deep and exhaled rings of smoke before continuing. "Jake and Hildie have been playing between the sheets for over a year. I know 'cause I followed them to Jake's place. The neighbor lady told me what they were doing."

"Told you what?"

"Well, you know, always alone in Jake's room. Howling and making so much racket that they—"

"Enough." Gus held up a fleshy hand. "This is not good. I guess we will have to cut short Hildie's chase since she could not wait to give goodies 'til after the wedding."

He clenched the pipe between his teeth, narrowed his fish-colored eyes into a squint. Hildie, his favorite ... Hildie, with more gumption than the other two combined. Knowing his little girl had crossed over the virginity line rankled his already constipated bowels. Worse yet, she'd been busted by that weasel wop.

"Wait, there's more, Pop." Harold took his time lighting a second cigarette. "Jake's working another woman, you know, besides our Hildie. I seen him with this other one more than once. But I don't think he's poking her yet."

"Poking her yet?" he yelled, spraying Harold's face. "For crissake, how many women does the shit need to poke?" He slammed his pipe into the ashtray, spewing ashes over the table. "Enough. I've heard enough. Him I want out of Hildie's life now and forever out of Chicago."

"What about his brother, Pop?" Harold leaned forward.

"Use your head. Where one brother goes, the other soon follows. And if the bellyacher don't follow soon enough, we'll show him the way. Them damn wops, they're all alike. They got this family thing about living around each other."

Harold crushed his Lucky Strike in the ashtray stand and lit another. "Let me work on this, Pop. Maybe I could get Elio Seppi to make a connection for us. There's this guy called Garlic Joe Bonetti. He could show Jake hell on earth."

"Another dago? What's he gonna do, breathe on him?"

"Sort of, he rubs his bullets with garlic and aims for the legs."

"Better the *schwanz*."

"Hold on. I didn't get to the best part. Garlic in a wound produces gangrene. Gangrene means amputation. There's just one problem. I hear Garlic Joe expects a bundle for rendering such services."

"Christ. Has living with an iceberg sent your brain to the North

THE FAMILY ANGEL

Pole?" Gus slammed his hand into the smoking stand. "Don't act surprised that I know what's not going on in your bed. That wife you despise—all puckered up from too much douching with vinegar. And I done seen you eyeing what's next door. Never mind about taking care of Hildie's problem. You take care of your wife. I'll take care of Jake."

*****

Later that week Elio Seppi sank into his parlor chair, content while his wife and daughters bustled in the kitchen, cleaning up from their usual five-course supper. Elio folded his hands over his round belly and closed his eyes to better appreciate the Italian opera his radio emitted. Periodically, he unfolded his hands and cracked one eye to navigate his left hand to the grappa sitting nearby. He drank with caution, allowing the potent spirit to ease down his throat so as not to curl his toes before performing its magic.

The Italian immigrant from Bologna had put in twenty years as a padrone, helping his paesani secure first-time jobs at Chicago's brickyards, butcher shops, bakeries, and restaurants. For a little extra he secured their housing and even wrote their letters. Later he served as godfather to their children and pallbearer at their funerals. But after the war strict immigration quotas had forced Elio to find additional employment, as a foreman with Becker Brewery.

He'd just finished the last of his grappa when Gustav Kramer's knock at the door brought an unpleasant problem.

"Si, si," Elio nodded to his immediate supervisor. "I know this Garlic Joe though I never had occasion to call upon his services. Avenging your daughter's honor could turn her against you forever. This I seen happen too many times with those hot-blooded Siciliani."

Kramer wavered, conceding that he wanted Hildie safe under his roof until she could be properly married.

"Leave this to me," Elio said. "I see to it that Jake Baggio leaves Chicago. There's just one thing …."

"How much?"

"Not a penny. But I gotta do it my way."

Chapter 20
Losing Jake

Elio hated losing Jake Baggio, a hard worker who showed up every day and did his job without complaining. At least Gus hadn't brought up Jake's brother who worked rings around everybody, including Jake. Like Carlo, Elio would soon be a father too, but he already had three daughters. Already his wife had told him, boy or not, there'd be no more bambini.

At the end of work the next day he called Jake into his cramped office, a former supply closet he'd procured through a bit of clever persuasion. But this was no time for pussyfooting.

"Jake, I gotta let you go." Elio shuffled papers that didn't need shuffling. "I hate firing any man, especially a good worker."

Jake slammed his hat on the desk. "Hell, Elio, I thought me and you was friends. Paesano you called me, even moved me up."

"I got my orders, kid. It ain't about what you do at work. It's about the other fourteen hours. This I tell you for your own good: Gus Kramer knows you been messing with his daughter. Says there's some other girl too. Consider yourself lucky. He wanted to sic Garlic Joe Bonetti on you"

"Who?"

"You ever see that guy begging for a living on Maxwell Street, the one with no legs riding around on a little cart."

"Madonna mia, Garlic Joe did that?"

Elio opened his palms and shrugged. "Gus wants you out. Out of

THE FAMILY ANGEL

his daughter's life, out of Chicago. Now. Better to hear it from me than Garlic Joe." He handed Jake an envelope. "I put a little extra on your paycheck. Use it to leave of town. You got 'til noon tomorrow."

Jake turned the envelope over several times before he spoke. "Chicago's all I know."

"I hear there's jobs in Southern Illinois."

"Oh, yeah? What brewery?"

Elio shook his head. "Forget the breweries. They ain't hiring in Belleville and the St. Louis mucky-mucks don't hire outsiders."

"Not even for a little grease?"

"Don't waste your time or money. You gotta be related to somebody already working there. I'm talking coalmines, Jake. They're all over Southern Illinois. And the money's decent."

"I don't know—"

"You got no choice, kid. Go to the Dearborn Station and buy yourself a one-way ticket to St. Louis. You'll find the mining jobs posted there at Union Station." Elio came from behind his desk to shake Jake's hand before pushing him out the door.

For a split second Jake felt like a caged animal set free. What better way to wiggle out from under Hildie and her family? His relief short-circuited as soon as he walked out of the employee exit. POW! Jake's nose ran into the brass-knuckled fist of Harold Kramer.

"This is for fuckin' my sister. You damn bastard wop." Harold removed his blood-spattered fist from Jake's nose. Another blow came from the left. "Don't ever come back to Chicago." Followed by one to the right. "And don't never try to contact Hildie. You're dead if you do." A ram behind the knees dropped Jake, inviting a kick to the groin. Harold walked a few steps away, and came back for one more to Jake's kidney. "Lucky for you Pop didn't want to call in Garlic Joe."

The assault to Jake's balls kept him grounded. He lay on the gravel pavement, writhing in pain as his nose grew with every gasp from his mouth. He lacked the strength and desire to soothe his throbbing face. Each breath felt like his last. His first move was to pull a red kerchief from his back pocket and dam up the blood dripping into his mouth. His nose had turned to mush taking a new direction. As the fog lifted from his eyes, Jake saw a leather sole heading toward his face.

"What the hell." Elio Seppi did a quick sidestep. "That you, Jake? Sonofabitch, this wasn't part of the deal. Here, take my hand."

Jake's knees wobbled into an upright position. He leaned on his former boss. Together they walked to Elio's Ford Coupe where Elio pushed him into the passenger seat. After the short drive to Carlo's apartment, Elio offered to help him up the stairs.

Jake refused. He crawled on his own.

*****

"Holy Mother of Mary, what truck hit you?" Carlo asked on seeing the swollen face and bruised eyes. "I don't know about that nose. Maybe a doctor ...."

Jake gasped between breaths as he explained what happened. No sooner had he finished when a very pregnant Louisa came home from her cooking duties. This time Carlo told the story while Jake slouched on a kitchen chair. With a cold washcloth on his nose, he leaned his head back, too distracted by pain to wipe away the uncontrolled tears trailing down his face.

After Louisa whispered a few words to Carlo, she opened the desk drawer, selected a sturdy pencil, and snapped it in half.

"Okay, Jake. Let's take a look at that nose," she said with the authority of a medical professional. "Maybe we can fix it." She sat before him, legs apart to accommodate her expanding belly. "I seen Ma straighten my brother's when it got broke in a fight."

"This was no fight ... dammit ... no, no, don't touch me."

While Louisa kept reassuring Jake, Carlo moved behind him and immobilized his head. Before Jake could react, Louisa leaned over and maneuvered the pencil sections into his nostrils. Using her fingers as anchors, she held the stubs firmly in place. With an index finger on either side of Jake's nose and one swift pop, she repositioned his nose. Jake opened his mouth to let out a yell. He stopped. He sniffed. He sniffed again.

"You fixed it. I can breathe without it hurting." Still shaky, he stood up. He circled the room and came back to Louisa. He stretched out to hug her. He kissed her cheeks. "Bella, bella," he whispered, extending his laced hands to compliment her pregnancy. "So full of life with Carlo's baby. Someday I will find a bride just like you."

"But not in Chicago," she reminded him. "Tonight, you eat supper with Carlo and me—a nice *zuppa*—uh, minestrone, your favorite. Then you go home and pack your suitcase. Good thing Carlo is off tomorrow. He can go to *la stazione* with you. Right, Carlo?" Louisa looked at her frowning husband. "I know, I know. It's the first time you and Jake ever been apart. Don't be sad, my love. It won't be forever. Nothing lasts forever."

*****

The next morning Carlo weaved through the Dearborn Station crowd with Jake, his black eyes and puffy nose attracting the curious and the amused.

"At least it's on straight," Jake said, sounding like he had a head full of snot.

As they passed Roscoe Johnson's shoeshine stand, the bootblack called them over. "Mister, didn't you come through with your intended bride a while back?"

"Si." Carlo grinned and repeated Jake's earlier description of Louisa's belly.

"I knew it. I knew she was the one for you." Roscoe cocked his head. "Say, what wrong with your friend?"

"He's no friend; he's my brother."

"Damn, that no way to treat kin."

Holding a handkerchief to his nose, Jake managed a few words. "Ever hear of Garlic Joe?"

"Say no more. Mister, you lucky to be leaving Chicago on your own two legs."

"Catch you on my way out," Carlo said, tossing Roscoe a quarter.

The brothers approached the Illinois Central platform in time to hear the conductor shout the final boarding. They lingered at the end of the passenger line, and Carlo cleared his throat. "So, how long you staying in St. Louis?"

"I already told you, long enough to figure out my next step. Elio said the mines are in Illinois, across the Mississippi."

"You gonna be okay, Jake?"

"Hell no." Jake managed a half-hearted grin. "Don't worry about me. How else was I gonna get out from under?" He wiped his dripping nose. "You just take care of Louisa."

The brothers hugged until Jake pulled away and jumped onboard. Carlo walked alongside the train as it slowly moved down the track. "Don't forget to write," he called out over the clatter. As the train picked up speed, he kept his eyes on Jake's passenger car until it disappeared into the tunnel. Then he headed toward the exit. And home to Louisa.

*****

On Wednesday Hildie went to Fabiola's where she cornered Carlo and

Louisa during their salad course. "What's going on?" she asked with pouty lips that weren't faking. "I haven't seen Jake all week."

"He didn't talk to you?" Carlo asked.

"If he had, I wouldn't be asking. What's more, I don't appreciate the brush-off. After all, I've done for—"

"Jake ain't coming back," Carlo said.

"So he finally wised up. I kept telling him the food here was lousy. Sorry, I just meant … never mind."

"I meant Chicago. He ain't coming back to Chicago."

Hildie looked at Louisa. Louisa dug into her lettuce.

"My wife don't know a thing so keep her out of this."

"Your wife knows everything." She reached over the table, stopped Louisa's fork in mid-air. "Tell me where he went, please."

"It might've been St. Louis," Louisa said. "But don't go making any more trouble for him. If they find Jake …."

"If who finds Jake?"

"I ain't saying."

*****

Hildie went home in tears. She found Gus on the front porch, sucking his pipe. "Poppa, what'd you do to Jake? He's gone and my life's ruined." Hands to hips and stomping her foot, she gushed a flood of angry tears. "The only man I ever loved who loved me back and you made him go away."

"This man was not fit for the favorite offspring of Gustav Kramer. My little girl deserves nothing but the best."

"Jake was the best, Papa. You said I could have him and then you changed your mind. That's not fair."

Harold had been raiding the icebox when Hildie's ranting disrupted his evening ritual. Pork chop in hand, he edged closer to the action and overheard his father's high appraisal of Hildie. With that, he stormed out to the porch, told Hildie why Pop had Jake run out of Chicago, and how the weasel wop was lucky to still run on his own two legs.

Elsa joined the ruckus, waving a doily she'd been embroidering. "What's this you say, your sister making whoopee, playing house like a common trull? Show me the engagement ring."

"One more week," Hildie wailed. "That's all I needed."

Laying the doily over her forehead, Elsa feigned a swoon to the couch that everyone ignored.

"I want Jake back, Poppa. Don't believe Harold's lies. Even if Jake had somebody else, he still loved me best."

"Hildie, where is your shame. With another woman you would share that weasel?" Gus slammed down his pipe. "This is not the way of a Kramer."

Elsa's quick recovery came with a pair of blazing eyes. "Out, I want you out." She pointed her embroidery toward the door. "For the house of Kramer you are not fit."

"She stays!" Gus shouted, his voice mellowing with the next words. "Hildegard, please. Whatever I did, for you I did. What this festering boil needed was a proper lancing. He hoodwinked you, hoodwinked all of us."

"Not me," Harold said. "I always knew."

"Shut up!" chorused the other three.

*****

In the end the Kramers agreed to a moratorium: not another word about Jake Baggio. Hildie gave up Fabiola's and for the next two weeks she ventured out only to perform her duties at Western Electric. At home she moped over magazines until Gus showed up with a slick Southern Italian from the brewery. Enzo Tarro may have lacked brain matter but made up for that with a powerful physique and handsome face. He charmed Hildie into forgetting the unspoken one and she convinced him to Americanize his name.

Chapter 21
Good Days and Bad

Shortly after midnight on March 1, 1926, Louisa's water broke. Carlo telephoned Midwife Licia Spilari and made his next phone call to Louisa's brothers.

"We'll come after the baby makes its entrance," Massimo said. "It's been twenty-six years, but I still remember our Ma's pain when she birthed Louisa. I'd offer to send Tillie to sit with you but she's holed up in the bedroom ... something about her nerves."

Tillie, as if Carlo or Louisa wanted Tillie poking her nose where it didn't belong. Other than the midwife, Louisa wanted only Noreen. "Show me the baby as soon as it's born," Carlo told Noreen when he was sent to the parlor.

Noreen assisted the efficient Licia Spilari with the delivery of Louisa's first child, born with relative ease and minimum pain. While Licia waited for the afterbirth to discharge, Noreen carried the newborn into the living room. "Papa, 'tis a wee colleen," she said. "I hope you don't mind your first not being a boy."

"Mind, are you kidding? I'm the luckiest man alive. Already I can tell she resembles my mama."

"Come to Licia, so I can make you clean," the midwife said. "Oh, little baby, you are so special."

"They say she predicts the future of her newborns," Noreen whispered to Carlo. "Not that I believe such nonsense."

Holding the infant in the crook of her arm, Licia washed its mouth and eyes with small linen squares saturated in boric acid. When a squeaky cry erupted, Lucia hummed a lullaby to accompany her next words. "Time for your first bath, Baby Baggio." Using a soft cloth and olive oil, she removed the baby's protective coating. The crying soon stopped.

While Louisa murmured her gratitude, Noreen worked around her to remove the soiled sheets and pads protecting the clean linens underneath. After that she gave Louisa an antiseptic sponge bath and helped her into a fresh linen gown. "Well done, Louisa. 'Tis a proud father you've made of that husband of yours. I'll tell him you're ready."

Carlo tiptoed into the room. He sat beside the bed and pressed Louisa's hand to his lips. "*Grazie, mi amore*, for giving me this precious gift." He leaned his head to her breast.

"Better than the watch and chain?" Louisa asked, referring to her wedding gift to him. She ran her fingers through his hair.

"Better than my own life. I love you, Louisa."

"I know. That's why there's something I need to tell you."

"No way can you love me more than I do you," Carlo said. "Nothing else matters."

Holding back a yawn, she closed her eyes and fell asleep.

*****

Carlo and Louisa named the baby Maria after his mother and Anna after hers. He wanted to call her Anna Maria, but Louisa contended an American daughter should have an American name. They agreed on Mary Ann.

After Mass on Easter Sunday the proud parents tucked Mary Ann into a new perambulator, imported from England and one of several pricey gifts from her Valenza uncles. The sidewalks hosted a rotogravure of fashion with Chicagoans of all ages promenading their spring finery. Carlo didn't bother with a new outfit but insisted Louisa should, a two-piece pale yellow crepe he'd bought for her at Carson's.

"Carlo, would you look at that lady coming toward us," she whispered, along with a hand gesture. "Bella, bella ... maybe she's the wife of a very rich man, perhaps a banker."

The fine lady carried herself in the manner befitting royalty. She wore a silk chemise, the color of burnished rose, and matching T-strap pumps. A string of pearls, Louisa thought genuine, cascaded to the waist of the woman's trim frame. Hair the color of bricks bordered her rose-tinted straw cloche. As did everyone else, she stopped to admire the adorable Mary Ann.

"Ah, Carlo, what have we here, the new family?"

Carlo bungled through an awkward introduction.

"And what is the baby's name? Mary Ann ... how lovely, after your beloved mother, right? And those bluest of blue eyes, indeed."

"From my side," Louisa said.

"Ah-h, but of course." She stepped back to observe Carlo's face, one that showed no emotion other than pride. "So nice to finally meet the lovely family ... well, I must get back to my books."

"What are you reading?" Louisa asked.

"Only my financial reports," she said with a laugh and resumed her stroll.

"So that was the famous Giulietta Bracca," Louisa said.

"Blue eyes run in my family too, in case you didn't know ... from way back."

She slipped her arm through his, and together they pushed their daughter down Taylor Street on that glorious spring day, an Easter worth remembering.

*****

Later that week Monsignor Flaherty telephoned Louisa, asking her to stop by whenever it was convenient. She left the sleeping baby with Carlo and went to the rectory.

"Two meals a day, Lass, is all I'm asking." pleaded Noreen. "I could take care of little Mary Ann right here while you do the cooking. You needn't stay and serve the evening meal. I've been cursed with this silly girl who can't lick a stick when it comes to food preparation but she'll do for the serving and cleaning up."

"'Tis a great service you'd be performing for St. Sebastian's, Louisa," the monsignor chimed in. "And, of course, you would be fairly compensated. Did I tell you: the archbishop came to dinner last week and asked about you?"

"Cardinal Mundelein?"

"In the flesh, and picking at spicy Mexican food prepared by a well-meaning parishioner."

Sean Flaherty did not elaborate on the extent of his embarrassment that night when the Cardinal asked when the Italian cook would return. Nor did he tell Louisa that the archbishop reminded him of the favor he'd granted, allowing Father Connelly an unearned sabbatical to Rome. Indeed, the chain of circumstances Sean

Flaherty set forth had moved beyond his control.

"And don't forget Fathers Grady and Alvarez," Noreen said, referring to Terry Connelly's replacements. "They've quit asking for seconds, which makes me suspect they're also eating on the sly."

Louisa nodded. "At Fabiola's. What I mean to say is—"

"Now don't be making excuses for them," Noreen said. "It just proves how much you're needed here. Not that I'm saying things will ever be as they were before, what with Father Connelly and all."

"Father Connelly?"

"Did I not tell you," the monsignor said. "He's staying in Rome, to further his studies at the North America College."

The request had come from Terry, after the monsignor told him Louisa had married Carlo and was expecting an early baby. Sean Flaherty dreaded the unpleasant task of having to approach his supervisor on Terry's behalf. The Cardinal, one of the most authoritative of American archbishops, did not favor his young priests finding their inspiration elsewhere. In fact, it was only due to a restricted bequest from a wealthy Chicagoan and aficionado of Rome that Chicago diocesan priests had been permitted to travel abroad. But before the Monsignor could present his petition, he received a directive from the Office of the Archdiocese. The Vatican had requested Terrence Connelly be reassigned to the Roman Curia until further notice. Sean Flaherty's dilemma had resolved itself. His troubled assistant was destined for a far different role than that of parish priest.

Father Connelly not returning? Louisa didn't so much as allow herself a single blink but she did give a silent thanks to Blessed Mother and Sweet Jesus. She left St. Sebastian's after promising to discuss the offer of reemployment with her husband. When she mentioned the news about Father Connelly, Carlo reacted as she knew he would, saying the decision to work again was hers. His pride wouldn't allow him to acknowledge their financial difficulties, but she'd seen his pained expression when he put off her request for a new cook stove.

With Jake out of Chicago Carlo had inherited the Kramer curse. Every other week Harold brought a new complaint to Elio Seppi: *Carlo was getting sloppy; twice he caused a slowdown; once he nearly stopped production. And so on.* Accusations never proved but they resulted in Carlo's responsibilities being curtailed. Then he lost his overtime. When Carlo's immediate supervisor cut his workweek to four days, Carlo started shining his own shoes. At three work days he changed barbers: Louisa instead of Amerigo. If Gus had a hand in the petty harassment, he never showed it. And Carlo knew better than to ask.

*****

Still miserable in a marriage brimming with antiseptic, Harold was determined to garner the favor of Alice Jean Armstead. He went so far as to approach her on the street one dark, blustery evening.

"Uh-h, fancy meeting you here," he said, brushing his bulk against her slender frame.

"Oh, it's you, Harold." She stopped under the streetlight. "You startled me."

"That wasn't my intention. I just wanted to talk."

"What a coincidence," Alice Jean said. "I've been meaning to ask you something."

"You have?" His face flushed. "So ask away, I'm all ears."

She smiled ever so sweetly, and said, "Please don't think me forward but …."

"But what, just say it."

"Of course, I was wondering if you knew what happened to that nice friend of Hildie's."

Harold's lip curled, as did his fingers into a tight fist. "Hildie's friends come and go."

"Now, what was his name?" Alice Jean paused, finger to chin. "Yes, I remember now. Jake. Jake Baggio. And his brother was called Carlo."

"I heard Jake left Chicago in a hurry, something about his legs."

"I see. Well, nice talking to you, Harold."

She walked away. He followed.

"Say, Alice Jean, I was wondering …."

"Yes?" She kept up her pace.

He put his hand on her shoulder, slowed her down. "Ever hear of the Green Parrot?"

"It's not my kind of place."

"Then we'll go someplace classy. You pick."

"Harold, please." She stepped out of his reach. "After all, you are a married man."

"Prim and me ain't been hitting it off so good. Not like you and me could. Just give me the word, as in yes."

"Certainly not, I could never do that to Primula."

"She-it. You didn't mind doing that to my sister, did you?"

Alice Jean resumed her pace. This time Harold blocked her way. "You and Jake—that's right, the Jake whose name you couldn't remember. I know all about you and that wop. If he was good enough for you, then I'm a whole lot better."

"No, Harold. You are not good enough for me. You are a coarse, boorish clod who turns my stomach whenever I see you. The fact that we are even having this conversation confirms the accuracy of my assessment of your defective nature. What's more, if you ever bother me again," she paused to level her forefinger at him, "I shall tell your mother."

Harold spit a wad of sour grapes on the sidewalk before stomping away. He sought consolation at Night School. Tolerated by only a few teachers, the regular was neither exemplary nor popular. Twice, he'd been reprimanded and later suspended for excessive roughness. Before he could be reinstated, Giulietta Bracca had required substantial donations to the Holy Guardian Angels Children's Home. And so, for a short time Harold Kramer's sexual appetite and precarious ego were kept under control.

Chapter 22
The Messenger

"Wake up, my love," Louisa whispered into Carlo's ear one September morning, his face buried in the pillow as he slept.

He rolled over.

"Mary Ann's going to have a little brother ... or, maybe a sister, only God knows for sure."

Her words flung Carlo into an upright position. "But the baby, she's only six months old."

Indeed, *bambino secondo* in the oven so soon after Mary Ann was not what either of them expected. Nursing one baby was supposed to prevent the conception of another, or so Louisa thought. She worked her fingers into Carlo's tight shoulders, trying to soothe away the tension. "*Non si preoccupi, mi amore*," she said, urging him not to worry. "Who can say—maybe this time we'll get our boy."

He pushed Louisa down and snuggled into her. "Boy or girl, the new baby will be as special as our Mary Ann. Whatever makes you happy, makes me happy."

"You're my happiness, you and Mary Ann." She giggled. "I thought this was the best year of my life, but next year will be even better."

The cook stove she'd inspected at Newman's Appliance Store would have to wait. Isaac Newman even took measurements to make sure it would fit in her kitchen. All she had to do was ask Carlo. For her he would buy the stove, even if it meant a second job to pay for it.

If only there hadn't been that trouble between Jake and the Kramers. Thank God for Elio Seppi. Twice, he'd saved Carlo's job.

In the months that followed morning sickness and constant fatigue plagued Louisa, but she ignored both to prepare meals for Monsignor Flaherty, his clerics and guests, while Noreen, who'd accepted the honorary title of Nonna, fussed over Mary Ann. Fathers Grady and Alvarez received permanent assignments to St. Sebastian's, but according to Noreen neither priest could ever measure up to their predecessor. Only once did Louisa comment on Father Connelly: her hope that he'd found his heaven on earth in Rome. She'd relegated him to the deepest recesses of her mind, along with that farewell evening. As for Mary Ann, the baby had but one true father: the one who cradled her in his arms and lulled her to sleep.

*****

On a night in late February, a full month before the due date estimated by Licia Spilari, Louisa awoke to amniotic fluid oozing between her legs. She tried moving away from the wet spot that would soon soak the mattress but excruciating pain circled from her lower back to her pulsing belly. When the pain subsided, she tried to get up. Her legs cramped and weakened under her pregnant weight. Sharp pains came and went with relief.

"Carlo, wake up. The baby, he's coming ... dear God, not now."

Only two days before Licia Spilari had examined Louisa and said everything appeared normal. Licia explained she was going to Milwaukee for a short visit but would return to examine Louisa again before the due date. Still, Carlo telephoned the Spilari house, just in case Licia had changed her plans.

"Licia won't be back for two more days," her husband said. "I'll call another midwife."

Silvia Mansino was involved in a difficult breech birth and couldn't leave her patient. She suggested Olimpia Taglio. The new midwife was contacted at the home of a patient who had just given birth. She rushed through her post-delivery cleansing routine and hurried on to Licia Spilari's patient. By the time the second substitute midwife reached the door of the Baggio apartment, she was greeted by the wailing of a newborn infant.

Noreen had arrived thirty minutes earlier and took charge of the delivery with Carlo's assistance. Both were relieved when Olimpia took over the delivery of the placenta. When it failed to emerge in a reasonable time, she pushed one hand deep into Louisa's birth canal and with the other hand, applied pressure on top of Louisa's belly. At last, the afterbirth expelled.

Tucked away in the parlor, Baby Mary Ann slept throughout the birth of the boy infant who arrived on the first anniversary of her birth. Although he didn't arrive in the orderly manner of his sister, Michael John was healthy but tiny, barely weighing five pounds.

Vincenzo and Massimo rushed over to see Louisa and the baby. They passed Mary Ann back and forth but kept their distance from the newborn. Louisa too, although they stood in the doorway of her room and made small talk.

"Tillie's still in Italy," Vincenzo said. "It's been four months."

"Her ma's still dying?" Louisa asked.

"Nah, as soon as Tillie arrived, the old lady made a miraculous recovery."

*****

Twenty-four hours after Michael's birth Louisa hemorrhaged and Carlo called the Spilari house again. This time Licia answered the telephone. She'd returned early, claiming a premonition of impending disaster. The midwife nearly wept when she saw Louisa, shivering from a high fever that kept her drifting in and out of lucidity. Her pulse had slowed, sapping her strength. The telltale odor of old blood and rotting flesh signaled childbirth fever.

The midwife called an American-born physician whose parents had emigrated from Sicily. Before Dr. Molini arrived, Licia employed the standard treatment for puerperal bleeding. Using extreme care and properly sterilized instruments, she removed the remaining tissue from the infected womb before administering a warm water douche. Hot swipes soaked in turpentine applied to Louisa's belly eased afterbirth contractions that were more severe than yesterday's labor pains.

Carlo and Noreen carried their own pain of undeserved guilt. "Get the wine," Licia told Carlo. "For Louisa, to give strength to her blood, you could use some too." To Noreen she said, "Cool water compresses might reduce the fever."

Busy work kept the family strong, for Louisa's sake. Licia sensed her patient was moving beyond medical help. Early in her profession she'd learned not to suggest prayer as a last resort to the grieving family. Too often they blamed God for not hearing their prayers when His was the answer they couldn't accept.

THE FAMILY ANGEL

After Noreen applied cool wet cloths to Louisa's forehead and neck, she retreated to a far corner, one hand clutching the rosary she always carried. Her lips moved without sound as she fingered the crystal beads.

Carlo held a small glass to his wife's parched lips. "Louisa, take some wine. It'll do you good."

She managed two sips before closing her eyes again.

"Okay, okay, you win. Do this for me and we'll get that new cook stove you been wanting. But first, you gotta get better."

"Let her rest, Carlo," said Licia, her hand over his. "Soon the doctor will be here."

*****

Dr. Molini arrived in a rumpled suit and carried a black satchel. After a brief discussion with Licia he examined Louisa and then followed Carlo into the kitchen. A foreign dialect spilled from the doctor's mouth.

"*Non Siciliano, Dottore*," Carlo said.

The doctor cleared his throat and started over in English. "Sometimes, but very rare for our modern time, a great fever can overtake a new mother, perhaps from improper sterilization. Infection spreads throughout the body. Because of her weakened state from childbirth …."

"Yesterday we were laughing. Our little girl—"

"Mr. Baggio, I regret nothing more can be done. Your wife is in God's hands."

"God's hands will save her?"

"Not for this life. I am sorry."

Carlo buried his face in his hands, shoulders heaving with silent sobs. He heard Noreen making the dreaded phone calls to Louisa's brothers, the monsignor, and Sister Barbara, a nun he didn't know. "Holy Mary, Mother of God …." he began but couldn't go any further. Instead, he squared his shoulders and went to Louisa's bedside.

She opened her eyes, managed a faint smile. "*Mi amore*, do not be sad for me. I dreamed of waiting for you … in heaven." Her voice trailed off.

"Louisa, don't leave me. I need you now, more than ever."

"I'd stay if I could, but God already dispatched *L'Angelo Nero*. A black angel, he was, dressed like a Western Union messenger. Imagine that, me getting a telegram."

His poor wife had lost her senses. Carlo choked back tears. "I can't make it without you."

"You will—for our babies. *L'Angelo Nero* ... he sat at the foot of my bed ... said he'd watch out for you. I should've been scared but ... but ... dying ain't so bad."

"Don't talk that way. You gotta know how much I love you. More than I ever let on. More than you ever knew."

"About Mary Ann ... God forgive me. I should've told you."

"Sh-h-h. Don't tell me what I already know. Mary Ann is mine, same as Michael."

Carlo felt a hand on his shoulder. He shuddered. Could it be Louisa's angel?

"'Tis but a few minutes alone with your beloved I'll be needing," Monsignor Flaherty whispered. He pulled a purple stole from the slit in his cassock, and said, "For her confession."

Carlo let Noreen push him into the hallway. She fingered her beads while he paced, unable to gather one lucid thought. After a few moments the door opened and they hurried back inside. Louisa seemed at peace when Carlo pressed his lips to hers. He gave up his spot to the monsignor and moved to the foot of the bed. He watched Noreen light a candle and held his eyes to its eerie glow of flickering shadows dancing on the wall. What better way to block out the one ritual no father with two babies should ever have to endure.

Thus began the Last Rites for Louisa Valenza Baggio, with Monsignor Flaherty making the sign of the cross to accompany the rhythmic words of his blessing.

"In nomine Patris, et Filii, et Spititus Sancti. Amen."

Chapter 23
Or Else

In less than three years Carlo had evolved from bachelor to husband and father to widower unable to care for his babies. Until he could work out a more palatable arrangement, Mary Ann and Michael were under the care of untouchable women who wore black robes and starched white collars. The Guardian Angels Foundling Home had been Noreen's idea and Carlo had gone along with it, at least for now.

Every conversation and lovemaking ritual he once shared with Louisa now haunted his bittersweet memories.

"I promise to love you with all my heart every day of my life," he'd told her on their wedding night.

"And I will love you longer than the day I die," she'd said. *"If I leave this earth first, I'll wait for you in heaven."*

"Don't talk like that," he'd whispered, skimming his lips over her face. *"It's bad luck to talk about dying, like reminding God in case he forgets."*

God didn't forget. And now Carlo wanted to fold, to cash in his chips, but the necessity of a paycheck prevented him from giving up. That and the promise he'd made to Louisa, for the sake of their children.

Mary Ann's blue eyes and pale skin remained a mystery Carlo wouldn't allow himself to contemplate. Her curly dark hair could've come from either side but the toddler's temperament most certainly matched that of Louisa's. Extracting favors from Mary Ann required clever negotiation, even the simplest kiss. Often, it required little more than one from him first. Before she relinquished any toy, a suitable replacement had to be offered. Carlo loved the challenges, the constant tweaking of her independence. This child, his and Louisa's first born, was now his alone. And nothing or no one would ever change that.

Baby Michael, with his personality still developing, had inherited Louisa's best features: same chestnut hair, same almond-shaped eyes.

"He is his mother's child, Mr. Baggio," confirmed Sister Barbara, placing the infant in Carlo's arms. "I don't have to tell you the many wonderful qualities your beloved Louisa possessed. Monsignor Flaherty often sent her to the Guardian Angels for special events. Of course, my sisters in Christ miss Louisa and her cooking skills, but we must also rejoice for now she is with our Lord in Heaven."

For Carlo there was no rejoicing. Had it not been for the babies, his heaven on earth would've turned into hell. Instead, he found himself wallowing in limbo. He missed the camaraderie only a brother could provide. Jake's presence would've helped fill the gap. When Louisa died, they'd talked by telephone twice. Empty words that couldn't express what either felt.

*****

Several weeks later Jake called again. "You oughta come to St. Gregory. I can get you on at the mine."

"You mean six hundred feet under the ground?"

"It ain't as bad as the picture painted in your head."

"How's the pay?"

"Not as good as the brewery but the living's cheaper. And for the right money you get used to not seeing the light of day." He went on to describe the prairie town, where gardens and grape harbors thrived like the Garden of Eden. "You should see the tomatoes, some as big as my fist."

"Any mountains?"

"Hell, we're talking Illinois, not Colorado. Think rolling hills and fishing lakes."

"What about the saloons?"

"On every corner and more wine then you or I will ever drink," Jake said with a laugh that lifted Carlo's spirits. "This guy I'm boarding with has vineyards and a vat in the cellar. In my opinion, his table wine's better'n Vincenzo's best. But don't tell the bastardo I said that. So, whadaya say?"

"I don't know, Jake."

"It ain't the Old Country, but there's our own kind here. Would you believe, this town's overrun with Piemontese. The guy who owns the mine brought them over before the war. Now we all but run the coal company. For crissake, Carlo, what's holding you back?"

"My babies. They're too young to shuffle off to someplace new. The nuns I trust, but I can't have strangers looking after them while I work. Besides, I worry about Michael. He's got some breathing problems. The doc says it's asthma but not to worry. In time he might grow out of it."

*****

Time. Time ruled his life. In time he'd get over losing Louisa. In time he'd get his babies back. Time was working against Carlo. He was twenty-four and going nowhere. After a while he resumed his Wednesday and Saturday routine at Fabiola's. It helped, letting Louisa's brothers bend his ear reminiscing.

"Did Giulietta come to Louisa's wake?" Vincenzo had asked one evening.

"She sent flowers," Carlo said.

"That funeral spray must've set her back a couple hundred," Massimo said as he refilled Carlo's wineglass, on the house. "Reminds me of the one Dion O'Banion did for Berto Marconi."

"O'Banion the gangster?" Carlo asked.

"The same. O'Banion could well afford the show, what with him owning his own flower shop."

"They say over the years O'Banion killed more than his share," Vincenzo said. "He probably went straight to hell when he met his own maker. Can you believe, gunned down in his place of business? The dumb bastard, he thinks the guys coming in to pick up a $10,000 funeral order are real customers. Instead, they feed his belly five bullets and one more to the head."

"For good measure," Massimo said. "I don't know about that Giulietta. She's messing with trouble by answering to Capone. With him she better have the right answers."

"And if he don't like what he hears, the right answers are still the wrong ones."

*****

One evening about four months after Louisa's death Carlo returned from Fabiola's to find Giulietta waiting in his living room. He kissed her on both cheeks and asked how she got in.

"Does it really matter?"

He hated when people did what he often did: answer a question with another question.

"Where are your manners, Carlo? I taught you better than that."

"I'm sorry. Please sit. Would you like some wine?"

She sat but refused the wine.

"It's only Wednesday," he said. Her usual time away from the business fell on Sundays when Night School wasn't in session.

"Hmm, so it is." Giulietta gave his parlor the once-over.

For his benefit, Carlo figured since she must've seen an eyeful before he came home. Her eyes stopped at the crucifix hanging over Louisa's statue of the Blessed Virgin.

"How quaint," she said, "straight from the Old Country."

"How nice of you to stop by; I never thanked you in person for sending the flowers."

"It was the least I could do. That Easter, seeing you with your wife and child, I realized you'd made the right decision. What a pity fate intervened."

He and Louisa had been so smug then. Like all young lovers, convinced they deserved to live forever. He took a seat across the room, next to the rosewood end table holding the photograph of his parents. He lifted his ankle to the opposite knee and started drumming his fingers. "Business has been good?"

"Never better. New faces, old faces, it's the favorites I miss." She smiled. "And you?"

"Could be better. At the brewery, I mean."

Her pink tongue curled out, wetting her cupid lips. "Excuse me, Carlo. May I have something to drink now?"

He jumped up and poured two glasses of Chianti.

Mindless small talk filled the minutes, easing tension until Giulietta laid this on him. "Carlo, my pet, I've come as a concerned friend." She folded her hands in the manner of a gentlewoman, holding in check the subtle body language he found hard to resist. "Rumor has it that a certain Harold Kramer blames his current troubles on the Baggio Brothers."

"Current troubles, you mean his sister and the Siciliano?"

"An embarrassment already rectified at the altar."

She inserted a cigarette in her rhinestone holder and motioned Carlo to come over and light it. He wound up sitting next to her.

"So what about Harold?" he asked.

"A pathetic student, one of Night School's least desirable. He went haywire after a certain repressed virgin rejected his advances. It seems Harold's frigid mate recently learned of his extracurricular activities. The iceberg filed for divorce last week."

"I ain't surprised." Carlo said, recalling dinner with the Kramers.

"I should think Harold would welcome his freedom, even with the alimony Mrs. Kramer is demanding and no doubt will be awarded. Instead, he let her departure wound his Teutonic pride."

"So what's this got to do with me?"

"According to the scuttlebutt, your sweet brother also pursued the eternal virgin who rebuffed Harold. He still blames Jake for botching his chances for a side dalliance. And since Jake is no longer around … well Harold feels the next of kin should pay for grief he brought upon himself."

"Pay with what? Thanks to Harold, I lost my overtime. I barely make a living."

"Money is not what he has in mind."

"So we're back to Garlic Joe."

She laughed, in the old familiar way. "Harold being Harold may want to resolve this without incurring outside expenses. He's such a fool, which makes him all the more dangerous. Perhaps you should consider a temporary relocation, at least until Harold finds a new playmate."

"Merda! That could take forever and I ain't leaving Chicago without my babies." Carlo pounded the upholstery with his clenched fist. "How much more shit do I have to take." He fumbled with the smoking stand, held a match to his cigarillo. He stood up, paced and puffed and paced some more.

"I realize this is sudden and quite disturbing, my pet. But you don't have much time to weigh your options."

"Don't try changing my mind."

"Better those babies have an absentee father than no father at all. Think of their welfare."

He shook his head.

"I have discreet connections with the foundling home."

"Anything but this, Giulietta."

She stood and sandwiched his face between her hands. "Listen to me. On the watery grave of my dead mother, I make this promise to you: your babies will receive the best of care. For as long as I live and then some."

For Giulietta to invoke the memory of a past she seldom discussed gave Carlo some comfort. He sighed. "How much time you think I have?"

"Maybe two days, but don't push your luck."

She removed the cigarillo from his mouth, kissed it in the old way guaranteed to arouse him. Neither of them made an effort to move toward the bedroom he'd shared with his wife. Why compete with a ghost, a perfect one no less. The living room would do just fine.

*****

Nothing came easy, especially when it involved Mary Ann. She would not go to Sister Barbara after Carlo kissed her goodbye. Although he held back his tears, the screaming toddler sensed his new level of distress. She wrapped her chubby arms tighter and tighter around Carlo's neck while Baby Michael slept in the nursery down the hall.

"Mary Ann, please. Release your papa," Sister Barbara said.

Carlo did his magic with a tiny book, a Cracker Jack prize Elio Seppi had passed on to him. Mary Ann snatched it from his fingers and quit crying.

"Do not worry about your children, Mr. Baggio." Sister Barbara kept a firm grip on Mary Ann. The toddler snuggled into the warmth of the nun's heavy bosom and tugged at the impressive black rosary hanging from her waist. "My Sisters in Christ and I cannot take the place of you or their beloved mother, but we will love your little ones as the children we shall never bear. Of course, there's also Monsignor Flaherty and Noreen. And the Valenzas, God bless both of them."

"There's another friend …."

"Ah yes, a most generous and loyal donor," Sister Barbara said. "We count Miss Bracca among our earthly angels who provide for the little orphans or those children with parents experiencing temporary misfortune."

At least Giulietta hadn't exaggerated her sincerity. And last night had been a touching farewell. Carlo relaxed the kink in his neck. "I should be going, Sister."

"And may Our Lord go with you in love and peace."

Mary Ann gave one final tug to the rosary, sending a flood of beads to the polished floor. Carlo slammed his fist to his forehead and was prepared to apologize when the nun motioned him to leave.

"I'll write every week," he said, bending down to gather the scattered rosary.

"Leave the beads. One of the older children will take care of them."

He straightened up. "I'll send money too. Right now this feels like forever but trust me, it ain't. It's just 'til I get settled."

"Of course, Mr. Baggio. Perhaps if you just walked away and not look back ... so as not to upset the child."

Chapter 24
Chicago's Other Side

"Where to?" the cabby asked, addressing the rearview mirror.

"Dearborn Station. I'm in a hurry." Relieved to have hailed a cab as soon as he left the apartment, Carlo expelled a deep breath. He'd only allotted a few minutes to buy his ticket before the train's departure.

Two blocks from the station the cabbie stopped, again spoke to Carlo through the mirror. "There's a traffic jam up ahead. I suggest you get out here and go through the rear entrance. Polk Street's bound to be clogged with drop-offs who wait 'til the last minute."

Carlo paid the fare, along with a good tip. He grabbed his suitcase and high-tailed it toward the station, passing a familiar face who was toting a wooden box and heading in the same direction.

"Hey, mister, where you go this time?" asked the bootblack.

If Roscoe Johnson had kept his mouth shut, Carlo might've glanced across the deserted street, maybe seen the stocky man with sandy hair aiming a gun in his direction. Instead, Carlo heard the sound of a firecracker. POW! A sharp ping zapped his lower right leg. He stumbled to the pavement, stunned but feeling no pain.

"What the shit!" Roscoe yelled. "We under attack."

The alley, Carlo had to make the alley. He crawled five feet before hearing the second shot. Hugging the sidewalk, he waited for the accompanying ping. It never came.

"Just hold on, mister," Roscoe said while dragging Carlo by his armpits. "You been shot and needs a doctor."

"To hell with the *dottore*, just get me to the station. I got a train to catch."

Roscoe shoved Carlo against a brick wall. "To hell with the station, mister, you ain't catching no train this day."

"If I don't wanna lose the other leg, I gotta leave Chicago now." Carlo struggled to one knee before clattering into a garbage can.

"Mister, shut your mouth for one minute and lemme take a gander." Roscoe pulled up the blood-soaked trouser leg. "God is good: that bullet done gone in one side and out the other." He dropped the bullet in Carlo's shirt pocket. "You be okay after couple days. 'Til then, you best come home with me."

"Hell, I don't even know you. And I sure as hell don't know your part of town."

"The way I sees it you ain't got much choice. Either piss a shitload of blood waiting for the cops, or take your chances with me."

"Some damn fool's trying to kill me."

"Not any more. A better shooter done shot the man what shot you first."

Carlo's eyes followed Roscoe's outstretched arm, finger pointing across the street. Had it not been for Giulietta's earlier warning, he wouldn't have recognized the man sprawled on the distant sidewalk. Blood oozed from under Harold Kramer's head, a pool of thick mahogany creeping over the gray concrete.

"He one dumb sonofabitch."

"Never saw him before," Carlo said.

"The look on your face tells me otherwise. He some Eye-talian, like you?"

"Hell no."

"Well whatever he was, he ain't no more. You can bet on that. 'Course if he got friends or family …."

Merda! What about Gus. Carlo had to make the train, any train. Just then he heard the braking of tires, saw a set of wire spoke wheels come to a halt, ten feet away curbside. The driver of the chrome-plated Pierce Arrow wore a chauffeur's cap and raced the motor without looking in Carlo's direction.

"I think reptile face is offering you a ride," Roscoe said. "What you think, mister?"

"Yeah, I know him." Carlo couldn't have managed the touring

car's rear seat without a shove from Roscoe but he didn't expect the bootblack to slide in beside him. "Get me to the station, and hurry," Carlo mumbled. "The cabby let me out here because the traffic—"

"Was lighter than usual," Frog Sapone said. "I just passed the entrance."

Carlo wanted to ask Frog why he showed up, but he lost the words somewhere between his brain and his mouth. Frog wouldn't have told him any way. After a while the Pierce Arrow stopped, Carlo thought to let him out at the station. Instead Roscoe was flagging down another cab. Between Roscoe and someone called Elijah, they moved him and his suitcase into the taxi. Carlo couldn't remember if he thanked Frog.

"You know, mister," he heard Roscoe say, "that driver done saved your life."

"*Io sono Carlo*, Carlo Baggio."

They drove deep into the South Side, where Elijah parked at a taxi stand near Thirty-fifth and State Streets. A groan erupted from Carlo's throat when the two men pulled him from the car. Sandwiched between them, he faltered. His legs turned to rubber as they headed into a neighborhood teeming with the excitement of theaters, cabarets, and cafes. Bright neon lights illuminated the buildings, and nearly blinded Carlo, a blessing that shielded him from the mixed reactions his bloody trail brought. Pedestrians moved aside. Some grumbled. Others shook their heads.

"All right folks, no gawking on The Stroll," said Roscoe. "White folks bleed same as the rest of us."

Just when Carlo didn't think he could go any further, they turned into a building and stumbled up one flight of stairs. He felt his weight and suitcase shifting to Roscoe. He managed a nod when Elijah tapped his shoulder and said goodbye.

Roscoe spoke up. "I thank you. My friend thanks you too."

"Say no more," Elijah said on his way down the hall. "I knows he would if he could."

"*Grazie ... io sono Carlo ... Carlo.*"

"Hold on, lemme unlock the door so's I can move you inside. And whatever you do, don't make no mess. There, now I'm turning loose so don't do anywhere." After throwing a rag rug over the couch, he eased Carlo onto it and then called out in a cheery manner, "Essie Mae, we got us some company."

Carlo saw the woman through a blur of rheumy eyes: taut and proud, her skin the color of light caramel.

Essie Mae Johnson had already changed into her chenille robe and floppy slippers. After finishing her night shift at the post office, she wanted the comfort of a soft bed. She stopped cold at the sight of Carlo leaning back on her couch, his pale face screwed up in pain. "Lawdy mercy. No peckawood ever set foot in my home. Not here in Chicago. Not on the farm in Mississippi."

"He hurt, Essie Mae."

"That I can see: white blood dripping on my brand new carpet." She shoved a towel under Carlo's feet. Her chocolate eyes narrowed into slits and conveyed an unmistakable message of displeasure to her husband, one that transcended position and race.

Carlo leaned forward and dropped his head.

"This here my good friend, Mister Carl. He from Rome, as in Italy." Using one arm, Roscoe backed Carlo into an upright position. "I know him for two years, a regular at the station and a good tipper. He ran into troubles, but not with the police. Or with do-gooders."

"Hold on, you talking about Black Hand?" Essie Mae pursed her lips. "Crazy folks who don't wannabe colored, but like showing their Black Hand."

Carlo grunted.

"Mister Carl said no to Black Hand. He just got in the way of some crazy guy who ain't even Eye-talian, leastways that what he say, and I believe him."

"*Non Siciliano, non luna*," Carlo said through clinched teeth. "*Io sono Carlo Baggio*. Car-r-lo, as in Charles."

"Hells bells, why didn't you say so? Essie Mae got a cousin down in *Missippi* name Charlie. Got a white daddy, that one. You be Charlie too." Roscoe put his arm around Carlo but his eyes never left Essie Mae's. "Whadaya say, Sugar Tits?"

"Shush, none of that sweet talk in front of strangers."

"You spend hours listening to Preacher George talk sweet charity. Now it's time to show some."

Her eyes drifted from Roscoe to Carlo and back to Roscoe, pondering before she spoke. "Ezell's sheets are clean. Put the cracker in his bed."

"Crackers make crumbs," Carlo mumbled, having passed out while Roscoe and Essie Mae Johnson were arguing his merits.

"Forget the cracker shit, Mister Charlie," Roscoe said with a chuckle. "Essie Mae just funning you. We gonna fix that leg."

*****

When Carlo woke up again the woman was dumping poison into the crater in his leg. "Holy Mary and Joseph!" he roared, unable to move from his spread-eagled position. Four gaudy neckties secured his wrists and ankles to the bedposts. Blessed Mother, the butcher woman was going to cut him up. Flush chunks of his flesh down the toilet. And no one would ever know.

"Hold on, Mister Charlie. Just lemme clean out them holes." Essie Mae used a light touch to swab the festering wounds. "Ain't no better use for Roscoe's moonshine than a mission of mercy." Her voice had a soothing nature, different from when she'd argued with her husband. "Sorry 'bout the ties. I didn't know how you be awake. Some folks make themselves crazy."

Crazy, hell. Carlo lifted his brow to hold up his eyelids. He wanted to ask about her man but couldn't recall his name. She must have read his mind.

"Roscoe done back at Dearborn. The man can't bring home bacon if he don't polish shoes. Right, Mister Charlie?"

Who's Charlie he wanted to ask, but couldn't form the words. Not that he'd understand the answer. English was hard enough; colored talk was impossible. He dropped his lids while the woman worked her black magic. The strange bed engulfed him and for the first time since Louisa died, he knew some measure of peace. Maybe it meant he was dying.

"You're a long way from dying, my friend."

The bootblack's witch must've conjured up a helper. The man's words emitted from a baritone voice, melodious and refined. Carlo strained his eyes to follow the voice until they focused on another black man. This one sat at the foot of the bed, cocksure with one hand resting on his bent knee. He wore a broad pinstriped gray suit, a bright yellow shirt and purple tie with white dots.

"Husband of Louisa, your time has not yet come," the black man said. "You must be strong, for the children."

Angelo Nero. Carlo nearly choked trying to expel the words trapped in his subconscious.

"For now, get on with the living," the angel said. "God has a plan, one that must be followed."

"Like hell, I didn't like the first one." There, he got the words out. Or did he only think them. At least he could move again. "Don't leave yet. Since you're so good at delivering messages, how 'bout taking one to my wife."

"She knows what's in your heart. For now that's good enough."

From far away, Carlo heard a woman's voice, but not Louisa's. The woman—he forgot her name—asked if he felt better. He wanted to ask if she'd seen what he saw but changed his mind. Instead, he let himself drift off, hoping to meet up with the angel again. So he could ask about Louisa.

*****

Like any other twenty-year-old, Ezell Johnson belonged on The Stroll, not sitting beside his bed watching some loony white man mess with the clean sheets Ezell wouldn't be enjoying later. Enough, he'd been playing nursemaid for half an hour longer than his sister gave. He poked the loony in his ribs, poked him again and again until he moaned and then stirred.

"Hey, Ma! Mister Charlie's waking up,"

Ezell jumped up when his ma came running.

"Hallelujah. You finally awake," Essie Mae said, clapping her hands. "Roscoe be home soon and glad to see you better. We was worried 'bout you, Mister Charlie."

Carlo threw off the covers, rolled to his side, and let out a groan. "I gotta go."

"Ezell, get that bucket so's he can relieve hisself."

"No, not that. I gotta catch my train. God has a plan ...." His voice drifted off as he tried to finish the thought. His feet hit the floor but couldn't hold his legs. He teetered before falling back on the mattress.

"Ezell, why he say that about God?"

Ezell shook his head. "Mister Charlie, you ain't going no place for a couple days."

"That's right," his ma said. "God plans for you to stay in bed. Food and rest what you need. Let that leg heal good." Carlo started to protest; she pushed him down. "Ezell, get Ruby Lee and a fresh bottle of your daddy's stuff. Hurry, now." She clucked her tongue and wrinkled her nose. "Whewy, such a mess of wicked pus."

Ezell returned with his sister and they held Carlo down while Essie Mae applied more shine. After the ordeal ended, Carlo rolled over and pounded the pillow.

"Merda, merda."

"What that merda mean?" Essie Mae asked.

"Shit, it means shit."

"Then say what you mean, you in America now."

While Essie Mae puttered around Carlo, Ezell motioned for Ruby Lee to follow him. They stood at the kitchen sink, Ezell threatening to tell Mama that her precious daughter had lifted the covers to check out Mister Charlie's private parts.

"I did no such thing," Ruby Lee said.

"His manhood can't hold a candle to the likes of any black man."

"Not that I would know. But you go ahead and meet your friends. I'll sit with him and read my book."

Earlier that day Ruby Lee had been alone with the feverish cracker when he started shaking. She did what her mama might've done if he hadn't been a cracker; she crawled into the bed. She held him close, spoon fashion, warming his body with hers, and stayed that way after he stopped shivering and muttering foreign words. And yes, she had lifted the covers.

*****

By the end of the next day Carlo was able to sit up in bed. Ruby Lee fed him chicken soup, a humiliating experience, more so when he tried feeding himself and the spoon slipped from his fingers. Something about the young girl made him think they'd met before, in a dream or another life. Maybe it was the perfume teasing his nose whenever she bent over to ram the spoon into his mouth. He saw a younger, darker version of her witch mother, the dispenser of moonshine and wisdom.

The girl's slick hairstyle reminded him of the new Louisa. Her American haircut damn near ended their romance. After a while he got used to it and gave into her on everything else. Not that she'd ever asked for much.

"You keep looking at me," Ruby Lee said, wiping his mouth with a flour sack towel. The feeding ended.

"Do I know you from some other place?"

"Only in your dreams, Mister Charlie."

"I am Carlo. Carlo Baggio."

"Looks like you be with us a couple more day, Mister Charlie," Roscoe chimed in from the doorway. Carlo didn't know how long he'd been standing there. "You feel like talking?"

Carlo shrugged. "About what?"

"I gotta know, mister. Where that nice foreign lady you marry?"

The question brought more pain than any gunshot wound. Carlo fixed his eyes on the wall, searching paper flowers for the right words.

"Let it out, Mister Charlie. Just like Essie Mae drained that festering wound."

Carlo allowed Roscoe to take the place of his brother, just for a while. He talked about Louisa's death and his children in the foundling home. Roscoe listened, adding nothing more than an occasional shake of his head. Ruby Lee brushed away her tears with the back of her hand. And in the far corner Essie Mae swayed to a rhythmic beat heard by no one else, her head turned upward as she sang a gospel prayer.

"Shush, wife."

She kept on singing.

Roscoe raised his voice. "What about your brother? He escape from Garlic Joe?"

Carlo explained why the Kramers ran Jake out of Chicago. With Jake gone, Harold had targeted him. "If Gus Kramer ever finds out Harold was after me …."

"Mister Charlie, leaving town's your only choice but what about those babies?"

"Besides the nuns, they got Louisa's brothers. And some priests and their housekeeper. And there's this lady friend who runs a moneymaker if ever there was."

"What kind?"

"Ever hear of Night School?"

"Who ain't? And if you friends with the boss lady, she gonna look out for you and yours. With all that help, I'd say your babies will be okay."

*****

A week after the shooting Carlo felt strong enough to travel. On the way to Dearborn Station, he sat in the back seat of the cab and Roscoe rode in front to reminisce with Elijah Washington about their sharecropping days in what they referred to as Missippi.

"We always had 'nuff food," Elijah said. "Daddy saw to that. But I wanted more so I came up here. No way am I ever going back."

"Me and Essie Mae declared our love when I was fifteen to her fourteen. 'Ain't gonna be no shotgun wedding,' she said. 'You waits for the good stuff 'til we wed.'"

"How long that take?" Elijah asked.

"Four years."

"To become a man?"

"No, just with Essie Mae. That same afternoon we went to the county seat at Charleston, caught the train to Chicago. She carried a shoebox of her mama's guaranteed belly fillers: fried chicken, fatback with lard biscuits, sugar and cinnamon piecrust, and plain teacakes—enough to hold us the entire trip."

"Amen, that dining car for white folks only."

While they were talking, Carlo said goodbye to life on The Stroll, one that had fascinated him from the Johnson's front window. When the familiar sights of his Chicago came into view, he said another goodbye, not knowing when he'd return. At the Polk Street entrance he stuck his hand over the front seat and shook Elijah's.

"Better luck this time, Mister Charlie."

"I couldn't have made it without your help." Carlo got out. He leaned down to pick up his suitcase but Roscoe beat him to it. Together they walked into the station, at a pace to accommodate Carlo's limp. As they neared the ticket window, Roscoe stopped.

"Damn, I almost forgot. Something for you, Mister Charlie—five sawbucks, I knows 'cause I counted them."

"You're paying me?"

"Hell no. This money came from the Pierce Arrow driver. Three days ago he dropped it by my stand. Got his shoes shined too."

Carlo shoved the money in Roscoe's pocket. "He meant it for you and Essie Mae, not me."

"No shit? Well you didn't cost us anywhere near that much. And we didn't expect a thing in return."

"I won't forget what you and yours done for me. If you ever need—"

"Say no more, Mister Charlie. I knows where to find you."

BOOK TWO

Chapter 25
St. Gregory

"Irene, meet my brother from Chicago," Jake said with a grin stretched to his jawbones. "You said Carlo could stay here as long as we share my room, right?"

The petite woman stepped away from a gray enameled range, pots and pans spewing on its six burners. After pushing a strand of dark hair from her forehead and wiping her hands on a sauce-splattered apron, she welcomed Carlo with a kiss to each cheek. "Put your suitcase in with Jake," she said. "Supper'll be ready soon. We're having roast beef and risotto."

"I can hardly wait," Carlo lied. He had no appetite for one of Louisa's specialties prepared by another woman.

"Already Irene likes you," Jake said after she left. "She never welcomes new boarders in the Italian way."

Jake must've relayed the story of his brother's miserable life to the woman. Pity from a stranger, Carlo didn't need. What he did need was sleep. As they walked down the center hall, two little boys wearing denim overalls and no shirts ran down the stairs, bouncing a rubber ball. The older one tugged on the sleeve of Jake's chambray shirt.

"Can you play with me and my brother?"

Jake grabbed Tony Roselli under one arm and Frankie under the other. While they squealed, he pretended to knock their heads together. "I got my own brother to play with now," he said with a laugh. "This here's Carlo."

Carlo preferred meeting them eye to eye but the stiff leg prevented him from kneeling. Instead, he bent over and slipped each boy a nickel. "Buy yourself some candy."

"Wow, this is way bigger than a penny," Tony said.

"Way bigger," Frankie added. "Let's show Mommy."

Carlo felt a tug at his heart, watching the wiry boys hurry off. "They remind me of us when we was little."

"Yeah, I knew I seen those kids somewhere before," Jake said, motioning Carlo to follow him upstairs. "Tony just turned four. The little one's almost three. You sure made a hit with those nickels."

Jake's room was half the size of their studio in Chicago. "Not bad," Carlo said, standing in the doorway.

"I moved up to *numero uno* just for you. It cost me four extra bucks a month."

"And what else?"

"That's all, no greasing the palm. No nookie—Irene ain't the type."

"Not like our landlady in Chicago, eh? Remember when her husband came home early?"

"Forget Chicago."

"I can't as long as the *bambini* are there." Carlo took off his jacket, loosened his tie, and adjusted the Morris chair into a leaning position before he plopped down.

"The chair didn't come with the room," Jake said, sliding an ottoman under Carlo's legs. "The damn thing's mine ... ours now, bought with my own money."

Carlo closed his eyes. "Feels as good as it looks."

"Can't say the same for you." Jake tossed his cap over the gooseneck lamp and knelt beside the ottoman. "No sawing logs 'til I look at the leg."

"So look." Carlo didn't move.

"I want the big picture."

Carlo sat up, wiggled out of his trousers. "Make it quick. I'm beat."

Jake whistled a sigh when he saw the healing wound. "I'll make this up to you, I promise."

"Starting now ... just leave me alone." He laid back and dropped his lids again. "I oughta skip dinner tonight."

"If you don't show up, Irene'll worry. She'll bring food on a tray. If you don't clean your plate, she'll think it's her cooking."

Carlo opened one eye. "Look, I'd rather sleep than eat. I'm tired of being poked and jabbed and force-fed like an invalid. Believe me, my lack of hunger is no reflection on the landlady."

"She's more than a landlady. She's a friend."

"And I ain't putting my pants back on for her or anybody else. Now toss me that cover on your way out."

Jake obliged and Carlo wrapped himself in the crocheted afghan. Instead of leaving, Jake pulled up the only straight chair and sat, elbows to knees. "Don't get the wrong idea about me and Irene," he said. "She's got a good man."

"You mean the winemaker?"

"Yeah, you'll meet him later. But just so you know: don't ever mess with Mario."

"Right now I ain't in the mood for messing with nobody."

"Down in the mine Mario's the guy we trust with our lives. He's what's called a timber man. He shores up the ceiling so the damn coal don't fall on our heads. I ain't talking about a few lumps making a headache. I mean a ton of coal and SPLAT!" Jake slapped his hands together, and then sandwiched Carlo's face between them. "Damn, it's good having you here. Just like old times ... well almost."

"Yeah, I missed you too. So eat without me, and with no hard feelings."

"You gonna be able to start work on Monday?"

"Yeah, yeah. Now get the hell out of here."

Carlo fell into a sleep without dreams or tossing or the uncertainty of new surroundings. He would've slept until morning had it not been for Jake shaking his shoulder. He opened his eyes to the dimly lit room.

"Trust me, that chair ain't gonna feel nearly so good after eight more hours," Jake said. "You better hit the bed. But first, go down the hall and take a piss."

Carlo forced his feet to transport him to a spotless bathroom where he peed until his mouth went dry. Back in his room he crawled into bed and returned to his deep sleep. He didn't wake up again the smell of chicken frying in bacon grease filtered up from the kitchen. Jake was standing over him, a kid anxious to play.

"Get a move on, sleepyhead," Jake said. "I want you to meet Mario before we eat. You two are gonna like each other."

After a hot shower and clean shave, Carlo strolled around until he found Jake in the backyard with an Italian who stood almost six feet tall. Mario Roselli thrust out his dry, coarse hand and pumped Carlo's. "*Benvenuto*, Carlo. Jake told me all about you."

Mario's grip held nothing back. Neither did his face. He had the nose of a paesano, the kind that takes over the whole face, and dark hair giving in to gray earlier than his years warranted. The eyes: lumps of coal sunk deep in their sockets, darting here and there from years of constant vigilance.

"You'll like Irene's chicken and mashed potatoes," Mario said. "She's a good cook, the best around."

"That's what Jake said."

Mario put his hand on Jake's shoulder but kept his eyes on Carlo. "Your brother's a good worker." He motioned his hand toward the gravel driveway. "My car," he said, introducing Carlo to the Model T Ford. "This afternoon I take both of you for a ride. You have to meet St. Gregory, your new home."

*****

Indeed, Irene's cooking lived up to Mario's assessment, with Carlo eating enough to compensate for the supper and breakfast he'd slept through. At Sunday's noonday meal he met the other boarders, all miners who said little but ate until the serving bowls and platters were empty. Afterwards while Irene cleaned up the monumental mess, Mario drove Carlo around St. Gregory. Jake too, but he sat in the back and let Mario do most of the talking. Aside from the magnificent trees lining every street, the sooty town of St. Gregory was neither picturesque nor charming. Still, it did present a sense of stability despite the mismatched of bungalows, Victorians, and narrow shotgun houses that spanned three generations and were situated on large, uncluttered yards. Even the company cracker boxes were arranged in tidy rows although the mine could've splurged for some much-needed paint.

Mario pointed to the right. "There's All Saint's Catholic. You probably saw its steeple from the train. The Italians go there, some of the Germans too, the others to Bethany Lutheran. The rest of the town attends Grace Methodist, or one of two Baptist churches—Mount Calvary for the Southerners and Freedom for the Negroes."

The church-going preferences of St. Gregory's inhabitants didn't interest Carlo. Sluggish from a full belly, he stifled a yawn. "How far are we from St. Louis?"

"Ninety minutes by train, less by car," Jake said. "The damn train stops for every whistle."

"St. Gregory has just about everything," Mario continued. "And what we don't have can be ordered from Sears Roebuck. 'Course some ladies still take the train to St. Louis every so often to shop like city folks. Even my Irene."

The heart of the town's business district formed a four-block square jammed with buildings, most of them two-storied. In the middle of the square a circle of earth held three twenty-foot American Linden trees, five lilac bushes, and a scattering of park benches. Mario pulled into a parking slot facing the common green, turned off the motor, and got out, as did Carlo and Jake.

"The park ain't much," he said as they strolled through it, "but it's where everybody comes to watch everybody else. Those crowded benches remind me of Italy: old men trying to outdo each other, young ones hoping to arrange a date, or maybe some nookie, depending on the girl."

Jake lifted his brow. "So that's where the action is."

"As if you didn't already have your own connections," Mario said with a wink.

At the bronze statue of three doughboys with bayonets drawn, Mario tipped his cap, and said, "In memory of three St. Gregory men who died in the Great War."

"You fought?" asked Carlo.

"Nah, my lungs couldn't pass the physical."

They shared a bench and watched the parade of Sunday drivers circling the park. The beep-beep of horns reminded Carlo of Chicago's quieter streets, a thought he quickly dismissed. "So everybody's got some kind of car."

"Except me, and now you," Jake said. "The town's overrun with Model Ts, Chevys, Oldsmobiles, and Plymouths. Yesterday, I saw a Hudson." He motioned to a passing car. "Hey, Mario, ain't that your neighbor driving a Hudson?"

"Brand new, just off the showroom floor, he paid cash." Mario pointed out a row of hitching rails near the circle's outer perimeter. "Those are for the horse and buggy diehards."

"Times must be good," Carlo said.

"Booming, same as the coal company," Jake said. "Not just here, everywhere. Coal fuels the whole damn country."

"Since I first came over, the town has doubled in size, all because of the mines. Italians, Germans, even hardscrabble from the South. I tell you, Carlo, and Jake'll back me on this, won't you Jake?" Jake nodded and Mario continued. "Any man can make a good living if he ain't squeamish about the conditions. You know: the underground cave, the picking, chipping, shoveling, and hauling for eight hours a day, six days a week."

Carlo narrowed his eyes to Jake. "How much did you say?"

"Fifty to sixty dollars, every two weeks."

"And we owe it all to John L. Lewis," Mario said. "In case you don't already know, he's head of the United Mine Workers. I ain't going to whitewash what we do. Mining can be hellfire dangerous: cave-ins, fires, explosions, and methane poisoning. But it ain't as bad as before. Not like when I first came here. Not like it was for my pa."

Every immigrant has one story etched in his brain, his reason for coming to America. The brothers leaned back to hear Mario's.

*****

"Many years ago in Italy my papa saw this ad in a Torino newspaper: Free passage to Illinois for men willing to work at the St. Gregory Coal Company. The men were supposed to come alone and after getting a nest egg, send for the families they left behind.

"But not Antonio Roselli, my papa refused to leave his wife and two sons behind so in 1908 we all came to America and Illinois. At fifteen I followed Papa into the mine. Papa expected the same of Ernesto but not for another six years when he turned fourteen.

"On the morning of April 13, 1913 after finishing my night shift at the Little Eva, I went home, rolled into bed, and fell asleep as soon as my head hit the pillow. Later I woke up to the piercing sound every mining town prays not to hear: five whistle blasts signaling a fatal accident. I jumped out of bed, threw on my clothes, and raced through the kitchen scattered with laundry Mama had been folding. I ran the long mile to Little Eva; and before reaching the mine entrance, I heard one distinct scream above the others: Mama calling for her Antonio.

"For the next seven hours I stood with her, waiting for word of Antonio Roselli and twenty-six others trapped in the 15 North cave-in. One by one, the elevator brought up the broken bodies, some identified by little more than clothing or a certain scar. Wailing and moaning filled the air and will forever haunt my dreams. The body of my papa became number thirteen, a numerical match to the horrendous day and an ominous sign Mama could not overlook.

"The fourteenth body was that of Francesco Bosario, Papa's mining partner. Francesco left behind his wife, Appolonia, and Irene, who was but twelve. Appolonia, she was something that woman. To earn extra money she gave room and board to the miners. Three dollars per month bought each man a shared bed, one hot meal of polenta and garden vegetables in the summer or soup in the winter, plus a bucket lunch for work. For another two dollars Appolonia would launder their clothes, which all the miners paid because a deal like that they couldn't get elsewhere.

"Four of the ten miners boarding at the Bosario home lost their lives in the Little Eva Disaster. Of the twenty-six trapped in 15 North, two survived and returned to Eva after their injuries mended.

"Mama vowed her youngest would never set foot in a coal mine. She returned to Italy with Ernesto, insisting the dark cloud hanging over the Roselli family still hadn't passed. As for me, I belonged in America to honor Papa's dream. Mining, it's in my blood.

"I kept working at Little Eva and eventually helped sink the shaft for Little Eva No. 2. On the day the mine opened for work, it was me, Mario Roselli among the first shift miners who rode the cage to the bottom.

"Five years after the disaster I married Irene. She was seventeen to my twenty-five. We moved in with Appolonia since she needed help running the boarding house. Dammit, wouldn't you know: the Influenza Epidemic of 1918 claimed Appolonia, leaving me and Irene to run the business. First thing I did was buy Irene a new Maytag wringer washer to replace the scrub board and wooden tubs Appolonia swore by.

"We made us a good life; Irene and me, and like our parents, we made regular deposits to Italy's Bank of Torino instead of any bank in America. Our savings grew along with our family: two sons—Tony named for my papa, and Frankie for Irene's."

Chapter 26
Little Eva No. 2

On Monday morning, dawn had yet to break when Carlo felt Jake's foot poking his back.

"What time?" he asked.

"Doesn't matter, get up."

Five-thirty, Baby Ben said. After staggering to the bathroom and back, Carlo put on his new long-sleeved flannel shirt, denim overalls, and high-top work boots: items that had set Jake back four dollars at the general store. Carlo wiggled inside the roomy overalls, having dropped ten pounds since the shooting.

"Hey Jake, ain't this outfit too hot for summer?"

"Just you wait." Jake handed him a pair of gloves. "Where we go the temperature stays the same year round: fifty-four degrees." He lifted his nose to a pleasant aroma. "Smell them biscuits? Every morning the guys bury them under a glob of flour and water mixed with pork drippings. Sausage gravy, it's called. Irene learned how to make the stuff from a Kentucky miner who used to live here."

Carlo screwed up his face. He could've gone for a hunk of bread from Pané. Already he missed Chicago. Most of all he missed his children.

"Hey, don't turn up your nose," Jake said. "When you sit down to her table, eat 'til your stomach hurts 'cause by noon you'll be starving."

Carlo started out with the coffee and hot milk. He helped himself to the steaming grits, a pale version of polenta but without the sauce or proper consistency. He ate two warm biscuits smothered with grape jelly, but passed on the bowl of wallpaper paste that circled the table of six hungrier men and came back empty.

After breakfast he and Jake grabbed their lunch buckets and climbed into the front seat of Mario's car. Soon they were joined by the southern faction—Red Armstrong and Wilbur Shaw. Two other miners from breakfast—both Italians—had taken off earlier by foot.

"Well, another day, another dollar," said Mario, the last onboard. He started the engine, waved to Irene standing on the porch, and set off for Little Eva No. 2.

Ten minutes and two miles later Carlo followed Jake into the mine's office. Jake got him signed up and outfitted with a pick, shovel, and miner's cap with carbide lamp.

"Don't worry about paying now," Jake said. "It'll come out of your first pay."

Back in the yard Jake introduced Carlo to two miners from the third shift who also boarded with the Rosellis. No time for chitchat or comparing villages, the brothers walked over to the No. 2 entrance where they were the last of fourteen to step into the elevator cage.

"Already you're bringing us luck," Jake whispered in Piemontese. "No way would we have gone down with a total of thirteen." The only man he introduced was Rooster Williams, the hoisting engineer. Rooster released the lever to start their bumpy descent 600 feet into the earth.

Carlo clutched his stomach. "The elevator at Marshall Field's it ain't, that's for sure."

"Remember what I said before: stick with me and don't wander off on your own."

Carlo felt Irene's biscuits talking back. He swallowed hard as night engulfed the confined area. The singular lights emitting from the miners' hats reminded him of gigantic fireflies. Already he sensed a connection to the men standing with him. When the cage creaked to a stop at the bottom of the shaft, he followed Jake and the others exiting to the right. They trekked through cool tunnels that smelled of musty earth, the intermittent lighting supplied by carbide lamps attached to walls of coal. A shadowy critter slinked along the crevice, its beady red eyes darting around.

"Is that what I think it is?" Carlo whispered to Jake.

"Didn't I tell you everything grows bigger in the country?"

The miners paired off, every so often a team turning right or left.

After a long mile, Jake stopped at work area, 12 North. "Okay, Carlo. This here's what they call a room, ours for now. Stand back. I'll show you what to do." Jake demonstrated where and how to use a pick in order to extract the most coal from the wall. When he finished, he leaned his pick against the wall and stretched his arms overhead.

"Well, what are we waiting for," Carlo said. "The more we dig, the more we get paid. Right?"

"We can't start 'til the whistle blows. Union rules."

"Shit." Carlo adopted Jake's position until the seven o'clock whistle blew. Then he picked while Jake shoveled into a nearby pit car. Later when they reversed jobs to break the monotony and use a different set of muscles, they increased their production.

At noon the whistle blew again.

"Grab your bucket," Jake said. "We usually eat on a gob heap not too far from here."

They settled on a mound of discarded coal where Jake introduced ten lean miners. The men offered little more than a nod, reserving their acceptance until the newcomer had proven himself. Jake had been right about the eating: Carlo was famished. He unscrewed the lid of his cylinder bucket and from a nest of small compartments he pulled out two sandwiches—slabs of homemade bread packed with thin slices of salami—one generous hunk of brick cheese, and a thick wedge of apple pie. He gobbled his food, washing it down with water stored in the bottom of the bucket while listening to an exchange of bullshit.

"Hells fire," roared Amos Carter. "That boarding house witch done give me a liver and onion sandwich again." He slammed down the soggy combination. "That's it. I'm moving outta her place. I swear I am."

"Come on, Amos. You know your reasons for staying with that sweet woman go beyond affairs of the stomach," said his cousin Tom Carter. "You said her cooking didn't matter none so long as she kept you cooking."

Using his thumb and forefinger, Amos removed every bit of liver and pitched it in his lunch bucket. The bread he stuffed in his mouth and spoke through a splatter of crumbs. "Hey, Mario, you got room for another hungry miner?"

"Sorry, Irene's not taking any more boarders right now. Looks like you're stuck with liver and onions for a while longer."

Carlo stood up. He stretched his back, now aching from muscles unaccustomed to a new kind of work. He wiggled his bum leg. The constant throb of its healing hurt more than the injury ever did.

"About the food, Carlo, nothing stays behind, not even a single crumb," Red Armstrong said. He nudged Amos. "No sense in growing rats any bigger than they already are."

All the miners, including Carlo and Jake, returned to their coal rooms early so they'd be ready to work when the whistle blew. They didn't quit until the three-thirty whistle told them they had to stop. After retracing their steps from that morning, they waited in line for Rooster Williams to move up batches of the remaining day shift and bring down the last of the second shift. Finally, their turn came to board.

"Say Rooster," drawled a voice out of the dark. "That's a mighty unusual name. Is that what your ma called you at birth?"

"Hell, no, my real name's Will ... William Williams to be exact. After birthing five older sons, Ma ran out of names by the time I came along. My nickname I acquired on turning sixteen. Why even then I could have my pick of any chick at the Little Red Henhouse. Those little birds used to line up and fight over my pecker."

He slapped a hand on his scrawny thigh and let out a cockle-doodle-do. Jake nudged Carlo and spoke in Piemontese. "Consider yourself lucky. Not every new man gets the rooster story."

Minutes later they walked into the glaring light of day. Carlo blinked as if he'd never seen trees before. He turned to look at Jake, did a double take, and looked again. "For crissake! Are you what I look like? Am I what you look like?"

The whites of Jake's eyes stood out like pinwheels as he peered out from a face covered with coal dust. His smile reminded Carlo of Ezell Johnson's.

"Come on, there's even a place to wash up before we go home." Jake flung his arm over Carlo's shoulder and they headed toward the washroom, with Carlo's limp more pronounced than before. "I told you the money's good but the work's hard, a helluva lot harder than the brewery."

"I don't know if I got what it takes."

"What you got is two bambini waiting for you to bring them to their new home."

Chapter 27
New Boarders

01 July 1929
My dearest Mary Ann and Michael,
Your Papa loves you and misses you very much. I think about you every day and long to hold you and play with you. The good Sisters tell me that both of you are healthy and growing tall. I know they will put the enclosed money to good use. I cannot wait to see you again.
Love,
Papa
P.S. My English is still not so good. My friend Irene helped me write this letter.

After a year in St. Gregory Carlo had saved some money but not enough for the life he wanted instead of the one he had. For months the coal industry had been caught in the troughs of a steady decline. According to the St. Louis newspapers, lower profits, competition from non-union fields, mechanization, and coal users converting to gas or oil had impacted the strong, union-controlled mines of Southern Illinois, and likewise the entire country.

And according to St. Gregory's head honchos, in order to stay afloat the mine had to cut its employees down to three days a week. Men with no ties to the community, including most of the Roselli boarders, moved on to look for work in the non-union Kentucky fields. Lousy pay but steady work, they told Mario. The rumor turned out to be unfounded, but many of the itinerant miners did not return. However, Red Armstrong came back, along with a wife and new baby he settled in one of the company houses.

Jake convinced Carlo to stay put, insisting the mine would soon pick up. Like Mario and Irene, the brothers sent part of their savings to the Bank of Torino. The rest they hid under their mattresses. Carlo had acquired his own now since Jake's snoring forced him to move into one of the vacant rooms, the one extravagance he'd allowed himself. Saving enough to make a good home for his children was his ultimate goal, the promise he couldn't think of breaking.

Other than Carlo and Jake the only miners who didn't leave were Leno Gotti and Armando Sabino, otherwise known as Moon. Both bachelors were pushing forty and set in their ways. They talked about returning to Italy but after five years in America neither man seemed in any hurry.

"Why work so hard only to end up shouldering more and more responsibilities," Moon explained for both of them.

"Those women you left behind won't wait forever," Mario said.

"That's what we're hoping," Moon replied with a grin.

The economy had also devastated widows and orphans such as Margherita Falio and her 12-year old son, Sammy. Margherita's husband had been killed four years before, at Little Eva No. 2 when he fell down a mineshaft. Between the miner's union and the coal company, she received a total of five hundred dollars in death benefits, money deposited into a savings account at the St. Gregory Bank and Trust where she could withdraw funds as needed. But other than housekeeping, the widow had no skills and could no longer afford the two-room company house she'd come to as a new bride.

Irene Roselli's hands were shaking when she invited Margherita and Sammy to move into the boarding house. Irene's hands always shook when she was nervous, this time about asking for help she could've done without: cooking, cleaning, laundry, and gardening in exchange for room, board, and a small salary. Without hesitation Margherita accepted.

*****

Respectable ladies lived in boarding houses too. In late August a fire of undetermined origin had severely damaged the Wallace Home for Women and left a number of Lucy Wallace's boarders without lodging. One afternoon Lucy approached Irene for assistance in relocating her last two boarders. The two women sat on the davenport in Irene's humble parlor, Lucy imparting her sweetest smile.

"Please, Irene, a favor. I'd be most grateful if you could find it in your heart to accommodate several lovely teachers. They are absolutely desperate for lodging. What with the fire and all, I do feel responsible for helping them resettle."

Irene raised her brow. She poured lemonade with shaking hands chapped from hard work. "I don't know, Lucy. I'm used to miners, not teachers. Men don't make trouble as long as they got full bellies and clean clothes."

"But, these ladies don't eat much. And they do their own laundry. Besides you already have one female."

"Mrs. Falio works for me and has the only boarder's room on the first floor," Irene countered, her voice softening at the mention of Margherita. "The teachers would have to room on the second floor. Worse yet, share the miner's bathroom."

Lucy cleared her throat. "If these miners are gentlemen, they'll have the courtesy to lower the toilet seat. Irene, p-lease, I've exhausted my options."

Irene thought a minute. She twisted her fingers. "I won't tolerate hanky panky."

"Certainly not. The ladies are refined; they are teachers of the highest caliber."

"They have to eat what I feed the miners. It's nothing fancy—a mix of Old Country and just plain country."

"Irene, you are an angel." Lucy stood up, one hand clutching her handbag showing signs of wear. "God will bless you a thousand fold for your kindness. I'll send the ladies around this afternoon to settle the arrangements."

*****

Both teachers had been away from St. Gregory for the summer and only returned a week before the start of the new school year, two days before the fire. Since Lucy Wallace had given preference to her year-round boarders by placing them in the better housing, Ellen Waterhouse and Maude Simpson had little choice but to accept the Roselli Boarding House. The location was desirable, within walking distance to the public elementary and secondary schools. Still the teachers were skittish. After all, they'd be living under the same roof with immigrant miners.

Miss Ellen Waterhouse came from straight-laced Methodist roots and was protective of her reputation. While attending college in

Carbondale to secure her teaching credentials, she'd experienced a lapse in judgment that resulted in a thoroughly enjoyable, albeit hopeless, addiction to smoking cigarettes. Now, as a full-fledged teacher, Miss Waterhouse took care not to smoke in public unless she was visiting St. Louis where city attitudes were more liberal than those of St. Gregory.

She found the new accommodations acceptable, especially her window seat overlooking the vineyards, an ideal place for composing amusing stories for her fourth grade students while blowing cigarette smoke into the fresh outdoors. Attempts to mask the nasty habit did not always cover her own person so Ellen gargled Evening in Paris cologne, an effective mouthwash that made her more astute colleagues suspect she'd been imbibing a nip or two of forbidden liquor.

Maude Simpson occupied the room next to Ellen Waterhouse. For the past twenty years Miss Simpson had taught English to the sophomores of St. Gregory Township High School. Large-boned and angular, this woman of a certain age viewed life through the wireless pince-nez bridging her upturned nose. She possessed an air of mystery that discouraged any discussion of her personal life before moving to St. Gregory. In South Bend, Indiana, a much younger Miss Simpson had been humiliated on her wedding day when the only man she'd ever loved ran off with the preacher's wife. Like Miss Simpson, the preacher was by all accounts inconsolable. After a brief period of mourning the betrayed rejects found temporary comfort in each other, and Miss Simpson sacrificed her virginity in the name of lust. Soon realizing they shared nothing in common except rejection, the lovers agreed to go their separate ways, a journey that soon led Miss Simpson to St. Gregory.

*****

Dinner at the Roselli Boarding House did not occur before six o'clock or later than six-thirty but whatever the time, Irene allowed Tony and Frankie to ring a cow bell that could be heard in every room and throughout the Roselli acreage. On the teachers' first evening they promptly answered the six o'clock call and joined Carlo, Jake, Moon Sabino, and Leno Gotti in the dining room papered with large cabbage roses. Sitting at the head of the long oak table, Mario introduced everyone amidst a series of polite nods and little else.

Moon Sabino spoke first with a simple request. "Scusi, Miss Waterhouse, bread please."

"Certainly, Mr. Sabino," she replied, her back ramrod straight from an unyielding corset.

"Please, no mister, I go by Moon." He accepted the plate of sliced homemade bread. His hands, scrubbed as clean as the Lava soap with pumice allowed, still showed signs of coal ground into every crease of skin and under his ten nails.

Between Irene and Margherita, and with scant help from Sammy, a steady stream of food and drinks came from the kitchen: pitchers of water and *vino rosa*, carafes of red garlic vinegar and olive oil, a huge wooden bowl of salad greens, platters of thinly sliced tomatoes, roast beef laced with red wine and garlic, boiled potatoes, and fresh green beans sautéed in onions. After the food had circled once around the table, Mario made the sign of the cross, rubbed his hands together, and said, "*Mangiamo* everybody, dig in."

As usual the meal began in earnest, with singular purpose and lacking the distractions of polite conversation. After several minutes Miss Maude Simpson cleared her throat and said, "I do believe it may rain tonight."

"Nope, the moon ain't right for rain," Leno Gotti replied. "Neither is my shoulder."

She persisted. "But according to the Farmer's Almanac—"

"Who needs books," Moon said.

The red-faced Miss Simpson returned to the food on her plate. With that, Mario hopped up. "Here, Miss Simpson, try this nice wine. I made it myself."

Before she could protest, Mario poured a glass for her and one for Ellen Waterhouse.

"To Mario and the best wine in Southern Illinois," Carlo said. He lifted his glass and waited for the others to follow. They all did, including the schoolteachers who were last to oblige.

"*Salute*," the Italians said as one.

"Oh, dear, perhaps we shouldn't be partaking," Ellen Waterhouse said to Maude Simpson. "You know, what with Prohibition and all."

Moon wiped his hand across his mouth. "Wine is food, a part of the meal since before the time of Jesus."

"That's right. What's more, it aids in the digestion," Leno added. His brow creased to a furrow as he stared Miss Waterhouse down. "If you gonna live with Italians, you gotta learn to eat and drink like Italians. Otherwise …."

"Come on, paesani," said Jake, ever the peacemaker. "This is America. The ladies don't have to drink if they don't want to."

"Excuse me," Maude Simpson said with a lift of her chin. "Miss Waterhouse and I are quite capable of deciding what we will eat and drink. We are self-sufficient, independent women. Come, Miss Waterhouse. Throw caution to the wind." Miss Simpson took a sip, puckered her lips to savor the taste, and then emptied her glass. "Mario, the wine tastes very good indeed. I should like a refill, please."

By the end of the meal Miss Simpson had consumed three glasses of wine and was laughing at everything said, funny or not. Ellen Waterhouse, who rarely drank given her temperate upbringing, was well into her second glass before dessert had been served.

Having finished eating in the kitchen with their mother and the Falios, the Roselli boys came tearing into the dining room.

"Papa, Papa," they chorused. "Can we sit with you now?"

Without waiting for permission, the boys scrambled onto Mario's lap and wrapped their stick-like arms around his neck. With black eyes wide and dancing, Tony whispered in his father's ear. As soon as Mario nodded his approval, Tony and Frankie wiggled to the floor and hurried from the room. Minutes later they returned with their caps, those necessary props for performing their rendition of the popular "Me and My Shadow." Tony took the lead with Frankie tagging behind as his shadow. The little hams ended their performance on one knee, arms outstretched to encourage the ensuing applause.

Carlo laughed the loudest, his fingers still tapping to the beat. When they stopped, he turned away and brushed his palm across one moist eye.

"Not to worry," Jake said quietly. "You'll get your kids out of Chicago."

"Oh, your wife and children are in Chicago?" Ellen asked, to which Carlo gave a brief explanation of his situation.

"How very sad," Miss Simpson blurted out. She dabbed her watering eyes with a crisp handkerchief trimmed with rows of lace tatting. "Please excuse me," she said, leaving her serving of angel food cake untouched. As soon as she disappeared through the doorway, Leno Gotti laid claim to the cake.

After finishing dessert, the boarders carried their empty dishes to the kitchen on their way outside, anything to escape the lingering heat of the house.

"So what do you think?" Irene asked Mario when they were alone. "About the schoolteachers, I mean."

He laughed and wrapped his arms around her slender frame. "Those two teachers are gonna fit in okay. They like my wine."

"What about the food?"

"They ate what got passed and didn't complain."

Chapter 28
Prep and Harvest

Earlier that year Carlo and Jake had spent long hours with Mario and Irene, working side by side to plant a large vegetable garden of lettuces, spinach, zucchini, squash, eggplant, potatoes, corn, and tomatoes. By summer the resulting harvest proved so plentiful that Irene opened a vegetable stand and sold what they couldn't eat fresh or put up for the winter. Besides the garden, a healthy vineyard that Irene's parents had established years before stretched in long rows down one side of their five acres. Mario expected a bumper crop in September, red and white grapes he would press into fine table wines, a nice addition to the ample supply stored in his cellar.

One evening Carlo, Jake, Mario, and Irene sat around the kitchen table, playing pinochle to take their minds off the 90-degree temperature that should have let up when the sun went down.

"Well, I'm out," said Irene as she folded her cards. "Looks like another win for Jake."

Jake swept his hands over the coins. "Hell, with money so tight even forty cents makes me feel rich."

"We may not have much money but we sure eat and drink well," Mario grumbled. "I never thought it would come to this. *Too many mines, too many miners*: that's what the newspapers say. There's plenty of coal waiting to be mined and now the country don't need it." He poured more wine for himself and passed the jug. "So, Carlo, whadaya say, any ideas how we can make some extra dough?"

"We're looking at it." Carlo poured to the level of his three fingers. He took in the aroma and held up the glass to admire the wine's color and clarity. "I say, sell your wine to Benny Drummond. What he can't bootleg in St. Louis, he'll sell on the Illinois side. This vino rosa beats any that Pete Venuta supplies."

"No shit." Jake held up the bottle Carlo had passed to him. "So that's how Pete bought his new truck."

Carlo took a sip, smacked his lips "Hell, Pete does more than bootleg cheap wine. He waters down whiskey and makes his own hooch."

"Hooch?" Irene asked. "What's hooch?"

"*Christo*, where you been all these years?" Mario said. "Carlo means bootleg whiskey."

"Well I don't like this talk about bootlegging." She stood, walked behind Mario, and pressed her fingers into his shoulder. "And you know better. Bootlegging is against the law."

"Well, it's still a free country and just talking about bootlegging ain't against the law. Besides, it's a dumb law that nobody follows." Mario ignored her massage as he directed his words to Jake and Carlo. "I say it's worth a try. We already have a head start in the cellar. Jake, about the Drummond fella: how 'bout asking Pete to put us in touch him."

"You don't know about Benny Drummond?" Irene applied more pressure with her fingers. "For god's sake, he's one of the biggest gangsters in all of Southern Illinois, maybe the entire state. He took over from that Jewish bootlegger out of Harrisburg. You know: the one who got himself hung for killing a state trooper and his wife. Poor girl, found buried under a slagheap. They say she was in a family way."

Mario grunted. "Come on, Irene. Don't believe everything you read in the Weekly Wipe. Anyway, that cop probably got paid back for shitting on Charlie Birger. I heard rumors about stolen car rackets and insurance fraud."

"And what about his wife and unborn child," she said. "It's not worth your life or mine, this mixing with gangsters for some extra money. After all, we're not going to starve."

"No, but we ain't getting ahead either." Mario slammed his fist on the table, spilling his wine over the flowered oilcloth. "Not with the mine working half time, this threat of shutting down hanging over our heads."

"Look, Mario, Irene's right about not starving," Jake said. "I've

THE FAMILY ANGEL

had my share of Chicago bootleggers. That's why I came here, Carlo too. Right, Carlo?"

Carlo replaced his faraway look with a sigh. "Yeah, but what the hell, I sure could use the money. Maybe get my babies sooner, or at least go back to see them."

"Stupid me," Jake said, slamming the heel of his palm to his forehead. "I forgot about the babies. If Carlo's in, so am I."

Mario reached over his shoulder and patted Irene's hand. "A few inquiries can't hurt. It makes sense; this wine as good as ours should be worth something to those less fortunate." He opened his palms into a shrug. "So we make a little money."

Irene threw up her hands. "You won't make much with that dinky set-up downstairs. Just remember this: if you make wine to sell, the government says it's illegal. And that makes the three of you bootleggers too."

"Irene, honey, we're talking small potatoes."

She stomped out, banging the screen door in her wake.

Carlo leaned over his elbows. "You know, Mario, Irene's right about one thing: your setup, it's way too small. Jake and I could help you build a bigger one, like what our parents had back home, with vats and barrels taking up the whole cellar."

"Sounds like more than I can handle. If you and Jake help me all the way, I'll give each of you part of the profits."

"No shit?" Jake said. "You'd do that for us, even though we don't share the same blood."

"Blood ain't everything and so what if I don't make a killing the first go-around. I ain't up to messing with this by myself."

Just the words Carlo wanted to hear. He could almost smell the ripe grapes, taste the infant wine, and revel in its maturity. All of this and then his babies—they needed him, but not as much as he needed them.

*****

Over the next ten days the three men worked as a team, digging out two more feet of dirt from the cellar floor and then carting the dirt in wheelbarrows to feed the gullies located at the far side of the Roselli acreage. After leveling out the floor to a smooth finish, they bitched and cussed and nearly came to blows but still managed to construct a gigantic wooden vat called the *latina*. It measured eight feet deep by ten feet across and occupied an entire corner. By that time Mario was calling Jake and Carlo partners; they regarded him as their older brother. Next, they installed a galvanized metal trough from the cellar window directly into the vat, which was accessible by way of a wooden ladder on the floor. In the opposite corner they built a second vat, smaller at one hundred gallons but just right for fermenting white grapes as good as the purple but not as plentiful.

*****

Six weeks later the grapes were ready for picking, a crop so prolific Mario enlisted some trustworthy helpers, a dozen miners and for the most part, Italians. His friends readily agreed to work in exchange for all the cheap beer, good wine, and home cooking they could consume during harvest day. At six o'clock on Saturday morning he stood at the end of the driveway and greeted each man with a shot of whiskey and a slap on the back. As soon as the dew lifted in the vineyard, Mario lined up his workers on both sides of long arbors filled with firm, luscious, reddish purple grapes. Using their favorite knives honed to fine, sharp edges, the volunteers severed the fruit clusters from their vines and tossed them into bushel baskets. Mario and Carlo lugged the first of the filled baskets onto a horse-drawn sled and circled around to the outside cellar window where Jake waited with a grin on his face.

"What a sight," he said, rolling his tongue over his lips. "Already I can taste the vino rosa."

"And the money," Carlo added.

Mario unloaded the remaining baskets, Jake dumped grapes into the grinder connected to the trough, and Carlo cranked the handle, rotating the four rollers inside to crush the fruit. Juice and pulp poured from the trough into the vat, its bottom lined with straw that served as a filtering agent. While Jake and Carlo were getting more grapes, Mario went down to the cellar. He wrapped string around a straw bundle, and pushed it into the spigot of the vat.

"Whatcha doing that for?" cracked a youthful voice. Sammy Falio stepped out from the shadows of the cellar.

"When the moon is full and clear, I'm gonna pull this out to check on the fermentation," Mario said. "Now, here's a question for you."

"Yeah?" Sammy asked, the fat cheeks of his round face overtaking his eyes.

"What're you doing down here when I gave you the best job up there?" Mario pointed to the stairs. "Now get a move on before my thirsty workers start griping."

THE FAMILY ANGEL

Sammy hurried up the cellar steps and into the morning sun. He had a knack for ducking work whenever he could but had begged for the coveted job of keeping the workers supplied with buckets of beer. Using Tony's little red wagon, he started lugging the buckets back and forth. By ten o'clock the beer was lagging and so was Sammy. Mario found him barfing behind a tree so he alternated the beer distributor's job between two of the thirstier miners, and Margherita sent Sammy to his bed.

While the men were busy with the grapes, Margareta helped Irene prepare lunch: fried chicken, beef stew, pork *salsiccia*, polenta baked with cheese, risotto, garden-fresh spinach and hard cooked eggs laced with vinegar and olive oil, firm, sweet sliced tomatoes, crusty fried eggplant, and a mix of tuna, cannellini beans, celery, and onions with more vinegar and olive oil. Margherita's specialty was *frituro dusa*, creamy pudding dumped in a pan to set firm before cutting it into diamond shapes that were rolled in cracker crumbs and fried in equal parts of butter and oil.

Neither Maude Simpson nor Ellen Waterhouse participated in the harvest day's activities, on the grounds that such involvement would be inappropriate conduct for schoolteachers expected to set an example for the youth of St. Gregory. They did, however, observe the scene from their bedroom windows. Closer observation would reveal a steady stream of cigarette smoke making its way from the window of Miss Waterhouse's room.

Five hours after the harvest began, all the grapes, including the whites, had been picked, transported, heaved, and ground into the vat to begin the fermentation process. The men lined up at the outside pump, using lava soup to scrub purple stain from hands already stained with coal. Those who couldn't wait for the outhouse hurried behind the barn to piss away their beer. When order seemed restored, Irene nodded to Tony and Frankie. Together they clanged the bell and yelled, "Mangiamo, mangiamo!"

Sitting at sawhorse tables under the shade of Linden trees, the harvest workers devoured the bountiful spread, washing mouthfuls down with jugs of wine and more buckets of beer. When they had their fill of food but not of drinks, the men remained at the table to bend their elbows and chew the fat. After the stories turned stale, Leo Gotti brought out his guitar and strummed the familiar songs of his youth. Thirty minutes of singing and little else brought Moon Sabino to his feet.

"Dammit, Leo. What you trying to do—send us back to the Old Country."

"Hells bells, Moon. Ain't it time you went back?" bellowed Rooster Williams. "How many years you been telling us about that little filly waiting in Italy? She'll be too old to trot by the time you're ready to mount her."

"Christo, look who's talking. I don't see no ring attached to your nose."

"No, and you ain't about to either. As it says in the Old Testament, God meant for certain men to please more than one woman. And I'm one of the chosen." Rooster paused to raid his mind for a good yarn. "I ever tell you 'bout my Uncle Jeb?"

"Not that I recall," Amos Carter said, setting up the story.

"Well, sir, according to Uncle Jeb, Beelzebub stuck him with the meanest, ugliest old lady this side of the Mississippi. That would be Aunt Oma. Uncle Jeb always said he couldn't stand the sight of the bitch, although some thought he might've exaggerated a bit. Well, sir, one day she sent him to the drugstore for her spring tonic. On the way back Uncle Jeb poured out half the tonic. The old fart peed in the bottle to fill it up again. Lemme tell you, Aunt Oma done away with that special potion in three days time, said it were the best she ever drunk. After that, she couldn't keep her hands off poor Uncle Jeb."

"Come on, Rooster. That's pure disgusting."

"You better believe it was. Poor Uncle Jeb like to never got over that ungodly smell oozing from the pores of Aunt Oma."

Rooster slapped his knee and spewed out a spray of beer along with his belly laugh. After that each story got raunchier than the one before. And when the beer went dry and the sun went down, the contented miners went home.

Chapter 29
The Winemakers

While the wine continued to ferment, the volatile stock market started to decline. Then widespread panic selling created further decline, causing the market crash on October 24. Black Thursday, the newspapers labeled the disastrous day. Panic spread, even to the cautious who had not invested. They lined up to withdraw their entire savings from banks and savings and loans associations that paid out what money they had on hand, which wasn't enough to meet the demands of every customer. Although Herbert Hoover declared a bank holiday to allow the banks recovery time, it came too late for customers such as Margherita Falio, who lost the remainder of her five hundred dollars with St. Gregory Bank and Trust. Ellen Waterhouse lost her small savings, as did Maude Simpson. But the Roselli Boarding House miners got a pass, having managed to hang onto their money invested in Italy and the nest eggs stashed under their mattresses.

Nor did Mario Roselli or his partners suffer any fallout from Black Thursday. Mario sold half of his aging wine to Benny Drummond, including the older bottles destined for Irene's vinegar. In return, Benny gave Mario a standing order for the fermenting wine as well as next year's production. Rather than water down the Roselli wine for Southern Illinois roadhouse customers who tolerated cheap whiskey and wine, Drummond distributed the unadulterated version to St. Louis's finer restaurants and hotels that still drew a well-heeled clientele.

Those eight weeks following the grape harvest were crucial to producing a fine wine. Every few days either Mario or Jake or Carlo climbed the ladder to the top of the vat. While straddling the board that spanned its diameter, that day's inspector made sure the mash was fermenting and the liquid staying on the bottom. If any seeds and stems floated to the top, he used his long pole to push them down. Whichever man was on the board downstairs could count on Irene praying for his safe return upstairs.

One Saturday morning after checking out the vat, Mario came back to a bustling kitchen that brought tears to his eyes. Carlo and Jake were chopping the last of twelve fat heads of garlic while Irene stood over the stove, using a wooden spoon to slowly sauté the minced garlic and tins of anchovies in olive oil and butter. Their team effort involved the making of *bagna caôda*, gravy they used for dipping fresh vegetables, so potent it opened up the sinuses and lingered in the pores longer than any tonic Rooster Williams had imagined.

Mario took an appreciative whiff before nuzzling the soft spot between his wife's neck and collarbone. "Ah-h, nectar for the gods."

Irene lifted her shoulder to brush him away, all the while stirring the simmering garlic. "Don't try softening me up," she said, "the three of you inviting trouble with that percolating monster downstairs. I remember Mama telling how her uncle disappeared one day. After Zia Anna cooled her heels for twenty-four hours waiting his return, she thought to look in the cellar. Need I say more? The poor man had fallen off the board and into his latina—*che pasticcio*."

"What a mess, oh yeah," Mario said, holding back a grin. "All that hard work and good wine wasted."

"Sure, make fun of me and mine." Irene shook her spoon at him. "But I hear that's how gangsters do away with the winemakers who don't cooperate. Good men, no different from the three of you, hog-tied and drowned in their own vino."

"Dammit, Irene, how many times I gotta say this: we're a small potato operation, and we ain't getting in trouble. Now give it a rest, will you."

"You bet I will." She slammed the spoon down and once again stomped out of the kitchen.

"Holy shit," the three men chorused as they scrambled to the stove.

"Don't let the bagna burn," Carlo said. "I ain't about to peel another batch of garlic."

*****

During the many weeks of grape juice bubbling through its fermentation process in the cellar, the partners worked outside to season fifty-gallon whisky barrels. From the Roselli peach trees they gathered branches, leaves, and stems which they cooked in a washtub of water simmering over a backyard wood fire. Then they poured the peach liquid into twelve oak barrels that were later sealed with the care given to precious cargo. To permeate the sweet, fruity flavor into the wood, they rolled the barrels back and forth over the rungs of a ladder positioned on the ground until Mario determined the seasoning complete. The barrels were emptied of peach juice, fitted with spigots, and brought to the cellar where they were hoisted to rest sideways on wood braces along the wall.

One cool evening in late fall, the three men stood outside in their shirtsleeves and with heads lifted to the full moon. "Not a cloud in sight," Carlo said. "We got us a clear sky."

"And a clear fermentation in the cellar," Jake said.

"Harmony, that's what we got," Mario said, with legs spread as he lifted his arms to the heavens. "Tomorrow we fill the barrels."

God, I love that man, Carlo thought. Jake must've been reading his mind because he said, "Didn't I tell you Mario was the greatest."

The next day they took turns at the vat spigot, filling their buckets with wine and funneling it through holes on top of the barrels. "No moving those barrels 'til the wine turns clear and mellow," Mario said. "I figure sometime after the Ides of March."

They waited until the end of March. As senior partner and the most experienced, Mario tapped the first barrel and filled a pint jar half way. He swirled, sniffed, and sipped before sloshing the wine around his mouth and swallowing. He passed the jar to Carlo who repeated the ritual before passing the jar to Jake. After Jake finished it, he looked from Carlo to Mario and back to Carlo before he spoke. "Somebody say something."

Mario stretched his mouth into an ear-to-ear grin. "This here's the best Illinois wine I ever tasted. If I didn't need the money so bad, I wouldn't even sell it. My thanks to the two of you 'cause I never coulda done this on my own."

"Maybe we should give our product a name," Carlo said.

They thought a minute, kicked around a few suggestions, and

finally decided on *Tre Paesani,* Three Countrymen.

Within two weeks Tre Paesani's first wine had been bottled and sold to Benny Drummond. Later that day the winemakers gathered around the kitchen table.

"Let's see," Mario said as he calculated their profit on a tablet pad. "Twelve barrels times fifty gallons, that's six hundred gallons at fifty cents each. Three hundred dollars minus the material to build the latinas and barrels, and then there was the harvest day. That leaves two hundred sixty: one thirty for me and sixty-five for each of you."

"Not bad," Jake said, "considering the twenty bucks we pull down for three days of mining."

"It'll take me to Chicago and back," Carlo said. "But I'd feel better if we had some extra to set aside. How about another pressing?"

"I was hoping you'd ask," Mario said. "Let's use part of our profits to buy ripe grapes. We'll squeeze them into the sediment left in the latinas and add some sugar for fermentation."

"Bingo," Carlo said. "The second wine."

"So, Mario, what kind of grapes you have in mind?" Jake asked.

"The best Concordes and Tokays, shipped all the way from California to St. Louis. Understand, this second wine won't match the first, but it'll be decent enough for Benny Drummond's customers."

*****

The St. Louis wholesale market opening at two in the morning required the partners to leave St. Gregory no later than midnight. Mario had borrowed a truck from Drummond and opened it up to forty on the highway. While Jake sawed logs, Carlo kept one eye on the road and the other on the driver. Not that Mario needed watching; he was riding high and enjoying every minute of the bumpy, two-hour drive. After crossing the Mississippi into St. Louis, he made a quick right and cruised along aging three-story structures lining the illuminated streets that led to the area known as Produce Row. Carlo poked Jake as soon as Mario parked next to a red brick warehouse. They hopped out of the truck and Mario pointed to a century-old sign painted on the side of the building.

"Look, this used to be a fur trading post when the land was still virgin pure."

"Think we'll see any Indians?" Jake asked through a yawn.

"Okay, enough history. Now pay attention and maybe you'll learn something else."

"I'm here to deal," Jake said.

They hurried to join the hectic market scene. Crates of fruits and vegetables lined the walkway as buyers and sellers negotiated for what they considered fair prices, the lowest in years given the economy. Crisp spring air sprouted occasional pockets of seasoned warmth generated from coal and wood burning in tin barrels; but the riverfront's most distinct pungency came from the melding of fresh and rotting produce, wet cobblestones, animal waste, old bricks, brazen rats, river water, raw sewage, and human secretions.

At one busy stand Mario stopped to pick several grapes from an open crate. He popped one grape in his mouth and tossed the other to Carlo. "What do you think?" he asked in Piemontese.

Carlo gave a slight shake of the head; Mario concurred with a nod. They left empty-handed, to circulate among the other stalls, evaluating quality to price. Carlo was blessed with the most discriminating palate whereas Jake proved to be the best negotiator, a role for which Mario had no patience. At the end of an hour they agreed on Concordes from one vendor, Tokays from another. They made their purchases, loaded the crates onto the truck bed, and before dawn were crossing Eads Bridge into Illinois.

Chapter 30
Visit to Chicago

While June's second pressing of grapes perked in the Roselli cellar, Carlo caught the train to Chicago—his first trip back since leaving three years before. After a brief shopping splurge he went by taxi to the Guardian Angels Children's Home. Alone in the parlor he leaned back in a wingback chair, drumming his fingers on the doily covering its arm. Considering Gus Kramer's warped sense of justice, Carlo knew his visit couldn't last longer than the weekend. Even though he hadn't fired the shot that killed Harold Kramer, in Chicago he was still considered a wanted man, at least in the eyes of Gus Kramer and that's all that mattered. Every month he sent money for his children. In turn, the nuns kept him informed of their progress. They even rewarded him with several photographs of Mary Ann and Michael, including a studio portrait Giulietta had arranged and paid for. Still, all the letters and sawbucks couldn't make up for the lost years or buy his children's affection. Mary Ann was four; and Michael, three. They deserved better. He heard the squeals of toddlers and stood up, tall and straight. But when his children ran into the room, he fell to his knees.

"Papa! Papa!" Mary Ann and Michael yelled.

He grabbed one in each arm, and let his tears flow while they let loose with hugs and kisses.

"Children, please, not so rough," Sister Barbara said with a shake of her finger. "Whatever will your Papa think?"

"It's all right, Sister," Carlo called out from under the barrage of

THE FAMILY ANGEL

affection. "I think they have not forgotten me."

"Certainly not, Mr. Baggio. My sisters and I will not let them forget how hard their papa works so you will all be together someday. The little ones pray for you every morning and evening."

"That's good," he said and gave each child another kiss.

"I might add, your family is also remembered in the prayers of Monsignor Flaherty and his sister Noreen, and also those of Father Connelly. Many people are interested in Mary Ann and Michael." She paused before adding, "You really must call on the monsignor while you are in Chicago."

"Si, Sister," Carlo said with a courteous nod but in his mind he ruled out a visit to St. Sebastian's, not wanting to open painful memories. Under different circumstances any mention of the priest in Rome would have angered Carlo, but this precious weekend would not be marred by petty jealousy. Nor by the color of Mary Ann's hair, which had lightened to a reddish brown.

He turned to the flurry of packages his children were tearing open: a dress and Raggedy Ann doll for Mary Ann, a romper set and Tootsie Toy truck for Michael, purchases made at Marshall Field's earlier that day. When the excitement of new toys wore thin, Carlo took the children outside. They walked to the same park where he'd courted their mother, and when the children played on the swings and teeter totter, he imagined Louisa beside him on the bench, both of them watching and laughing over their remarkable children.

*****

That evening after tucking Michael and Mary Ann into bed, Carlo gave in to nostalgia and the irresistible pull of another time. Another cab ride brought him to Pané, where he asked for the daily special.

"Special? Whadaya mean special," answered a clerk unfamiliar to Carlo. "All bread same price, five cents a loaf,"

"What about upstairs, don't I need a password?"

"Not any more. Business ain't so good. Just go to speakeasy and ring buzzer. Someone will open."

At the building's side door the name of Carlo Baggio still carried some weight. And inside, jazz music still filtered from The Playground. But its personnel had changed, the bar monitored by an old geezer with questionable ability to bounce any riffraff. Carlo took the stairs two at a time up to the next floor where Frog Sapone met him at the landing.

"Come, come," the lizard lips commanded as he led the way. "Miss Giulietta is expecting you."

"How'd she know I was back?" Carlo asked. Getting no answer, he figured one of the Guardian Angel nuns must've told her. He caught up with Frog and tapped his shoulder. "Wait a minute, will you. I never got the chance to thank you."

"Thank me?"

"For the rescue, you know, that day outside the train station when I took a bullet."

"I just happened to be passing by. And did nothing more than give you a ride. It was just a ride, understand?"

"Yeah, sure, thanks for the ride."

Giulietta's office hadn't changed since he last visited it, the month before his marriage. Window blinds separated the outside world while subtle lighting and shadows softened the inside. Behind the mahogany-inlaid desk sat Giulietta, going over the books, a routine he'd observed many times.

"You changed your hair," he said. "I like it."

The bobbed hair had given way to blonde finger waves and bouncy curls, making her appear as unsophisticated as a small town matron. As did the rayon shirtwaist dress, closed down the front with mother-of-pearl buttons to show off her trim figure. For the moment, he ignored the graceful fingers waving him to the sofa.

"Ah, Carlo my pet, it's been such a long time. And here you are, still handsome but with much broader shoulders. Digging coal must agree with you."

Glib talk, with Giulietta some things never changed. "It's a living," Carlo replied. "But judging from the operation downstairs, I'd say your business ain't so good."

"Good enough to keep me in furs. However, I am my teachers. We're down to ten and those who leave won't be replaced."

With brow furrowed, he snapped his fingers. "Now what's that called?"

"Attrition, my pet—a-t-t-r-i-t-i-o-n, I'm pleased you're still eager to learn." She came out from behind her desk and stood before him. "In any case I've been exploring new business opportunities."

"You in some kind of trouble?" He gently traced the faint swelling on her cheek, a bruise artfully covered with make-up. "This time I'd like to help you."

She lifted her head and projected a throaty laugh. "My pet, how very cavalier of you but do give me some credit. I did not get this far without knowing when to shield myself from those who would see me fall and not get up."

Giulietta's lips puckered into an air kiss. Her mascara-trimmed lashes camouflaged eyes he did not remember as so distressed.

"Enough about me," Giulietta said. She moved to the plush sofa and patted the cushion. "Sit. I want to hear all about you and life in Podunk with Jake."

"Podunk? No, no, we live in St. Gregory."

"Oh, my pet," she laughed. "I'd almost forgotten just how much I miss you."

The next two hours they spent getting reacquainted. On the sofa … on the floor … on her bed … anywhere except her desk. Carlo had tried the roadhouse whores beyond St. Gregory's city limits but none could match Giulietta's ability to please him. He could've stayed the night but Giulietta told him she needed to prepare for her evening clientele.

*****

After stepping into the early evening, Carlo hailed a passing cab. Alone in the back seat he allowed his senses to reel from the magic Giulietta had exuded. After a while he let her go because she still couldn't give him the life he wanted. He'd been lonely by choice. He'd sized up every decent woman around St. Gregory but none seemed right to mother his children. There'd never be another Louisa. Dear sweet Louisa. He'd disciplined himself to only recall those memories that brought some measure of happiness, not those leading to her death. He couldn't blame Michael for the unclean birth or Mary Ann for the blue eyes.

Carlo set aside his thoughts when the taxi came to an abrupt stop. "Thirty-fifth and State, mister," the cabbie said. "That'll be a buck even."

Carlo added a quarter to the dollar before stepping onto the sidewalk. Neon lights lit up The Stroll, burning bright as ever. Ragtime and blues still sent out their distinctive melodies from nightclubs and jazz bars and street corners. Skinny little boys, more agile than Tony or Frankie, danced and turned cartwheels and back flips alongside a hatful of pennies. The Hoover years had made little impact on Roscoe Johnson's neighborhood. Either the Depression had bypassed The Stroll, or The Stroll had chosen to ignore it.

Chapter 31
Ruby Lee

Earlier that morning at the train station Carlo had looked around for Roscoe but another bootblack told him to come back later. A personal visit made more sense. Carlo knocked on the apartment door, half-hoping Ruby Lee would be on the other side. Instead it was her mother.

"Lawdy!" Essie Mae cried out. "Roscoe, looky who's here. We got us some company. It's Mister Charlie, that's who." She grabbed Carlo by the arm and ushered him into the living room.

The two men shook hands. They stood back to size up one another before Carlo made the first move to embrace Roscoe.

"Good seeing you, Roscoe. I couldn't come back without thanking you and Essie Mae one more time. You know, for taking care of me."

"Hey, mister, no need to thank us again," Roscoe said, his voice choked with emotion. "We just glad you got outta Chicago in one piece. Police never did find who shot the guy what shot you. Good thing you got away clean 'cause that shooter's daddy still out for revenge. Anyways, let's not talk the bad times. How's it going with you and that brother of yours?"

Carlo explained about the lack of work forcing them into bootlegging wine with Mario.

Roscoe shook his head. "Mister, you best watch yourself. I hear those downstate gangsters every bit as mean as Chicago's. You take

Scarface Capone. His bagmen beat up on barkeeps and madams The Man figure might be holding out. Never mind their business being down, what with the Depression and all. Couple holdouts even got themselves killed."

Carlo listened with half an ear as he recalled the swelling on Giulietta's cheek and how she'd refused his help. He decided to see her again before leaving Chicago, something he hadn't planned on doing before Roscoe mentioned Capone. For now, he forced himself to concentrate on the Johnsons. Giulietta could wait one more day.

"How's Ruby Lee and Ezell?" he asked.

"Ezell staying out of trouble, thank God," said Essie Mae. "Can't say the same for Ruby Lee. The wrong man set his eye on her. And she lap up his bull-skating like some cat with a bowl of cream."

"That shit got more than his eye on her," said Roscoe. "It just ain't right."

"Roscoe mean the shit's a cracker, a rich ofay at that. Every bit as white as you, Mister Charlie. We can't do nothing with Ruby Lee. And then you come knocking on our door, like some angel sent from heaven. Talk to her, will you?"

Angel. For sure Essie Mae had never seen Carlo's angel. Nor had he since that day three years ago, which was a good thing. "Ruby Lee won't listen to me."

"Oh, she listen all right. She like you."

"She be home soon," Roscoe said. "If Ruby Lee gotta be seen with a cracker, best it be one we know."

"You want me to take her out?"

"Just for a good talk," Roscoe said. "Two blocks from here's the Black Pearl. Serves up jazz and the best soul food in all Chicago."

"Soul food?"

"That's down home cooking for black folks, straight from the heart."

"We counting on you, Mister Charlie," Essie Mae said. "Make Ruby Lee see the light, whatever it take." The apartment door opened and packages rustled from the hallway. Relief crossed Essie Mae's face. "Ruby Lee, is that you? Get in here, girl, and see who come to visit."

One look at Ruby Lee explained her parents' concern. The spunky seventeen-year old Carlo remembered had matured into a beautiful woman, dressed to the nines in the latest fashions he'd seen on the white mannequins in Marshall Field's windows. Her animated face invited lust, as did her black eyes when she spoke. She smiled, showing off teeth as perfect as Louisa's had been.

"That you, Mister Charlie?" She laughed and threw her arms around him. "You back for good?"

Carlo shook his head and explained the purpose of his visit.

"Listen up, Ruby Lee," her father said. "We needs a favor of you tonight. It's my poker night and your Ma going to Preacher George to pray for our redemption. How 'bout you taking Mister Charlie to Black Pearl so he can save his own soul with good food and music."

Ruby Lee raised her eyebrows. "The Black Pearl, are you sure?"

"Anybody ask, say he your kin ... uh, from N'Orleans."

"Sure, Daddy, you mean my cousin the octoroon, or maybe the quadroon?" She stepped back to appraise Carlo. "I guess he could pass for one quarter Negro."

"Now don't be so smart, girl," her mother scolded.

"Maybe next time," Carlo said. "It's just that—"

"I have a date tonight but you can go with us."

Roscoe put his arm around Ruby Lee and hugged her. "Mister Charlie need a friend he can talk to ... you know, alone."

"Oh, sure, I'll just call and change my plans to another evening."

She whirled around and walked out of the room, leaving behind the same fragrance Carlo remembered from his week of recuperation. He started after Ruby Lee, to tell her not to change her plans, but Essie Mae grabbed his arm in that familiar stronghold.

"Let her go, Mister Charlie. She don't need cracker this evening, or any other."

*****

Standing at the teak wood bar of the Black Pearl were two men wearing brightly colored double-breasted suits and white spats over black patent leather shoes. The men had focused their attention to the mirror wall behind the bar, which reflected this odd couple occupying a booth, some cracker sitting across from Ezell Johnson's sister.

Neither Carlo nor Ruby Lee appeared aware of this scrutiny. Conversation took precedence over food as they picked at the blue-plate special: fried pork chops smothered in gravy and onions, mashed potatoes, and boiled mustard greens. By the time their waiter had removed the half-eaten food and filled two coffee mugs, Carlo and Ruby Lee were head to head in a tension-filled exchange. With a sympathetic hand over hers, Carlo focused his attention on Ruby Lee's every word. The tears rolling down her cheeks he dabbed away with the linen handkerchief from his breast pocket. Still unaware of their two-man audience, the uncommon twosome played out an emotional scene, one no doubt mistaken for a lover's quarrel.

When the mirror show ran out of steam, the two spectators put some coins on the bar and left without so much as a glance toward the couple. Only then did Carlo take note of the men and their pricey garb. The dandies were at home on The Stroll but in St. Gregory they'd have stood out like strutting peacocks.

"I love Guy and he loves me," Ruby Lee repeated for the fourth time, anything to convince him she'd already made up her mind. "What's more, he's taking me to Paris where they don't look down on mixing races."

"And he will marry you?"

"In Paris we won't need a marriage license. Not like America, where everyone is so provincial. By the way, I asked Guy to meet us here. I hope you don't mind." She looked beyond Carlo's shoulder, to the entryway, and her demeanor changed as she waved one hand. "Here he is now."

Hardly what Carlo envisioned from the excitement Ruby Lee had shown. The man for which she professed such love was groomed in the manner of wealth, and paunchy from good food and middle age.

"Mister Charlie, meet my darling Guy Durand."

Carlo stood to shake the soft, damp hand. "I am Carlo Baggio."

"Sorry, I keep forgetting," she said. "I'm just so nervous. Mister Char—I mean Carlo is an old and dear friend of the family."

Guy Durand slid in beside Ruby Lee. He held her hand to his lips, and continued to hold it when he spoke. "I hope you'll be my friend too, Carlo. This may be difficult for you to understand, but I love Ruby Lee and want to take care of her."

"Then marry her."

"That's out of the question, for more than one reason. Aside from the racial barriers, there is the matter of religion. As a proud Jew, I will not abandon my heritage. Nor do I expect Ruby Lee to give up hers. Although compared to Judaism, Christianity is still in its infancy."

Ruby Lee closed her eyes; she rested her head on Guy's shoulder. Her mind would not be easily changed. And Carlo wasn't sure he should even try. Durand was droning on and on, obviously annoyed at having to justify himself to a stranger.

"Ruby Lee will want for nothing. I can oversee my business from abroad. In fact, I plan to open a second office in Paris."

Carlo listened without comment, searching Guy's face for some sign of deceit to confirm his unworthiness. What did she see in this man too old, too self-important? And why should he risk so much for her, this Guy Durand who didn't care what others thought.

"Help me make my parents understand, Carlo."

"This is not how you were raised."

"Who clings to the life of their childhood? After all, my parents left Mississippi; and what about you, giving up Italy for America. Now it's my turn to live where I choose."

Carlo shook his head. "It's not where you live; it's what lives in your heart."

"There! You just said what I've been trying to explain."

Durand spoke up, his voice softer now. "Ruby Lee will have everything. Most importantly, my love."

Carlo leaned forward and opened his palms. "Your mama and poppa don't approve. I guess that goes for Guy's family too since he's not proposing marriage. For me, it's not to say one way or the other. But I will talk to Roscoe and Essie Mae on your behalf. If they hear your words coming outta my mouth, maybe they'll get used to the idea before you do what you gotta do."

Carlo left the Black Pearl, his mind in turmoil contemplating how to report failure to friends counting on better. He walked about a block, ignoring the curious stares but wishing Roscoe or Ezell walked beside him. As he passed the entrance of a dark alleyway, he caught a whopping slam from behind. He gasped for his next breath. Somebody stretched his arms back into the unyielding lock. He couldn't see the bastard holding him but the one punching his stomach and ribs came from the Black Pearl.

"We bring a message from Ezell." Wham! "Stay away from his sister." Wham! "You got that, ofay?" Wham!

Before Carlo could reply, he took another blow to his gut. He dropped to the sidewalk, received several well-placed kicks. Doubled up in pain, he vomited his soul food onto four white spats encasing four black patent leathers. The shrill of a police whistle ended the attack, prompting his assailants to run off, all the while cursing the souvenir Carlo had sent with them.

A brass-buttoned blue uniform poked Carlo with his nightstick, to make sure he was still conscious. "Here now, young fellow. What the hell would you be doing in this part of town?"

"I'm okay. Just help me up."

The cop bent over and offered his arm. "Now would you be seeing who done such a thing to you?"

"I don't know. Two men came from behind."

"Well, no point in filing a report if it's okay you are. But heed my warning: once the sun goes down, The Stroll is no place for the likes of a fellow such as yourself."

The words sounded familiar, somewhat on the order of those he'd heard during the Night School raid of long ago. Carlo limped down the street, stopping twice to spit up blood before making it to Roscoe's. He announced his arrival with a loud thud.

As soon as Ezell Johnson opened the door, he let out a low whistle. "Holy bejeebers, Mister Charlie. Who did this to you?"

"Your friends from the Black Pearl," he muttered through gritted teeth. "I guess they got the wrong idea, seeing me with Ruby Lee."

"Hells bells, they must've thought you that ofay Durand." He helped Carlo to the sofa. "Ma, come quick. Mister Charlie's hurt again."

Armed with her first aid box, Essie Mae hurried from the bedroom.

"Look, we ain't doing this again," Carlo said, trying to make light of the pain in his belly. "Just let me rest here a minute, then I gotta go. I mean leave."

He waited for Roscoe to come home before explaining his failure. Without expressing his own doubts, which were considerable and shamefully intolerant considering his own attraction to Ruby Lee, Carlo presented a convincing case on behalf of the two lovers.

Roscoe and Ezell paced the room like caged panthers.

"My little girl with that ofay," Roscoe muttered. "He ain't good enough to clean a shithouse."

Ezell smashed his fist against the kitchen door, leaving a smear of blood. "That fucking fairy, I'll break his legs."

While he rubbed his knuckles, Essie Mae cleaned the door. Sobbing, she dropped to her knees. She lifted her face and arms to the ceiling. "Oh Lord, Lord in heaven above, snatch our Ruby Lee from the jaws of Satan. He put her under a spell and now she stuck there. This all about a peckawood who ain't even accepted Jesus Christ as his personal savior. Drive that good-for-nothing cracker from her life forever and ever. Sweet Jesus, spare us from disgrace."

After all the anger and tears were spent and nothing had changed, the Johnson family took a breather so they could conserve their energy for a direct confrontation with Ruby Lee. And when Essie Mae insisted Carlo stay the night on her sofa, Carlo didn't argue with her. The next morning he awoke to a swollen face and stiff, aching body. When he left, Ruby Lee had not come home yet.

*****

Back on The Stroll Carlo caught a cab to the Guardian Angels home. Relieved that Sister Barbara ignored his bruised face, he collected his own little angels and headed for the park. After another play on the swings and teeter tooter, Mary Ann and Michael filled up on hot dogs and ice cream while their papa sat back to revel in their excitement. In the afternoon they napped with their heads on his lap. It was the sweetest of days, one he would carry in his heart forever.

When he brought his children back, he expected to see Sister Barbara. Instead, Mother Superior swept through the parlor door. Her starched white coif encased a stern, oval face that softened to smile at his children. Lifting her imperial chin to Carlo, she announced in a tone demanding obedience that Monsignor Flaherty expected him at five o'clock. Carlo knew better than to disregard such a command; the careful nurturing of his children ultimately rested with her and the monsignor. After another heart-wrenching farewell with his children, he walked the nine blocks to St. Sebastian's.

Noreen opened the rectory door and smothered him in a maternal embrace of genuine fondness before stepping back for a better look. "A good thing it is you're a wee bit early since a minor emergency has delayed the Monsignor. Now into my kitchen with you ... I won't have him thinking you an unfit rowdy. Let's see what a bit of raw meat will do for that banged-up face."

"It was all a mistake ...."

"No excuses, Carlo Baggio. And don't you be trumping up a tale about getting beat up while trying to perform a good deed."

Ten minutes later in the parlor Carlo and Monsignor Flaherty greeted each other like old friends.

"Ah, Carlo, 'tis good to be seeing you, lad." The monsignor patted him on the back, pushed him into the nearest chair. "Sit down, sit down." He went to the door and called out for Noreen. She was already in the hall, which didn't surprise Carlo. "Now sister of mine," the monsignor said, "would you be so kind as to bring that special wine I saved for a day such as this."

The two men spent the next hour over a bottle of Barbaresco, a fine Piemontese red beyond Carlo's means. They talked about the children and his struggle to eke out a living as a coal miner. Carlo never brought up Tre Paesani. Either Noreen's cosmetic first aid had worked its magic or the monsignor chose not to comment since the matter of bruises never came up either. When the conversation drew to an end, the monsignor put his arm around Carlo and walked him to the door.

"Now would you be remembering Father Terrence Connelly? My assistant he was when your beloved Louisa first came to St. Sebastian's."

"I think we met once or twice," Carlo said, wanting to end any further mention of *The Priest*.

"In Rome Father Connelly has been for almost four years now, at the Papal Office of the Vatican. Doing the work of Our Lord he is, but in a different capacity than his original intent. I doubt he'll every return, except to visit."

"I should be going, Monsignor."

"God works in strange ways, now doesn't He? For all our encounters in life there are reasons, even those that touch us in the most painful of ways."

*****

Having done his St. Sebastian's duty, Carlo put aside thoughts of Terry Connelly in favor of a return visit to Night School. He wanted Giulietta one more time. More importantly, he wanted to make sure she wasn't in any trouble. He got as far as the outer door, only to hear Frog through the intercom.

"Sorry, Carlo, Miss Giulietta's busy with an important client and can't see you any more today. She said to tell you not to wait so long next time."

"Just tell me this: has she got troubles with Capone?" Carlo asked into the speaker, neither expecting nor receiving a response.

Since Giulietta gave him the brush-off, he followed his original plan of paying his respects to Massimo and Vincenzo. Other than dropping the food and liquor prices in order to keep their regulars, the brothers had suffered few effects from The Depression. Sitting at the bar, Carlo took his time reviewing the menu. Against his better judgment he ordered the veal, only to regret his choice when the meat arrived overcooked. Not tender like Louisa used to fix it, nor as good as Irene's. After endless chewing on what could have passed shoe leather, he pushed his plate aside in favor of the wine. Still Fabiola's best. The remainder of the evening he spent reminiscing with Massimo and Vincenzo, mostly about the Old Country since talk about Louisa brought too many tears.

Chapter 32
Giulietta and Mr. Smith

Giulietta had known far too many men in her life, most of them unforgettable, which was not the case with Carlo Baggio. If only she was younger or him older. If only he could've stayed in Chicago instead of dirtying his hands in the coal dust of Podunk. She should've disposed of his nemesis before now. Perhaps when the dust of Chicago settled, she'd call in a favor or two. But not tonight; tonight she owed Fingers Bellini or so he thought. And what he thought mattered more than disappointing Carlo. She'd received two visits from Capone's bagman within the same week, one more than his usual. On Monday, Bellini accused her of holding out on the Big Man's take; and when she wouldn't cough up an extra five hundred, he applied the flat of his hand to her face. Fortunately, Ugo had come to her rescue—with a powerful cuff across Bellini's pointy scalp. Giulietta handed Bellini a cold pack, and threatened to tell Capone that if the take was short, he should consider his man holding the bag instead of her. Bellini backed off, and before he left, they both agreed to forget the incident. Not so easy for Giulietta since she still had to deal with a throbbing cheekbone. Of course, Carlo had noticed the nasty bruise. Not that she expected any less from him.

This morning Bellini made his second visit, bringing a special request on behalf of the Big Man. Would Giulietta personally entertain an important friend of his? She'd granted Capone such favors before. To refuse could invite disastrous consequences to her business. In any case, the clients Capone recommended were big spenders with the right connections; and this one had Bellini deliver an envelope containing ten C-notes, payment for a single night of her undivided attention. Giulietta didn't take long to consider the offer; one could never have too many rich friends.

Had Giulietta known Carlo would return for an encore, she'd have arranged a later time for Big Al's big spender. Too late now—business was business and Giulietta was in business to make money.

In her dressing room lined with mirrors Giulietta inspected her body from every angle with the same discriminating eye she knew the big spender would also use. She still conveyed a glamorous image, but didn't have many years left as a high-class whore who indulged special interest clients. Granted, she'd lost money in the stock market crash but other cautious investments provided sufficient financial stability to keep Night School operating. Barely out of the red, but she hadn't resorted to selling street-corner apples. Selective work on her back had filled the monetary gap in her coffers as well as the emotional gap of Carlo's absence.

Last night's encounter with him had stirred old passions put to rest when he took his marriage vows with that mousy immigrant. God rest her peasant soul. The only good thing about Carlo's quick departure from Chicago had been the necessity of leaving Mary Ann and Michael behind, which allowed her a discreet role in their upbringing. Although she harbored no doubts about the good intentions of Holy Guardian Angels, Giulietta had sweetened the pot which ensured the Baggio children would want for nothing. In return, the sisters provided her unlimited access to Mary Ann and Michael, with the understanding that Carlo not be informed of the full extent of her involvement. On Sundays she took them to the zoo, puppet shows, or the circus. Once she arranged for a few clowns to visit the orphanage. Wherever the three of them went, heads turned. As with the nuns, Carlo's precious tykes had become the children she'd been denied.

Thirty minutes after turning Carlo away, Frog knocked at her door to announce the arrival of the latest Mr. Smith. This Mr. Smith fell short of what Giulietta had come to expect from a Capone referral. This Mr. Smith must've just stepped down from a barber college chair: amateurs prepping an aging peacock for a new hen. Giulietta counted four bloody razor nicks. His barrel chest strained the seams of an ill-fitted tuxedo, most likely rented or borrowed. New money acquired under the table, not that she cared. Mr. Big Spender risking first-time naughtiness, perhaps a beer distributor from Milwaukee who pulled off a coup for the Big Man. Giulietta put on her thousand-dollar smile.

"Come in, come in. Don't be shy, Mr. Smith," she said in her low, sultry voice. Taking his hand, she led him to the sofa in her salon. "Can I get you something to drink?"

The red-faced man shook his head. Perspiration dotted his forehead like drops of urine on a burrowing pig. She half-expected him to snort. Later, that would come when he fell asleep, his putrid sweat drenching her silk sheets.

"Here, let me loosen your tie, Mr. Smith. You'll be much more comfortable." With a tease of rose-scented tits past his thick, dry lips, she bent over to undo the bowtie and top button of a constrictive shirt, his massive neck all but thanking her as it filled the expanded space. So far he hadn't said a word. Another embarrassed john who couldn't get it up, hoping she could work some miracle. No problem. Miracles were her specialty. "Why not put your feet up, Mr. Smith. Just relax and let Giulietta massage those tired, aching muscles."

He took a deep breath and closed his porcine eyes.

When coddling Mr. Smith's fallen arches became tiresome, she moved to his trouser fly.

Pushing her hand away, he spoke his first words. "No, not yet."

"Perhaps some entertainment? We have talented ladies capable of contorting their bodies into remarkable positions."

"Just with you I want to be. Please, a little more time like this."

Another German, talking backward in that damn guttural manner. Oh well, she'd turn him around with a night to remember. Afterwards, he'll take flowers and candy to a dumpy wife grateful for the attention. And never be the wiser. "Would you like to see the rest of my salon?" she asked. "The evening's young but shouldn't be wasted."

Without waiting for his answer, she tugged Mr. Smith off the sofa and guided him into her bedroom. She turned to fluff her bed pillows, presenting a well-practiced wiggle of slender hips to nudge any man's sluggish libido.

"Your stockings," he said, "I want to see you take them off." He sat on the edge of the chaise lounge and folded his arms.

Giulietta knew she could bring him around. She lifted one leg to the dressing table stool, raised her skirt, and slowly peeled silk down to her ankle. "Oh, my stocking's stuck," she murmured. "Could you help me unbuckle my shoe, please?"

He closed the gap with two hesitant strides. His coarse fingers fumbled with the buckle until with a flip of her thumb, Giulietta released it. She slipped off the shoe and the stocking, handing both to him. "Would you mind holding these?" she asked before propping up the other leg.

He came from behind to wrap his arms around her, to nuzzle his ruddy cheek next to hers, like sandpaper against porcelain. His breath was heavy with stale beer. For an old goat his nudge surprised her. She forced a laugh and turned around. "Whoa. Something tells me little Smitty's ready to play."

His grip tightened, holding her fast. She made a mental note about slipping a Sen-Sen into his mouth when she entered it with her tongue. His red face had turned a weird shade of purple. The blustering fool choked on words he couldn't wait to spit out. "Take it easy, Mr. Smith. Why don't you just relax a little?"

"Why? Why you say? Better I should ask why my boy should die. This I do not understand. For three years now his mother talks of nothing else."

"I don't know what you mean, Mr. Smith, but may I express my deepest sympathy for your loss. Now let's move over to my bed where we can talk." She kept her voice calm, anything to ignore the wild pounding in her ear.

"Not Mr. Smith, you stupid bitch ... Mr. Kramer, Gustav Kramer. Word on the street is the Night School madam saved her fucking teacher's pet. For a damn wop, my only boy winds up dead."

"Your boy ... who is your boy? Please, Mr. ... Mr. Kramer. I don't know what you mean."

As soon as she said the name Kramer, Giulietta understood why the fool kept blubbering. Her mind raced to that morning Carlo was leaving Chicago.

Concerned for his safety, she had Ugo drive her to Carlo's apartment. Just as her car turned the corner near his building, Carlo drove away in a taxicab. They followed him. Two blocks from the Dearborn Station Carlo got out. Ugo slowed down but before she could offer Carlo a ride to the entrance, Harold Kramer emerged from a doorway, holding a gun. The one shot he fired sent Carlo to the pavement. She stayed calm, for Carlo's sake. While Harold took aim for a second shot, she pulled a revolver from her handbag. She fired once, into Harold's head. After instructing Ugo to help Carlo, she left the car and walked away.

For that, she now faced the distraught papa. She struggled to free one hand from his grip, to reach the faithful stiletto that never left her bed. But the clumsy beast reacted quicker than she expected, grabbing her before she reached the mattress. He twisted her around so they faced each other. She hated him for sensing her fear.

The first blow knocked Giulietta off her feet, the shock of it so disabling she couldn't make a sound. The heel of his shoe slammed into her mouth to abort any screams for Ugo. She felt the silk stocking wrap twice around her throat; and while he knotted the stocking with her hairbrush, she raked her nails down the side of his face, breaking two nails in the process. Damn ... where was Ugo ... Ugo. Tighter and tighter the bastard twisted until she gave up and used what little time she had left to make her peace with God.

Gustav Kramer held the hairbrush tight against Giulietta's throat for a good six minutes, much longer than needed. If she were to arise now, it would've been a miracle. After Gus released his grip, he remained kneeling beside her body. And wept, unaware that Ugo Sapone had entered the room.

*****

The next morning Carlo worked his way through a throng of Dearborn Station travelers before meeting up with Roscoe Johnson at the bootblack station. As soon as Roscoe finished his spit and polish shine, he grabbed Carlo by the elbow and pushed him back into the crowd.

"Here we go, Mister Charlie. I'm taking you straightway to the Illinois Central platform. Just making sure you get out of Chicago with no trouble."

Carlo left that day without seeing the Chicago Tribune. An article on its lower front page reported the murder-suicide of a well-known figure in the underworld and her deranged, unnamed suitor. No photographs of the gruesome scene had been published, thanks to the newspaper's editor, a former student of the deceased Giulietta Bracca. Instead, the photo Ugo Sapone provided revealed a striking woman, the sophisticated headmistress of Chicago's most popular school.

Chapter 33
Risky Business

With half the country burdened by unemployment, most adults and children over the age of nine spent their days dreaming up innovative ways to make money—from flagpole sitting to dance marathons and lemonade stands. The Southern Illinois miners considered themselves fortunate, what with working three solid days every week. St. Gregory's more industrious housewives took in sewing or sold freshly baked bread or a variety of pies. Some opened their homes to lodgers and their dining rooms to outsiders, which created competition for the newer boarding houses—but not for Lucy Wallace or Irene Roselli. Like Lucy, Irene pampered her loyal boarders with a decent spread of food. But unlike Lucy, Irene went one step further, pampering her boarders with an unlimited amount of wine.

During every grace Mario offered thanks for the blessings of good harvests and unsurpassed wines. He even asked God's blessings for the *have-nots*, without naming names since only one mattered: Benny Drummond. The *have-not* of Mario's prayers enjoyed no wine of his own making but he did have a monopoly on the Tre Paesani wine. Benny had already bought the wine processed from the previous fall and was expecting the second wine, two weeks away from drawing.

One evening that had settled into an unforgiving night found most of the Roselli boarders either working or involved in bedtime preparations. But not Carlo and Jake, they were sprawled out on the back porch steps while Irene and Mario creaked back and forth on the swing. The only other movements came from the buzzing mosquitoes or an occasional slap to ward off their attacks.

"If that drought the caterpillars are predicting comes to pass, there won't be enough wine for our own table," Irene said. "It's God's way of punishing us."

"What the hell are you talking about," Mario said. "Punishing us for what?"

"You know, for desecrating our wine by dealing with that bootlegger."

"For god sake, open up that family bible in your parlor shrine to the Virgin Mary. Show me where it's a sin to make wine, or to sell it to the *have-nots*. We got the ground. We got the grapes. We got the equipment. Right, Jake ... Carlo?"

Carlo gave careful thought to his words. "Not to share would be selfish but to give it away, a crime." He nudged Jake, who agreed with a slight nod so as not to rile Irene.

"What about your middleman, that Benny Drummond," Irene went on. "The man's a known hoodlum."

"But a cash and carry one with the connections and trucks we don't have. Our wine's located in some of the best places in St. Louis. Hotels like the Lennox and Mayfair and Jefferson."

"Yes, but—"

"We need the money, Irene. And fifty cents per gallon goes a long way, even after expenses."

"That's all he's paying you? No wonder he drives a Cadillac and lives in a fancy house. Not that I'm complaining."

"Look, you got a better idea, spit it out. If not, stick to your cooking and laundry."

*****

Several days later Lucy Wallace telephoned and invited Irene to spend the day with her in St. Louis. Irene hesitated, embarrassed by the luxury she couldn't afford. But Lucy insisted the day would be her long overdue treat, for Irene taking in the schoolteachers. Irene put on her best dress, the all-occasion navy rayon with white organdy collar she wore for every Sunday Mass and holy day. She left Margherita in charge of her boys and met Lucy at the depot. From there, they caught the interurban to St. Louis. Late that afternoon she returned in a better mood, changed into a print housedress, and helped Margherita prepare supper: platters of sauce-covered ravioli filled with beef and pork leftovers, spring lettuce and green onion salad, sautéed green beans, and juicy strawberries that drenched sweetened biscuits. No whipped cream.

Later, after tucking Frankie and Tony in bed, Irene wandered out to the back porch. Carlo and Jake were stretched into their usual positions on the steps; Mario was creaking the swing. He patted the wood slats, and Irene sat down.

"So, how was St. Louis?" he asked.

"Lucy took me to the Lennox for lunch. A fancier place I never saw: fringed drapes, thick carpets, and so-so food—something called tomato aspic followed by chicken salad with walnut halves. I even had a glass of wine, our wine. At forty cents a glass I nearly choked on every swallow. You did say Benny Drummond pays you fifty cents for a whole gallon, didn't you?"

Carlo gulped. He felt Jake's leg stiffen. He didn't have to look at Mario to know what their partner was thinking. Mario's voice cut through the silence.

"So what are you saying, Irene, that we bypass Benny and make our own deals?"

She jumped up, hands flapping like the wings of a startled wren. "Certainly not, I only meant that Benny's a worse crook than I first thought. He's buying cheap and selling high. If you ask me—not that you ever do—I think you should give up bootlegging with Drummond. If you need the money that bad, sell our wine to a few choice friends." She left in her usual huff but her words lingered.

"I hate it when she's right," Mario said. "All that work for lousy peanuts."

"You didn't think so our first year," Jake said. "This go-around there's not as many expenses so we'll show a better profit."

"Not enough to make a difference," said Carlo. "Maybe we should deal direct with the hotels while they still need us. Prohibition won't last much longer."

"What about Benny?" Mario asked.

"So we tell him some barrels went bad," Carlo said with an open-handed shrug. "A little of this, a little of that—we'll dilute the wine with water. Sell half to Benny, half to the hotels."

Mario raised his brow. "That's too risky ... two thirds to Benny, one third to the hotels. That way, the hotels still have to order some from Benny."

"What about the deliveries?" Jake asked. "Sure as hell we can't borrow Benny's truck."

"For a couple of bucks Amos'll let us use his pickup," Carlo said.

Mario appointed Jake negotiator, a role the smooth talker relished and Carlo agreed he deserved.

*****

The next day they didn't have work at the mine but still ate breakfast with those who did. Everyone, including the teachers, gobbled up the meal Irene served with teary eyes that either went unnoticed or were politely ignored. Afterwards, the three partners piled into Mario's car and drove downtown to Chamber's Drugstore. After splurging on nickel donuts, Carlo and Mario stood outside the telephone booth while Jake fed coins into the slot. One by one he called the three St. Louis hotels serving Tre Paesani wine, and insisted on speaking to no one except the head chef. Each decision maker hemmed and hawed, reluctant to consider a change until Jake presented the offer: three dollars a gallon compared to the six Benny charged, delivered in six ten-gallon barrels a week from Saturday. Early in the morning, which meant Benny and his watchdogs should be sleeping although Jake didn't elaborate on that with the chefs.

The partners made their hotel deliveries in Amos Carter's beat-up truck, a trial run that went off without a hitch, except for two flat tires, one repaired outside East St. Louis before they crossed the river and the other east of Belleville on the way home. The next week when Benny came for his wine, he grumbled about the number of barrels going bad but accepted Mario's explanation. He even agreed to the watered down wine, after a taste test revealed little difference to his unrefined palate. The partners knew better but the extra money alleviated any guilt they might've harbored for compromising their product.

Three weeks passed. One afternoon they were driving home from work, Carl beside Mario and Jake in the back. As soon as the Model T turned off the road and rumbled down the long driveway, Carlo spotted the black Cadillac parked up ahead. The familiar car used to mean another deal or money in their pockets, but not this time. Benny Drummond was leaning against the front passenger door, a fat stogy jutting from his mouth.

"Remind you of anybody?" Carlo asked from over his shoulder.

"Capone without the scar," Jake replied. "Or the potbelly."

"Let's hope he ain't as mean."

Mario hadn't said a word. As they neared the house, he slowed down to wipe his brow. When the approaching scene registered in his brain, he let out a gasp, followed by, "What the hell."

There, perched on the hood of the Cadillac were Tony and Frankie, inspecting a Tommy gun one of Benny's henchmen had cradled in his arms. On the porch, a second henchman sat on the swing, a Tommy gun on his lap and Irene to his right. Squeezed into the arm of the swing, she clutched its chain links in one hand and a handkerchief in the other.

"Easy," Carlo said when the Model T came to a halt. "Let Benny do the talking and don't piss him off any more than he already is."

As soon as Mario got out, Tony and Frankie hopped off the Cadillac's hood and ran over to him.

"Waldo let us touch his gun," Frankie yelled.

"And Emmet gave us chewing gum," Tony said. He lowered his voice to add, "Mom let us keep it, the whole fucking pack."

Benny cracked a half smile. "You'll have to excuse Emmet's language. When it comes to kids, the man shows no restrain."

"How 'bout checking out the henhouse," Mario told his boys.

"We already did that," Tony said.

"So do it again and fill the water troughs—*now*."

Carlo's stomach turned a dozen summersaults. No trip to Chicago—those precious hours with his kids—was worth this. Nor that night with Giulietta, God rest her soul. Massimo had written him about the scuttlebutt that never made the newspapers.

Time and motion stood still until the boys took themselves out of sight. Only then did Mario speak. "So Benny, we're kinda surprised to see you."

"No more than me when I found out you three stooges were dealing directly with my hotel customers. You shoulda come to me first, Mario."

Jake spoke up. "It wasn't Mario's fault. He didn't even know what was going on until the barrels wound up in St. Louis."

"Shut up, Jake. I oughta splatter that nice nose over your pretty boy face. However, I am a reasonable man." Benny cocked his head to the porch. "Right, Irene?"

"My wife's got nothing to do with this," Mario said, clenching his fists as Irene buried her face in the crumbled handkerchief.

"Then you don't know her as well as you oughta. It's a done deal, Mario. The Missus and me already worked out the details after visiting the setup in your cellar."

The blood drained from Mario's face; resignation filled his sunken eyes. Never had Carlo seen him display such desperation.

Benny's lips crept into a half-smile, more like a sneer. "Not to worry, Mario. In exchange for my fireproofing your entire house, I get all the wine you held back … at no charge, of course, for my inconvenience. Oh yeah, and about the St. Louis hotels. You can keep the fifty cents a gallon. I get the rest, in exchange for saving your lives. Like I said, I'm a reasonable man. And your wife offered me a fair deal. Hands down, the best I ever negotiated."

Chapter 34
Fire!

Although Southern Illinois' stifling summers were as common as its flies and mosquitoes, the drought-stricken summer of 1932 had still managed to set record-breaking temperatures. Absent were the occasional rain showers that provided temporary relief until the humidity took its turn at provoking misery. Once healthy vegetables from the Roselli garden withered before they matured, forcing Irene to deplete her stockpile of canned goods from the cellar. Mario didn't expect the thirsty grapes to yield much more than a lackluster crop, which meant there'd be no wine for Benny Drummond. He'd already surveyed the vineyard and taken his business elsewhere, much to the relief of the partners. Irene too, she'd developed the annoying habit of chewing her nails to the quick.

With money so tight, Irene agreed to take in another miner, Amos Carter. He finally gave up the liver and onion sandwiches his former landlady enjoyed foisting on him. When forced to decide between his appetite for sex and his appetite for food, Amos had reached the stage in life when the latter made more sense. In spite of the weather and the economy, food at the Roselli table remained good and plentiful; and the eclectic mix of teachers and miners tolerated their differences, some more than others.

One hot evening after a solitary stroll around the sorry garden, Maude Simpson went upstairs and bathed in a tub of cool water. She patted herself dry and slipped into a lightweight cotton batiste nightgown, a recent purchase in St. Louis. After checking to make sure the hall was clear, she hurried to her bedroom and locked the door behind her.

As part of her nightly ritual, Maude stroked Noxzema Cream into her face and neck, removed the excess with a cotton ball, and applied a splash of witch hazel to close her delicate pores. She massaged Jergens Lotion, the hand cream of movie stars, into her freckled arms and hands to combat an ongoing battle with the aging process. Her feet and legs received extra attention as she rubbed long and deep with a special blend of glycerin and rosewater prepared by Ned Chambers, the local druggist. She stretched her arms to the large hairpins binding her hennaed twist and released a tangle of wispy hair that tumbled below her bony shoulders.

Baby Ben displayed ten-thirty when she turned out her reading light fastened to the headboard. Maude lifted the top sheet, and let it float down to barely cover all she held dear. Surrendering to the darkness, she extended herself with a long, feline stretch; and concentrating on one limb at a time, she eased into a state of complete relaxation.

From out in the hallway came the slight sound of a key rattling in the lock. The opening door squeaked, as did the floorboard near the foot of her bed. From under the sheet a groping hand sought her foot. A hungry mouth sucked her toes, one by one. Maude shuddered on feeling a tongue move over to tickle the inside arches of her feet. Fingers marched to the top of her inner legs and took command of her trimmed fortress. Giggling with the excitement of the ingénue she once was, Maude reached down to bring the face of her intruder to loom over hers. Smiling, she asked, "What took you so long?"

"No shower, no nookie, ain't that what you always tell me," said Leno Gotti. "I had to wait in line for the outside shower. With this damn heat everybody needed a cooling off."

"Let me feel how cool you are."

Maude Simpson explored every inch of Leno Gotti, in great detail and with uninhibited enjoyment. When she murmured her journey was complete, he settled into her to complete their combined journey with a climax so satisfying both of them wept with relief.

Their intimate relationship had started a year earlier, brought about when Maude insulted Leno at the dinner table by correcting his poor English. Later that evening she invited him into her room with every intention of apologizing, which she did before inviting him into her bed. Their initial encounter proved so rewarding that he came to her twice a week thereafter, more often if she asked.

Poor Ellen Waterhouse, ever the bridesmaid. Not only did she have to endure the heat but also the audible pleasures erupting from Miss Simpson's room. Hoping to capture a light breeze, Ellen opened the window. She propped herself up in bed, her books and cigarettes for company. Earlier at dinner she'd exceeded her customary two glasses of wine which may have accounted for the unfinished cigarette in one hand and her book in the other when she finally drifted off.

Meanwhile, Jake and Carlo were playing cards at Sugg's, a popular roadhouse located just beyond the city limits and the police chief's jurisdiction. An easy walk from the boarding house, Sugg's filled the role of social club, a place the brothers frequented twice weekly—once for back room rummy and once for upstairs sex. They left Sugg's around eleven and were within a block of their boarding house when Carlo saw flames shooting from a second floor window.

They both ran: Jake to the nearest house where he banged on the door and yelled for Remy Baker to call the fire department; and Carlo to the burning house, where he took the stairs two at a time, yelling, "Fire! Fire! Everybody out!"

Smoke was filling the entire house as Carlo pounded on doors, opening those unlocked on his way down the hall to Tony and Frankie's room. He scooped up the sleeping boys and handed them to Mario and Irene who were climbing up his back.

By the time Carlo had hurried into yard and everyone from the house was presumed safe, Jake and Remy Baker had a water hose aimed on the house, trying to wet it down until the volunteer firefighters arrived. Mario was clad in pajamas and slippers. His barefoot wife had thrown a cotton blanket over her nightgown.

Maude Simpson had taken on the appearance of a Greek goddess, wrapped in her bed sheet as she wandered around with words no one wanted to hear. "Oh, dear, oh dear, wherever is Miss Waterhouse? I can't seem to find her anywhere."

Mario groaned. "Jesus, Mary, and Joseph, don't tell me that fool woman was smoking again."

"I warned Miss Waterhouse: no smoking after nine o'clock," Irene said. "She promised not to do it anymore. Maybe Benny Drummond set the fire."

"Benny, hell, forget about Benny." Mario grabbed Irene's blanket, skimmed it across a barrel of rainwater, and raced toward his burning house.

"No, Mario, it's too late," Irene shouted. She looked at Carlo, tears streaming down her face. "Don't let him in there alone, please."

Carlo heard the clanging bell from the fire truck getting louder, but he knew by the time it arrived and the men set things up, there'd be nothing worth saving. After dunking his head and arms in the rain barrel, he ran like hell and followed Mario into the back door. They were almost to the top of the stairs when Carlo heard a loud cracking noise above his head. Before he could look upward a burning beam came crashing down in his wake. It hit the steps, sending Mario and him down to the first floor hallway. Thick, dense smoke blinded Carlo. He struggled to get up but couldn't move. His leg carrying the bullet scar was wedged under the beam.

"So, *buon amico e partner*, this is how it ends for us," he said although he couldn't see Mario. "Not so different from dying in a mine explosion, except there's more time to think."

"You don't have to go yet, Carlo."

The voice did not belong to Mario. Carlo strained his watering eyes until they focused on a black man, outfitted in fire gear yet making no effort to fight the blaze. "I thought I knew all the volunteers," Carlo said. "But you I never saw before."

"Of course you have. Chicago, how long has it been?"

"You again ... so this is it."

"Did I say that? Your children still need you."

"Dammit, if my time ain't come, then how about helping me."

"Help yourself, Carlo."

"Any ideas, Angelo Nero?"

"Yanking on that leg won't help. Work it back and forth 'til the beam loosens up. Then give one quick jerk."

Carlo did as he was told but nothing happened. He let out an unexpected moan. "I can't make a miracle. I'm done for."

"Don't give up so easily. Try again." The voice came across firm but encouraging.

Once more Carlo tried, this time setting his leg free. He called on all his strength to stand up but only got as far as his knees. "Mario ... dammit where'd you go? Let's get the hell out ... now." Carlo coughed the words out. "Say something, Mario." He started crawling, feeling his way until his hand moved into a sticky puddle. "Sweet Jesus, not this."

Carlo slid his fingers over to the gaping wounds in Mario's head and chest.

"Save yourself, Carlo. Your friend is dying."

"He's more than a friend. And he ain't dying here."

"As you please but I can't help you any more than I already have."

"Then go back to wherever you came from ... wait, not yet. About Louisa—never mind, we'll talk later."

Carlo grabbed Mario by the pajama top and crawled toward the door, every inch a painful reminder that he couldn't find the air his lungs were demanding. No matter how close the door may have seemed, it kept moving further away.

Outside, Leno Gotti had taken the water hose from Jake and told him to check on Irene. She was kneeling in the middle of the yard, praying through a torrent of tears. Jake tore off his sweaty water-soaked shirt, and covered her shoulders. "Irene, it's me, Jake. Where are the boys?"

"With neighbors, I think. I know they made it out."

"And Mario?"

She pointed to the burning house. "In there. Carlo too."

"Holy Mother and Jesus!"

Ignoring Remy Baker's warning to stay back, Jake didn't stop running until he reached the back door. Eight feet inside, he stumbled over Carlo, and then Mario. Taking the back of one shirt collar in each hand, he dragged both men through the door, down the steps, and into the yard.

By that time the fire truck had arrived with six men. Ten more came by car and on foot. As the firefighters readied their hoses to blast water on the half-burned house, orange-red flames lit the midnight sky and silhouetted the outbuildings. Windows popped like Chinese firecrackers as they shattered from the heat.

It didn't take long for the fresh night air and deafening racket to bring Carlo around. He rolled over and saw Irene sitting on the ground, holding Mario in her arms as Jake knelt beside her, a bucket nearby.

"Mario, Mario ... don't leave me," she wailed. "Dear God, don't take him from me. Not now."

"Don't cry, Irene. Mario's gonna make it," Jake said as he kept ladling water over Mario's face. "He's way too tough to die."

Carlo sat up. He tried to speak but couldn't, not with his throat feeling like raw meat. He wanted to tell Jake not to give Irene any false hope. But why bother—Jake wouldn't believe him anyway. For their *compare* ... *their amico,* the fight was over. *L'Angelo Nero* had already called Mario's death.

Chapter 35
A New Partnership

The day after Mario was put in the ground, Irene and Jake sat in the lobby of the Commercial Hotel, where they'd been staying ever since the fire. The clothes they wore were new but cheap, donated from the discount rack at Saunders General Store. Irene pulled the lace curtain aside and looked out the window to where her boys and Carlo were playing stickball in an empty lot across the street. The curtain fell back in place when she curled her fingers around a wet handkerchief.

"If it wasn't for Tony and Frankie, I don't think I could go on."

"What about insurance?" Jake asked.

Irene blew her nose. "Two policies, one on the house and one on Mario—double indemnity since his death wasn't related to the mine."

"Hell, Irene, you could rebuild."

"No more boarders, please. If it wasn't for that fool teacher, my husband—God rest his soul ... I suppose hers too—Mario would still be here. My boys would still have a father."

"You gotta think about the future."

"You're so right, Jake, but I don't want it filled with near strangers depending on me when it's all I can do to take care of myself and the boys." She took the clean handkerchief he offered. "What about you and Carlo? Did you lose much, in the way of money, I mean."

"Just what we kept under the mattress. Oh yeah, and some pictures of our folks, and Carlo's wife and kids. Those he took pretty hard, not that I'd expect otherwise."

She shook her head. "Memories, and dreams of what might've been. What about the other boarders? I guess some of them lost everything."

"Money and clothes can be replaced, Irene."

She started crying again, into Jake's handkerchief.

"Dammit, I'm sorry, Irene."

"So far, everybody's found a place to stay except Margherita and Sammy, and I'm working on that. Instead of another big house I'm thinking about something simple, maybe a duplex. You know, the boys and me on one side, renters on the other. Non-smokers, of course."

"Sounds good but rental income ain't enough to get by on."

"I know, I know. But with the insurance I'll be okay for a while, at least 'til the boys are older. And there's always next year's garden. I'll sell the produce again. Surely God wouldn't send us another summer like this."

Jake cleared his throat to bring up a topic he and Carlo had already discussed. "Irene ... about the latina in the cellar, I think me and Carlo could clean it up. Not for wine to sell but to enjoy around the table. Next to you and the boys, it was Mario's greatest pride."

"Not now, Jake. If you and Carlo really want to help, then help me rebuild."

"We know how to make wine and we know how to mine coal. Carpenters we ain't."

"Just think about it, will you?"

*****

The next day Irene paid a visit to the Wallace Boarding House and thanked Lucy for the nearly new clothes she'd sent over to the hotel, including the cotton seersucker Irene was wearing. She refused Lucy's offer of tea and went straight to the nature of her call. "I'm sorry to bother you, Lucy, but you did say, 'if I ever needed anything.'"

Lucy flushed. "The best I can offer would be kitchen work in exchange for room and board. I'm sorry, I wish it were more."

"What about Margherita Falio and her boy Sammy? Would there be a job for her?"

"Oh, Irene, I just don't have enough boarders to justify more than one additional worker. You do understand, don't you?"

"Then give the job and the room to Margherita."

"But what about you?"

"I'll need one room for me and the boys, just until my house is finished. Of course, I'll pay, same as everybody else."

"Irene, what a kind friend you are."

"Don't tell Margherita, okay? She needs the money more than I do. What with Sammy wanting to finish high school, and no work to be had even if she asked him to quit, which I know she wouldn't do."

*****

After a series of lengthy discussions Jake and Carlo agreed to undertake the construction of Irene's new house. They enlisted Red Armstrong as lead carpenter and to teach them basic skills since Red had built his own house. When the men weren't mining coal, they worked on the duplex, a project that took almost seventeen months to complete. By coincidence, Jake hammered the last nail on the same day Prohibition was repealed—December 5, 1933. Although Illinois had already repealed it statewide in April, there was still reason to celebrate. During the construction Irene had paid Red Armstrong once a month for his work but neither Jake nor Carlo would accept any money from her. That afternoon as they sat around her new backyard table, Irene held out two envelopes.

Carlo showed her his palms. "We agreed not to charge."

"Out of respect for Mario's memory," Jake said, "out of respect for you, and all that the two of you done for us."

Irene shook her finger. She almost smiled. "Don't be in such a hurry to refuse the envelopes until you see what's inside."

"I don't understand," Carlo said, taking one envelope. Jake took the other. They both inspected a set of legal documents, unsure of their meaning.

"For your work and your friendship, I've deeded each of you a half acre of ground that borders the vineyard."

"Carlo, did you hear that?" Jake picked Irene up and twirled her around. After her feet hit the ground, Carlo bussed her with a kiss that made her blush.

"Wait, before you get too excited," she said. "Certain conditions go with the deeds."

"Anything you say," they chorused.

"Agree to rent the other half of my duplex. That is, until you build your own houses."

"You bet. Right, Carlo?"

Carlo nodded, too pent up with emotion to say anything worthwhile. In a most uncomfortable way Mario's death had given them this incredible moment.

"There's just one other thing," Irene said. "No smoking in the house, okay?"

"We promise, Irene," Jake said. He managed a hug and kiss before Carlo snatched her away to dance around the yard.

"Our own land," Jake shouted. He leapt from the chair to the table. "Hey world, look at the Baggio brothers. We got our own piece of America."

Carlo watched with his feet grounded, remembering an earlier evening in Chicago when his brother had stood on another table to announce he was changing his name from Giacomo to Jake. Now, four hundred miles away and ten years later they were first-time landowners. So much had happened since he and Jake left Italy, good and bad: his beloved Louisa, then Giulietta and Mario—even Harold and Gus Kramer. All had touched his life, brought him to this moment. He and Jake had finally found their place in America, right here in St. Gregory. First things first, he'd build his own house, and then he'd bring his children home.

Chapter 36
The American Dream

The Repeal of Prohibition brought a resurgence of the corner tavern, which meant Sugg's Roadhouse had lost many of its regular customers including Carlo and Jake who'd been so busy with Irene's duplex they lost touch with the old crowd. After finishing the building project, the brothers made time for an important issue that should've been addressed years before. They became United States citizens, after long evenings with Irene who helped them study for the demanding test.

With the two families comfortably situated in each side of the duplex, the men took it upon themselves to look after Irene and her children. That is, as much as Irene would allow such liberties. In any case the boys adored Jake and Carlo and came to regard them as substitute fathers. At the same time an unspoken understanding developed between the Baggio brothers—Jake decision to pursue Irene with the intention of marriage.

For Carlo to even consider horning in on Jake was unthinkable. Besides, Irene's nerves got on his, not that he would've admitted as much to his brother. Instead Carlo returned to a sanitized version of his old ways, playing the field with the most attractive ladies in town, promising nothing but an entertaining evening.

After a respectable courtship Jake and Irene exchanged their vows in early June of 1935. He was a mature thirty to Irene's thirty-four. When they returned from a three-day honeymoon in St. Louis, Irene offered to look after Carlo's children while he worked at the mine, which was now operating at full capacity—five days a week with occasional overtime.

Had platters of food not been covering Irene's table, Carlo would've jumped on it. Danced like Jake, and shouted to the world that soon he would make a real home for his children.

*****

The next day Carlo sent a wire to Sister Barbara, informing her of his good news, and the day after that he caught the *Abraham Lincoln* to Chicago. He arrived at Holy Guardian Angels to find Mary Ann in tears, not the welcome he'd expected. "Why so sad, little one? I'm taking you and Michael home. I'm just sorry it took so long."

"I don't want to leave, Papa," the nine-year old said between sobs, each one heaving her slender shoulders.

Mary Ann's hair had turned darker than he remembered Louisa's. Damn the fire for destroying the family photographs, for daring to play tricks with memories he didn't want to fade. Carlo smoothed his hand over the curls bouncing from his daughter's head. "What pretty hair. For me, I hope."

"Banana curls, I hate them. *'For special occasions only,'* that's what Sister Barbara said when she pulled and twisted my hair around those silly rag strips." Mary Ann kicked the small suitcase holding her few possessions. Hands went to waist like little ears on a cup. "And this is not a special occasion. What about my friends?"

"You can make new friends. Uncle Jake has two boys now. His wife, your Aunt Irene, promised to look after you while I'm working."

"We'll be a real family?"

"Si. I'll take you on your first train all the way from Chicago to St. Gregory, Michael too." He looked around, eyes settling on Sister Barbara. "Where is my son?"

"Michael's been running a fever for several days, Mr. Baggio." Her face appeared drawn, with an expression speaking more than any words could have.

One of the other nuns whisked Mary Ann away, something about helping with the altar cloths, and Carlo followed Sister Barbara down a long hallway, passing numerous doors until they stopped at the one marked ISOLATION.

"The sign, what does it mean?"

"Just a precaution, Mr. Baggio, to keep the other children from getting sick."

Carlo entered the room, saw that Michael was sleeping and tiptoed toward the bed, only to have Sister Barbara block his path.

"I don't advise physical contact, until we know the extent of Michael's illness."

"Nobody's coming between me and my boy," Carlo said, sidestepping her. He leaned over and kissed Michael's forehead—so warm it reminded him of Louisa's last hours. "Michael, it's me, your papa. I'm here to take you home, just as I promised."

The boy opened his eyes. "Papa, it's really you." Tears trickled down his thin pale face. "I hurt all over. It even hurts to walk and I'm so cold. But I'll be okay tomorrow. Stay one more day, please. Don't leave without me." Michael's feverish hand slipped into his father's, and stayed there until he fell back unto a restless sleep.

Carlo choked back a sob. *Dear God, don't let this happen, not again. Wasn't it enough to take their mother from me?*

The physician who ordered the sign placed on Michael's door told Carlo he'd seen too many similar pediatric cases not to be mistaken.

Michael Baggio: age eight.

Diagnosis: infantile paralysis.

Polio, a parent's worst nightmare, Carlo loosened his tie; his heart started to pound. He wanted to drop to his knees, pray as he'd seen Essie Mae do for her daughter. How could God have played such a cruel trick on him. Worse yet, Michael—so young, so innocent, it was God's way, punishing the child for the sins of his father.

*****

"Proper care will require long-term hospitalization," Doctor Unger told Carlo as they stood outside Michael's hospital room. "If it's any consolation, at least the boy can touch his chin to his knee. In the worse cases … well, some children can't even do that. I can't say how long the treatments will last, or if Michael will ever be cured."

"What about me taking him to a hospital in St. Louis?" Carlo asked, his mind already racing to the logistics of making arrangements.

"You want the best, don't you? Chicago Children's Hospital has one of the most prestigious pediatric facilities in the country, an entire ward dedicated to children with polio."

"I'll get a second job, whatever it takes. I'd move here but there's nobody I trust to look after my little girl. She's nine and I can't leave her alone. There's only a year between her and Michael."

"Leave everything to me, Mr. Baggio. The hospital will waive all fees if you agree to Michael receiving innovative, experimental therapies not being used anywhere else."

Carlo had no choice but to go along with the doctor's advice. He called Fabiola's from a telephone booth at the hospital and told Massimo about Michael.

"Vincenzo ain't here right now," said Massimo. "But I speak for both of us. We will look after Michael as before. For now, take your daughter to her new home and come back when the boy can travel."

After Carlo hung up, he dug in his wallet for a scrap of paper scribbled with another telephone number and placed a second call.

"Roscoe? It's me, Carlo. I'm in Chicago."

"Mister Charlie, what you doing here? Tell me you finally getting those sweet babies of yours."

For the first time in years, Carlo broke down and cried. Then he told Roscoe about Michael.

"Mercy, Almighty God. Not that precious little boy. Now, don't you worry none. Me and Essie Mae'll visit him. Just like we done at the orphanage."

Shortly after Giulietta Bracca's murder the Johnsons had visited Holy Guardian Angels, bearing gifts for Mary Ann and Michael. At first the nuns seemed leery of the Johnsons' interest in the Baggio children; that is, until Carlo vouched for the couple. Soon their periodic visits meant gifts for the other children as well.

Carlo let Roscoe do most of the talking. Near the end of the conversation, Roscoe said, "Mister Charlie, I needs a favor. I knows this ain't the right time to be asking, but it ain't for me I'm asking."

"Anything, Roscoe—you know that."

"It's for Elijah Washington. You know, the cabby what helped the day of your shooting."

"Elijah Washington, I could never forget. What does he need?"

"A job for his nephew, Abraham Washington. He's in Chicago now. Can't go back to *Missippi*. Gots a heap of trouble back there. But not with the police, you understand. Hard working fool, that one."

"I'll do what I can when I get back home."

"Mister Charlie?"

"What?"

"Take Abraham with you."

*****

A week later aboard the *Abraham Lincoln* Carlo closed his eyes to the lull of the train's steady motion and thought of his son. Leaving Michael behind had been the toughest decision he'd ever made. Having put aside his differences with God for now, he prayed this latest setback would soon be resolved. As least he was returning to St. Gregory with his precious Mary Ann. He felt a tug on his sleeve and marveled at the wonderful feeling.

"How much further?" she asked with a yawn.

"We just passed Kankakee. There's still a long way to go."

"Those two boys, my new cousins, what're they like?"

"They promised to look after you, which makes them A-okay with me. Just remember, boys are tough. Girls are special. Right, Abraham?"

"Right Mister Charlie," replied the muscular black man in the seat facing theirs.

He reminded Carlo of *L'Angelo Nero*, only not so cocky. Besides, The Black Angel only showed up when times were bad. Thank God, the angel had seen fit to overlook Michael, at least for now.

"Were you named after this train?" he heard Mary Ann asked Abraham, "or was the train named after you?"

"Train's younger'n both of us," he said. "My name came from President Sixteen. How 'bout you, Mister Charlie?"

"Don't call me Mister Charlie, okay? Not if you want me to get you a job in the mines."

"Nuff said, Mister ... uh, just what is your name?"

"I am Carlo, Carlo Baggio." *Citizen of America and owner of my own piece of the land.*

BOOK THREE

Chapter 37
Michael, 1941

Michael Baggio rarely traveled the nine blocks to St. Sebastian's unless Monsignor Flaherty ran out of altar boys and had to call Mother Superior at Holy Angels for back-up. Today, however, had been Michael's last time to accommodate such a request since this occasion marked the funeral Mass for Monsignor. Only one hour since the final ritual at the cemetery and already he missed the old man, his constant oversight that kept the nuns in line, not that Michael ever gave them reason to reprimand him. He missed Nonna Noreen too. God had called her home the year before. Still, he could rely on Essie Mae and Roscoe who always created a stir at Holy Angels because they never arrived empty-handed. Neither did the uncles—Vincenzo and Massimo, generous to a fault, but at their best when entertaining him at Fabiola's. What a pair. Vincenzo had taught him how to appreciate wine; and Massimo had this thing about noses, always tilting Michael's chin to inspect his profile. "A nose worthy of Michelangelo's David," Zio often said. "Thank God, you were spared the Valenza beak."

Too bad God hadn't spared Michael the aftereffects of polio: pesky breathing problems, weak neck muscles, his left leg withered and one inch shorter than the right; a slight limp made worse when he was tired. Two years living in a hospital, sharing a ward with other kids, some worse off than he was. Two years waiting for the weekly letters from his father and sister, two years without a visit from them. Their lives revolved around coal. When the mine was busy, Papa needed to work; when it wasn't, he couldn't afford to make the trip.

When Father Connelly was on leave from Rome, he made time for Michael. Father Connelly also wrote long letters. So did Mary Ann and Papa. But they wrote about gardening and homework; Father Connelly's letters described the wonders of Rome. Father Connelly had a swell life, serving God and the Vatican in the world's greatest city. Not like Papa, always struggling, hanging on to his little piece of the world—his place in the sun.

Michael wanted his own place.

This afternoon he shifted in a padded chair facing the late monsignor's desk. The door opened and he quickly stood at attention. One comforting hand wrapped around his shoulder, and Michael shook the other hand of Father Connelly. At five feet eight, Michael was as tall as the priest, and still growing. He looked into the blue eyes behind those round spectacles, trying to place their familiarity.

"I'm so glad you requested this quiet time together—what with the funeral and Monsignor's many friends. Sit, Michael, sit."

"You first, Father."

"Ah-h, the nuns have taught you well. I'm impressed."

After both of them took their seats, Michael rested his bony arms on his equally bony knees and leaned forward. "Father Connelly, I have this problem."

Terrence Connelly settled his haunches into the chair. He removed his bifocals and began a meticulous polishing with his handkerchief. The gesture reminded Michael of Monsignor Flaherty, a subtle tactic the old man often employed to gain time before pontificating on what he called erstwhile wisdom. But this time belonged to Father Connelly.

The priest returned his spectacles to his nose. He cleared his throat. "I'm pleased you came to me for advice, Michael. I still remember you and Mary Ann in my daily prayers and will continue to do so after I return to Rome."

"Thanks, Father. I knew I could count on you."

"How old are you now?"

"Going on fifteen, Father."

"Ah, yes, for young men, a difficult age. No longer a child, yet not an adult, so many physical and emotional changes. I suggest you involve yourself in some type of sport." His eyes wandered to Michael's leg before he added, "Even as a spectator, which in itself can be rewarding."

Michael blushed, not for himself but for the priest. "Oh no, Father, it's nothing like that. I was thinking maybe you could help me get into a preparatory school. More than anything, I want to be a priest, just like you. I wouldn't be bothering you about this, but since you're here for the funeral—well, I just thought …."

Michael's voice trailed off. He went to the window and focused his attention outside to the street: some boys batting an old tin can with a broom handle. It was the least he could do for Father Connelly. Any grown man blinking back tears deserved a moment of privacy.

*****

May 1, 1941
Dear Papa,
I send my love to you and Mary Ann and hope you are both well. I know you expect me to move to St. Gregory this summer and go to high school there but I want to stay in Chicago and go to Quigley Prep instead. It's a school for boys who are thinking about becoming priests. Father Connelly took me to visit Quigley during Holy Week. Don't worry about the cost. He can arrange a scholarship to cover most of my expenses.
I pray you will understand and give me permission to serve Our Lord.
Your loving son,
Michael

*****

May 15, 1941
Dear Michael,
My heart is broken that you don't want to come home. Those short summer visits to St. Gregory were never enough. But you needed special treatments and the hospital in Chicago was better than any place around here.
I will not stop you from trying out the seminary if this is what you really want. Just be sure it's not what someone else wants for you.
Your loving Papa
P.S. Mary Ann feels the same as me.

*****

There was a time when Michael wanted nothing more than to crawl after his father and sister, make them take him to St. Gregory. There he was, so sick he couldn't get out of bed and didn't know which hurt more—the pain overtaking his body or the one in his heart. But that was then.

*****

October 4, 1941
Dear Papa,
Quigley sure is swell, and not too different from regular school, except no girls, which I never thought much about until I got here. Now I pray not to think about them.
Guess what? One of my buddies is a fellow named Bobby Seppi. He said you and Uncle Jake used to work for his father in Chicago. Is that so? I never knew you worked at a brewery but I guess there's a lot I don't know. Maybe someday you can tell me how things were in the Twenties.
Thanks for letting me go to school here. I promise to do well and not to let you down.
Your loving son,
Michael

Chapter 38
Mary Ann, May 1942

Mary Ann Baggio gently pulled the brush through her long strands of dark hair. After flipping it from side to side, she winked at her image in the mirror. Blue eyes, what a break, she considered those aquamarine marbles her best feature. Her teeth weren't bad either—not a single cavity, thanks to a diet rich in fruits and vegetables that Aunt Irene insisted she eat before munching on the sweets that called to her every day. She wandered out to the kitchen, checked the wall clock, and decided to wait another two minutes before racing out the door for school, her departure timed to coincide with that of Tony and Frankie Roselli who lived next door. Both were handsome enough to be movie stars—maybe Tyrone Power or Errol Flynn. The brothers could've passed for Uncle Jake's real sons, only taller. Their mother, Aunt Irene, had been the only female in her life since the Ursuline nuns. Poor thing, she'd turned into the world's worst worrywart, which Mary Ann quietly disregarded out of respect for the sweet woman. Living in attached housing made for one big family, although with certain disadvantages—too many people looking after her too much of the time. Just like Holy Angels.

Sometimes Mary Ann felt closer to Tony and Frankie than to her own brother. Dear Michael, stashed away in a preparatory seminary, being told what to do and where to go every minute of his life, now and forever. Of course, she loved him best, but in the seven years since she left Chicago, they'd only seen each other at Christmas and for short vacations. Now that Michael was at Quigley, he couldn't even come home for Christmas—some silly rule about the seminary not wanting their future priests attached to family life. As bad as that bugaboo about keeping them away from girls so they wouldn't fall into a pit of temptation. Now, Michael came in January when everyone else was back in school.

Tony and Frankie and Mary Ann: tight as a trio playing solo, Uncle Jake used to call them. Then, last year Tony turned seventeen and started dating so he didn't have time for her anymore. Worse yet, he treated her like a kid, something Frankie would never do. She and Frankie were the same age, sixteen. They talked about everything, until Tony dragged him away from her. What a dope. At that rate their trio may never play sweet music again, especially with Tony leaving for boot camp after graduation.

Damn the war—already going on for six months, ever since Pearl Harbor. Papa said the whole country's behind President Roosevelt because he pulled us out of a depression. And now these posters of Uncle Sam, pointing his finger at every young man and saying, "I want you!" All the newspapers agree America's going to beat the Japs and the Nazis, even the Italians. Beating the Italians seems strange. Papa doesn't have any family left over there, but there are uncles and cousins on Mama's side. Tony and Frankie have cousins in Italy too. What if Tony winds up fighting his own blood and doesn't know it?

Time. Mary Ann shoved the war worries into her closet, along with the slippers Aunt Irene wanted her to keep out of sight. She hurried outside, ran down the steps, and called out to the brothers.

Neither turned around although Frankie did slow down.

"Come on, Tony," he said. "We'd better wait for Mary Ann. You know how she gets when we ignore her."

"Yeah, same as when we don't. She'll tell Papa and Papa will tell Jake and Jake will tell Ma …."

They both stopped.

"And Ma will bawl us out," Frankie said with a laugh.

"So, what else is new."

"Aw, Mary Ann's not so bad. Besides, she thinks you're the tops."

"Me? She's still a kid. More your size, little brother." Tony gave him a friendly shove.

"Hey, I ain't lagging that far behind you." Friendly shove returned.

"I meant your head, Frankie ... the one sitting on top your shoulders." Tony maneuvered Frankie into a headlock and using his knuckles, applied an invigorating dutch rub to Frankie's scalp that didn't end until Mary Ann caught up with them.

"Thanks for nothing." she said. "I told you to knock on the wall when you were ready to leave. You know Papa doesn't like me walking to school by myself."

*****

The plans for Tony's commencement celebration soon evolved into that of a farewell before his departure for boot camp. On the day of the party Jake and Carlo assembled their jugs of Dago Red, as they fondly referred to the wine Irene had finally consented to their making, two years after Prohibition had ended. For this special day and between frequent outbursts of tears, she pushed herself to roll out enough pasta dough for seven hundred ravioli filled with ground meat, spinach, and a domestic version of the Romano cheese they used to buy from Italy. Besides the ravioli, she planned on serving salami, ham, potato salad, green salad, and a variety of breads and locally produced cheeses. Although the government started rationing sugar in April, she had squirreled away enough to bake Tony's favorite chocolate cake. Butter cream icing decorated the sheet cake in the form of an American flag, which she somehow squeezed all forty-eight stars into the blue section.

Irene assigned Carlo and Jake the task of stringing Chinese lanterns and patriotic decorations in the backyard. While Carlo held the base of the ladder and tossed up supplies, Jake moved between the second-from-the-top rung and various tree limbs, tacking crepe paper streamers onto the posts and corners.

"Watch your step," Carlo said. "Watch it ... not there ... to your left more."

"I only got a couple more pieces to connect," Jake said. "These red, white, and blue colors are just the right touch."

"Dammit. Tony and Frankie oughta be doing this shit."

"Irene gave Tony the day off so he could bum around town. She put Frankie to work cleaning windows with Mary Ann." Wobbling on the ladder, he connected paper to a distant post. "Okay, that's the last streamer."

"So get the hell down before you kill yourself, and me."

After Jake bounced down the ladder, he stepped back to view his handiwork. "Not bad, not bad. I just wish the party was for a different reason. Remember the two of us coming to America to start a new life? We were younger than Tony."

"And never had to fight a war."

They moved the ladder away from the house, maneuvered it onto the grass, and Carlo lifted one end. "Grab the other end," he told Jake. "You're lucky you didn't get killed."

"If anything happens to Tony, I don't know what Irene would do, me either for that matter. Him, I love like he was my own. Hell, he is mine. Frankie too."

"You're damn lucky," Carlo said. "Me too."

"Not lucky. Blessed."

"If you say so."

*****

That evening Tony said his goodbyes to nearly one hundred guests: classmates and their parents, miners who first worked with Mario then Jake and Carlo, Irene's friends from church, even Father Clancy, pastor of All Saints.

"That corner piece with all the icing will do just fine, thank you," Father Clancy told Irene while she was cutting the flag cake into precise squares. "So, is there a special girl Tony's leaving behind? I've not seen him at Mass with anyone."

"No, no, Father. And it's just as well." She handed him the slice he requested and excused herself to reach for her trusty handkerchief. "Leaving family is tough enough without worrying about a girlfriend too. You heard about Sammy Falio, didn't you?" Before the priest could answer, she went on, "He received a *'Dear John.'* Can you believe it? While he's in the Pacific fighting for our country, his wife finds herself another man, a 4-F at that. Poor Sammy, he deserves better."

By ten o'clock most of the guests were giving Tony their final best wishes, which consisted of backslapping, awkward hugs, and more stilted words.

"Looks like the party's breaking up," Carlo said. He poured himself another glass of Dago Red and raised his eyebrows to Jake.

Jake responded with two vertical fingers to his empty glass. "It's just as well. I'm setting the alarm for four, which should be enough time to get Tony to Scott Field by six."

"Irene, you going with us?" Carlo asked, ignoring Jake's poke to the shin.

"I'll make breakfast, but I'm saying my goodbye from the kitchen door." She pulled out a fresh handkerchief and started another cry.

*****

Mary Ann was among those drifting away from the party, along with a friend from school named Gayle Chambers. Wearing her hair in a shoulder length pageboy, a la Veronica Lake, Gayle had turned heads in her flowered sundress with spaghetti straps, wedgie shoes and an ankle bracelet, a sharp contrast to Mary Ann's navy blue swing skirt and white blouse trimmed with a peter pan collar. Mary Ann had told her papa that Gayle's parents owned Chambers Drugstore, which boasted the town's only soda fountain counter. For extra leverage, she was prepared to explain how Mr. and Mrs. Chambers worked twelve-hour days, six-day weeks, but she didn't have to go that far. Papa didn't even balk about giving her permission to spend the night.

She and Gayle had strolled to the yard's end when Frankie came dogging after her. "Hey, Cuz, where're you going at this hour?"

Mary Ann rolled her eyes. "Sorry, Gayle. This'll just take a minute." She walked over to Frankie. "Uh-h ... to spend the night with my friend."

"Maybe you should sleep in your own bed. Gayle Chambers is wa-ay too fast for you."

"I know what I'm doing, Frankie. Gayle is a whole bunch of fun. Besides, Papa doesn't care."

"Well that's 'cause your papa doesn't know beans about Gayle."

"Get your finger out of my face. It's only for one night."

"She has a reputation."

"Mind your own beeswax. How many times do I have to say this: you are not the boss of me."

Mary Ann stomped off, grumbling about Frankie acting like a big brother, which he wasn't and never would be.

"Oh, pooh on Frankie No Fun," said Gayle as she flipped the peek-a-boo wave from her eyes. "Kid, you and me will have one super duper time tonight. I hope you don't mind: I told some fellas they could catch up with us later."

"How much later?"

"What's the diff? This one guy's crazy to meet you. He saw you coming out of the drugstore last Friday, said you had nice gams."

"No kidding? He said that about my legs?"

"Cross my heart." Gayle crossed hers.

"It's almost ten-thirty," Mary Ann said. "Maybe we should do that another time. Besides, what about your parents?"

"Silly. We tell Momsy and Popsy goodnight on the way to my room. As soon as they hit the sack, we sneak out the window."

"But what if they catch us?"

"Trust me, they won't. Consider tonight our patriotic duty. Uncle Sam could call up these guys and pfft, they're gone."

"I don't even know them."

"Oh but you will."

Mary Ann fell into step with Gayle and as they walked she thought about Papa being too strict, too Old Country. Worse yet, Aunt Irene throwing a conniption if she ever found out, what with Tony going away to God only knows where. If Frankie hadn't acted like such a know-it-all, Mary Ann might have backed down, but not now. Anyway, this boy had admired her from a distance; it might be fun letting him admire her up close.

*****

At the Chambers stucco bungalow Mary Ann parroted Gayle's cheery goodnight to the middle-aged Momsy and Popsy sitting in the living room, their ears cocked to the radio for the latest war news. After Gayle closed her bedroom door, she tuned in the radio to Raymond Gram and his swing music.

"Stuff those pillows under the covers," she told Mary Ann. "You know, to look like we're sleeping. I'll scatter some clothes around, just in case my folks check on us."

At eleven o'clock the light under the master bedroom door went dark. Another ten minutes passed before Mary Ann followed Gayle through her bedroom window. As they walked down the deserted street, Mary Ann caught a glimpse of two flashes in the distance, followed by the red glow of cigarettes. Two shadowy silhouettes came into focus.

"Our dates," Gayle said.

"Not dates, acquaintances of yours," Mary Ann replied.

When Gayle introduced Coy Eaglestone and Rollie Tyler, Mary Ann didn't recognize either name from elementary or high school. Rollie put his arm around Gayle; he hugged her in a familiar way. From what little the moonlight revealed Mary Ann wasn't impressed with his fleshy wet lips, pasty skin, or stringy brown hair.

Or when he said, "Let's go someplace where we can dance."

"I'd better not. If this ever got back to Papa ...."

"Don't worry," said the guy called Coy. His voice rambled behind the cigarette. His face she couldn't make out. "This place is more like a private club. There's even a jukebox. A pretty girl like you, I bet that skirt of yours has some swing to it."

"I do like to dance, especially the jitterbug. But it's kind of late." She nudged Gayle. "Maybe we should go back."

"For crying out loud, Mary Ann, it's okay; they're okay. I wouldn't say so if I thought otherwise."

Mary Ann's silence was taken as a yes. They walked in pairs down McKinley Street with Rollie and Gayle in the lead. Coy slipped his arm around Mary Ann; she wiggled free. He sulked through one cigarette and lit another before he spoke. "You hang out at Chamber's, don't you."

"Sometimes," she said. "I never saw you there."

"That's 'cause I'm across the street, working at the hardware store. I ain't no drugstore cowboy, you know. Some of us have to work for a living."

When they turned onto the hard road leading out of town, a streetlight gave Mary Ann a better view of Coy: limp hair the color of straw and dirty dishwater; husky enough to play football player, but not much taller than her five feet five. "I work at home when I'm not in school," she said.

"I quit two years ago. I'm joining up when I turn eighteen."

A set of approaching headlights came barreling down the road. Mary Ann shielded her eyes from the glare, and Rollie told everybody to move back into the bushes so they wouldn't get hit. As soon as the car passed, they returned to the gravel easement.

"How much further to this place?" Mary Ann asked.

"Hold your horses, kid. We're almost there," Gayle said as she leveled her finger forward. "See, up ahead."

What Mary Ann saw was a dilapidated roadhouse, its broken windows crisscrossed with nailed boards. "Didn't this used to be Sugg's? The place is falling down."

"Don't be silly," Gayle said. "I've been here before and had loads of fun."

"You girlies wait here," said Rollie. "Me and Coy'll go in through a special entrance. We'll come back for you."

They disappeared around the side of the building, and Mary Ann swiped her hand across an exposed windowpane.

"I don't know, Gayle. It looks kind of creepy inside."

"As in Bella Lugosi? You watch too many movies, kid."

Their discussion ended with the toot of a horn: Dennis Briggs driving by in the family Chevy. Not a good sign; Mary Ann had seen him earlier at the party. "Shoot. If he tells Tony or Frankie …."

"Don't worry," Gayle said. "Denny won't say a word. Not with what I know about him."

"Denny? What'd he do?"

Before Gayle could answer, Rollie opened the door and motioned them inside. "We'll use these candles instead of the electricity. It's nifty lighting for dancing and afterwards."

"Afterwards?" Mary Ann walked through a door that closed before she could change her mind.

"Mary Ann, quit your worrying," Gayle said. "There's nobody here but the four of us."

Mary Ann looked around the one-time stopover for the town's men. The top of the sorry bar bore the scars of hard use and good times. The shelves were stripped of the usual assortment of glassware and colorful bottles of liquor she knew from the family taverns Papa favored for fish on Friday evenings. Behind the bar, a smeared, dusty mirror reflected the need for re-silvering. Chairs piled on top of black square tables resembled contrived displays of art. At least there was a dance floor—its once-glossy varnish now worn down to bare wood. Off in one corner the loaded jukebox waited for the sound of clinking nickels to make things happen.

"Didn't I say it was real private," Coy said. "Damn. We can't play the jukebox if there's no electricity, but that don't mean we can't dance." He started poking through some rubble in the corner. "But first, let's have something to drink—on my favorite uncle."

"Your uncle?"

"Uncle Jack Daniels, who'd you think?" Rollie held up the fifth with one hand. He took a swig before passing the bottle on to Gayle. She had a gulp, big enough to show it wasn't her first, and passed it on to Coy.

The Jack Daniels stopped in front of Mary Ann. She shook her head. "I don't drink that stuff."

"Whadaya mean? All you dagos drink, don't kid me." Rollie grabbed the bottle for another swig.

"Yeah, what about all that Dago Red?" Coy said, taking his turn before Gayle. "You grape-stomping Eye-talians drink more wine than milk."

"Maybe with our meals …."

"You don't have to chug-a-lug. Just take a sip," Gayle said. "See, watch me."

"I've seen enough." Mary Ann headed for the door only to be cut off by Coy, arms crossing his chest as he blocked her way.

"You ain't going nowhere," he said. "Least ways not 'til you have one little drink. Just one."

"Okay, one sip, then I'm leaving."

Rollie grabbed her hair from behind, pulled her head back. Coy shoved the bottle to her lips and sent a swallow down her throat. She gagged and sputtered and coughed it up. "Don't … ever … do … that again."

"Come on, Miss Goody Two-Shoes, take another swig."

Mary Ann knocked the bottle out of Coy's hand. He let out a cuss word, lifted her swing skirt and snatched the crotch of her panties. No one had ever touched her there before.

"Holy Mother!" She yanked free, ran for the door.

"Hey, not so fast," Coy said. "Where do you think you're going?" He lunged forward, catching the back of her blouse. From the front every button bounced to the floor, scattering like so many marbles.

"Now how am I supposed to explain this to my aunt?" Mary Ann clutched her blouse; Coy gripped her arm.

"Come on, don't be a scaredy cat," he said. "Didn't we promise you a good time?"

"Gayle, please. Let's get out of here."

"Hey, speaking of good times, where's mine?" Rollie said as he steered Gayle toward an open doorway. "Come on, I got the red hots for you."

Gayle stuck out her lower lip, pouted in mock disappointment. "But I wanted to watch the cherry bust."

Mary Ann could've smacked her, if only Coy ….

"Not tonight, Gayle," said Rollie. "This dickie of mine is itching for some scratching. Let's do a boing, boing on the sweet green."

Arm in arm, Rollie and Gayle strolled into the billiards room, leaving Mary Ann to grapple with Coy. Locked in his grip, she could feel what she'd only heard about from others—the pressure of an erection. She wanted to throw up. When Coy managed to plant a sloppy kiss on her tongue, she chomped down on his lip as hard as she could. Coy yelped like an injured dog. She spit out his blood. He slapped her across the face, hard enough to bring tears.

"Cockteaser!"

After hitting him, she almost made it to the door but he tackled her from behind. She was crawling when he flipped her over, pinned her down, and yanked her blouse open. "Please let me go, Coy. I won't tell a soul. I promise."

"What's to tell? You sneaked out. Nobody dragged you here. Come on ... don't be such a baby." He ripped through her petticoat, reached down into her bra, and squeezed tight with both hands.

"Oh, ba-a-by, you are so ready."

Not her *pupe*—no way, those gems she'd been saving for a precious moment. Basta! She jammed her knee into his crotch.

Coy moaned. He freed up one hand to check his fading erection.

Then the door flew open with a bang. Mary Ann saw Frankie, his face like that of a wild man

"Let go of her," he yelled, "you no-good dirty bastard."

Tony was right behind him. "I'll kill you. I swear I will by all that is holy."

Mary Ann scrambled to her feet, blouse hanging from the elbows, her skirt covered with dust balls. While Tony and Coy were exchanging punches, Frankie's face registered disbelief as he stared at Mary Ann until she turned and ran outside.

She found Denny Briggs sitting behind the wheel of his Chevy. He motioned her to get in the back and had the courtesy to keep his eyes on the windshield while he flipped a windbreaker over the seat. "Here, you better put this on."

"Denny, thank God you came back. Gayle said you wouldn't tell anybody, but I'm awfully glad you did."

"Gayle's full of it," Denny said. "I came here with her and Rollie one time. Once was enough. I figured you were headed for trouble when I saw you with her."

"Don't tell anybody else, Denny. You won't, will you?"

Before Denny had a chance to answer Mary Ann, the back door opened and Frankie slid in beside her. She couldn't bear to look at him, not if it meant seeing what she'd seen before.

"Dammit, Frankie, don't say I told you so. Don't tell my father.

Don't tell your mother. And don't tell Uncle Jake."

"Hey, it's me: Frankie. What do you take me for?"

She started crying when he put his arms around her. For the first time that night she felt safe. With Frankie, she'd always feel that way. "About Gayle ...."

"Forget about Gayle. She's riding some guy on the billiard table."

"Oh my gosh ... I forgot about Tony."

"Don't worry about Tony. He's wiping the bar clean with that other jerk."

Chapter 39
June 1943

The setting sun had cast an array of red-orange over the Roselli vineyard as evening breezes stirred trees surrounding the two-family duplex, now in its tenth year of housing the combined Roselli and Baggio families. Carlo sprawled his ropey frame over the porch steps and Jake leaned forward, both smoking banned-from-the-house-cigarillos, a comforting routine they still enjoyed at the end of every day. Carlo's eyes wandered over to the creaking swing that placated Irene, strands of gray streaking through her dark mane. She gazed into the sunset, her lips silently moving as she fingered the beads of her crystal rosary, a comforting routine she began the day Tony left for basic training. According to Tony's last letter, which arrived in late February, he was somewhere in France, which could've meant a battlefront, behind enemy lines, or worse.

And now Frankie's turn had come. He was due to report to Scott Field in the morning, thirteen months after Tony's departure. For Frankie, there'd be no farewell party; he told his mother to save the celebration for when he returned. Irene seemed relieved, not that anyone blamed her since some of the farewell party honorees were now returning in flag-draped boxes. Thank God Irene had married Jake. He kept her grounded and made a good father for Mario's boys. Carlo hardly thought about that horrible night anymore, unless he heard the clang of the firehouse bell. Nor did he think about *L'Angelo Nero* who only showed up when times were so bad they needed fixing.

The screen door banged and the swing stopped creaking as Frankie strolled onto the porch. He barely pecked his mother's cheek and she patted his with one weary hand. To Jake, he grinned and held out his open palm. Jake tossed him a ring of keys, for the Ford he bought used three years before.

"Be careful," Jake said. "You know how your Ma worries."

"Not too late," Carlo said, withholding his usual smile for the young man, more like a son than his own Michael. "I worry too, about my Mary Ann."

She came running out of the house, blew a flurry of mid-air kisses, and hopped into the car with Frankie. The two of them took off, leaving a trail of dust in their wake. If only Louisa could've lived to see Mary Ann—their American daughter with the sassy mouth and confident strut. She just needed to keep her head on straight. Was that asking too much of her or God or whoever was in charge of such things.

After Irene finished with her Godly beads and the Blessed Virgin, she went into the house to pour some lemonade, not that he or Jake cared one way or the other. Carlo blew a few smoke rings before he said what was on his mind. "So, whadaya think, Jake?"

"About what?"

"About those two—Frankie and my daughter."

"Let's get through this damn war before we start thinking about those two."

"I mean about those two, tonight."

"Come on, Frankie and Mary Ann?" Jake said. "They're practically brother and sister."

"Brother and sister, they ain't. Never were. Where you been the past year?"

"You know he'd never do anything to hurt her."

"This much I know for sure: tonight they're alone; tomorrow he goes to soldier school."

"For crissake. If you feel that way, you should've stopped her."

"She's growing up, Jake, this I can't stop."

But Carlo had extracted a promise from Frankie, one he knew Frankie wouldn't break.

*****

In the back booth of Chamber's Drugstore Frankie and Mary Ann sat huddled over two straws stuck in a cherry coke ice cream soda. The place was jumping with their high school friends: jitterbugging to the jukebox Andrews Sisters and later slow dancing to Glen Miller's Band. Without exception, every person stopped by to shake Frankie's hand and wish him luck. Mary Ann tolerated the usual pats on the shoulder, sometimes accompanied by a sympathetic squeeze.

"I need fresh air," she finally said. "Let's get out of here."

Frankie checked his watch, a graduation gift from his mother and Jake. "Okay, but we can't stay out too late. I promised your papa."

"How sweet," Mary Ann said with a wink, "that leaves just enough time for a drive through Morgan Woods."

Back in the car Frankie kept his hands on the wheel and his eyes on the road while Mary Ann messed with his hair and talked nonstop about things that didn't matter. Her chatter petered out when he turned off the hard road. After driving another mile, he pulled into a secluded clearing, near the edge of a wooded site named after one of the town's founding fathers. In the course of fifteen seconds, he turned off the motor, set the emergency brake, and took her into his arms. He closed his eyes to the sweet fragrance of the Ivory Soap she always used.

"There's more room in the back, what do you say?" she whispered, as if the trees and creatures of the night might hear and register their disapproval.

Not waiting for his answer, she crawled over the seat, and Frankie followed. When he held her again, she starting crying the tears she'd been choking back at Chamber's.

"Oh, Frankie, I can't believe this night is finally here. Our last chance to share the love we have for each other."

"Don't say that. I'm coming back, God willing."

"But just in case you don't, I want to remember this night forever and a day." She knelt on the seat, leaned over, and pushed her tongue in his mouth. While they exchanged saliva, her hand slipped down his waistband and she wrapped her fingers around his balls. God, he loved the feeling, so much that he forced himself to pull her hand out, broke the suction of their kiss, and pressed his head against the steamy window.

She sat back. With tears rolling down her cheeks, she spoke between sobs. "Don't … do this to me, Frankie. I … love you…with my whole heart and soul. You're … the center of my life … my hero … every single day since we first met."

"I love you too. There could never be anyone else." They kissed again, with the same intensity as before, which brought more tears from Mary Ann. Frankie straightened up and forced a soft laugh. "Hey, enough with the waterworks, okay? This is no way to end our last night."

"I'll show you how it should end, Frankie."

She grabbed his hand and guided it under her dress, held it to the inviting warmth between her legs, a place he'd only dreamed about until that moment. He wanted to stay there, to bury himself inside her. God knows he wanted every inch of her. But he'd promised Carlo, more than once. And his mom expected as much. So did Jake. He pulled his hand free, brought it to the surface, and patted her dress back in place.

"Chicken shit," Mary Ann blurted out. She followed up with a stinging slap to his face.

He grabbed the offending hand, kissed her damp palm. "Come on, Mary Ann. You have to know how much I want you—more than anything in this whole damn world. But it has to be the right time, the right place. You're too special for the back seat of a jalopy."

"The place doesn't matter. Our love would make it special."

"When I come back, we'll have the whole nine yards—a big church wedding and all of St. Gregory celebrating with us."

"And what about me? I want you, here and now. Tonight, Frankie, tonight. How can you leave me like this?"

Frankie answered by moving back to the front seat. He turned the key in the ignition, trying to drown out Mary Ann's spiteful words from behind.

"I hate you, St. Francis ... St. Francis the Sissy. I hate you for turning me down. For treating me like some pathetic tramp. I'll never forgive you, Frankie No Fun. Never, never, never."

Chapter 40
Normandy, France 1944

Dear God, any place but here. Not that PFC Frank Roselli had any choice as to where he would be fighting his first battle—in this case, Omaha Beach on June 7. Dawn had yet to break on D-Day Plus One when Frankie jumped from his LCI into the chest-high waters bordering Normandy's coastline. The nineteen-year-old was one GI among the thousands of reinforcements assigned to follow General Omar Bradley's 29th Division. Those poor bastards had landed the day before, the unfortunate casualties of Bradley's First Army.

Frankie held his M1 Garand overhead as he waded in the direction of sand. The sun had yet to come over the horizon, not that it mattered. Sporadic mortar and sniper fire from the enemy's rear position managed to illuminate the gray sky, giving Frankie a clear view of water strewn with the 29th, plus too many of those who had just landed. *Dear God, bodies everywhere.* He brushed past his dead comrades, nudged a combat boot. Shit, the foot was still inside. His stomach flipped and churned, producing an indigestible mix of disgust and shame.

Damn the flying shit. Keep moving, or wind up like these poor, broken bastards—he'd pray for them later. Frankie's immediate concern was the beach, getting there in one piece. God willing, he wouldn't take any shitfire, enemy or friendly, along the way. What the hell, survival boiled down to the luck of the draw. Move the wrong way and walk into a random shot. Bang, you're dead.

Up ahead, water rolled into sand, exposing a graveyard of mutilated GIs. Their numbers too great to comprehend; their bloated remains scattered among the remains of landing crafts and military paraphernalia, an eerie testimony to what had transpired twenty-four hours earlier. Frankie hit the sand running. The stench of burnt flesh assaulted his nostrils. He stumbled and fell, onto what? Sweet Jesus, a baby-faced soldier, history now. Vacant eyes stared in astonishment, as if relaying the horror they'd been forced to witness. Frankie rolled to his knees and out of respect, turned his head. After heaving up yesterday's k-rations, he made a sign of the cross, as much for himself as for the fallen heroes.

Their fleeting mortality reminded Frankie of a bizarre place he learned about in the eighth grade. He pictured Sister Agnes strolling around the classroom, rosary beads swinging from her ample waist. She spoke in an Irish brogue that distinguished her from the town's other immigrants. This day she lowered her voice to a near whisper as she described a certain church in Rome.

"It's called the Chapel of the Bones, boys and girls. Housed within the Church of the Immaculate Conception is a crypt dedicated to centuries of deceased Capuchin monks." She stopped at Frankie's desk, opened a large book of photographs, and held it up. "As you can see, their bleached bones—too numerous to count—have been assembled into the walls and floors of various room displays. Even into chandeliers. Some skeletons remain intact and wear the Order's coffee-colored habits." Sister directed her plump finger to the pointed hoods concealing skulls and profiles. "Outstretched skeletal hands beckon the curious visitors to indulge themselves. No need to hurry here they seem to say."

Frankie leaned forward for a better view, but one row over Charlotte Evans gasped and uttered two words, "How disgusting."

"No, Charlotte, 'tis the reality of our physical existence," Sister replied. "Now, if you please, allow me to continue. Here in the museum, among the Capuchin, time is no longer of the essence." She turned the page to more bones. "Posted on a wall in the last room is a Latin inscription, written in flawless calligraphy. The monks left us this message; one I challenge all of you to remember." Swishing in her long black habit, she went to the blackboard and using the Palmer Method—which none of the boys could master—she wrote in chalk, transcribing the words into English:

What you are now, we used to be; what we are now, you will become.

Enough, Sister Agatha, PFC Roselli thought, someday yes, but not this day. He banished the prophetic verse from his brain and scrambled to his feet.

"Move it, soldier. Head for cover," a voice called out from behind. "Don't look at them. Don't think about them. We're not going to be them."

The order came from Sergeant Lawrence Winters. He and Frankie first met in England, where Sarge was recuperating from an injury sustained in Sicily and Frankie from an emergency appendectomy that had separated him from his unit. Sarge had enlisted in the army the day after Pearl Harbor and Normandy would be his second tour of duty. The Montana cowboy wore a face ten years older than its twenty-one, but the early aging didn't result from constant exposure to the Western sun or the bitter winds. "No amount of R & R could ever return my lost youth," he once told Frankie, "not after Sicily."

Frankie continued to dodge bullets while friendly machine guns and mortars punctured the sides of cliffs that created a natural backdrop for the beach. The barrage went on for hours, allowing the infantry to continue their steady infiltration. In the afternoon when the shelling had temporarily subsided and before the removal of bodies began, three chaplains conducted a service for the dead. Sharing a makeshift altar, they led prayers in the Protestant, Catholic, and Jewish faiths.

Frankie prayed too, for those folks back home who were praying for the safe return of their loved ones, not knowing the time had come to pray for their souls instead. Heart-wrenching reality would come in the form of regrets from the military. He made another sign of the cross for his own family—Mom and Jake, the best stepdad a guy could want, and of course for Tony. He crossed himself again, this time for Mary Ann. She wrote the day after he left, begging forgiveness for her silly behavior on their last night together. Frankie No Fun, she called him when he turned her down. He'd wanted her but she was such a kid. So was he, then.

And what was with Tony, no word from him for months. Had his first taste of war been any worse than this? Damn, Frankie missed his brother as much as he missed Mary Ann, but in a different way. Prior to enlisting, he and Tony hadn't traveled beyond the coal mining towns of Southern Illinois. They knew their place, and had always bummed with their own kind. Not like the soldier who stood beside him now—his new best friend, PFC Ato Racine.

The half-Cherokee from Oklahoma pronounced his name A-toe but some guy had shortened it to Toe and the new handle stuck tighter than wallpaper paste. During a barroom brawl in Alva, he came to the aid of a down-and-out drunkard getting knocked around by a guy half his age and twice his size. Toe wrestled away the bully's knife and managed to get in a few nicks before the sheriff broke up the fight. He gave Toe a choice of early enlistment or jail time. The next morning Toe signed up at the local recruiting station and by nightfall he took his first train ride to basic training.

Next to Toe, Private Gordon Dean of Bay City, Michigan was performing his usual tic, a lifting of his right shoulder to massage the neighboring ear. Rub ... two, three ... release. Rub ... two, three ... release. Once more, now scratch the nose. Again, the nose. Dean stood five feet six, same as Toe, but he could never measure up to the Cherokee. From behind coke-bottle spectacles Dean's darting green eyes magnified fear the rest of the platoon tried to hide. To them, he spelled d-u-d, a bona fide, casualty-prone reject that had no business on the frontline. Dean didn't seem to mind their rejection, so long as he could hang close to Toe.

Because Toe Racine allowed Dean to walk in his footsteps, Frankie tolerated him too. What the hell, so the guy ranked lower than most earthworms. Every family was cursed with some version of Dean, every family except his. This war had dumped a bunch of mismatched guys together and out of desperation they formed a pseudo family that shared one common goal—staying alive long enough to make it back to the real thing.

Frankie tuned back into the prayer service.

"We'll close with a reading of the Twenty-third Psalm," one of the chaplains said. Not the priest, Frankie thought maybe the rabbi.

Rabbi got as far as, 'Surely goodness and mercy shall follow us,' when a shot erupted from a fissure in the bluff. Some second lieutenant—who once bummed a cigarette from Frankie the non-smoker—dropped with a hole between his eyes. A machine gunner fired his round into the narrow opening. The sniper fell screaming from his bushy perch while several more ground shots, including one from Toe, nailed Jerry before he hit the sand. A chorus of simultaneous *amens* concluded the ceremony as units hurried to the base of the cliff.

"Dig those foxholes deep, twice as deep as you think they ought to be," ordered Lieutenant Lancaster. "Later tonight we'll work our way up the bluff. When we reach the plateau, there's less than a quarter mile between them and us. Those Jerries are bottled up in what's known as hedgerows, or as I prefer—hellrows. Our job is to flush out the enemy, like shit from a toilet."

"How we gonna do that, sir?"

"Rush and attack, soldier. Rush and attack."

"How many of these hedgerows we gotta take, sir?"

"All of them, however long it takes."

Everybody knew the lieutenant had graduated from Yale and taught European history, not that he bragged about either. He did acknowledge some understanding of hedgerows and a fair amount of experience fighting Germans, but when it came to fighting Germans holed up in French hedgerows, he didn't have much to offer. According to certain scuttlebutt, neither did any other American officer leading troops in this invasion.

"Sir, about these hedgerows—"

"Dammit, Dean. Shut up and keep digging."

"I am, but I just thought—"

"Don't think," Sarge growled through the Camel dangling from his mouth. "It's bad for morale.

"He's twitching again."

"About the hedgerows," Lieutenant Lancaster said in his teacher voice. "Think square, rectangular or irregular land boundaries and cattle holdings. Centuries-old mounds of earth, taller than most of you and covered by vegetation. And tunnels and mazes with singular entrances."

"What's our chance of penetrating them, Sir?" Frankie asked.

"Nearly impossible but that never stopped hell-bent GIs before."

*****

Two days and a quarter mile later Frankie counted himself among twelve men advancing on their first hedgerow. While artillery from both sides lit up a sky gone dark with the setting sun, rifle and machine gun coverage from the rear failed to budge the enemy from within. Three lead soldiers dashed in a zigzag pattern through the open area, trying to get close enough to launch an assault. Frankie nearly shit when the first two scattered into the wind, blown away by their own grenades. The third lay moaning in the open field. "My legs ... dear god, help me, my legs. Somebody ...."

"Cover, me, Frankie" Toe Racine took off on his belly. "I'm going after him."

"Dammit, PFC, stay where you are!" shouted Sarge over the steady barrage of artillery.

Toe kept moving.

"Bastard Krauts!" Dean yelled while Frankie continued firing. Other than Toe, Frankie considered himself the platoon's best marksman but shooting into an overgrown brush fortress was no way to show off.

While machine gunfire sprayed within inches of his helmet, Toe crawled toward the injured soldier. He grabbed Kern under one arm and retraced his route, ignoring an endless volley of bullets erupting from the hedgerow. Not once did he look back. When he reached the safety of his trench, he cracked a half-smile. "Damn rough out there, Sarge, but I got him."

"Let go, soldier." Sarge said. Frankie knew why but couldn't bring himself to speak up.

"He'll be okay, don't you think?" When Sarge didn't answer, Toe glanced around, and realized he'd been pulling a dead man.

"Don't ever do a stupid-ass thing like that again, Racine," Sarge said, loud enough for every soldier within earshot. "You'll get plenty of chances to play the hero when it counts."

The aborted first charge served its purpose by drawing enemy fire and locating their positions. The rear retaliated with an all out offense of mortar and machine gun fire. Meanwhile, Frankie, Toe, and five others repeated their advance—first running, then creeping, moving closer and closer until they gained enough ground to toss grenades into the hedgerow sides and open them up. With help from a constant barrage of artillery and hand grenades, they finally charged the barricade.

Frankie went in screaming senseless obscenities, as much to fuel his courage as to distract the Jerries. When he looked into the face of a young German, the soldier's fear mirrored his own. Like gunfighters out of a B Western, both men froze, each waiting for the other to make the first move. Frankie couldn't pull the trigger, not like this. In his moment of doubt a shot fired from behind. Ato Racine had relieved him of his first kill. Frankie would not have the luxury of hesitation the next time, or the next. Soon after he killed two Jerries, the skirmish ended. He slumped down and ran his hand over beads of sweat prickling his face. Squinting through cloudy eyes, he checked out his hand. Blood! At least it wasn't his. He rubbed his hand into the dirt, clawed his nails even deeper.

"First time's always the roughest," said the Lieutenant. "After that, you learn not to think about it."

Frankie couldn't even muster a nod. Already he felt nothing but fatigue and overwhelming relief. He was still alive. Seven of his comrades were dead. His squad had captured its first hedgerow. They took no prisoners.

Two days and four hedgerows later after settling into a recently commandeered maze, the GIs understood why their attacks had been so frustrating and the natural defense of the hedgerows so valuable. Every man listened when Lieutenant Lancaster reiterated his earlier objective. They were going to push back the German front by taking the damn hellrows one by one. However long it took.

*****

For the next seven weeks the GIs captured two hedgerows a day, each time advancing further into the German occupation. Besides the hedgerows, they fought for control of any structure dotting the fertile countryside—stone farmhouses, stone barns, and stone walls—whatever provided protection. Their aggression improved with experience and the arrival of Sherman tanks. These American vehicles lacked the power of German Tigers or Panthers, but were more plentiful, and their smaller size proved advantageous for maneuvering in compact areas separating the hedgerows. By the end of the eighth week Frankie considered himself a seasoned infantryman, one who knew his fate rested on the whim of enemy fire. He was one of twelve riflemen from his original platoon of thirty-six. The rest were either dead or hospitalized with serious injuries.

On one overcast day the battle-weary survivors trudged behind a Sherman as it advanced on the next hedgerow. A radioman rode low on the tank's back and transmitted target areas he spotted from the enemy's return fire. The Sherman repeatedly took aim and fired, creating gaping holes in what once had seemed impenetrable. After the band of men got closer, Frankie pulled the first pin and hurled his grenade into the stronghold. More grenades followed, creating a chaotic scene of dismemberment and agonizing screams amid artillery fire from overhead. The Sherman started ramming the barrier at ground level, and GIs rushed over the crumbling mound to finish off those Jerries who refused to lay down their weapons. When the skirmish ended, two of Frankie's comrades were dead along with five Jerries. Four others raised their arms and surrendered.

Every fear and uncertainty plaguing Frankie accelerated as dusk eased into dark. A full moon or clear night could become a soldier's best friend or his worst enemy, especially with the Krauts playing their unnerving games. One night after a quick but sincere *Our Father* Frankie burrowed into his coffin-like foxhole, five feet deep and six feet long, and next to the men he knew—Sarge, Toe, and even Dean. God bless the little shit.

By now Dean's shoulder tic had evolved into a rhythmic shrug of cocking head and bunny-twitching nose. Somehow the spastic d-u-d had managed to stay alive, bringing up the rear while Toe and Frankie took care of the forefront. In fact, Dean had gained a minute degree of acceptance. When not in immediate danger, he operated a successful barter service by negotiating K rations. Usually his cigarettes, which he never could inhale, for everyone else's canned egg yolks, a product so foul it was rumored to have been the brainchild of upper echelon—to keep the troops lean and mean. Anyone brave enough to ingest the eggs developed acute halitosis. Naturally, Dean's case proved by far the worse.

"Psst, Frankie," he whispered. "What're you doing?"

"Drying out my stinking feet, you oughta do the same."

"Like I told you before," Sarge said. "Healthy feet are a foot soldier's best defense."

"Yeah, but what if we get hit."

"Then we die with our pissing boots off," Toe said. "It ain't like we're living in the Old West."

At least we're living, Frankie thought. He yanked off his boots, massaged his feet, and changed his socks. With the boots back on, he now wanted some shut-eye. Dammit, he deserved some shut-eye. His catnaps were usually as sporadic as the distinctive shelling erupting from both sides. This time a loud, wailing missile sailed overhead from the other side.

"A fucking Moaning Minnie," Toe said.

No one challenged him. They all knew friendly fire from enemy fire. So did the Jerries. Minnie landed two hedgerows away. Frankie curled up and waited. Cries of the injured and dying violated the night.

"Damn the Krauts."

*****

During the third week of July Lieutenant Lancaster gathered his men in the remains of an old farmhouse. A hunk of cheese sitting on the plank table reminded Frankie of his mom's kitchen. He could almost taste her home-baked bread. "Listen up," he heard the Lieutenant say. "I just received word from command headquarters. We're pulling back."

"What?" said a guy who rarely complained. "After busting our rear ends to take this ground?"

"General Bradley's orders. He needs a wide buffer zone between our lines and the Kraut's. We're getting help to open the remaining hellrows so Patton's men can access the paved roads."

"What kind of help, sir?" Dean asked.

"Expect all all-out air attack from P-47s and B-17s, with Piper cubs targeting radio points. This could be the start of something big."

"As in THE END."

A loud cheer went up; Frankie offered a silent prayer of thanks.

As soon as Frankie stirred on July 25, he grabbed his pocket calendar and circled the date. He was thinking about Mary Ann when the P-47s piloted by young daredevils appeared in the sky. He smacked a kiss from his fingertips when those planes began dropping five-hundred-pound bombs over the German occupied countryside. With each precision dive their target zone moved closer to the American lines.

"Whoa! Don't they know which side we're on?"

"To hell with this."

"Ain'tcha glad we pulled back, Toe?"

"Everybody down!" Sarge yelled. It was an order he did not have to repeat.

Frankie pushed further into the deepest foxhole he'd ever dug. The unrelenting bombardment played havoc with his eardrums. He mouthed his next words. "Dear God, please keep this helmet on my head."

During a brief interlude the band of GIs surfaced again.

"God, I'd give anything for a one-way ticket back to Oklahoma."

"When it's over, I'm going home."

"He's going to his Mary Ann."

"Ain't this beautiful, Toe?" Dean twitched. His eyes grew round as pancakes "We got front row seats in the final game of the World Series."

"More like the Fourth of July."

"A Busby Berkley musical."

"Remarkable aerial choreography."

Toe grinned with pride. "Just look at that sky. It's like swarms of bees buzzing and swooping in formation."

Somewhere behind American lines a friendly bomb exploded into the ground. "What the shit!" Sarge yelled. "They're bombing short! They're bombing short! Everybody down!"

First came the deafening noise, worse than any before. Then the good earth shot into the sky and rained down like a summer shower. Shrapnel crisscrossed in all directions, cutting and slicing whatever blocked its path.

"Toe, you okay? Toe? Answer me."

"Dammit Dean, get your ass down! Toe's okay."

Frankie lied but what the hell, Dean would never know.

Every second counted, so little time before another B-47 dropped its load. Frankie shouted his next prayer, an act of contrition.

"Oh my God, I am heartily sorry...."

He couldn't hear the rest but he did see the Capuchin monk, its hand of polished bones reaching out and inviting him to join the holy order of dead. The words, what were the words? Frankie shouldn't have banished them from his memory. He tried to resurrect the prophetic inscription but his brain wouldn't let him.

Or maybe, just maybe, it wasn't his time to go.

Chapter 41
St. Gregory, August 1946

A summer storm passing through the heart of Southern Illinois had climaxed in the late afternoon, scattering fallen limbs and downed power lines over the streets of St. Gregory. In the storm's aftermath, calm serenity greeted a mud-spattered Greyhound coach that rolled into town. The bus stopped in front of the bustling depot, one block off the square. Its door swung open for the only passenger, a weary soldier who stepped onto the curb and dropped his duffel bag as soon as he saw his waiting family. He leaned over and took the older woman into his arms. They clung to each other, their silence communicating a bittersweet mix of joy and sorrow.

Tony Roselli pulled away from his weeping mother. He moved over to the warm handshakes of Jake and Carlo; and when that didn't seem enough, he followed up with a crush of bear hugs. He turned to the young woman standing off to the side, her brave face masking sadness. He'd not seen her since that night of the deserted roadhouse. He lifted Mary Ann off her feet, avoiding the teary eyes that would've preferred gazing on the face of a different soldier. Instead, he chucked her trembling chin.

"Hey, you're not a kid anymore."

"Neither are you." She gave him a peck on the cheek.

"Maybe I was a kid when I left but I sure grew up in a hurry."

"Don't talk that way," his mother said. "It makes me sick thinking about all you've been through. And what about Frankie, God rest his soul, dying in some godforsaken hellhole before he ever had the chance to live."

Jake put a protective arm around Irene's shaking shoulders. "Today we should thank God for the son who returned. Today we celebrate life."

"Come on, soldier," Carlo said. "Wait 'til you see the garden, tomatoes as big as your fist." He slipped one arm through Tony's, the other through Mary Ann's. Pulling them toward the car, he cocked his head upward to Tony. "I think you grew some more. You're taller than your pa ever was, but now I see his eyes in yours."

Tony remembered those eyes, dark and brooding yet capable of dancing with pleasure. The horrors thrust upon his own eyes had been relegated to the deepest recesses of his brain. Never to be resurrected, he vowed.

"The town's planning a big bash for the returning servicemen," Jake said, "sometime in September."

Tony nodded but said nothing.

For now, out of respect for the son and brother who would never come home, for the house displaying a gold star in the front window, Tony's homecoming celebration would consist of a simple meal around the family table. His mother prepared an array of fresh garden vegetables. And spaghetti topped with fresh tomatoes and grated cheese, which reminded him of a few meals he'd eaten in Europe.

"The government's still rationing meat so I fix this at least once a week," she said. "Even though it's Southern Italian, Jake and Carlo can't get enough of it."

The brothers rolled their eyes and Tony's shoulders relaxed with his first chuckle of the evening. There were more, brought on by stories about him and Frankie that resulted in a mix of outright laughter and occasional tears. Good tears, that much he owed to his brother. By ten o'clock Jake and Carlo called it a night in order to get up in time for the seven o'clock shift. His mother held out until she finished praying her rosary. When she left, Tony took her seat on the back porch swing, next to Mary Ann.

"I'm sorry for my stupid remark at the depot," she said, "about your not being a kid anymore. It was—"

"Hey, this is Tony you're talking to. You don't have to pussyfoot around me."

The swing creaked back and forth for another minute before she spoke again. "You know, I loved him—Frankie, I mean."

"We all did."

"No, I don't mean like a brother or a son. I really loved him with all my heart. I'm sure we would have married if only …."

"I know what you mean. Frankie wrote and told me how much he loved you too."

"He said that?"

"He couldn't help but love you. You were … you are so pretty. Seeing you today, for the first time in over four years, I had forgotten just how pretty." He leaned over to brush his lips over her thick mane of hair. She lifted her shoulders to welcome the sweet intimacy.

"Me? Ah, come on. I was just a punk, the silly cousin begging for attention."

"What about me," Tony said. "When we got older, I became the outsider. You and Frankie always with your heads together, sharing little secrets. I couldn't break into your tight circle. It just big enough for two. "

"Frankie adored you," she said. "Tony, the big brother who could do no wrong."

"Remember my last evening before Boot Camp, how we found you with that creep?"

"Sweet Mother, how could I ever forget." She giggled into her hands. "God bless Denny Briggs for suspecting the worse. Me with my clothes half off, scared stiff and so relieved to see you and Frankie. Papa never did find out, neither did Uncle Jake or your mother. Thank God, or I'd have spent the rest of high school confined to a remote convent."

"What ever happened to those shits?"

"Coy Eaglestone lost his leg at Argonne. He's been in and out of the VA Hospital at Jefferson Barracks ever since. Rollie Tyler never made it back. He died somewhere in the South Pacific. As for Gayle Chambers … well, she married a pharmacist by the name of Walter Haley. They have a baby boy, Little Wally. Big Wally works his head off at the drugstore, right alongside Mr. and Mrs. Chambers. Some day he'll take over the business."

Tony nodded to the trivia of everyday life until she ran out of steam. A summer serenade of locusts and crickets accompanied the steady creaking of the wooden swing to fill the ensuing silence. He cleared his throat and asked what he'd been thinking about for hours.

"So, you dating anybody now?"

"No one special, if that's what you mean." Creak ... creak ... creak went the swing. "I just can't get Frankie out of my head, or my heart. More than anything, I regret we never did *it*. I wanted to, that last night, but he turned me down. Can you imagine that?"

"No, I can't." But he did. Frankie always kept his promises.

"He actually pushed me away," Mary Ann said. "Frankie was so incredibly honorable. He thought we should wait until after the wedding vows. What did I save myself for? Not a damn thing, pardon my French."

"I'm glad you waited. But had I been in his shoes, I would've made love to you. All night long, until I got it right."

Chapter 42
Mundelein, March 1947

Daily Mass at six, followed by a decent breakfast, then, a well deserved smoke outside regardless of the weather. Michael Baggio allotted five minutes for the enjoyment of his pipe and to scan the remnants of winter giving way to the greening of spring. A cloudy sky had cast its pallor on the distant lake, misty with vapors rising to greet the chilly morning. The afternoon promised sunshine for Pop and Mary Ann, a visit predisposed to prick and prod and grumble. To what extent depended on the phase of the moon, or the trials of Harry Truman and John L. Lewis, or Mary Ann's monthly cycle, or—Time.

Leaning against a red brick wall, Michael bent his shriveled leg and tapped his pipe bowl against the oversized sole of a sturdy black oxford. Ashes scattered to the ground. He shoved the pipe into a soft leather pouch and slipped it into the side pocket of his black cassock. Copping one more view of the lake, Michael eased away from the smoking area. He fell in step with the expanding group of seminarians hurrying along a path of Neo-Georgian structures that led to the various dormitories. The orthopedic shoe that added an inch to his shorter leg made his limp almost undetectable and enabled him to push to the front of the pack. He entered his dorm before anyone else, which gave him more study time before leaving again for the solemn High Mass at ten o'clock. On Sunday there were always two Masses at St. Mary's of the Lake.

*****

That afternoon in the visitor's room filled with sofas and tables and chairs, the seminarians formed tight circles with their families. Most of the people kept their voices low, a practice ignored by Michael's father and sister.

"Are you still smoking that pipe?" asked Mary Ann, her voice reminiscent of the nuns from Holy Angels. "It seems like every time we visit, I smell tobacco on your clothes."

"That's because you always visit right after our smoke break."

"According to Aunt Irene, insatiable sucking is the result of not having nursed at the breast."

"Mary Ann!"

"Sorry, Papa."

Heads turned, and Michael took a second piece of homemade fudge from the box Mary Ann had brought. He let the candy melt slowly in his mouth, savoring the melding of chocolate, butter, and sugar as it dissolved.

"Don't eat it all at once. According to the latest findings too much chocolate is the leading cause of sore throats."

"He deserves some pleasure in life," Pop said. "Smoking and candy, that's all he's got. They took everything else away from him."

"Ah, but not the wine. There will always be the precious wine." Michael managed a smile. "Come on, my life isn't so bad. I have everything I need."

"What do you have? No girlfriends. No radio. No newspapers. No books. No holidays. You come home in January, after the Christmas tree drops the last of its needles."

Home. Michael didn't think of home as the duplex and land his father loved more than a spoiled mistress. "You're talking about things, Pop, worldly things. I'm trying to concentrate on the spiritual, not the material."

Pop stood up, to stretch his back and wiggle stiffness out of the leg he always favored. "My Chicago souvenir," he said, "seventeen years ago and forty miles south of your sheltered world here in Mundelein. Come on—let's get the hell out of here, take a walk in the warm sun."

"Sorry, Pop. As I told you before: this is where we visit with our families"

"Dammit, don't they ever let you outside your cocoon?" Carlo opened his arms to the expanse of the room. "Why all the trees and the lake and the bridge if you can't enjoy them?"

"I do, every day. We play outdoor sports or stroll around the lake. In the summer we swim and go boating. Exercising the body is almost as important as exercising the soul."

In spite of the gamy leg, Michael participated in every physical activity, excelling in none except swimming, thanks to the years of therapy. But he showed his greatest strength in the classroom, where all lectures and exams were conducted in Latin.

"I guess these priests are afraid we might talk Michael out of taking his vows," Mary Ann said. She stood up to stretch her legs too.

Ah, the Baggios ... ever united when it mattered. "It would take more than a walk around the lake to change my mind," Michael said. "Discipline and obedience enables me to free my mind for prayer and meditation."

Mary Ann wiggled the ring finger of her left hand, a reminder of the diamond Tony had given her on Christmas Eve. "Any chance you can come to St. Gregory for the wedding?"

"Not a prayer. You know how much I'd like to, but there's no way I can get excused from my studies."

"Only if I die,' Pop said. "That's a legitimate excuse."

"Don't talk that way, Papa, even if you're just kidding."

"Who's kidding. So Michael, what time you get up in the morning?"

"Five-thirty, Pop, same time as you for the mine. We're already in the chapel before six for morning prayers." He made a mental note for his daily examination of conscience: to accuse himself of two venial sins—impatience with the marginally faithful and a constant lack of humility.

To Michael's relief a stocky seminarian came strolling over. Michael had attended Quigley with Rob Seppi, one of the few students his family could relate to.

"Excuse me, Mr. Baggio." Rob extended his hand to Pop while nodding an acknowledgment to Mary Ann. "I just wanted to say hello."

"Ah, Roberto, good to see you again." Pop smiled as if he really meant it. "Everybody sit so Roberto can talk to us." They found their chairs again. "So, how's the old man?"

"Pa couldn't make it today but sends his best to you and your brother. He's still with the brewery. In fact, he's been promoted to

Head of Personnel."

"Personnel?"

"Somewhere between management and rank and file."

"Ah-h, a position made for Elio Seppi. To him my brother owes his life," Pop said, opening his palms. "Twenty years, it seems like yesterday."

"No kidding, is there a story I should know about, maybe the Roaring Twenties." Rob smoothed down his unruly hair and leaned forward.

Mary Ann tapped her watch. "Papa, we only have fifteen minutes."

"Whoops, maybe next time." Rob jumped up and extended his hand again. "I'd better return to my own family, Mr. Baggio. Good seeing you again."

After Rob left, Pop shook his head. "Elio's only son, another family name that won't survive. It just ain't right." He leaned over, kissed Mary Ann's cheek before he stood up. "*Permisso, Maria Anna*, I need a few minutes with your brother before they kick us out."

Michael felt the firm hand on his shoulder, guiding him toward an unoccupied corner. He towered a good four inches over Pop but Michael still knew his place. The man had a way about him that demanded respect in spite of their differences. They sat down again.

"Dammit, I shoulda brought some wine."

"We haven't much time, Pop.

"When did we ever." He lifted his shoulders into a sigh. "About your uncle and me, we each own a piece of ground on the far side of the grapes. At first I planned on building a house there but now I'm content to stay where I am, next to Jake and his wife. We all get along, even though Irene ain't been the same since Frankie died. Still, she's a good cook. And me, I don't like eating alone."

"God bless Aunt Irene."

"Amen. She kept a tight rein on Mary Ann. Now the tables are turning. Jake and me do the gardening. It's too much for one man so we only plow the Roselli land. But before we offer our ground to your sister and Tony, I need to be sure you won't want my share—your share—someday. You know what I'm saying? In the Old Country the son inherits the land."

"Thanks, Pop. But in my world I have no need for land."

"No chance you changing your mind about this church thing?"

"No chance, Pop. Don't be sad for me. It's what I want."

"If that's what you want, that's what I want for you." He tapped a row of coal-stained fingertips to his chest. "We won't speak of this again."

The tension eased in Michael's neck. "What about you, is there someone special in your life?"

"Lots of nice ladies—widows and divorcees anxious for another marriage. When they push too hard, I quit calling. Not one could take your mother's place. God was cruel to have taken her when he did ... before she saw you open your eyes ... before she—"

"God has a plan for everything, Pop. Those painful times often bring our greatest strength. How old are you, forty-three? That's way too young to spend your life alone. You could start another family."

"A sermon I don't need. Nor a second family, you and Mary Ann are my life."

Chapter 43
The Wedding

Terrence Connelly preferred his annual holiday in August when the scorching heat of Rome gave him nasty headaches and his Vatican position as an English interpreter demanded fewer hours. But this year he made an exception and returned to Chicago in early June. The phone call he only dared to anticipate came a few days later. He closed his eyes and listened to the excited voice of Louisa's daughter.

"Please say yes, Father Terry. It would mean the world to me if you'd come to St. Gregory for the wedding, especially since Michael can't. I guess you understand those strict rules better than we do."

"Indeed, the seminary imposes many sacrifices. But Michael will preserver, of that I am sure."

"Anyway, Tony and I would be greatly honored if you would be co-celebrant at our wedding."

"Well, Mary Ann, just being there to see you as a bride, remembering your saintly mother and how very much she loved you, would be a great privilege. Your pastor is—"

"I'll talk to Father Clancy and he'll make a place for you. Please, Father Terry. I've never asked anything of you until now, except, of course, to look after Michael."

Indeed, Terry Connelly had been looking after Louisa's son, which was how he'd always thought of Michael. He'd sat at the boy's bedside during his illness, sent him letters filled with inspirational messages, arranged for him to study at Quigley—no small feat considering the pricey tuition. Whenever he returned to Chicago, he always visited Michael at Quigley. And now at St. Mary's of the Lake—always careful not to overstep his bounds with the seminary faculty of Jesuits who would not tolerate interference, especially from a Vatican priest, no matter how insignificant his role.

After receiving Mary Ann's letter about the wedding, Terry restructured his vacation schedule. Although he hadn't seen her in the twelve years since she left Chicago, they still kept in touch by letter, an exchange that began with her sixth birthday. He wrote about life in Rome, sent postcards of the Roman ruins and other places of interest. She wrote back about school and her favorite subjects. As with Michael, she became the child he would never have. To be more accurate, the child he could never claim as his. Nor would he ever know for sure.

During the war years, their communications had stopped and when it resumed, the little girl had left Mary Ann. It was the teenager who wrote about her love for Frankie Roselli, and when Terry received her distraught letter regarding Frankie's death, he wept for her grief and prayed for Frankie's soul, just as he did for so many other victims of the war. Several years later Tony Roselli made it home and Mary Ann found love again. "You're the first person to know, Father," she wrote. "I haven't told Papa yet, although I know he'll share my happiness."

Perhaps the petty bootlegger had made some progress toward his salvation, only time would tell.

*****

In the anteroom of All Saints Catholic Church Carlo waited with his daughter for their cue from the organist. Mary Ann stood before the full-length mirror, turning her slender neck over one shoulder for a final critique. Never had he seen a lovelier bride, except for his own.

"Bella, bella," he said with a choke in his voice. "As beautiful as your mama on the day we married."

"Papa, all brides are beautiful." She twirled around to show off her ivory satin gown trimmed with lace and seed pearls. "I just love the *velo di matrimonio*. It makes me feel so-o special, wearing a traditional veil instead of this year's sweetheart headpiece. Aunt Irene went all out, ordering everything handmade from Italy."

A justifiable extravagance for a worthy event—the only wedding this dual generation of Baggios and Rosellis would know. He patted the fancy swivel stool and told Mary Ann to sit.

Obedient as a child, she humored him. Facing the mirror of a small dressing table, she dropped her lashes and wiggled on the velvet upholstery. "Hurry, Papa. We haven't much time."

"Without us, they can't start so quit squirming." He slipped a lavaliere around her neck, fingers fumbling as he fastened the clasp from behind. "There, so whadaya think?"

She leaned toward the mirror. It reflected a diamond set in black onyx. The oval pendant hung from a gold chain.

"Papa, it's beautiful. Where did you find such an unusual piece?"

"My gift to your mama, the day we married."

He kissed the top of her head. "Make your husband happy. And give me more than one grandchild."

She blushed and wiped away a tear just as the organ music swelled into a dramatic overture. "Come on, that's our cue."

He helped Mary Ann stand up and after slipping her arm through his, Carlo was ready to let his daughter make a new life. As they walked down the aisle, he scanned the gothic church and then focused on the waiting groom—Tony, standing tall and proud in his military dress. Ambitious too, going away to college with his bride. Mario would've approved. Another generation in the mines, but this one would use his head instead of his hands. After Carlo kissed his daughter and turned her over to the smiling groom, he moved to the front pew that faced a statue of the Blessed Virgin, He knelt for a quick Hail Mary before sitting back.

His eyes drifted to the ornate altar and the guest priest performing the Sacrament of Matrimony rituals with Father Clancy. Figuring Terry Connelly to be five years older than his own forty-three, he felt gratified to observe the auburn hair had faded to salt and sand, as had the brows and lashes behind those round spectacles. As with Carlo the few extra pounds of middle age had done little to alter the priest's wiry frame.

Terry Connelly may have found his place in Rome but no earthly distance is far enough to suit me. Like a thief in the night this priest put one foot under the tent and crept into my world. Seduced my Louisa with books and words. Enticed my children with flowery letters. Stole my only son with promises of everlasting chastity. Denied me grandchildren bearing the Baggio name. That name may not live on, but the seed I rightfully claimed as mine will live on. Mary Ann's someday babies will make up for what I missed when my own were little. And from that cushiony job in

Rome, the priest will have nothing to hold but empty dreams.

How Louisa would've loved this day. Too bad her brothers couldn't make the wedding. Massimo with his arthritis and Vincenzo, a bad case of gout. Their gift of five hundred dollars will help the newlyweds survive that college town.

Still, there were other guests from Chicago. While Carlo was marching in with Mary Ann, he noticed Roscoe and Essie Mae Johnson sitting with a row of black miners. The Johnsons had arrived the evening before and were staying with Abraham Washington, the nephew he'd brought from Chicago as a favor to his Uncle Elijah. Roscoe hadn't exaggerated when he described Abraham as a hard worker. After Carlo got him on at the coal company, it fell to Abraham to prove himself. This he did, and soon sent for Hannah Montgomery of Corinth, Mississippi. She came with John, their six-year-old son. They married at the Freedom Baptist Church and became respected members of St. Gregory's black community, which seldom mixed with St. Gregory's white community.

*****

After the formal ceremony had ended, Carlo did his duty at the back of the church. When the Johnsons came through the receiving line, he kept pumping Roscoe's hand. "It's good to see you, Roscoe."

"No way would we miss this day."

"That sassy girl turn out fine, Mister Charlie," said Essie Mae. "You right to be proud."

Carlo responded with a grin. Before his friends moved on he whispered, "After the reception come to my house. Bring Abraham and Hannah too. We'll drink and talk the night away."

The wedding hoopla ended with the newlyweds on their way to honeymoon in St. Louis. By ten o'clock Carlo's old friends gathered around his table. Dago Red flowed for the Italians, moonshine for Roscoe and George. Essie Mae and Hannah indulged in the Hires Root Beer. After two rounds, Irene excused herself for the night, as did the Washingtons.

"How's Ezell doing?" Carlo directed his question to Roscoe but it was Essie Mae who answered.

"Right good. Moved to Memphis, he drive a bus for the city."

"Any family?" asked Jake.

"Wife, two girls."

"That's a good woman you got, Jake," Roscoe said. "She look at you with love in her heart. Now ain't you glad you saw the light and skipped Chicago with no help from that Garlic Joe?"

"I hear he wound up in the Chicago River," Jake said.

"Sure did, 'bout fifteen years ago. That wicked Joe lasted a helluva lot longer on this earth than he ever deserved."

"Indeed he did, yes indeedy." Essie Mae rocked back and forth on the kitchen chair. Carlo directed her to the bathroom and opened another Hires for her return.

As the night wore on he refilled glasses and prompted new toasts until the conversation started to lag. After the Seth Thomas chimed its twelfth time, Jake said his goodbyes and backed out the door. Then Roscoe and Essie Mae scooted their chairs closer to Carlo's.

Roscoe took the lead. "You ain't asked about her."

"Not because I forgot or didn't care. How is Ruby Lee?"

"She marry the cracker. Can you believe that?" Essie Mae said. "He wait 'til his folks in the ground, then say 'marry me.' Kind of late for a proposal, I say, what with three babies already born outside."

"They're still in New York?"

"No, back in Paris," Roscoe said. "They only did New York because of the war. Essie Mae, pull them pictures outta your pocketbook."

She did and passed them to Carlo. He flipped through a few ragged snapshots before setting them aside. He focused his attention on a black and white studio photograph of the Guy Durand family, more European than American, the kind who wore money on their confident faces. The man hadn't changed much in fourteen years, except for losing his perpetual scowl along with a good chunk of hair. Three children, two girls and a boy with corkscrew curls and close in age, had inherited their father's fine nose and fair skin, their mother's wide-open black eyes and captivating smile. Carlo saved Ruby Lee until last: more beautiful than he remembered, more elegant than any model posing in his daughter's fashion magazines. Ruby Lee would've been about thirty-six, a sophisticated young matron accustomed to the best of everything. Guy Durand had proven to be a man of his word.

BOOK FOUR

Chapter 44
Florence, Italy 1950

The boy known as Santo lived with his widowed mother in Florence's Old City where she managed a small pensione which provided living quarters and enabled her to keep him under her thumb during those war-torn years of Nazi occupation. As Santo grew older he learned to cherish what little freedom she gave him, always knowing that someday she'd expect him to live his life for her. True, he wanted for nothing within reason. He went to a good school within walking distance from home and never gave the nuns any grief. His playground alternated between the streets of cobblestones and those of the *Piazza della Signoria*, where he scrambled among the sculptures of David and of Perceus holding Medusa's head. But unlike the other boys, he never stole coins from the Fountain of Neptune. Instead he demanded a share of their take in exchange for his silence.

In his thirteenth year Santo came home from school one day to find his mother sitting in the living room with a priest he'd not seen before. The priest stood, took Santo's slender hands in his, and scrutinized every inch of him. Santo remained motionless, watching the expression on the priest's face soften. The boy glanced over at his mother, her eyes wet but not sad. After a while the priest released Santo's hands in order to retrieve his handkerchief. His was the softest evacuation of a nose Santo had ever seen or heard.

"Santo, this is your papa," his mother said.

"I don't understand," Santo replied as he picked up the framed photograph of his father. "*This* is my papa. He died before I learned to walk. Didn't you teach me to pray for his soul every single day?"

"I did and you must continue to do so. Giorgio came to my rescue when you'd already started to grow inside my belly."

Giorgio, so now his papa was Giorgio. Santo gave the priest a look befitting that of a lowly criminal. He couldn't bear to think of the woman standing before him as his mama. Olga suited her better.

"It's not what you think," the priest said. "Had I known at the time, I would never have taken my final vows. Giorgio was my friend, as well as your mama's."

"The poor man knew he was dying," Olga said. "He could have no children of his own. Still, he wanted his name to live on, even if his seed could not. Giorgio gave his name to you, my unborn child; I, in turn, gave him an heir."

Tears streamed down Santo's cheeks, at his age an uncontrolled weakness he detested. "What about my nonna and my nonno? Do they know I'm nothing to them?"

Olga slapped him, so hard it brought fresh tears. "You are what they live for," she said. "What you now know would break their hearts to learn. Do you understand?"

Yes, Santo understood about the money that someday would be his. He stared at the face of this priest, searching for some likeness to his own, perhaps the dark eyes, closely set and brooding behind those scholarly spectacles. Those eyes should brood, those eyes of a hypocrite. Maybe the nose—he refrained from touching his own—or the high forehead he so detested.

"Shouldn't he be exposed as a fraud?' Santo posed the question to Olga while focusing his attention on the priest.

Her lip trembled when she said, "He gave you life."

"A dog can give life. This man was never my father."

"He only learned of you recently," she said. "He has financial resources and influence."

Santo and his mother had been speaking of the priest as if he were invisible. When he finally interrupted, it was to plead with open hands. "Think of your future, Santo," he said. "Your mama tells me your grades are excellent."

Santo listened to him while examining the scuffed toes of his shoes. The priest grew more confident with each word.

"I'll be staying in Florence for three more weeks," he said. "The only opportunity I'll ever have to help decide your future."

"Nobody but me decides my future," Santo said.

"So be it. Instead we'll get to know each other. Do you agree?"

*****

During the next month, one week more than the priest had promised, he spent every day with Santo, showing him the churches of Florence and explaining the historic significance of each fresco and statue. Visiting hospitalized children and those in orphanages accounted for a few more hours as did short trips into the countryside, Santo's first glimpse at the vineyards and endless rows of olive trees. The remaining hours included Olga, the three of them dining together at home or in nearby trattorias. To appease the curiosity of their neighbors Olga explained the priest was a cousin on sabbatical, and for a short time able to give attention to a boy growing up without a father.

Santo learned more than he'd ever expected to learn and on that final morning, he begged the priest not to go.

"My staying is not an option," the priest said, once again evacuating his nose. "The bishop needs me."

"Not as much as I need you," Santo said. "The bishop has other priests. I have but one father."

"On earth, yes, but you must never forget your Heavenly Father. As for the bishop I have pledged allegiance to him and must obey his every command. Anything less would be tantamount to a serious sin."

"I should hate you but I cannot," Santo said. Instead he kicked Olga's cat.

"Santo!" she said, picking up the hissing animal.

"It's not fair," the boy said. "I'm losing another papa—all because of you, Olga."

"Don't call me Olga." She drew back her arm for another slap but before she could administer it, the priest stepped between her and Santo.

"Please, Olga," the priest said. "Perhaps I can provide further assistance."

Chapter 45
Frank, April 1966

Frank Mario Roselli acquired his name from two fallen heroes he never had the chance to meet: the uncle who died during the Normandy Invasion and the grandfather who died in a house fire. Still, the sixteen-year-old figured he'd lucked out with two more grandfathers: Grandpa Carlo and Grandpa Jake—both wiser and with more on the ball than his own parents who were hopelessly square but still looked good for their age.

Frank looked good too, trim and athletic at six foot two and one hundred seventy pounds. His Mediterranean features may have reflected that of his parents, but not his attitude. Frank already knew he was going places, anywhere but St. Gregory. As the only son sandwiched between Michelle, a year older, and Jamie, two years younger, this hotshot enjoyed his status as *numero uno* in the family and elsewhere—classroom, playing field, and dating game.

As a seventh grader at All Saints Elementary, Frank had entered puberty and discovered girls. So impressed was Sister Mary Thomas with his natural leadership ability and keen attention to any topic on religion that she scarcely noticed his preoccupation with the budding breasts of female students. During his sophomore year Frank lost his virginity as a reward for scoring the winning field goal—an incredible shot from half court—in the regional basketball finals. Thereafter, he indulged himself with some of the prettiest girls in town. Following the advice of his two grandpas, who claimed more youthful escapades than the entire male population of St. Gregory, Frank kept his conquests discreet and answered to no one except himself.

On a Saturday afternoon in late April he and Michelle were lounging on the grassy slope bordering the family vineyard, out of sight from their home to the north and the grandparents' duplex to the south. Frank leaned back on his elbows and bent one leg to rest his ankle on the other knee while Michelle wiggled her back into an arbor post and stretched her bare legs to the sun. Fluffy white clouds floated across the sky while closer to earth the air filled with scents of blooming wildflowers and billowing puffs of smoke.

"Sweet, innocent Michelle, what a crock. Mom and Dad would blow their tops if they knew their precious little girl could blow such fine smoke rings."

"Yeah, and Grandma would have to pray another rosary."

"Hey, watch your mouth. The old gal has had one tough row to hoe."

"Not any more but that doesn't stop her from that damn worrying, what she calls her insurance against the evil eye. It gives me the creeps."

"Don't knock what works. We've had twenty good years since Uncle Frankie died." He closed his eyes. "Did you know Grandma prayed that you'd get a date for the spring prom?"

Michelle jabbed her finger in his ribs. "I did not need Grandma's help and you know it, Mr. Hotshot."

He grabbed his side and faked a moan.

"Let's make a deal." She paused to create four smoke rings. "You quit humping every girl in town and I'll give up my weeds."

Frank straightened up. "What do you mean, me humping every girl?"

"Cut the act, little brother. You may have conned Mom and Dad but not me. Your old girlfriends could start their own club: Roselli's Honey of the Hour: Susan, Betsy, Sandy, and What's-her-name."

"You mean Dana."

"Yeah, every one of them broke up with you but still think you're the greatest." She paused to light a fresh cigarette from one smoked down to the filter. "What'd you do, claim to have a contagious disease?"

"Hmm, not bad. But in my case I let the girls think they let me down easy."

"You mean after they went down so easy with a couple romps in the hay, or the back seat."

"Go back to what you said before: about keeping my private life private in exchange for covering up your bad habit."

"Let's see: you have a private life; I have a bad habit."

"You can smoke 'til your nose caves into your tonsils for all I care. Just don't dump my personal stuff on Mom and Dad."

"It's a deal." She gave him a thumbs-up. "So who are you taking to the prom, Corrine Haley?"

"Yeah, we're doubling with Gary and his latest, Bonnie Baker."

"I thought he was taking Venetia Sims."

"Venetia got a better offer."

*****

On prom night Bonnie Baker fluttered her lavender lace over taffeta from one end of the living room to the other, her ballerina-length gown tickling like a feather duster against the toned skin she'd nurtured into a golden tan while helping her dad with farm chores.

"This is the opportunity of a lifetime for me," the youngest of seven explained to her stodgy parents. "Not only am I going out with Gary Albers, the richest boy in school, but we're doubling with the most popular girl in the junior class. Her date is the class president. Did I tell you Frank Roselli starts as a guard on the basketball team?"

"I don't understand why this dance has to turn into an all-night activity," Oren Baker grumbled from the comfort of his maroon vinyl recliner. "A midnight curfew seems plenty reasonable."

His wife looked up from her post at the picture window. "Today's young people are never satisfied. Fried chicken served by the Parents Club is the proper way to end a grand evening. You'd be home by midnight, safe and sound."

"With my social life ruined," Bonnie whined. "For the in-crowd, there's a marathon of house parties followed by a sunrise breakfast at Posey's."

"That twenty-four hour diner on the interstate?"

"Come on, Daddy. You know you can trust me."

"We trusted Maggie too. Nine months later she gave us our first grandchild."

"My goodness," Lurleen Baker said, patting her heart. "Would you take a gander at the carriage pulling into our driveway. Oren, get over here and see for yourself."

"Mother, p-lease. Move away from the window."

"Now don't he look cute as a bug."

Gary Albers wasn't a standout athlete or a top student but he did possess a sense of humor and a generous allowance. Having a father who owned a luxury car dealership also enhanced Gary's popularity. He stepped out of a powder blue 1967 Cadillac, one he personally selected to coordinate with his powder blue tuxedo and matching ruffled shirt. Completing the ensemble from Tux and Go Rentals was a pair of shiny black vinyl shoes, stiff enough to have been cast in industrial-strength molds. Gary shrugged his suit into place and ran a pocket comb through a modified Elvis Presley with skimpy sideburns he'd been cultivating for months.

Meanwhile, Frank Roselli relinquished his shotgun position and was headed for the back seat. Tux and Go offered limited choices for formal wear so Frank's outfit matched Gary's but was in gray. Somehow Frank managed to look better. Maybe it boiled down to his hair, shorter and less flamboyant than the current style. Or maybe the way he carried himself.

"Wish me luck, Frank. Bonnie said her folks were on the provincial side, whatever that means."

"Stay cool, man. You can handle them."

Frank leaned his head against the window. To kill time he thought about Corrine and how long it would take to get in her pants this evening. Maybe they'd go all the way. Just thinking about it made him hard—until he heard fingers tapping on the glass. Damn. He rolled down the window.

"Frank, come with me," Gary said. "I need you in the house."

"What the hell. Bonnie's your date, not mine."

"And she ain't staying out all night unless you can convince her parents otherwise."

Frank entered the farmhouse with a broad smile for Mrs.

Baker and his hand outstretched to Mr. Baker. *"How do you do, sir. I'm Frank Roselli. I usually see you at seven o'clock Mass on Sunday mornings ... it's my favorite Mass too—early in the morning and at peace with God. Yes, my grandparents still have the vineyard and the produce stand. Of course, their garden's nothing compared to the farm you have here. They've always spoken so highly of your family. I believe both my grandfathers worked with your father in the mine. Yes, you're right, sir. That would've been Grandpa Jake who carried Mr. Baker Senior out when he broke his leg. Yes, sir, I can personally vouch for Bonnie's safety. We'll have her back home right after breakfast. You have my word. Thank you, sir. Nice meeting you, Mrs. Baker."*

As they walked to the Cadillac Frank helped Bonnie negotiate her spiked heels through the patchy front yard while Gary trailed behind them.

"You were positively wonderful," Bonnie told Frank. "If it hadn't been for you, my parents would never have agreed to the all-nighter."

"Hey, no problem," he said. "Here, let me get the door for you. Be careful of your dress." Frank scooped the remaining lavender into her lap and whispered in her ear, "You look like a dream, Bonnie." He closed her door with a gentle push, climbed into the back seat, and tapped Gary's shoulder. "Put your pedal to the metal and let's get Corrine. You know how I hate being late."

Corrine kept them waiting fifteen minutes. Their fashionably late arrival turned into a distinct advantage. With Gary and Bonnie serving as second bananas, Frank and Corrine were able to make a grand entrance. Wearing her one-of-a-kind yellow and green chiffon, Corrine floated straight off the pages of Glamour onto a field of look-a-like pastels from *Seventeen Magazine*. Frank made a dashing Prince Charming, allowing Corrine to hang on his arm as well as his every word.

Doubling as chaperones and chicken dinner helpers were a handful of students' parents who sat in the upper bleachers of the gymnasium, a respectable distance from the prom festivities below. They oohed and aahed and tried to appear impartial, certain their own children were the brightest stars that lit up the night. Even the decorations merited a second glance. In keeping with the Americans in Paris theme, third and fourth year art students had designed and painted theatrical backdrops that transformed the basketball court into a turn-of-the-century Parisian scene.

"Oh, Mary Ann, to be that young and that thin again," sighed Gayle Chambers Haley as she basked in the glow of her daughter Corrine's beauty, her own having faded long before the forty-second birthday she recently celebrated.

"And to know what we know now," Mary Ann Roselli said, without going into the ancient history of Sugg's Roadhouse.

"So, tell me. Where's Frank going to college after he graduates next year?"

"Hopefully, U of I in Urbana. Michelle's been accepted for the fall semester."

"With Frank's brains, he'll probably be a mining engineer like his father," Gayle said.

"God only knows. How about Corrine?" Mary Ann asked with eyes scanning the scene below. "What's she going to do after graduation?"

"If she graduates." Gayle lowered her voice. "She's not the smart ass I once was, in more ways than one, if you get my drift."

"Oh really?"

"Last week she wanted to be a model, this week a psychologist. Considering her grades, she'd better find herself a rich sugar daddy or a handsome go-getter." Gayle nudged Mary Ann and winked.

Handsome go-getter, please. Mary Ann's weak smile coincided with the school orchestra's change in tempo.

"Oh-oh, looks like they're bringing back an oldie." Gayle meant the invigorating action on the dance floor. "One crazy twist was enough for me. Last month I pulled a muscle that put me out of commission for three long days, even after Wally brought home a muscle relaxant from the drugstore."

While Mary Ann feigned interest in the gyrating display of youthful hips, Gayle groaned about the benches being too hard. Getting no sympathy, she moved four rows away to sit with a notable purveyor of local gossip.

Mary Ann didn't remain alone for long, "Thanks for nothing," she said when Tony sat beside her. "You waited for Gayle to leave, didn't you."

"As if you needed any help."

"Gayle I can handle, but I don't like Frank dating her scatterbrained daughter. I don't care how pretty Corinne is, or what Gayle says about her sweet innocence. The apple never falls far from the tree."

"Don't make a big deal out of something that isn't. Next week Frank'll be dating a new face. Give him some credit. After all, he is our son and a good kid."

"I was a good kid too, but I came this close to real trouble." She measured an inch between her thumb and forefinger. "When you get in over your head …."

"Careful. You're turning into my mother."

"Scary, isn't it. She taught me too well."

The parents of Frank and Michelle Roselli leaned over the railing to watch their children. Before Frank danced with anyone other than Corrine, he always made sure she first had a partner. Given the splash Corrine was making, this should not have been a problem, but Frank always seemed to be prying her from his arm. More than once he looked toward the bleachers and offered his little boy grin. The one his mother couldn't resist.

"He reminds me of you," Mary Ann told Tony. "Frankie too at that age."

"But our Frank knows a helluva lot more than my brother or I did at sixteen."

"Look who's telling me not to worry?"

"Not tonight. Not with our Michelle stealing the show from every other girl on the dance floor."

Michelle had taken a cue from Frank and was alternating dances between her date and the other boys who hung around the Roselli house, both her friends and Frank's. With dark, bouffant hair styled to add extra height to her five feet, four-inches, she graced the ball in the elegant simplicity of a rose-colored empire gown.

"I can't help what I see," her father said. "Michelle has that special something."

"Oh, Tony, I hope it's not too special for St. Gregory. You know how she feels about small towns." Mary Ann reached for his hand and stifled a sniffle. "I can't believe how fast our kids are growing up. One more year of this with Frank and then it will be Jamie's turn."

"Don't go weepy on me. Jamie's only a freshman." He stood, pulling her with him. "Come on, time for our shift in the cafeteria."

*****

The removal of plates with the remains of strawberry shortcake brought an official end to the 1966 prom of St. Gregory High School. The students strolled into the moonlit parking lot, piled into their fathers' cars, and took off with spinning tires and sprayed gravel. Frank and Gary made the party rounds with their dates. At three-thirty they arrived at a ranch house, lit up like a prairie showboat and filled with sleep-deprived revelers who had shed their tuxedo jackets and three-inch heels.

Corinne started circulating to let everyone know she'd arrived so Frank detached himself from her arm on the excuse that he needed a drink. Soda in hand, he worked his way over to the corner of a brown and orange sofa and sat down. His eyes were about to close when a petite brunette plopped onto his lap.

"Whoops, we'd better be careful or Corrine might get jealous." Venetia Sims tickled his palm with her fingertips. "Of course, I could be wrong."

Riding high from a supercharged evening, Corinne had surrounded herself with the unattached males who'd lost their dates to rigid curfews. Even so, Frank did have certain standards to maintain.

"I'm leaving with the girl I brought. But that doesn't mean I can't call you next week."

As soon as Frank separated himself from Venetia, Gary stumbled into the room and christened the green shag rug with Stag Beer.

"So, Frankie-boy, grab your date or maybe two, or three," Gary said, rubbing his shoeless foot into the wet carpet. "Everybody's heading for Posey's."

"Maybe we should skip breakfast," Frank said.

"Hell, no. Not after all that stuff with Bonnie's folks."

"Then let me drive." Frank held out his hand for the keys. "You must be on your fifth beer by now."

"Are you kidding? I may be a little woozy, but I'm still Gary Albers. The old man would have my hide if he knew I turned over the Caddy keys to any old shit, even the great Frank Roselli."

"Okay, okay. Just don't toss your cookies all over that upholstery." Frank wrapped his arm around Gary's shoulder. "Come on, let's round up the girls. I got an itch that needs some serious scratching."

"Yeah, me too. Already I can taste Posey's pancakes and jelly doughnuts."

After they piled into the car, Frank suggested taking the long way to Posey's. "Over the country roads so we don't run into the sheriff."

Just as Gary had said, the back seat did have certain advantages. Frank leaned over to Corrine and kissed her shoulder. He worked his way over to her ear where he whispered what she already knew, "You were the prettiest girl at the prom."

"Oh, Frank. That's so-o sweet."

"Promise you won't get mad if I ask you something."

"Cross my heart and hope to die."

"Can I screw you?"

"Sh-h," she whispered with her usual giggle. "Bonnie might hear you."

"If Bonnie does, she might say yes. And where would that leave you?"

"I can speak for myself, Frank I'm not stupid."

"That's not what I meant. Uh ... never mind." He trailed one finger over her soft shoulder, felt her skin shudder with goose bumps. "Come on, Corrine. Don't make me beg."

"Gee, I don't know, Frank. I've never ...."

"Your first time? Mine too. You and me, we'll learn together."

"You make it sound so-o romantic."

"Because it is, just tell me when."

"My parents are going out of town next weekend."

"I can hardly wait. Wait a minute, maybe we won't have to."

He checked out the front seat. Gary and Bonnie were preoccupied with the radio, singing off key but having fun as they tried to harmonize with Elvis on "Love Me Tender." As soon as Frank got down on his knees, Corrine started giggling again. He was in over his head, surrounded by yellow and green blossoms and working his way to paradise when Bonnie went from Elvis to high-pitched hysteria and Gary started yelling for Jesus.

Damn, not now. Frank came out from a tangle of chiffon. Corrine screamed and he shielded his eyes from the blinding light engulfing their car.

"What the hell …."

Frank bore witness to hell on wheels and Gary had been right to call on Jesus to save them. But that night the Illinois Central showed no mercy. Frank went numb to the sounds of screeching brakes and grinding steel. He found himself riding a careening roller coaster like some hapless Charlie McCarthy snapping out of control. Inside his pseudo woodenhead, a volley of crazed pin balls started setting off whistles and bells and flashes of color. Then a gigantic burp erupted. The mountain ride derailed and hurled him head over heels into a black abyss.

Frank thought he was descending into Hell, having died while planning to deflower the chiffon queen: the just consequences of intent, as much a mortal sin as the act itself. Not to mention his other sexual transgressions: confessed and forgiven, but knowing they would be repeated. Maybe God would consider his youth, although well past seven years, the age of reasoning. He'd loved his family, respected adults, and never missed Mass on Sundays or Holy Days. Sometimes his face didn't reflect the depths of his soul. Neither did his words. But he wasn't the only hypocrite. Maybe he'd qualify for a timeout in Purgatory, that temporary detour to cleanse his tainted soul.

"Enough!" he heard a voice called out. "You're not in Heaven or Hell, so stop with the self-righteous malarkey."

Frank had just been exposed as a fraud. He rubbed his eyes to clear the fog engulfing his mind and body.

"Over here," said the voice. "Not there, to your right."

Sitting on a boulder no more than six feet away was a black man wearing the uniform of an ambulance driver. "Get up, Frank. Your time has not yet come."

"You mean I'm not going to die?" Frank stumbled to his feet and fell back down. He looked around, relieved to recognize the gully of the Illinois Central track.

"Well, not yet. But don't get any ideas about immortality," the black man said. "For now, just stick to God's plan."

"Plan? What kind of plan? I don't have a clue what you're talking about."

"Patience, Frank. You'll find out soon enough."

"Find out what. Dammit, don't play games with me."

"Look who's talking." The driver stood, brushed gravel from his white pants, and walked into the fog. "Make the best of what time you have on Earth."

"Wait!" Frank called out. "What about my friends? They might need help. Maybe some first aid, a ride to the hospital."

"Your friends don't need my help, and certainly not yours. You've already done too little."

*****

First arrivals on the accident scene proclaimed Frank's survival as miraculous, considering he'd been ejected from the car and incurred nothing worse than heavy lacerations and a broken leg. They found him leaning against a tree, his right femur jutting through the Tux and Go trousers. He mumbled something about a black man no one else had seen. Later at Memorial Hospital one doctor set Frank's leg, another removed his damaged spleen, and another supported his whiplash with a neck brace. The two-inch gash on his chin was stitched tight to heal into a lasting reminder of prom night.

Indeed, his friends were beyond help. The coroner pronounced Gary Albers and Bonnie Baker dead at the scene, their bodies intertwined with the crumpled steel and metal of what had once been the showroom Cadillac. Corinne was found twenty feet from the car and bleeding from massive head injuries. She died two hours later at Memorial while being prepped for surgery.

Although the sheriff ruled the tragedy an accident and no mention of drinking made the newspapers, Frank couldn't hide from the truth. He should've scrapped breakfast at Posey's. Instead of making out in the backseat, he should've convinced Gary to let him take the wheel. And if he, or Gary, had stuck to the main road, they wouldn't have crossed the Illinois Central railroad tracks. Frank welcomed the two-week hospital stay that qualified as a legitimate excuse not to attend funerals, not to face distraught families, not to accept the undeserved compassion of his peers. Flat on his back and with his leg in traction, he wrote letters of sympathy to the grieving parents, the most shame-felt to Oren and Lurleen Baker.

*****

May 15, 1966
Dear Mr. and Mrs. Baker,
Please forgive me for not taking care of Bonnie like I promised. She sure was a hit at the prom. I will remember the sound of her voice and will pray for her soul 'til the day I die."
Sincerely,
Frank Roselli

Frank went home weaned from the painkillers that kept him sedated in the hospital. Alone in his room he obsessed about wanting nothing more than one night of uninterrupted sleep. As soon as he dozed off, Gary's cry for Jesus, Bonnie's screams, and Corrine's giggles overwhelmed his brain, robbing him of any relief from guilt he felt obliged to bear for having survived.

Chapter 46
Did you see him?

On a Saturday morning in late June Tony and Jake left at five o'clock for crappie fishing in an old quarry mine south of St. Gregory. Carlo rarely stayed behind but this morning he'd allowed himself the pleasure of sleeping until seven. After a quick coffee and hard roll he guided the power mower over the backyard grass so Irene could hang out her precious laundry. White sheets were fluttering in the warm breeze by the time he strolled over to Mary Ann's kitchen.

Jamie was sitting at the round oak table, flipping through the latest issue of *Vogue*, a magazine her mother said celebrated excess but still allowed her to read. He planted a kiss on top of chestnut hair styled to flip up around her shoulders.

"How's my little girl? After Michelle goes away, are you gonna turn into another sassy?"

"Oh, Grandpa, I'm not little and I could never be as sassy as Michelle." The fourteen-year-old stood and towering over him, returned a kiss to the top of his head. "I'm off," she sang out and blew a fingertip kiss to her mother.

"She's off?" he asked.

Mary Ann didn't bother to explain. She'd been wiping over a spotless kitchen counter ever since he came through the door. As soon as he sat down, she filled his cup with extra strong coffee and hot milk.

"It's been six weeks since the accident, Papa. The doctor said Frank's leg is healing fine. With proper therapy he said eventually it should be as good as before."

"Good enough for him to play sports again?" Carlo stirred two spoons of sugar into his coffee. He tasted it, added another spoonful.

She sat down. "Frank said 'no more basketball,' He refuses to wear the neck brace, says his neck is okay."

Carlo opened his mouth but yielded to Mary Ann.

"He won't go outside, won't see his friends. The phone doesn't ring for him anymore. He stays in bed all day and can't sleep at night. Tony and I tried talking to him. He nods and agrees with whatever we say just so we'll leave him alone."

"The body heals quicker than the mind." He patted her arm.

"You'll talk to him?"

"After my coffee." He took a long sip, making certain not to slurp, a habit of Jake's he considered as offensive as dunking. At sixty-two Carlo was still fit and trim from years of physical activity. He enjoyed his role as family patriarch, a position that allowed him to impart a wealth of wisdom, mostly unsolicited and acquired through the mistakes he regretted.

He walked down the hall, knocked once on his grandson's door, and received an okay to enter.

"I need to talk to you, Frank," he said, closing the door.

Frank was still in bed. He mumbled another okay from under a pillow wrapped around his head.

"I ain't talking to no lump," Carlo said. He tore away the rumpled sheet covering Frank.

Frank rolled over and swung his feet to the floor. He yawned, scratching one hairy armpit, and then the other before flexing his broad shoulders into a slump. He wore briefs, and a four-day growth of whiskers on a face demanding a daily shave, an inconvenience inherited from both sides of the family. "What's up?"

"Not you, that's for sure. The only reason for lolling in bed at ten in the morning is if you're sick or working the night shift. You ain't neither. Being on the mend don't count."

Carlo pulled up a straight back chair and sat down. Leaning forearms to knees, he looked into Frank's face. "Your mother, she worries about you."

"My mother worries about everything, just like Grandma Irene."

Carlo opened his palms. "That's 'cause they're women. And women show their love through worry. It's a curse handed down from generation to generation."

Frank rolled his eyes. He ran one hand through his snarled hair and pushed it off his forehead. "I've been thinking about going away to school this fall."

"What do you mean? There's another year before college."

"I mean I want to finish high school away from home."

"You can't run away from what can never be changed."

"Why not." Frank massaged the healing wound on his chin, a comforting habit he had no intentions of breaking. "Right now, all I want is to close my eyes without seeing my friends' faces. Close my ears to shut out their screams. You don't know what it's like, Grandpa."

"Says you. After all these years my past still haunts me." He paused, taking his thoughts beyond Frank. "In Chicago there was this woman I once loved, before the grandma you never knew. This woman saved my life when I got this." He patted his leg and straightened it out. "Years later when I went back for my kids—that's when I had to leave Michael behind with polio—I saw her again. Bella, bella," he said with his hands, "like a movie star she was. But because she once saved my life, she wound up paying with her own. This I never knew 'til after I put Chicago behind me. I often wonder if I coulda done more, saved her like she once saved me."

"I'm sorry, Grandpa. But maybe now you'll understand what I have to do." Frank gave the scar a rest. With laced fingers he stretched his arms overhead and then dropped them between his legs. He took a deep breath. "I've been thinking about spending my senior year in Chicago, at Quigley Prep."

Not another priest. Carlo stood and went to the casement windows. "Dammit, don't tell me you want to go the way of your Uncle Mike." He kept his eyes on the distant vineyard while searching for the right words. "Don't do this, Frank, not to yourself or the family. Quigley ain't the answer. Besides, you'll never get into that seminary. You ain't from Chicago."

"Uncle Mike can make it happen." He limped to the window, took in Carlo's view of the vineyards. "I already asked him."

"Uncle Mike can make you a lonely man. What's he got? No wife. No children. No home."

"He has God."

"So do I: in my family and in the land. Why he chose such a life, I could never figure. We got all this and he lives in a cubby hole in holier-than-thou Rome."

"Mom said Rome was a great opportunity for him, thanks to Father Connelly."

"Thanks to that priest, I hardly see my own son. Do I mean so little to him?"

"No, no, I'm sure it's not like that for Uncle Mike. Nor would it be for me."

"How would it be for you? Like jail, only no bars."

"There's nothing binding about going to a prep seminary. I just need to sort out my life."

"Living in a monastery, it ain't natural."

Frank put his hand on Carlo's shoulder. "Will you talk to Mom and Dad for me?"

"Maybe your Uncle Mike should do the talking."

"They'll listen to you, Grandpa. Please."

"Yeah, I'll talk to your Ma and Pa." Carlo turned to face his grandson. "There's just one more thing I gotta know. About the night of the accident, they said you kept talking about some black man saving your life. By chance, did you see *L'Angelo Nero*? You know, The Black Angel?"

"The what?"

"Never mind, I guess you didn't."

Chapter 47
Decision Time

May 1, 1967
Dear Mom, Dad & family,
I hope you're sitting down when you read this because I've taken the giant leap and decided to become a priest. Since I'm not really from the Chicago archdiocese, it might be hard getting into St. Mary's of the Lake. So, if it's okay with you, Uncle Mike has offered to speak to our bishop about my enrolling in the North American College in Rome.
Don't be mad at me for not telling you in person. I thought it would be easier if you had time to get use to this before I graduate. The past nine months at Quigley have given me time to decide what to do with my life. I'm giving it to God. I can't explain exactly what I'm feeling. All I ask is for you to be happy for me.
Love,
Frank

Most Catholic families celebrate a son's decision to enter the priesthood. Frank's family gathered in the kitchen to mourn the loss of their dreams for him.

"It wasn't enough to give up my Frankie for the glory of this country, now we give up his namesake for the glory of God," Irene said. She buried her face in her hands and cried, just as she always did when speaking of her dead soldier son.

Jake patted her shoulder. "Frank will make us proud. Who knows how far he can go as a priest? Some day maybe a parish that's close to St. Gregory."

"I don't think so," Tony said. "Priests in this diocese usually come from St. Henry's in Belleville."

"Damn. Chicago was bad enough but did he have to pick a seminary in Rome," Mary Ann said as she went through the routine of filling the coffeemaker with Old Judge and water. "Remember Michael at St. Mary's, how complicated a mere visit was? I think Frank's trying to get as far from us as possible."

"From bad memories, not from us," Jake said.

"Oh, Uncle Jake, surely Frank's beyond that. No amount of knee bending will ever bring those poor kids back."

"I'll take some coffee when it's finished perking," Irene said, having finished her cry. She fished in her pocket for a clean tissue.

Carlo banged his hand on the table. "There's just one thing I want to say and only to the family, not Frank. When Jake and me first came to America, more than anything I wanted a wife and children. I got what I wanted but not for long. I lost my wife to God, my son to the Church. I still have Mary Ann and her family. I still have Jake and his wife. If one grandchild leaves, I still have two more. Before, my only regret was that the Baggio name would not go on. Now, the Roselli name will also end. First, no children from Michael; now there'll be none from Frank."

Irene choked up again. "Jake, is this how you feel too? I'm sorry I couldn't give you children. You've been so good, raising Tony and Frankie like they were your own."

"Tony and Frankie are mine. My heart broke for Frankie, same as yours. But with time it healed, especially when Tony and Mary Ann married and had kids."

Tony reached over to Jake, squeezed his hand. "We'd better pull ourselves together before Frank's graduation. I don't want to lay any new guilt on him. My son's going to be a priest so get used to it."

The back door opened and the kitchen went silent as Jamie walked in. "What's going on? Is something wrong?"

"No, sweetheart, everything's fine," Tony said. "It's just ... well, we heard from Frank. He's decided to follow Uncle Mike's lead."

"So Frank's heading for the seminary. I figured he would. So did Michelle. No guy goes to a prep school for priests unless he's seriously thinking about becoming one.

Chapter 48
Rome, September 1974

Father Michael Baggio sat behind the desk in his office at Gregorian University, sucking on his pipe and drumming his fingers when the telephone rang for the first time that morning. He grinned on hearing the one voice he'd been anticipating, that of Bishop Tomaso Martinelli. Although the bishop could speak English, they conversed in Italian, the language of the Vatican.

"Of course, Your Excellency," Michael said after listening for several minutes. "I understand ... yes, of course ... I'm honored by your sponsorship. Indeed, whatever I can do."

After the conversation ended, Michael leaned back, held a match to the bowl of his pipe, and propped his feet on the desk. "Mission accomplished," he said through clenched teeth. "I just hope the payback won't be hell."

Tomaso Martinelli became the last of four clergy who agreed to sponsor Michael's special assignment at the Vatican. An ad hoc committee of priests was being formed to study turmoil brewing within the Church since the convening of Vatican II Council in the early sixties. At forty-seven, Michael felt honored to join the select few who would be making significant recommendations to the Holy See—recommendations that would ultimately affect Church policies.

For centuries the concept of sin had been as uncomplicated as black and white. But ever since the Council abandoned some age-old traditions to address the needs of a modern world, shades of gray began creeping in. Twenty-two years as a priest—the last fourteen in Rome--had taught Michael that the political system within the Roman Catholic Church, from the humblest parishes to the Holy See, differed very little from any other governmental body. The Church just moved slower and with greater diplomacy.

Two soft taps on the door interrupted Michael's thoughts.

"Entrate," he called out, annoyed for having to put his feet down and assume a dignified position. His attitude improved as soon as he saw the young seminarian crossing the threshold. He stood and embraced his nephew.

At twenty-four, Frank's face had chiseled into youthful maturity and still attracted females of all ages. Since coming to Rome, he'd fallen from grace numerous times—temporary gratification with young women who wanted to please and expected nothing in return.

"Are we still on for lunch, Uncle Mike?"

Michael glanced at his watch. "Absolutely, but I have a curriculum meeting at eleven. How about Pierluigi, shall we say one o'clock?"

"No problem. It's still okay if I bring the new transfer?"

"Hell, yes. I'd like to meet him."

"One more thing, Uncle Mike?"

"Make it quick. You have two minutes."

"About the Vatican Diplomatic Corps ...."

"First—get ordained. After that, the archbishop will expect you to put in a stint back home. The experience will do you good." Frank started to object, but Michael held up his palm. "For now, patience and more patience, it's the name of the game. After all, it took eight years and a recommendation from Terrence Connelly before I made it this far."

"How is Father Terry?"

"Back in Chicago as a Vatican liaison and monsignor. Not a day passes that I don't think about him." He leveled one finger to Frank. "But don't tell your grandpa I said that."

"What do you take me for? My mother didn't raise a fool. Any chance the old man could help me?"

"Show some respect, you twit. Monsignor Connelly sits at the right hand of the archbishop."

"Somehow I can't see myself back in Chicago."

"Sure you can. Now quit whining; your two minutes are up."

*****

Three hours later Michael's taxi crossed the Tiber River and into The Ancient City, an area where with narrow streets and the youngest buildings older than America's oldest. At the Trattoria Pierluigi Michael's only meal of the day would be taken in the Italian style—simple food and good wine enjoyed in a leisurely manner.

From his seat in a far corner of the trattoria Michael watched Frank working his way through a maze of tables with the other seminarian, a six-footer who walked with his shoulders hunched, as if they were supporting all the woes of the world. That, coupled with his massive bulk, made the young man look more like a linebacker for Notre Dame than a candidate for the priesthood. An interesting duo, Michael thought as he stood to greet them.

"Uncle Mike, I'd like you to meet Andrew O'Keefe. We'll be making our subdiaconate together," Frank said, referring to the upcoming rite in which they'd take their vows of celibacy.

Andrew O'Keefe possessed a head of reddish-brown hair, hazel eyes punctuated by premature crow's feet, a nose begging to be repaired, and a ruddy complexion that belonged outdoors. Indeed, a remarkable face, one that could be perplexing or deceiving but not easily dismissed.

"Thanks for inviting me to lunch, Father Baggio," Andrew said as they shook hands.

"Welcome to Rome, Andrew," Michael replied. Given his rugged appearance, the softness of Andrew's hand surprised Michael although it typified a student's: smooth and callus-free, except for the fingers that supported a writing tool.

The priest motioned his guests to sit and poured more wine from the carafe.

"Cin cin." They clicked their glasses together and leaned back to enjoy the scene. As always, Italians and Americans pretending to be Italians filled every table in Pierluigi. Efficient waiters moved about like thwarted thespians bent on displaying their talents to a captive audience. From time to time a waiter would belt out an operatic aria to the delight of his customers, most often Americans who bestowed generous tips.

The three men in black, Michael distinguished by his clerical collar, walked over to a sideboard laden with hot and cold antipasto dishes. After much musing, they settled on hard-boiled eggs with capers; roasted green, yellow, and red peppers; garlic-stuffed artichoke hearts drizzled with olive oil; fresh tuna with fava beans and more olive oil; plus tomatoes with anchovy fillets.

"So where are you from?" Michael asked after they returned to their table.

"Boston, Father. Oldest of three boys." He gripped his fork and lunged into the peppers as if they might escape from his plate.

"Any other religious in the family?"

"Mom has two sisters, both Ursulines, plus a Jesuit uncle, my Dad's brother."

"Quite a family."

"That it is. My parents are the God-fearing Irish variety. When I was a kid, we spent hours on our knees praying for vocations. Every evening after dinner the entire family said the rosary together, a rarity for my generation. Even so, I'm the only son who chose the religious route."

Frank popped a tomato slice into his mouth and shook his head. "No matter how much the Italians are known for good food, their tomatoes can never compete with those back home. Right, Uncle Mike?"

"Amen."

"Anyway, sorry for the interruption," Frank said, raising his glass to Andrew. "Back to the O'Keefes of Boston, What are your brothers doing now?"

"Carving out their own niches. Ted—he's a year younger than me—is in his second year of law at Georgetown. Sean just graduated from the Police Academy. I guess you could say we did a complete about-face." The crow's feet creased even deeper when Andrew grinned. "In our neighborhood the O'Keefe brothers were known as The Holy Terrors."

"Not so fast Andrew. I'm not so sure it was an about-face, at least not in your case," Frank said. "Tell Uncle Mike how you and your brothers earned that title."

"You know—kid stuff, like graffiti on the parish hall one summer. Naturally, we got caught and spent the next two weeks painting the whole outside. Dad saw to that."

"What about Sister Mary Rita?"

"I guess I scared the bejesus out of the good sister when she saw Sean hanging by his ankles from our attic window. Ted and I had a good grip on him but the little shit was still yelling bloody murder."

Andrew paused to wipe the napkin over his wet lips. "Of course, I must admit: my biggest problem was always my mouth, same as my brothers. Our folks encouraged us to speak up for what we believed in, even if we went against the mucky-mucks."

Michael looked up from the olive oil he'd been mopping up with a crusty bread heel. "What do you think, Frank? Any different from growing up in St. Gregory?"

"There's no comparison."

"Well, maybe you weren't so wild," said Andrew. "But like me, I'm sure it took a lot of family prayers to get you here."

"Prayers, yes, Uncle Mike's and mine."

After they finished the antipasto, their waiter removed the soiled plates and scraped breadcrumbs from the crisp white cloth. Guido, so thin he looked as though he never ate what was served his customers, was a fixture at Pierluigi, having worked there for the past twenty years, and Michael requested his table because Guido didn't sing or try to upstage the food. He set down three steaming bowls of *spassatelli in brodo*. Conversation went on hold temporarily as the trio concentrated on the broth with bits of cheese pasta.

Michael had already ordered the main course, one he felt certain the seminarians had never tasted: *triglio*—red mullet stuffed with fennel, wrapped in prosciutto, and cooked in white wine and lemon juice. Before Guido served it, he presented a bottle of Frascati for the priest's approval.

"Compliments of the couple across the way, Father Baggio," he said in Italian. "They also wish to pay for your meal and those of your companions."

Guido opened the bottle and handed the cork to Michael, who sniffed the wine-stained end. He sucked it, and then nodded. Guido poured one finger measure into the goblet. Holding the base of the goblet with his thumb and forefinger, Michael lifted it to the light. He swirled the white wine to examine its color and clarity before breathing in the bouquet. Only then did he partake, rolling the liquid through his mouth and holding it briefly before swallowing. Satisfied with a wine that had been the choice of popes for centuries, Michael smiled and lifted his glass in the direction of Arthur and Claire Bannister.

"Please express my thanks to the kind couple," Michael told Guido, "but I cannot allow such generosity to include our meals."

After filling the other two goblets, Guido left, and the young men followed Michael's wine tasting ritual. "The Bannisters are a dynamic twosome," Michael said, "hell-bent on championing concerns of Catholics in the United States. I just finished participating in a Catholic Cleric and Laity Conference with them several days ago."

"Could we ask them to join us, Uncle Mike? I'd be very interested in listening to their views on Vatican II and its effect on the laity."

"By all means, but take what they say with a grain of salt. I don't recommend your returning to the seminary primed to take on further reformation of the Church."

"Excuse me, Father Baggio," Andrew said, "but why not? Isn't it important that we relay what's going on in the trenches, so to speak?"

"Not at this phase of your education. If you do and it gets back to your rector, this might be the last outing before your final vows. Just listen and learn. The Bannisters can join us when we're ready for our coffee."

They agreed to forgo salad greens to refresh their palates, instead opting for baked pears and figs along with wedges of Parmesan cheese. Sensing his guests were hurrying their meal, Michael asked Guido to invite the Bannisters to his table.

Claire Bannister was a slight woman who carried herself with the confidence of old St. Louis money. Her ash blonde hair, parted to the side in a soft bob, set off a delicate pale face and smoky blue eyes that complemented her husband Arthur's silver gray hair, dark eyes, and golden tan. Although Arthur came from modest beginnings, through wise investments and Claire's connections he had parlayed their small real estate firm into a prominent development company. Management of the company was gradually being turned over to their only son, Bart. Semi-retirement had enabled the Bannisters to channel their enthusiasm into the study of modern Catholicism, mainly the effects of Vatican II on American Catholics. Their project soon evolved into a fulltime activity, which they pursued with the zeal of first-time missionaries.

Introductions were made and Michael instructed Guido to bring everyone espresso. A round of Sambuca followed and the party sat back to let the cordial ease their digestive tracts. Soon, idle conversation turned to a discussion of the meeting Michael and the Bannisters recently attended.

"What do you see as some of the key issues from Vatican II that effect the laity, Father?" Claire asked.

"Most were received with hardly a ripple, such as turning the altar around for the celebrant to face the people during Mass." Michael swirled the last of the Sambuca and drained his glass, leaving the customary coffee beans at the bottom. "However, I'm not so sure doing away with Latin has improved the Mass."

"And why not," Andrew said. "Latin was never the language of the people."

"Of course, what you say is correct. I guess I'm too much of a traditionalist at heart."

"You mean like giving up meat on Friday," Frank said.

"Well, yes."

"I have to agree with you on that one, Father," said Arthur. "Was it too much to ask for Catholics to set ourselves apart from the rest of the population?"

The question came to Michael while he was ordering another round of Sambuca. Before he could respond, Andrew jumped in.

"*The rest of the population*, would you be referring to the non-Catholics?" He didn't wait for an answer. "Of course, now we are told to acknowledge their role in Christianity, as well we should. The Jews too, given Our Lord was one himself. We should no longer think of them as his persecutors."

"A good thing too," Frank said. "The Jews have experienced more than their fair share of persecution. But from what I understand, the Council didn't go far enough. Vatican II ignored the whole issue of birth control. It won't go away, you know, regardless of what Paul the Sixth dictated. The laity will do as they please."

Andrew nodded. "The pill's more reliable than rhythm. Just ask any parent with more than three children."

"That would be my sister Martha," Claire said with a laugh. "Six children in eight years before the pill—only one since."

"As for the shortage of priests, The Church is in denial." Andrew's face flushed with excitement. "At some point priests must be allowed to marry."

Arthur managed to say, "That might present some problems."

"You bet," Andrew interrupted, "without effective birth control. Isn't that right, Frank?"

With a slight movement of his head, Michael caught Frank's eye, and narrowed his own.

Frank backed off. "Of course, the Church needs time …."

"Come o-on." Andrew cocked his head. "Don't be such a wimp. Say what you really mean. Picture this: a married priest with a wife and eight or nine kids for the parish to support. How will he tend his parishioners and his own family?"

"All right, fellows," said Michael. "You've made your point."

Andrew released an appealing smile. "Sorry, Father. Sometimes my mouth tends to move faster than my brain. I hope the Vatican doesn't have spies lurking behind potted plants."

"The Vatican has ears everywhere, Andrew."

"The Church needs to change, Father Baggio."

The table went silent, which gave Arthur Bannister a reason to check his Rolex. "Whoops, speaking of change: it's time for us to leave if we're going to change before dinner. We have an engagement at the Embassy tonight."

After a flurry of handshakes, Arthur and Claire left.

"Check, please," Michael said to Guido.

"I'm sorry, Father," Guido replied. "Your bill has been settled. The couple insisted."

*****

On the sidewalk outside Pierluigi Michael parted company with the young turks who insisted on walking off their meal, a grueling trek up Janiculum Hill to their dormitory. He figured Frank wanted to admire the women of Rome while they admired him. As for Andrew he was too full of himself to notice anyone else.

Michael lost no time in hailing a taxi. He climbed into the Fiat's rear seat and braced himself to experience modern Rome's version of an ancient chariot race. His driver, wearing designer jeans and a pencil-thin mustache above sulking lips, quickly merged into a lethal combination of compact cars and volatile Italians zigzagging and jockeying for the lead.

Don't give a single inch, Michael silently urged. *They're gaining on us from behind.*

He came close to whacking his nose on the front seat when the Fiat's squealing brakes stopped short of a fender bender. Waving arms and clenched fists backed up a torrent of exaggerated theatrics.

"Blind *bastardo!*"

"Your face belongs up your ass!"

Regaining the lead on an inside turn, the driver righted his taxi and passenger at the same time. Michael slid out from the corner and returned to the middle of his seat. On most days he enjoyed his position from the rear, bouncing and cheering on a spirited, determined driver. This afternoon his thoughts kept returning to the seminarians.

Andrew O'Keefe and Frank Roselli: a study in contradictions, not only their physical appearance but also their temperaments. Andrew the idealist, the crusader weighed down with unbridled passion. Pity the bishop overseeing Andrew. A religious order would better suit him, one that answered only to Rome. What about Frank, so ambitious and cunning. His nephew may be fluent in the Romance languages, but he had much to learn about the language of diplomacy: observe with discretion and reap the rewards.

Chapter 49
Michelle, St. Louis 1978

After centering three terra cotta pots of red silk geraniums on her pseudo Early American table, Nell Bannister started on the place settings—milk glass plates and ruby footed-tumblers over red and white-checkered placemats. Creating a festive mealtime ambiance was a loving ritual she performed every Sunday through Thursday, those precious evenings reserved for the family. First, we eat with our eyes; she'd been taught in a gourmet class, a lesson learned all too well. The meals she prepared and served with love always promised more than they delivered. Not that the actual food mattered all that much, she assured herself. What mattered was the family being together.

Nell didn't know her husband was even home until he came from behind to fold her body into his. When he started nibbling on her ears, she lifted her shoulder and murmured a weak objection. "Stop it, Bart. You're giving me the shivers."

"That's precisely what I had in mind, at least for starters." He took one more nibble before releasing her. "Don't set a place for me. I just came home to freshen up and then I'm on my way again."

The smile which minutes before had graced her heart-shaped face quickly faded.

"I'm sorry, Nell. It's that damn Lawson project. God, I hate missing another dinner with you and the kids."

Disappointment filled her voice. "Your children and I will miss you too." She completed a third place setting before turning to him.

"You're working too damn hard. This is not what your parents had in mind when they turned the business over to you."

"Sweetheart, please. Don't make me feel worse than I already do. Without you and the kids, I'm nothing but a pathetic shill."

Nell's smile returned but with less enthusiasm. She kissed him on the cheek and went back to the red and white display. "I want you back in time to kiss the kids goodnight. Promise?"

"I can't promise but I'll sure as hell try. You know how these things can drag on."

Bart showered and shaved. He dressed in business attire, jazzed it up with his favorite tie, a neoclassic geometric. He left in his green Mercedes coupe and meandered through the tony suburb of Ladue before turning onto the interstate. Heading east toward downtown St. Louis, he passed miles of commercial properties that were flourishing, in part because of his business savvy. He owed his success to parents who groomed him to use privilege to maintain the family standards, both moral and financial, and on a higher level, to provide aid to those less fortunate. Nell kept him grounded. They'd fallen in love while students at Chicago Loyola, and married the day after graduation. Two beautiful children completed their idyllic family. Yes, life had been good to Bartholomew Bannister, and not a day passed that he didn't thank God.

After taking the last downtown exit, Bart drove two blocks and pulled into the underground parking of a high rise overlooking the Mississippi River. He circled down to the lowest level, and after considering several options, settled on a prime slot between a late model Cadillac Seville and a Lincoln Town Car. Briefcase in hand, he got out, locked the car, and hurried to the elevator. Alone in the cage, he punched the number eight button and released his eyes to the gentle ascension. A bell signaling his floor jarred Bart from the brief respite. He moved with assurance down a well-lit hallway of thick carpeting and cherry paneled walls. Around the corner at Number 818 he inserted a key into the lock and entered a mirrored foyer.

"Honey, I'm home," he called out, tossing his briefcase and suit jacket on the upholstered bench. He checked his reflected image, liked what he saw, and walked down the hall.

"It's about time," said a pretty woman leaning against the door. Lounging pajamas, silky and yellow, set off the dark hair piled on her head. "You wouldn't believe the day I had, but enough about me.

Dinner's in thirty minutes."

"What are we having?" Before she could answer, Bart lifted her off the floor. He covered her lips with a wet kiss that lasted long enough for her legs to wrap around his tennis-trim body.

"Mama Mia's salad and pizza. So if you want a yummy appetizer, I suggest you shed those duds right now." She tugged at the knot of his tie. "Is the Hermés a coincidence, or in honor of our New York trip?"

"Neither," he said. "Consider it an incentive to exceed my New York performance."

She moved to the buttons on his shirt. He inhaled with appreciation. "M-m-m, you smell enticing."

"I ought to, for the seventy-five dollars an ounce you shelled out."

"Wow, you're some expensive date."

"Yes, and worth every dollar."

He kicked off the Italian loafers. She unbuckled his belt and peeled the zipper of his fly. "Careful there," he said. "Remember the last time."

"Silly boy, that was your fault for showing off."

Bart teetered as he stepped out of the briefs and trousers puddling around his ankles. He loosened her hair with one hand and with the other untied the belt of her lounger. "Gr-r-r," he growled into her neck as they eased down to the cushiony, plum carpet.

Yellow silk flew into the air. Simulated roars of the jungle interspersed with muffled squeals for the next ten minutes before she called a time out to catch her breath.

"Have you been smoking again, Michelle?"

"In more ways than the usual, and I have no intention of stopping until I'm good and ready. I've gained five pounds from all these damn eat-ins. Not there, Tarzan … m-m-m, there, that's better. So, you can either take me the way I am, or leave."

"I'm taking you, Baby, all the way to the very top. Ready or not, here I come."

*****

The first time Michelle Roselli met Arthur and Claire Bannister was during her brother's 1975 ordination in Rome. She'd been working in Chicago, a marketing executive on a secretary's salary. Stiff competition from those as good or better fueled her frustrations. She expressed an interest in relocating to St. Louis. To be closer to her family, she told Frank, which sounded better than having to admit she'd lowered her

Midwestern sights. The Bannisters said they'd be delighted to use their influence to help Frank's sister. They put her in contact with an old friend, the head of a powerhouse-advertising agency who hired Michelle during the first interview.

Shortly after moving to St. Louis, Michelle received an invitation to the Bannisters' annual Christmas party at their West County estate. An array of gold holiday lighting illuminated the drive through two acres of professional landscaping with a countrified theme before Michelle reached a Tudor-style mansion. She turned her aging Volkswagen over to a teenage valet and warned him not to disrespect it. At the entryway of large double doors boasting elaborate wreaths of evergreens and pinecones stood Claire, wrapped in red taffeta, and Arthur, tuxedoed with a plaid cummerbund and tie. Two little dogs posing as dust mops kept yipping and yapping as Michelle approached.

"Darling," Claire said, pursing an air kiss in the general direction of Michelle's cheek. "We thought you might've lost your way."

"Ouch," Michelle muttered as the bigger fluff nipped her ankle.

"Shame, shame." Claire tucked one mop under each arm and swished through the door.

After relinquishing her trench coat to a girl with metal-encased teeth, Michelle allowed Arthur to slip her arm through his. They walked into a reception area of soaring oak-beamed ceilings and leaded glass windows, where peach walls surrounded a display of fruitwood and chintz and muted stripes. In the far corner a golden angel hovered from the top of a Christmas tree covered with hand-blown German ornaments. Beyond the large doorway sideboards were laden with Christmas treats, eggnog, and spirits. Conversation and laughter flowed like bubbly champagne.

"You're looking at the elite of St. Louis," Arthur said, "at least from a purely Catholic perspective—Archdiocese clergy, Sacred Heart nuns and alumni from Maryville College, Claire's alma mater.

The older nuns were dressed in traditional habits dating from the establishment of their order. When religious clothing reflected that of the general populace, Arthur explained. Most of the younger nuns wore plain blouses and shoulder-length head coverings with matching skirts and jackets in assorted colors. One nun, the head of a small Catholic college, was decked out in formalwear comparable to that of well-to-do matrons.

Between the hole in her stocking from Claire's mutt and the two-piece fuchsia knit with bell-shaped sleeves, Michelle rated her fashion sense as one notch below the nuns in suits. But regardless of their clothing, the Maryville alums seemed to share a common dedication to liberal ideals. Their conversation centered on the shortcomings of Vatican II; and in keeping with the holiday spirit, they were kind enough to tolerate the opinion of any male who dared disagree.

"The Church does not recognize the breadth of our talents," said one, with others expressing their thoughts as well.

"Well, that's why we need to expand the role of female religious."

"We should be priests too."

"Had I not met Arthur, I'd have made a superb priest, better than some I know," Claire said, "present company excluded, Fathers."

"Now you go too far."

"That's not what Our Lord had in mind when he gathered the disciples. There were no chosen women, only men who left their families to spread The Word."

"Women of those times stayed at home."

"Times have changed. The Church needs to change."

The suppression of women in the Catholic Church didn't stir any passion in Michelle, other than her need for a smoke. She retreated to a glassed enclosure off of the dining room, a temperature-controlled conservatory filled with rattan furniture and exotic plants identified by markers noting their Latin botanical names. She stuck a cigarette in her mouth and while she rummaged in her evening bag, a hand came from behind a giant hibiscus and flicked a gold lighter. Monogrammed with the initials 'BAB', it belonged to Arthur and Claire's son, Bart.

She thanked him and turned her head to exhale. "You're not smoking?"

"It's bad for my health, but a great way to meet beautiful women."

"What a line," she said. "Is that how you met your wife?"

He laughed and spent the next five minutes talking about Nell and their children. They'd gone east to visit her family before Christmas.

Bart Bannister, you ought to be in movies, Michelle thought. What incredible genes: a younger version of his father but with his mother's blue eyes and blonde hair. And so devoted to his family, an admirable trait she respected, especially since her dating policy excluded married men.

*****

After the holidays Michelle reconsidered her stance when Bart waged an aggressive pursuit for her body and soul. What started as business lunches at Anthony's, where the well heeled gather to see and be seen, soon moved on to his giving her a first edition of Carl Sandburg poetry, which she displayed on her coffee table and pretended to understand. Next, elaborate French meals catered in her apartment. By the first of February they had progressed to imaginative lovers. Three weeks later she moved from the efficiency apartment on Twenty-Third Street to a luxury condominium on the waterfront.

When Michelle first told her parents she planned on moving to a condo, they offered to help with the financing. She declined, explaining a decent salary came with her new job, but failed to mention she already held title to the property. A gift from Bart with no strings attached, she rationalized to herself but knew better. She'd been bought and paid for, a rich man's working mistress, and worse than the Chicago madam Grandpa Carlo supposedly took up with in his youth. At least Giulietta Bracca had paid her own way.

*****

One Saturday morning in mid-August Michelle was finishing her weekly pedicure when an unexpected buzz from the outside hall gave her a jolt that smeared the nail polish and prompted a string of obscenities worthy of any sailor. With cotton balls separating her toes, she padded to the door, looked through the peephole, and let out a silent groan. But when she opened the door, it was with a broad smile plastered on her face.

"Grandpa Carlo, what a surprise. You're my first visitor."

"I was in the city on business," he said as they greeted each other with kisses. He scanned the well-appointed surroundings and shook his head. "Quite the place; that must be some job you landed."

"It's more than I ever expected." Feeling a rush of blood to her face, Michelle motioned to the glass and chrome dining set. "Please, sit. I'll make coffee."

"No coffee, thanks."

"With a little grappa?"

"*Si, con grappa.*"

They faced a large expanse of windows offering an uninterrupted view of the Mississippi. The overcast day neither enhanced nor disparaged the appearance of water that never advanced beyond its well-known murkiness.

"You see that, Michelle?" He pointed to a barge pushing aside floating debris as it slowly moved upriver. "Tons of coal going someplace where there's a need for it. Who knows, maybe that batch came out of St. Gregory."

She nodded to be polite, both sipping coffee and grappa until he spoke again. "All those years at St. Gregory Coal Company, me and your Grandpa Jake ... and before us, Mario Roselli, the grandpa you never knew. And before Mario, his papa—the one that died in a mine explosion. Nothing was ever handed to us. We busted our butts for everything we earned."

"Mind if I smoke?"

"This ain't Grandma Irene you're talking to."

She lit a cigarette without offering him one. Both grandpas had given up their cigarillos five years earlier after being diagnosed with mild forms of black lung, the result of inhaled coal dust.

He drained his cup and shoved it aside. "You know, Michelle, just 'cause your Grandpa Jake and me live in the country, we ain't no bumpkins."

"What do you mean?"

"I mean we know how this place came to you. Jake and me have ways of finding things out. Your mama and papa ... pfft." He shrugged them off with his hand. "They think you got yourself a big, fancy job."

"I do have a good job."

"Not good enough to afford all this." He waved his arms around to encompass the room. "Even a view of a dirty mud river, all because of ... what's his name? Oh, yeah. Bartolommeo Bannister, the rich shit with a wife and two kids."

Michelle felt the blood leave her face. She jumped up and tried to keep her voice from shaking. "This place belongs to me."

"This place was bought and paid for by him."

"Look who's talking, Grandpa. What about you and that girlfriend in Chicago, a high-class madam living off of other whores?"

"Fifty years ago and different times, people did whatever it took to survive. Besides, I wasn't married. She wasn't married. Nobody got hurt. Well, not at first." He stood, with effort to accommodate his seventy-plus years, and went to the window. "Giulietta didn't deserve what happened. Without her, I wouldn't be here."

Michelle joined him, put her hand on his shoulder. "I'm sorry Grandpa. I didn't mean to upset you."

"Your mama and papa, they made sure you went to college. Why? So you could take care of yourself. You can do better than this man."

"I love him, Grandpa."

"Because you love him, this is okay?"

"I can't let go, even if I only have part of him."

"That part you can get from any man. Think about what I say." He opened his arms to her. "So, give me a hug. I gotta go."

"You won't tell Mom and Dad?"

"Not a word from me. But that don't mean they won't find out some other way."

Chapter 50
A Good Cause

Several months later Frank received a telephone call from Claire Bannister who was in Chicago attending the annual Catholic Laity for Christ Conference. She invited Frank to tea at the Drake Hotel and he didn't hesitate to cancel an appointment to accommodate her. When they met in the tearoom, Frank thought Claire looked drawn and uncomfortable. Maybe she just looked her age, which must've been pushing seventy. She complained about the oversized chairs as she struggled to position herself on the crushed velveteen upholstery. Finally, she scooted to the chair's edge and contemplated the tray of tiny sandwiches before selecting a cucumber slice wedged between two rounds of bread.

She spoke before taking her first bite. "I regret Arthur could not be here today, Father Roselli."

He suspected the worse: Mrs. Bannister usually called him Frank or Father Frank. He sat back in the commodious chair designed for long legs and listened with a poker face as Claire recited a detailed account of the affair between her son and Michelle. She sipped the tea that had been poured ten minutes earlier. Turning up her nose, she sent the porcelain cup and saucer rattling to the table, a signal for the waitress to provide fresh service. With blue eyes lidded Claire patted her mouth with a dainty scallop-edged napkin. She folded the napkin, locked those eyes on Frank, and demanded an immediate resolution.

Frank tented his fingers, shaping forefingers and thumbs into a movable triangle, a gesture he'd developed to replace the finger drumming Uncle Mike called a dead giveaway for apprehension. "Michelle's always been willful, even as a child," he said with deliberation as Claire swallowed a dollop of cream cheese and pumpernickel. "What about your son?"

"Neither Arthur or I have spoken to Bart about this. Nor do we intend to unless it's absolutely necessary. Naturally, his devoted wife doesn't know but she's bound to find out, given St. Louis's small town mentality. The scandal would end their marriage, devastate my grandchildren." Claire waited until the waitress poured fresh tea and left before she continued. "To put it bluntly, neither Arthur nor I will tolerate an expensive scandal. Why channel money into a nasty divorce when it can be used for worthwhile charitable endeavors."

Frank straightened up. "Don't do anything for now, Mrs. Bannister. Give me time to consider some options."

"Consider this, Father Roselli. Your parish is dirt poor, the physical church in disrepair and soon will be condemned if necessary improvements aren't made. Arthur and I could manage a sizable contribution, establish a fund to alleviate this financial burden."

"Of course, a generous gift would be welcomed. Still ...."

"Don't toy with me, Frank, and don't underrate yourself. Should you ever plan on advancing your career, this would be an ideal stepping-stone. Training for the future, shall we say?" She lifted her brow. "In any case, to be quite honest I think your talents are being wasted here."

"You mean at St. Sebastian's?"

"I mean in Chicago. Of course, you must get your feet wet someplace but if you expect to be a general someday, don't stay too long in the trenches."

"How long and where is not for me to decide, Mrs. Bannister. That's the archbishop's role."

"All in due time, Frank. Of course, for now there's the matter of St. Sebastian's pastor suffering from inoperable cancer. Poor man, it's in his lungs."

"You know about Monsignor Logan?"

"We have connections, Frank. The right connections can move you beyond the Midwest. Chicago may be the heart of Catholicism in America, but you belong at the heart of the Universal Church."

"The Vatican?" He let the slight hint of a smile creep into his voice. "Ah-h, to be in Rome again."

"I'm quite serious. Arthur and I recognized your potential when we first met at Pierluigi, and we've followed your career ever since. You're learning how to play both sides and how to exploit discord to your advantage. There are forces out there to be reckoned with, Frank. Some believe the Church is moving too fast, others not fast enough."

"I don't understand, Mrs. Bannister."

"I know you don't, not from the shelter of your Chicago parish. But I'm giving you the opportunity to learn so don't disappoint me." She folded her napkin and stood up. "Don't bother about the check. I've already taken care of it."

*****

Frank waited a week before he caught an early morning flight to St. Louis. After a forty-minute cab ride to a renovated building on the waterfront, he met with Bart Bannister at his fourth floor office.

"Ah, Father Frank, it's good to see you again," Bart said, rolling his chair away from a cluttered desk. He stood to shake Frank's hand and motioned to one of four leather swivel chairs circling a teakwood pedestal table. "Please, sit. I'll have my secretary bring some coffee. Cream and sugar?" He picked up the phone.

Frank refused with the show of his palm. "I can't stay long, but thanks for seeing me on short notice."

"Glad to be of service." Bart cradled the telephone receiver and sat across from him. "Are you in the area on church affairs or to visit family?"

"Neither. I'm here to see you."

Bart laughed as he reached for his checkbook. "Okay, what's the cause and how much do you need?"

"It's about my sister Michelle."

Bart's smile started to fade. "I believe we met several years ago, Christmas at my parents' house. Didn't she move here?" He didn't wait for an answer. "Is she in some kind of trouble?"

Frank joined fingers and thumbs into their usual triangle and held Bart's eyes with his. "I recently learned of my sister's involvement with a prominent St. Louis businessman. Unfortunately, he's already married to a woman who deserves better. It's possible she may learn of this affair within the next two weeks. The scandal is bound to create tragic results, especially with those innocent families."

Bart swiveled ninety degrees to study a brilliant array of exotic fish

THE FAMILY ANGEL

swimming in their saltwater aquarium. A blue and white angelfish played hide and seek with a magenta dotty back while a red and blue goby weaved through the sea lettuce and ornamental shells. Bart gulped to relieve his throbbing Adam's apple before he stammered out a few words. "I ... uh, don't know what to say."

"Say you'll help me. Just as your parents did when they used their influence to help Michelle acquire a job in St. Louis. Now I'm asking you to arrange the offer of a better job, one back in Chicago."

Silence filled the room while the fish entertained Bart. He remained focused on them when he finally spoke. "Is this fair to Michelle? She may be reluctant to leave."

"Not if the offer is generous and non-negotiable. Agreed?"

"I suppose. But, with a timeframe so short, I don't know ...."

Frank stood. "Think about the wife. She's very close to learning the truth. You do understand, don't you?"

"I'll make some phone calls. Yes, I'll do that today." Bart swiveled away from the aquarium and stood up.

"By the way, Bart, about that charitable cause ...."

"Uh, yes, of course, which one?"

"Holy Guardian Angels Children's Home in Chicago," Frank said with a smile. "The building is in deplorable condition."

"How much, Frank?"

"Fifty thousand would go a long way toward its restoration."

Chapter 51
Jamie and Henri

Jamie Roselli discovered Henri during a crowded fundraiser for the Chicago Art Museum. From a distance the exotic man spelled intrigue with his black, curly hair, a mustache curving into his full, sensuous mouth, and skin the color of light caramel. M-m-m, she mused, licking her lips, Middle East. Perhaps in oil, judging from his expensive clothes, not that Jamie cared although she'd heard it was easier to fall in love with a rich man than a poor one. After he'd strolled over to the bar, she developed an immediate thirst and headed there too. Glass in hand he stepped back and into Jamie's path, christening her black velvet cocktail dress with bubbly sparkling wine. Karma, Henri later described their meeting, and Jamie agreed. After several failed romances, she had met the man of her dreams, even though she towered over him by a good two inches. Later when she learned his striking features resulted from a combination of French and Negro blood, she proudly conveyed the information to all her friends, thus avoiding any backlash of intolerance. As well as making sure they all knew how to pronounce Henri, as is, *ahn-REE*.

Like Jamie, Henri was the youngest of three. His sisters, both married and living in Paris, oversaw the European branch of Durand Enterprises, exporters of fine Parisian products, while Henri managed the Chicago and New York offices. Their mother had been widowed for ten years and still lived in Paris. On those occasions when she traveled to the States, she stayed at the Waldorf-Astoria, preferring

New York to her native Chicago. Without Henri's knowledge his mother had asked their lawyers to run a background check on Jamie Roselli. The extensive report, which listed Jamie's legal name as Giacoma Louisa Roselli, also included the names of her parents and grandparents.

*****

July 10, 1978
Dear Folks,
I think I'm in love. Erase that—I know I'm in love. Besides being handsome, he's generous, intelligent, and successful. Did I mention wonderful and kind? I want all of you to meet Henri but right now he's involved in the family business and can't leave Chicago. So-o, I was hoping you could come here instead—next weekend if possible. By the way, Henri says his mother knew Grandpa Carlo, years ago in Chicago. What a coincidence! Ask him if he remembers Ruby Lee.
Love,
Jamie
P.S. I took Henri to meet Frank. They really seemed to hit it off.

*****

Mary Ann still had the letter clutched in her hand when she telephoned her papa, demanding he come over right away. She met him on the screened back porch filled with country furniture and over the gentle hum of the ceiling fan, she read Jamie's letter out loud. He listened with closed eyes, as if in another time, another place.

"Ruby Lee, Papa? Didn't Roscoe and Essie Mae have a daughter named Ruby Lee? Papa, did you hear me?"

He cleared his throat. "Si, Ruby Lee, she had two girls and a boy."

"Oh, Papa." Mary Ann burst into tears. "Our Jamie wants to marry Ruby Lee's son? Call me a prejudiced bitch, but I just can't help what I'm feeling."

He patted her shoulder. "First, let's meet this Henri. Then we'll decide if he ain't right for Jamie."

"But if Michelle doesn't settle down, Jamie's our only hope for grandchildren."

"So her babies might be a shade darker than us. It ain't the end of the world, leastways not like before."

Mary Ann dabbed her tears and blew her nose. "To think Frank already knew. I could wring his neck for not warning us. When Tony comes home, we'll call and give Frank hell." She took a deep breath.

"Henri, hmm, the name sounds French. He's probably Catholic."

"Probably not, his papa was a Jew. His mama, a Baptist."

Later, after Papa left and Tony walked into the kitchen, Mary Ann thrust the letter into her husband's hand. While he read in silence, she watched his face, waiting for a break in its usual composure.

"I'd be more concerned if this were Michelle," he said, taking off his reading glasses. "Jamie's always been the sensible one."

"That's all you can say?"

"How about: these things have a way of working out. Isn't that what your papa always says? Look, Mary Ann, just don't get hysterical on Jamie."

"Hysterical? Please give me some credit. I am, however, extremely disappointed. Jamie was supposed to return to St. Gregory after college. Instead, she bolted to Chicago."

"And works as a buyer for … what's that store?"

"Carson Pirie Scott, one of the best."

"We can't run her life, Mary Ann, just like we can't run Michelle's. Now let's talk about Chicago."

"Papa promised he'd go. But don't count of your mom. Uncle Jake said she's not feeling well."

"Again? Do I need to worry about her?"

"Not yet. I'll tell you when."

*****

Early Saturday morning Carlo accompanied Tony and Mary Ann to St. Louis. From there they caught a flight to Chicago. Carlo's introduction to flying was so uneventful that when their plane touched down at Midway, he said he'd never bother with the train again. They stayed with Jamie, whose enthusiasm overshadowed the disappointment Mary Ann couldn't hide, and in the evening they went to Henri Durand's Gold Coast penthouse.

Henri and his mother held court in an immense living room decorated in polished steel and leather soft as butter. Abstract paintings, their number limited so as not to eclipse one another, hung against the stark white of plastered walls. Oak floors, bleached to complement the walls, bordered a variety of Oriental rugs. In one corner a marble pedestal served as the base for a large metal sculpture: man and woman locked in an embrace of intertwining arms and legs. One tuxedo-clad waiter circulated with a tray of drinks and another with canapés of Russian caviar on toast points and smoked salmon on miniature bagel slices.

After a series of cordial introductions Jamie and Henri gave her parents a tour of the condominium, which left Carlo alone with Ruby Lee. They talked about her folks, both dead for years and within months of each other—Roscoe from a heart attack and Essie Mae, a stroke. Then Ruby Lee produced her still-perfect smile and took Carlo's hand in hers. "We've both come a long way from 'The Stroll', haven't we, Mister Charlie?"

Mister Charlie. After all these years the name no longer irritated him, especially when it rolled off Ruby Lee's plum-colored lips. She was even prettier than he had remembered. Money can do that. He guessed her age to be around sixty-eight, six years younger than his seventy-four. She could've passed for fifty-five. Round curves filled every niche of her dress—a nice color, the same as Irene's prize roses. Nice body. Nice legs, even nicer in those high heels.

"And your leg?" Carlo heard her ask. He flushed under his collar.

"Your leg," she repeated, "does it give you much trouble? I noticed you were limping."

"A touch of arthritis," he said, "from the mine."

"Of course, all those years in the damp underground." She took a sip of champagne. "So, tell me: how do you feel about my Henri and your Jamie?"

"I'm just glad I don't have to defend them to Essie Mae and Roscoe."

"Oh-h … me too, Mister Charlie," she said with a laugh. "They'd be turning in their graves. Or maybe not, considering you were practically kin." She kissed his cheek and glanced across the room. "Oh dear, that daughter of yours looks positively miserable. I'd better go cheer her up."

*****

Mary Ann had steered Tony to the display of sensual artwork because its vantage point provided the best view of everyone else. She let out a groan on seeing Ruby Lee heading in their direction. "Brace yourself, Tony. Here comes Ms. Money Bags."

"And you behave yourself. She's probably a very nice lady."

Ruby Lee clasped Mary Ann's hand and nodded to Tony. "I'm so delighted to finally meet the daughter of Mister Charlie … I mean Carlo. You'll have to excuse my lapse of fifty years. Mister Charlie was our family nickname for your daddy."

"Yes, I know." Mary Ann eased her hand from Ruby Lee's and wrapped it around her wineglass. "Roscoe and Essie Mae ... I mean, your parents ... often referred to Papa that way."

"They held him in such high regard and they loved fussing over you and ...." Ruby Lee put one finger to her lips. "Let me think ... oh, yes, Michael. He had polio, right? And then became a priest. Where is he now?"

"In Rome, teaching at the North American College," Tony said, having been excluded from a conversation of two women sizing up each other.

"And I've already met your son." Ruby Lee raised her brow.

"Yes, another priest. As you can see, we're very Catholic."

"No need to apologize. If you'll excuse me, please," Ruby Lee said, adding her empty glass to a passing tray.

While Mary Ann and Ruby Lee had been bantering, Carlo caught up with his eldest grandchild. "You feel like the old Michelle," he said as they hugged, "not so stiff like a wind-up toy."

She popped a canapé into his mouth; he washed it down with wine. "I'm moving back to Chicago, Grandpa."

"This was your choice?"

She shrugged. "A job too good to pass up. You know the saying: If you want someone to leave, make an offer so good she won't want to stay."

"I heard about the fancy car."

"Part of getting dumped."

"You're okay with this?"

"The timing was right."

"It's all about time, Michelle. You made the right decision."

"I wish ... oh my god. Frank just walked in, and you won't believe who's with him."

Carlo turned to see Jamie greeting Frank and two other priests. The older one had a thatch of white hair that he remembered first as auburn and later peppered with salt. "Merda," he grumbled. "If that thief stays, I'm leaving."

"Please, Grandpa. Don't upset Jamie. It was her idea to invite Father Terry."

"Who's the young collar?"

"Never seen him before," Michelle said with a wave of fingers directed to the black suits.

"Basta! Don't encourage the pious bastard."

"Don't you dare walk away. Remember your lecture about time? Well, maybe it's time you and Father Terry buried the past."

Carlo wanted to bolt but Michelle had locked his hand in hers and the priest was on his way over. After an exchange of greetings, Michelle patted her lips with two cigarette fingers and excused herself for a smoke. The priest relaxed his shoulders and cracked a smile. "How long has it been, Carlo?"

Not long enough, he wanted to reply. But then the priest brought up his single visit to St. Gregory so Carlo half listened to him go on about Mary Ann and the wedding, as if he had some claim on her which they both knew he didn't. Then the conversation switched to Michael.

"Have you ever visited him in Rome?" the priest asked.

"Michael comes home when he wants to see me. Mary Ann I got living next door. Daughters have a certain loyalty, you know. They rarely leave the family."

"Indeed you are fortunate. I'm sure Louisa must be smiling down on you."

"What we had was special and just between the two of us."

"Forgive me, I didn't mean to imply otherwise. But I remember how much Louisa loved you."

"She told you that?"

"More than once, Carlo. Over the years I've seen that love manifested through Mary Ann and Michael—her blessed legacy. Yours too."

"No, Father. Mine has yet to be fulfilled."

*****

While Grandpa was matching barbs with Father Terry, Michelle wandered over to Frank and the other priest, a gaunt young man she thought looked vaguely familiar.

"Ah, my favorite big sister," said Frank, leaning over to hug her. "Michelle, this is my good friend Kevin—of the vast Clan Connelly—and great nephew to our own Father Terry."

"I knew I'd seen that hair in an earlier life," she said. "So now we have the pleasure of another Father Connelly."

"Please, call me Kevin. After all, I like to think of us as family by way of Uncle Terry. He holds your mother and Father Mike in such high regard."

"That's for sure. Mom kept all of Father Connelly's letters. She used to pass them on to us when we were kids. Right, Frank?"

"Those letters were my first introduction to Rome. I dreamed of going there someday, but not as a seminarian."

"First Uncle Mike, then you and his nephew," Michelle said. "Father Terry could've chartered his own religious order."

"Not quite," Kevin replied with a laugh. "We've all gone our separate ways and with our own agendas."

"Thank God. Houses built on the best of intentions have a way of tumbling, like so many rows of dominoes."

"Please, Michelle, no more tea readings. Did I tell you: Kevin is an assistant pastor at St. Therese of the Little Flower?"

"Really," Michelle said with a smile. "I'm relocating to Chicago in a few weeks. I'll have to catch one of your sermons, Father."

"Please, I really do prefer Kevin."

Before she could answer, her sister came by and whisked Kevin away. Michelle watched him make the rounds with Jamie and then she asked Frank to hear her confession at his convenience.

"We can do it now if you like. I'm sure there's a private area where we can …."

"None of that face-to-face stuff. I prefer the traditional way—behind the screen and in a closet where I can't see your shocked expressions."

"There's not much I haven't already heard."

"But not from me. Besides, I need time to think."

He took out a small spiral notebook. "In that case, tomorrow at two. You do know I'm at St. Sebastian's?"

Michelle cocked her head. "How on earth did you wind up in that godforsaken ghetto?"

"St. Sebastian's is an urban sanctuary, even if it is surrounded by a jungle of rejects and abandoned buildings." Frank squared his shoulders and looked down on her. "Actually, some nice families live in the neighborhood. Little kids who deserve better, parents who have nothing better to give. Sebastian's physical plant is quite magnificent, although it could use an overhaul. We still draw former parishioners who made the great exodus to the suburbs. On Sundays they come back in search of a simpler time."

"Dammit, Frank. I never dreamed you'd wind up in the twilight zone. You were going places."

THE FAMILY ANGEL

"Even the ambitious have to crawl before they can walk."

*****

When Carlo walked away from Terry Connelly, he managed to leave behind some of his old resentment. With or without help from the aging priest Michael had become his own man and had made his own choices. But Mary Ann would always belong to the man whose name she carried at birth; Carlo made sure of that.

He caught the scent of Ruby Lee, seconds before she slipped her arm through his and ushered him out to the terrace overlooking the Gold Coast.

"You surely have a wonderful family, Mister Charlie."

"My children and grandchildren are my life."

"That's obvious. Of course, I love my family too. But it's good to have other interests, especially when a mate has passed, as your wife and my husband have."

"Nice," Carlo replied, commenting on the scene below: a collage of lights from the piers and marinas and of vessels crisscrossing moonlit waters. "I'm seeing Lake Michigan like I never seen it before."

She put her hand over his. "So tell me, were the years good to you? Did you even think of marrying again?"

"I never found the right woman."

"Does that mean you're still looking?"

He grinned. "When I quit looking, I'll start worrying."

Carlo listened with one ear as she talked about her late husband and their children. Fifty years ago he and Ruby Lee had lived in different worlds. They still did but during the ensuing years she had moved far beyond his.

"Carlo, pay attention," she said. "I asked what you thought about—"

"Excuse me, Mother," Henri interrupted. "Could you and Mr. Baggio please come back inside? We're about to pop the cork."

Ruby and Carlo followed him into the living room. After the waiter filled every glass from a single bottle of Dom Perignon, Jamie clapped her hands.

"Could we all please gather in a circle," she said, taking Henri's arm.

"It's a tradition in our family," he said, "to gather around and welcome new friends into our circle—one that grows stronger as it grows larger."

He raised his glass with a *"Shalom!"*

"Salute!" came the reply along with a few, "Cheers!"

"What makes this evening so special is the joining of new and old friends into one family," Henri continued. "No date has been set for our wedding but Jamie and I don't believe in long engagements." He kissed her to the polite applause of everyone.

After the announcement Frank was among the first to offer his congratulations and best wishes. Then his mother pulled him aside. "I guess it's official, Frank."

"Don't make *it* sound so morbid."

"And why not? Was it too much to ask: for Jamie to pick a nice Catholic boy from St. Gregory? Or, for that matter a nice Catholic boy from anywhere? Just how are we going to resolve the religion issue?"

"The issue isn't ours to resolve."

"Coming from you, a priest? I thought resolution was your strong suit."

"Perhaps Henri is not so strong in his faith."

"After that Shalom?"

Frank shrugged. "For the Jews it's tradition."

"Perhaps he'll agree to raise their children Catholic."

"That's for Henri and Jamie to decide. I can provide guidance, but so far they haven't asked for any."

"Don't let me down, Frank. I want my grandchildren raised in the faith. You can make it happen."

Before Frank could answer, Michelle appeared at his side. "Frank can make anything happen. Right Frank?"

"You got the name right. It's Frank, not Jesus. And I'm not a miracle worker." He glanced at his watch. "Speaking of miracles, I'll need one if I don't leave right now. I have the early Mass tomorrow."

After the three priests left, Jamie and Henri wanted to show Michelle the newest disco. They took the next elevator down, leaving Mary Ann and Tony to wait in the penthouse foyer with Ruby Lee.

Tony clasped her hand in the warm manner she'd displayed earlier. "It was a pleasure meeting you, Ruby Lee, after all these years."

"The pleasure was Henri's and mine." She turned to Mary Ann and smiled. "We'll have such fun getting together again for the wedding, won't we?"

"Yes, of course, the wedding," Mary Ann replied just as the elevator door rolled open. Holding the door, she called out, "Are you coming, Papa?"

"Later," he said from the living room. When he blew a kiss from his fingertips, Mary Ann let the door close.

Inside the elevator she bristled. "Did you see the way that woman pushed herself onto poor Papa?"

"Her name is Ruby Lee, and your father loved the attention. After all, she is a very attractive woman."

"Oh really? I didn't notice."

"Back in St. Gregory the Dapper Dago still gets around. But I can't remember the last time I saw him this revved up."

"He's too old."

"I'll remind you of that in another twenty years."

Back at the penthouse Ruby Lee followed Carlo out to the terrace. "I'm staying in Chicago until the end of the week," she said. "Will I see you again?"

"Tomorrow I leave with my daughter and her husband. For him it's back to work on Monday."

"Why not stay a few more days? We could explore Chicago together." She squeezed his hand. "Come on, Mister Charlie. I have a two-bedroom suite at the Palmer House. There's plenty of room. And I won't bite unless you insist."

He thought a minute before answering, "If I stay with you, I pay for everything else."

She wrapped her arms around his neck. "You won't be sorry. We're going to have so much fun together."

*****

True to her word, Ruby Lee did not disappoint Carlo. After sleeping in each morning, they explored museums and the area surrounding Madison and State Streets. They agreed the Loop had changed considerably in fifty years, although some of the familiar places still evoked memories: Marshall Field's, Chicago Theater, Blackie's Restaurant, and Dearborn Station. Carlo's old neighborhood and favorite haunts—Night School and Fabiola's—had not survived the wrecking ball, all swallowed in a maze of interstate highways. Ruby Lee's once vibrant Stroll lost its pizzazz too, and wore the tackiness of a party guest that had outstayed its welcome.

Ruby Lee took responsibility for their dinner venues, a task done early in the day, after first conferring by telephone with Henri, then enlisting the hotel concierge to secure the right table and proper ambiance. In the evening as they enjoyed Chicago's best restaurants, Ruby Lee would offer menu suggestions and Carlo selected the wine. By the time the food and drink arrived, they were regaling each other with stories from their separate lives.

On their last evening together after returning to the Palmer House suite, Carlo readied himself for bed in the room he had yet to sleep in. He flipped out the light switch and crossed the parlor to Ruby Lee's room. She was waiting in ivory silk, sitting in bed with her back against the padded headboard. Carlo grinned before dimming the light. He bounced onto the bed.

"I'm going to miss you, Mister Charlie."

He felt her finger trail down his leg and stop at the bullet wound.

"If it hadn't been for this," she said, lightly tracing the scar, "we never would've met."

He closed his eyes to block out a succession of memories before whispering a single word, *"Destino."*

"How right you are. You were the first man I ever saw ... well, you know ... up close and personal."

"Up close? Personal?"

She giggled. "I peeked under the covers when you were dead to the world from that raging fever. The sight of you prepared me for what to expect later from Guy." Her hand slipped away from the scar and lingered nearby. "As you may already know, crackers aren't supposed to be as well endowed as their black brothers."

He squeezed her hand. "They say size ain't everything."

"They are so-o right. Did you ever think we would end up like this—two old fogies fuckin' at the Palmer House."

"*Too* old? I thought you liked it."

"Oh, Mister Charlie, I surely do. My only regret is our not getting together sooner. I'll bet you were some sweet daddy fifty years ago."

Chapter 52
Michelle and Frank

In a dark confessional of St. Sebastian's Michelle shifted her weight on the cushioned kneeler until she found an acceptable level of comfort. She cleared her throat and spoke in a whisper. "Bless me, Father, for I have sinned. It's been four years since my last confession."

"Go ahead, Michelle, but could you speak up a little?"

"Please, Frank. This isn't exactly a piece of cake." She sighed before coming back with a stronger voice. "For two and a half years I committed adultery with a married man. I did so willingly and with no regard for his wife or family. I thought I loved him, the bastard."

"What about now? Do you still think you love him?"

"I'm not sure but it doesn't matter. He had to choose; he didn't choose me."

"Are you asking God's forgiveness?" he asked, massaging the raised scar on his chin.

"That's why I'm here, Frank. But, you already knew all of this, didn't you?"

"I was aware of the problem."

"That figures. I should be ever so grateful, considering the jerk didn't hesitate to give me a golden heave-ho. Not in person, over the telephone."

"I'm sorry, Michelle."

"Hey, this is my confession and my sins. But in the future please stay out of my problems unless I ask for your help." Her voice softened. "There's more—after all, it has been four years."

After Michelle recited a litany of mortal and venial sins, Frank gave her a penance of prayers. She made a good act of contrition and he gave her absolution.

"Frank, one more thing: I've decided to give up smoking, my own self-prescribed penance."

"You've made a wise decision."

"It's the best I can do, for now anyway."

"I'll pray for you. Now go in peace."

*****

Several months after returning to Chicago, Michelle attended Mass at St. Therese's, not for the donuts and coffee that would be served afterwards but to hear Kevin preach.

"Stand up and be counted for what you believe in," he told his parishioners. "Open your hearts to those sheep that have strayed from God and bring them back into the fold."

Michelle felt drawn to Kevin's compassion and honesty. She went back the following Sunday.

"As Catholics, we've been brought up to repress our feelings," he said at the end of that sermon. "For those of you who want to loosen up and shout your love for Our Lord, come to the parish hall on Wednesday evening and sing His Praises."

After two lively Wednesday evenings with the charismatic group, Michelle told Kevin they were too theatrical for her traditional Catholicism. It's not for everyone, he agreed, but there were many ways to become involved in projects at St. Therese's. He suggested they meet downtown for lunch to discuss new banners for the church. Ten feet high by six feet wide, the adornments must be worthy to hang alongside statues of the Blessed Mother and St. Joseph. As usual, funding for the project was meager. Could Michelle use her contacts in advertising?

They met several times at her office to go over the layouts before Michelle apologized with a red face. Since their project was non-income producing, it needed to be separated from the office. Although she offered her apartment as a reasonable alternative, Michelle never doubted her intentions when he showed up. She made the first move, taking Kevin's hand and leading him into her bedroom. He started to protest; she quieted him with a finger to his lips.

"You want me as much as I want you," Michelle said. She

could've pulled back when he protested. She could have sent him away but she didn't. After a passionate lovemaking session equal to any she'd experienced with Bart, Kevin wept in her arms. Out of joy or guilt, she wasn't sure. Nor did she care. She'd brought Kevin to the top of the mountain. He'd savored the ride, his first. Surely God would forgive them for enjoying the gift of their bodies.

Her affair with Bart Bannister had been tainted by the crime against his family. But with Kevin, there was an undeniable sweetness in the loss of his innocence. Kevin said he loved her and that he'd give up everything, just to be with her. Everything.

Chapter 53
History Revisited

Meanwhile at St. Sebastian's Monsignor Logan's declining health from the effects of chemotherapy had forced Frank to assume most of the pastoral duties. On three different occasions the archbishop promised to send someone older and more experienced to take the lead, but the shortage of qualified priests resulted in their being assigned to more pressing responsibilities. Frank didn't mind. In fact, he welcomed the challenge. Staying busy every waking moment helped him sleep through the night.

His mother had quit writing him letters because he never found time to answer them. She now preferred the efficiency of telephoning, no longer an extravagance but a modern necessity. Three months after Jamie's engagement party she called, her voice choked with emotion as she blurted out her first words. "I feel like I've been slapped in the face." Frank waited as she blew her nose. "Your sister has married Henri, in a civil ceremony no less."

"I'm sorry, Mom. I didn't realize they planned to marry so soon."

"I hope this won't reflect badly on you with the hierarchy, Frank. You know, having a sister living in a sinful union, one you might've prevented if only you hadn't been so damn busy. It's not too late to straighten this out. You will talk to her, won't you?"

"Sure, Mom, but not right away. Let things cool for awhile."

"Just don't tell me you'll pray for her and that's all you do."

"How's everybody else?"

"Your father's fine. So's Grandpa Jake, but I'm worried about your Grandma Irene. She's slowing down, showing her age."

"Well, she's not exactly a spring chicken anymore. How's Grandpa Carlo?"

"Still kicking up his heels if you know what I mean. At least for now he's content with St. Gregory. Thank God that other woman has stayed put in Paris."

"That other woman?"

"Don't play dumb, Frank. They've been corresponding, which won't last long. Papa never was much of a letter writer. Oh well, enough of that. Have you seen Michelle?"

"I … uh."

"Don't tell me you've been too busy. She called several times. Seems happy to be back in Chicago but what do I know. I thought she loved St. Louis. She sold her condo, you know, before your father and I ever laid eyes on it."

*****

Several weeks after Michelle relocated to Chicago, Frank received two checks in separate envelopes, both postmarked from St. Louis. The first, from Arthur and Claire Bannister for $100,000, was earmarked for repairs to St. Sebastian's Church; the second came from their son Bart, $50,000 payable to the Holy Guardian Angels Children's Home.

"Careful, Frank, you'll soon develop the reputation as a leading fundraiser for the archdiocese," Kevin Connelly said when he heard about the donations. "On second thought, maybe that's a plus. Your talents won't linger in a parish better known for its frescoes than its humanitarian efforts."

"Hey, don't knock my efforts. We manage to draw a decent Sunday attendance from other parishes, mostly generous worshippers who support the traditional Church. They're pushing me to petition His Excellency for permission to celebrate a weekly Mass in Latin."

"Ask for a weekly, you might get approved for a monthly. That is, if you're lucky."

"Or, if I can show an increase in the collection plate," Frank said with a wink. "Not to change the subject, Kev, but have you ever heard of John Marconi?"

"Who hasn't—a bigwig in construction who prefers keeping a low profile."

"A low profile in construction, is that possible?"

"What I mean is he keeps his private life private. There was some trouble way back when and the family's been publicity-shy ever since. But as far as I know, Marconi's a legitimate contractor." Kevin assumed the voice of a petty mobster, and asked, "What's the matter, Frankie? Marconi been putting the squeeze on you?"

*****

John Marconi had called on Frank several days before. Short, balding and in his early fifties, Marconi had a dumpling face and bulbous nose wedged between blotchy, pitted cheeks. Below a beach ball belly his trousers hung low, their cuffs worn and frayed. He sucked on a cigar stuck in the corner of his mouth. Unlit, he explained to Frank, out of deference to a bout with throat cancer. They'd been sitting across a cluttered desk in the office rectory, making small talk when Marconi inquired as to the whereabouts of Frank's home parish.

"A mining town in Southern Illinois called St. Gregory," Frank said. "But my mother's parents lived in Chicago during Prohibition. In fact, her two uncles ran a saloon on the South Side. Fabiola's, you may have heard of it."

"You don't say? When I was a kid, my old man took me there. His old man used to be tight with the owners."

Frank nodded. "My great-uncles, Vincenzo and Massimo Valenza. They've been dead over twenty-five years. Your grandfather, what was his name?"

"Alberto Marconi. Berto, they called him. He died over sixty years ago, murdered on the streets of Chicago."

"Really? Did they ever find his killer?"

"Nah. Pop never wanted to talk about it. Still, I'd like to know what happened. The newspapers and police reports were pretty vague, only that he died from a knife wound."

*****

Later that evening Frank called his grandfathers. Both Carlo and Jake remembered the circumstances of Berto Marconi's death, a chilling tale they'd heard more than once from the Valenzas who swore both of them to secrecy. The Black Hand enforcer had made his living off the blood of paesani and only after retiring, did he pay for those crimes—throat slit and genitalia stuffed in his mouth, a punishment he often meted out on others.

Several days later Frank met with John Marconi again. "I wasn't able to learn much about your grandfather's murder," Frank said. "But my grandpas remember Vincenzo and Massimo Valenza speaking of their good friend, Berto Marconi. In fact, the Valenzas knew him from the Old Country. 'A good family man,' was how they'd always referred to him. Perhaps that's how he should be best remembered."

"You're right, Father. That's what my old man would've wanted." Marconi moved his cigar from side to side. "I've been thinking about doing something for the less fortunate," he said, "like establishing a shelter for the homeless. In the worst section of Chicago where it's needed the most, where people can stay 'til they get back on their feet. I'd like to do this as a way of honoring the Marconi family name. What's more, I'd like you spearheading this project. Consider me your not-so-silent partner."

"This is wonderful, Mr. Marconi, but …."

"John, my friends call me John. I'll speak to the auxiliary bishop about your role. For this, he'll give his blessing."

*****

The Marconi Shelter took less than a year for Father Frank Roselli and John Marconi to bring to fruition. Between overseeing the shelter's construction and implementation of staff and the restoration and pastoral duties of St. Sebastian's, Frank had managed to keep occupied every waking moment, an ongoing regimen that continued to serve him well.

Chapter 54
July, 1980

Michelle assumed her lotus position on the living room floor while talking into the nearby speakerphone. "I love you so much but I can't ask you to give everything up for me."

"I've gone too far to turn back," came Kevin's reply. "From the moment I held you in my arms, I knew what I was doing felt right."

"But your career, you've made a commitment."

"I won't be the first priest dispensed from his vows. I love you, Michelle, as much as I love the Church and the priesthood."

"That's not enough. You have to love me more."

"I'll request a dispensation, which will infuriate the archbishop, not that I blame him … so many priests have left the Church already. But I can't stay now. My whole life would be a lie."

"He'll talk you into staying or send you to some remote parish in another diocese or a third world country with no telephones."

"It doesn't work that way."

"We'll never see each other again."

"Just let me handle this in my own way."

"Promise me one thing: do not, I repeat: do not, go to Frank until this is a done deal."

"I don't understand."

"Just do as I say. If you go to him first, you'll never leave the priesthood and we'll never get married."

"Michelle, please. Give Frank some credit."

"Dammit Kev, you already told him, didn't you."

*****

As Kevin Connelly's confessor, Frank had known about the affair from its beginning. Other than counseling Kev to remember his vows and return to the chaste life, Frank had no intentions of interfering, not with St. Sebastian's and the shelter consuming all his time. Then he received a phone call from Monsignor Terry Connelly, a pleasant though brief conversation ordering him to the home of Chicago's Archbishop Regis Clement for a private meeting.

"You're on your own, Frank," Monsignor Terry counseled him. "I won't be there. Nor am I at liberty to discuss the agenda prior to your going."

Frank had never been invited beyond the formal parlors of the imposing mansion but he intended to accept whatever assignment his stodgy superior might offer. After exchanging pleasantries in the cherry-paneled study, he and the archbishop made themselves comfortable on pliable leather chairs.

Archbishop Regis Clement fastened his steely eyes on Frank and spoke in a raspy voice that commanded attention, if for no other reason than its grinding irritability. "I've just returned from the American Bishops Conference with some rather alarming, uh ... scuttlebutt, shall we say for lack of a better term. It seems a situation has been developing in the Northeast—some rabble rousers led by a misguided bishop trying to sow the seeds of discontent for Our Holy Mother Church."

"I don't understand, Your Excellency."

"Nor do I. Who'd have thought such an abomination could occur in the twentieth century. Anyway, according to rumors, there's an underground group attempting to challenge the Church's authority, dissidents who think Paul the Sixth didn't address enough reform during Vatican II."

Privately, Frank agreed the late Pope Paul could have done more but he knew better than to express these feelings to the conservative archbishop.

"You don't seem surprised, Frank."

"Excuse me, Your Excellency. I was trying to absorb the seriousness of such a movement."

"What these fanatics expect to accomplish on their own escapes my common senses. In any case, as lean as my ranks are, and those of several other bishops, we've nevertheless decided to slip in a few, er ... damn ... I hate to use the term *spies.*"

"You mean infiltrate the movement."

"Exactly, a few good men capable of deception." He raised one eyebrow and searched Frank's face. "Interested?"

Frank suppressed the urge to protest his fitness. "Of course, Your Excellency. How long do you think I'd be gone?"

"Six months, give or take. First, you'd have to get established in some plausible role. Perhaps teaching in the Boston area, romance language would be a possibility."

"I could handle Spanish, Italian, or French. The assignment sounds intriguing." Frank's enthusiasm was not exaggerated although he would have feigned it to satisfy the archbishop who could be petty and vindictive.

"I have a partial list of the activists: diocesan and religious priests, even some disgruntled nuns." He clicked his tongue and passed the sheet to Frank. "Recognize any of these?"

Frank scanned the list before returning to a single name near the top. "Only one: Andrew O'Keefe."

The archbishop wrinkled his forehead; jutted out his lower lip. "Are you telling me you know him?"

"We were at Gregorian together."

"Damn. I missed that when I glanced through O'Keefe's dossier. Just how well do you know him?"

"We haven't kept in touch since our ordination."

"Unfortunately, we need an unknown who wouldn't draw suspicion," the archbishop said, slumping his shoulders.

Frank swallowed his disappointment and tried to salvage something from the lost opportunity. "If I might make a suggestion, Your Excellency?"

The archbishop waved his fingers for Frank to proceed.

"What about Kevin Connelly from St. Therese's?"

"Connelly. What made you think of him?"

"Well, Kev's the right age. He's enthusiastic about changes within the church, but he's also levelheaded. He would keep an open mind. And he's excellent with details."

"Can he teach a Romance language?"

"I don't know but he could organize charismatic groups at various churches, a perfect cover for meeting progressive clergy and religious."

It was the first time Frank heard the archbishop laugh, which evolved into a series of quick snorts expelled through a nose ill-prepared for the attack.

"I'll consider your suggestion. In any case, since you were in the seminary with O'Keefe, tell me what you know about him."

"As I remember Andrew, he was absolutely passionate about the Church. Passion he displayed with reckless abandon and scant regard for stepping on sensitive toes. My Uncle Mike used to say Andrew was a loose cannon waiting to be fired. Knowing Andrew, I'm sure he believes his rebellion is in the best interest of The Church and Catholicism."

"He cannot buck the system, Frank. It's been around for too many centuries."

*****

Ten days passed before Michelle stormed into the rectory office at St. Sebastian's. "You're responsible for this, Frank Roselli. I know you are, you thieving bastard."

Frank looked up from the homily he was preparing for Sunday mass. "Now what?"

"You had Kev reassigned."

"Please, if I had that kind of pull, do you think I'd be sitting here? What I do know is this: Kev's involved in some project for the archbishop. It's temporary and—"

"This is all your doing, a ploy to break us up. Can't you just stay out of my life?"

"Of course," Frank said, his thoughts already drifting back to the homily. "We should get together for lunch, maybe toward the end of next week?"

He reached for his calendar. Michelle flipped him the bird, and left in the wake of a slamming door that rattled the rectory windows.

Chapter 55
March 1981

Although the unrelenting winds of late winter had blasted snow throughout Chicago's lengthy corridors, the sidewalks and street surrounding Holy Name Cathedral had been scraped clean to accommodate the visiting politicians, church hierarchy, and ordinary clergy. Frank Roselli still belonged to the later group. He arrived at the archbishop's mansion in a yellow cab, with the door open and one foot out before the vehicle could screech to a halting stop. Bracing his face to the pelting snowflakes, he hurried to the front entrance. From there a matronly housekeeper ushered Frank into the inner sanctum of Regis Clement's study where the two Connellys, Monsignor Terry and Father Kevin, greeted him like family. The monsignor he regarded as a mentor, second only to Uncle Mike. As for Kevin, in another time he would've made an ideal brother-in-law.

Frank accepted a steaming mug of Irish coffee. That and the warmth of logs burning in the stone fireplace soon lulled him into closing his eyes while the Connellys engaged in the latest diocesan gossip. He'd almost dozed off but jerked to attention when the monsignor poked him with his cane, and asked if he'd met Rob Seppi. Frank stood and greeted the middle-aged priest with short-cropped hair as coarse and gray as that of a wire terrier.

"Your uncle and I attended Mundelein together," Rob Seppi said. "So tell me, is Mike still knee-deep in Vatican politics?"

Uncle Mike, the quiet academician? "Not that I'm aware of,"

Frank said. He wanted to press Rob Seppi for more information but Regis Clement had just barreled into the room.

"Let's get started," the archbishop said. "I've no time for idle chitchat." With an impatient wave of his hand he ordered his subordinates to pull their chairs into a half circle around the fireplace, two on each side of him. "Before Kevin gives his report," he said, "I want to say a few words. Please understand that the report we are about to hear is highly confidential. From time to time, similar reports will be made to select dioceses throughout the country. We must not lose sight of this movement. I've already spoken to Father Seppi," he said, nodding to Rob, "about his taking on a similar challenge in San Francisco next month. I regret not being able to utilize Father Roselli in a similar role; but since he's acquainted with one of the dissidents, I believe his abilities would be best served elsewhere. Monsignor Connelly, of course, will be kept apprised of what's going on at all times." He turned to Kevin. "All right, Father Connelly. I haven't had a chance to read your written report so let's hear the condensed version of these past six months."

"Thank you, Your Excellency, I appreciate the opportunity to be of service."

"Just get to the point, Father Connelly."

"Yes, of course," Kevin said, running a finger around his stiff collar. "WOC is a young group, in the length of its existence and the age of participants."

"Perhaps you should explain what WOC stands for," said the archbishop.

"Western Orthodox Catholic."

WOC. It was the first time Frank heard the term. Evidently, a first for Father Seppi too, since he leaned forward to give Kevin his full attention.

"I want to emphasize this is not an official organization by any means," Kevin explained. "The term WOC is only whispered and with some degree of humor."

"So who belongs to this WOC?" the archbishop asked.

"Mostly priests and nuns who left the church in the past ten years, religious still teaching or preaching, and a mix of fence straddlers." Kevin looked into the face of each priest before he continued. "They believe they are acting in the best interest of Catholicism."

"Hmm, any priests from the orders?"

"Dominicans, Oblates, Franciscans. In their defense I want to say these people are quite sincere in what they're doing."

"So you've already told us," said the archbishop.

"Just what are they doing?" Terry Connelly asked.

"Trying to be heard by the Holy Father. If he's not open to listening, they're considering the establishment of an alternative Catholic Church."

"Too late, Martin Luther already did that almost five hundred years ago," the archbishop grumbled. "And WOC's reason for wanting their way or threatening to secede?"

"Mainly, the failure to recognize and resolve certain issues: birth control, ordination of women, divorce, annulment." Kevin tilted his head and with a shrug, submitted one more reason, "Married priests."

"Should the American bishops be concerned yet?"

"It's too early to tell, Your Excellency."

"You've met their leader?"

"I'm not sure. It could be Bishop Ian Dwyer, from upstate New York. I heard him speak, once from the pulpit—highly respected though not much in the way of dynamics. But then one evening I attended an underground meeting the bishop addressed. In that setting he mesmerized his audience, Your Excellency."

The archbishop heaved his shoulders. "Thank you for your report, Father Connelly. I shall take my time reviewing it before Father Seppi leaves for San Francisco."

"Excuse me, Your Excellency," said Rob Seppi. "After hearing Father Connelly's report, I wonder if I'm the right person for the West Coast. I refer to my age, of course. Would I fit in, or do we need a younger priest?"

"You make a good point." The archbishop turned to Kevin and posed a logical question. "Are you up to another assignment?"

"Wherever I can best serve you, Your Excellency."

"Then it's settled. Father Connelly will spend the next six months in San Francisco where he can carry on with his charismatic evangelism." The archbishop stood. "Thank you all for coming. We'll keep in touch."

As the group filed out, Frank trailed behind, hoping for extra time with the archbishop to request additional funding for St. Sebastian's.

The archbishop, however, had his own agenda; he asked Frank and Monsignor Connelly to stay for a while. He motioned to the cabinet behind Frank. "Top shelf to the left—Courvoisier and three glasses, please."

While Frank poured, Monsignor Connelly added four logs of cherry wood to the waning flames. The three men leaned back to enjoy the warmth of the fire and that of the brandy. After draining his snifter, the archbishop muffled a satisfying burp.

"Frank, my reasons for inviting you tonight are twofold. As you already know, I picked you as my first choice for Boston. Although that didn't pan out, I still wanted to keep you apprised of this minor blip on the radar screen. I avoid using the term *problem* since I doubt it will ever reach that stage. Right, Monsignor?"

Terry Connelly agreed with lowered eyelids. To Frank he imparted a smile so intimate the young priest took it to mean they were allies. Better yet, family. The archbishop signaled for more brandy and Frank obliged quickly, whatever it took to keep the old man talking.

"Secondly and more importantly," the archbishop said after fortifying himself, "I'm considering a new role for you, Frank, one that has put me in quite the quandary. Do I keep my most promising clergy in Chicago where I can best utilize their abilities? Or, do I send them where their abilities can be honed for more universal duties that would eventually benefit Chicago?"

Frank wanted to bolt from his chair, but he didn't. Nor did he so much as twitch a muscle.

"For someone with so few years of pastoral experience, you've achieved commendable results at St. Sebastian's, also at Holy Guardian Angels and the homeless shelter. It's unfortunate, due to the shortage of religious throughout the country, that we no longer have the luxury of advancing our priests in an orderly manner."

"The swift route was one I welcomed, Your Excellency."

"Perhaps too well. Yesterday, I received a telephone call from the Vatican Nuncio in Washington," he said, referring to the Papal Ambassador. "He extended an invitation for one of my priests to study for the Diplomatic Corps. It seems your name topped the list, no doubt recommended by the rector at North American College."

Frank gave a slight nod but did not comment. He recalled the head of the Gregorian University affiliate as a good judge of character.

The archbishop raised one brow. "Perhaps with a little persuasion from your uncle in Rome? It's no secret that nepotism runs rampant throughout the Vatican. Right, Monsignor?"

Terry Connelly smiled. "It's called the Italian way."

"Your thoughts, Frank."

"I'm obedient to your wishes, Your Excellency."

"You have so much to offer here in Chicago, and that's why …"

Whatever Frank thought didn't matter. The archbishop had already made up his mind.

"… it's been so difficult to reach this decision." The archbishop paused to sip his third Courvoisier. "Were I a selfish man, I could, of course, refuse to honor this invitation—a decision which, ultimately, would not be in the best interest of our diocese. Right, Monsignor?"

"The Nuncio never forgets a slight, Your Excellency."

"Therefore, I shall begin looking for your replacement. Be prepared to vacate St. Sebastian's by August 1. Do take some leave after that, Frank. You don't have to be in Rome before the first of September and I'm sure you already know how Europeans are about their August holidays."

Frank allowed a slight smile. This would be his first vacation in three years.

"You'll be studying for the Diplomatic Corps at the Pontifical Ecclesiastic College," Terry Connelly explained. "It's a long haul, Frank. Four more years of schooling just to become an attaché, and that's only the first rung of the ladder."

"Thank you for allowing me this opportunity. I'm deeply honored, of course."

The three men stood, shook hands, and the archbishop hurried off to another meeting.

"Call me tomorrow," Terry Connelly said. "I'll make all the necessary arrangements."

"About my Vatican appointment, Monsignor …."

"Let's just say it came about through the combined efforts of the Italian-Irish-American faction.

Chapter 56
San Francisco

"I can't, Michelle. No matter how much I love you—and, believe me, I do with all my heart—I cannot desert the archbishop now."

"You said heart but not soul."

"Sorry, I've so much on my mind right now."

To hell with Kev's lame excuses, Michelle wanted him now. Just hearing his voice over the telephone sent incredible tingles down her spine. "I have to see you."

"There's no time. I'm leaving for San Francisco this afternoon, but that's between you and me."

"And Frank. This is all his doing, I just know it is."

"He's a low man on the totem pole, same as me."

"Okay, then what happened in Boston?"

"Not now, Michelle. Maybe someday you'll understand."

"It's over, is that what you're telling me?"

"Don't make me choose, not like this."

*****

After five months had passed with no word from Kevin, Michelle took a leave from her job with the Archdiocese and went to San Francisco. Finding Kev proved almost too easy: a few phone calls to Catholic churches regarding charismatic groups turned up a Chicago priest on temporary loan to St. Mary's. On Thursday evening she watched Kevin leave the parish rectory and followed him to the basement of a dim sum restaurant in Chinatown.

Michelle made her way to a room crowded with men and women sitting on folding chairs. Some wore religious garb. Others, like Kevin, were casually dressed but had the demeanor of religious orders. She took one of the few empty seats, in a shadowy corner out of Kevin's view, planning to surprise him later. Upstairs, the clatter of dishes, scrapping chairs, and Chinese chatter competed with the distinct odor of hot peanut oil filtering through the water-stained ceiling tiles and challenged Michelle's ability to concentrate on the program.

At the lectern stood a soft-spoken nun. She wore a white blouse and blue jumper; a crucifix hung from a chain around her neck. "The ordination of nuns would alleviate the shortage of priests," she said, a point well made but that didn't stop her droning on about it for another ten minutes. From the front row another nun shifted on a wobbly chair until the speaker caught her sliding one forefinger across the throat.

"I should like to finish by introducing our next speaker," the droning nun said. "Regretfully, due to illness, Bishop John Dwyer will not be with us tonight." Grumbling erupted from the audience and she paused until it subsided. "However, Bishop Dwyer has sent Father Andrew O'Keefe instead and asks that we welcome him warmly. Father O'Keefe comes to us from the Northeast, the birthplace of our movement."

Polite clapping emitted from the front rows. At the rear those around Michelle continued to complain about the unknown replacement but no one was bold enough, or rude enough, to walk out.

"Brothers and Sisters in Christ," Father O'Keefe said, opening his arms to encompass the disappointed assemblage. "God has brought us together this evening for a purpose. He has so much more to offer than what we, as Catholics, are now receiving …."

Andrew O'Keefe, hmm, he looked familiar. Of course, Michelle recalled his being ordained with Frank. If only Frank could see him now. If only Frank could she her too. While Andrew spoke, she watched Kevin stretching his neck around, taking in the room. No doubt, taking a head count. When he started to scan her area, she bent over and searched the linoleum squares for litter. After counting ten crumbled gum wrappers, she straightened up. By then Kevin was perusing the other side, not that anyone else noticed since Andrew O'Keefe had memorized the entire group.

"As with all good Catholics, we've always had an obligation to lift our spirits in the glorification of God and to live each day as disciples of Jesus Christ," he said. "Yet, Vatican II has failed to answer the demands of the twentieth century ...."

Andrew's voice grew louder, almost loud enough to drown out the enthusiastic diners from the floor above. Michelle had to admit he projected an undeniable magnetism and when he broached the subject of priests being allowed to marry, she stopped looking at Kevin.

"Are there any questions?" Andrew asked.

Michelle's hand shot up. "Yes, Father. Could you please elaborate on the role of married priests?"

She saw Kevin's back stiffen, as if he'd been shot with a bolt of electricity. He did not turn around, even when Andrew said there was no reason for priests not to marry, other than centuries of tradition. Michelle sucked in his words like a thirsty child. Maybe there'd be a place for Kevin and her in this new Catholicism, this Western Orthodox Church called WOC.

After the meeting she decided Kevin could wait. Working her way through the crowd, she overheard snatches of conversation about Bishop Dwyer's dynamic protégé, Andrew O'Keefe, and the young priest's potential as their next leader. "Do you remember me, Father Andrew?" she asked after penetrating his inner circle of new admirers.

He gazed into her face and apologized for his poor memory.

"I'm Michelle Roselli, Frank's sister. You and Frank were in the seminary together."

He smiled as if to say yes but didn't convince Michelle. She wanted to talk but others demanded his attention. Instead, she felt herself being jostled over to the coffee and granola bars. Then, a familiar grip to her elbow: Kevin steering her to the only exit.

"Does this mean you're going to feed me?" she asked without turning around. Kevin didn't answer. They walked up the stairs and through a door that led outside. "I haven't eaten a single morsel since breakfast," she said. "Maybe someplace quiet?"

Looking up and down Grant Street, she belted out a laugh. The singsong music of China challenged the blaring horns of frazzled motorists. Green, yellow, red, and orange blinked and popped up, down, and sideways to provide a backdrop for hordes of irreverent jaywalkers. Under inviting neon signs Chinese men in dark suits and white shirts smiled and bowed a welcome for the hungry to enter and sample their ethnic cuisine. Tourists commandeered the sidewalk, four abreast and two rows deep, belching and groaning and vowing not to eat for another twenty-four hours.

"We should go where no one will know me," were his first words.

"How about my hotel off Union Square?" she said with a wink. "It's not much bigger than a phone booth but in a pinch the bed could sleep two."

"You said you were hungry."

"More like starving. I'm not talking meat and potatoes."

When Kevin suggested they take a cab to the Cowtown section, Michelle conceded. In the back booth of a trendy café she smoked a cigarette with her coke and ordered a cheeseburger with fries. Kevin drank coffee—black, no sugar—and said he wasn't hungry.

"You don't seem happy to see me," Michelle said, turning her head to exhale a puff of smoke.

"You can't stay here. In San Francisco, I mean. I'm on a special assignment for the archbishop."

"In other words, you're a spy, sent to tattle on an insignificant, little group trying to buck the Pope."

"It's not so little."

"A crowd of ninety-seven, I can count too."

He waved the smoky tendrils away. She knew he was annoyed about their invading his space. Finally, he grabbed her cigarette and crushed it in the ashtray. "Please, Michelle, just go back to Chicago."

"No one has to know about us. I could find a job, an apartment."

"I'll always love you, Michelle. You know that."

"I don't like the sound of this." She reached for another cigarette.

After she'd smoked half of it, he said they couldn't go back to what should never have been. Before she could slam him with a clever rebuttal, the waitress showed up with her order. Michelle ignored Kevin's discomfort while she quartered the cheeseburger and alternated its consumption with salty fries and runny catsup. After she ate the curly parsley and orange slice, Kevin paid the bill and they left.

*****

Michelle didn't see Kevin again until the following Thursday when she returned to the basement of the dim sum restaurant. After the opening prayer she stood and pointed Kevin out as a fraud. Red-face, he slithered out, accompanied by a volley of hisses and boos. One nun threw her shoe, which pleased Michelle to no end. Several days later she learned Kevin had high-tailed it back to Chicago where she envisioned him having to justify his failure to the archbishop.

"Good riddance, Kevin Connelly," she said to her image in the mirror. "You're no better than Bart Bannister. At least with him I received a golden parachute."

Michelle spent another month in San Francisco during which time her job with the Chicago Archdiocese vanished. No problem, by then she had committed herself to WOC and Andrew O'Keefe. WOC and Andrew O'Keefe: the two names were becoming synonymous. She also abandoned her plan to become a social worker—a career more appropriate for life with Kevin—and instead turned to freelance marketing. The money was decent and in her spare time she produced WOC promotional materials that looked more professional than the shoddy array previously distributed. Andrew seemed pleased although he didn't elaborate on the improved image. Nor did she expect him to. With Andrew she didn't expect a physical romance. Andrew lived on a higher plane.

Unlike her brother. By the time Frank learned of her latest involvement, he'd have missed the boat. What a shame, too late to stick his nose where it didn't belong. Frank, the favorite son … Frank, the ever-so-perfect priest … Frank, the perpetual shit disturber.

Chapter 57
Rome, September 1981

Frank Roselli had already missed the first ten minutes of a required lecture on ecclesiastical diplomacy when he creaked open the door to a small amphitheater at Gregorian University. On stage Monsignor Bruno Santini looked up from the podium, pausing longer than needed for Frank to slip into a mid-row seat and nod an uncomfortable apology. With no change of expression the monsignor continued his discourse in Italian, the official language of the university.

Bruno Santini originated from Florence and was rumored to be a descendent of the Medici family, which may have accounted for his noble bearing. The monsignor stood five feet nine inches, with a physique matching his narrow nose and tapered fingers. Behind gold-framed spectacles, his priestly eyes took in more than most people needed to know. An aristocratic forehead stretched into his dome of black hair, combed back to meet the base of a goose-like neck. He wore with ease a cassock tailored to his proportions and black loafers in the softest of leather, handmade to accommodate the double A width and high arches that distinguished his equally noble feet.

After the monsignor's lecture Frank worked his way down to the stage, bucking a traffic jam of students ascending the steep stairs that led to the nearest exit and their next class.

"Excuse me, Monsignor," Frank said in English. He waited for an acknowledgment but when none was forthcoming, he continued in Italian. "Please accept my apologies for being late. It won't happen again, I assure you."

"In Italy respect for time is not as important as respect for the faculty," the monsignor replied in English through thin, colorless lips. He unzipped his briefcase and placed his lecture folder inside. "Your name?"

"Frank Roselli, from Chicago." He extended his hand.

A long ten seconds passed before the monsignor allowed his to be shaken. "Forget Chicago," he said. "Here, you belong to an elite group; and when you leave in four years, wherever you are sent, you will introduce yourself as Father Frank Roselli, from the Vatican." He picked up his briefcase and headed toward the stairs.

"Excuse me, Monsignor," Frank said as he walked behind him. "Since you're listed as one of my advisors, could we meet some time at your convenience?"

Without turning around, the monsignor replied, "You may call my office for an appointment."

At fifty-three Bruno Santini had been primed for an impressive promotion within his beloved diplomatic corps. His twenty years of service in foreign countries throughout the world were exemplary—first as an attaché, then secretary and later, counselor. In his mind he'd earned an appointment to a leadership position as an apostolic nuncio; instead, he received a letter from the Papal Secretariat, recalling him to the Roman Curia. The time is not right: there are no appropriate openings, he was told on his return. Now, after five years at the Vatican and with a myriad of duties he knew his elevation to bishop was just a matter of time. Patience precedes rewards.

And so he taught. He especially enjoyed the younger students: the beneficiaries of his wisdom, those enthusiastic candidates for the priesthood. The older students, over twenty-five and already ordained, were, to a man, ambitious careerists, just as he had been. And still was.

*****

Later that week Frank met his Uncle Mike at a sidewalk *osteria* near the Vatican. While sharing a bottle of cabernet, they watched a colorful, international parade of religious garb spanning two thousand years intermingling with that of polyester tourist spanning the last twenty. Beyond the pedestrian area beautiful young Italian men and women straddled their Vespas, buzzing the streets like a swarm of frenzied insects. Even though Frank had managed to stay celibate since taking his final vows, he still enjoyed looking at the female motorini drivers:

young goddesses with hair tousled and skirts hiked up to round hips. From the expression on Michael Baggio's face Frank could tell he still appreciated the female form too. He often wondered if Uncle Mike struggled with the same temptations as he did. Or, did Uncle Mike have different issues.

"So you've met the great Bruno Santini," Michael said, breaking into Frank's thoughts.

"How'd you know?"

"I could say 'there are no secrets at the Vatican'. No doubt, you've already heard that one. But more to the point Bruno told me."

"I didn't realize he knew you."

"Bruno knows everyone and everything. I've been here twenty years and still don't know what Bruno knows. We became acquainted when he started teaching at Gregorian; but like me, Bruno has other duties at the Vatican."

"Such as?"

"Don't have a clue."

"That's scary. I hope I didn't get off on the wrong foot with the monsignor. He seemed rather arrogant."

"In other words, he's a testy bastard." Michael leveled a forefinger at Frank. "But never underestimate him. Bruno Santini can be as unctuous and persuasive as a deadly cobra."

"Please, Uncle Mike, no more riddles. Just give it to me straight."

"Ah-h, spoken as a true American; I guess I've been away from home too long. At the Vatican there's no such thing as straight talk—not among the Italians anyway. They may originate from every province in Italy but once they're entrenched in the Holy See, they all think like the *Mezzogiorno*."

"Southern Italians, you're kidding."

"You'll find out soon enough. The rest of the players, especially Americans, get frustrated until they learn how to play the game the Italian way."

"And how is that?"

"With patience and a sense of humor," Michael said. "Remember, in the world of diplomacy courtesy goes a long way."

"What about Monsignor Santini?"

"When he wants something—for now, the title of Bishop—he can charm the socks off a soccer player. Besides counting a number of cardinals as his allies, he's tight with the *Secretariat of State* and the

Sostituto, you know, the substitute—second in command. Those two come right after the Holy Father."

"Sounds like Monsignor Santini carries a ton of weight on those skinny shoulders."

"Not to mention money and prestige. One more thing: he might be homosexual but this I don't know for sure nor does it matter. What I do know is he doesn't respond well to rejection."

Before Frank could protest, Michael showed the palm of his hand. "Don't misunderstand what I'm saying, nephew. You don't have to compromise yourself in order to engage support from Bruno. Just cultivate his friendship and connections to your advantage."

"Speaking of connections, how much did you influence my appointment to the Academy?"

"You're here, aren't you? Not that I take all the credit. Our good friend Monsignor Connelly secured a recommendation for you from Gregorian. You must've made quite an impression on the rector. He still talks about your ability to sway the obtuse."

"Obtuse at the seminary, that's quite a stretch. In any case, thanks for the help."

"One more pearl of wisdom, an important one," Michael said. "There are easier routes to the right hand of the Holy Father than wandering the entire globe hoping to be noticed. For now I suggest you expand your languages to include Polish and Yiddish."

"Yiddish?"

"The Pope wants to make amends with the Jews."

"It's about time. Looks like I better move fast. As I said before, patience was never my strong suite."

"Enough already, it's good having you here," Michael said, putting his hand on Frank's shoulder. "I've missed the family. How's Uncle Jake?"

"Losing Grandma was tough on him, but he's managing. Thank God she went peacefully."

"Amen. What about Pop? Does he still have the lady friends?"

"Oh sure, especially the one from Paris. They meet in Chicago every so often. Mom thinks it's scandalous. Dad says the old boy has the stamina of a twenty-year-old."

"And your sisters?"

"Michelle's working on her Master's Degree in social work. Also employed part time for the Archdiocese, a rather odd though commendable choice. Jamie and Henri are still trying to make a baby."

Michael rolled his eyes. "So your mother tells me in her letters. Sounds like she's finally accepted Henri."

"After they remarried in the Church."

"By the way, whatever became of your friend, the one I met at Pierluigi?" Michael drummed his fingers as he tried to recall the name. "No, don't tell me. Andrew ... Andrew O'Keefe."

"He joined a religious order."

"Good choice for a rebel. Andrew would have been any bishop's worst nightmare. A voice demanding society's ears, his own unwilling to listen."

"That would be Andrew. He's a Dominican now."

"Ah, a preacher ... I pray to God he uses his powers of persuasion in a responsible manner."

"Ever hear of WOC?"

"I thought you'd never ask."

*****

Frank waited another week before calling Bruno Santini's office. Besides the student advisory appointment Frank also received an invitation to dine at the monsignor's home, which meant passing on tickets to a jazz concert in order to hobnob with the elite. On Saturday evening after leaving his apartment in the Stritch Residence, he strolled past graffiti-stained walls and arm-in-arm couples sharing gelato before reaching a quiet, narrow street off the *Piazza della Unità*. When he arrived at the address scribbled in his notebook, he didn't think the ocher-colored palazzo worthy of Bruno Santini, that is, until he stepped inside its elaborate entryway of marble and walnut. After checking out the resident names encased in polished brass, he circled three flights of broad, winding marble before reaching the monsignor's apartment. He knocked once and the door opened.

"Ah, Father Roselli," his host said through pursed lips that gradually extended into a controlled smile. "Do come in."

Frank followed Bruno through a thick, arched doorway and into a salon, spacious and airy with its fifteen-foot ceiling. Walls finished in stucco tipped with gold luster lacked any artwork other than an impressive wooden crucifix at the far end. Long windows with shutters on each side opened out to narrow balconies filled with trailing geraniums emitting their lemony fragrance back into the interior. Frank scanned the room and counted ten priests gathered around furniture designed for entertaining: a low table of burnished leather sandwiched between two massive sofas perpendicular to a marble fireplace and pockets of easy chairs grouped around ornately carved tables.

The monsignor handed Frank the Campari he'd poured from a crystal decanter and invited him to meet his other guests. Frank recognized two young priests from the Academy, standing off to the side entertaining each other until Bruno insisted they join the others. He turned Frank over to Milo Frederico, a slender man with razor-sharp features and probing eyes. Too young and handsome for celibacy, Frank's mother would've said, just as she did about Frank. So far he'd proved her wrong. Milo escorted Frank around the room, introducing him as a candidate for the Diplomatic Corps. Among the priests he met were the ferret-face Monsignor Flavio Bono, whose stooped posture signaled the onset of osteoporosis, and Bishop Tomaso Martinelli, a Mussolini look-a-like bulging the buttons of his purple-trimmed cassock. They'd been deep in conversation with Stanislaus Zarenski, who accompanied John Paul II from Poland. Except for the three Diplomatic Corps candidates, each priest held a position with the Vatican's Roman Curia.

Frank felt his mouth turn dry from too much small talk. He noticed the empty glass in his hand but couldn't remember lifting it to his lips. He excused himself and headed back to the sideboard for a second aperitif. No one was around except a new arrival dressed in the bright robes of an African nation, perhaps a priest from Nigeria. The man smiled, the white of his teeth contrasting to skin as dark as blue-black coal.

"I'm only here for a short time," he said in perfect English while extending his hand. "And you, of course, are Frank Roselli."

Frank could see his hand pump the stranger's hand but had the numbing sensation of not feeling its grip. "We've met before?"

"Not in Rome. I just arrived this morning, to escort the body of a martyred priest to its final resting place."

"A martyred priest, I hadn't heard."

"Not every death makes the newspapers," the stranger said. "Or, the Vatican rumor mill."

"Not that I'd be privy to the later, at least not yet." Frank's response had tumbled from his mouth as if he were conversing with an intimate friend. Had the man given his name? Frank couldn't remember. He dug deep in his memory bank, trying to place this stranger who seemed to know him. "Please excuse me for staring," Frank said, peering into the man's eyes. "It's just that you look so familiar. Have you been to the States, perhaps Illinois?"

"Ah, the heartland of America, I do know my geography. But to answer your question, you might say we met in another lifetime."

Frank's hands went from warm to clammy. More than anything he needed a stiff drink but settled for the bittersweet Campari. He grabbed the crystal decanter; it slipped from his fingers and crashed to the floor. The sound of shattering glass pierced his ears to resurrect the undeniable sound of screeching brakes. He watched in horror as red liquor pooled onto the speckled terrazzo, a reminder of the precious blood his friends had spilled along the cindered tracks of the Illinois Central.

"You've made another mess, Frank," the stranger said. "But not to worry, somehow it'll get cleaned up."

Frank released his shoulders into a heavy slump. "Angelo Nero," he said, unsure why that name had popped into his head. "I didn't expect you this soon."

"Settle down, Frank. You'll have your four years at the Academy—the doctorate in theology and the licentiate in canon law. After that comes the real test of your worthiness. Just remember what I told you before about following God's plan."

The angel stepped into the shadows; Frank didn't have much time. He considered tackling him, but didn't want to appear foolish. When the colorful garb started fading into gray tones, Frank pleaded, "Wait, please, I have issues that need resolution. I'm sure we could work something out. About my worthiness ...."

Too late, Frank was talking to a blank wall. He looked around. No one had witnessed the scene. He checked out the floor; the broken glass and spilled Campari had disappeared. In fact, the decanter was back on the sideboard, brimming with the herb-infused liquor.

The crisp voice of Monsignor Santini ordering his guests to the dining room brought Frank back to the moment. He forced himself to set aside the past three minutes—an inexplicable aberration, he reasoned—and joined the group strolling into the dining room.

Twelve priests sat down to an elegant table setting of white on white: fine white porcelain on Belgium white linen and crystal stemware. Overhead, a Murano crystal chandelier sent shimmering lights to dance across the ceiling, accompanied by the strains of

Vivaldi's *Four Seasons*. Suddenly, the clatter of pans in the kitchen interrupted the graceful ambiance, followed by a loud scream. An argument ensued in Italian. The voices belonged to two females.

"Ugly bitch! Who are you to give orders?"

"How else would a stupid cow know when it's time to move?"

"I can move out and then who will you boss?"

Bruno Santini lifted his eyes to angels painted on the ceiling. He made the sign of the cross and thanked God for the food they were about to receive. A silver bell tinkled from his fingertips; and two elderly women, no taller than four feet ten, pushed through the swinging door. In each hand they balanced a plate and bowl of steaming *ricotta tortellini en brodo*. Both women were round, with gray hair parted in the middle, knotted, and squeezed into the base of their necks. Both wore white aprons over long black dresses that grazed the tops of black oxfords. Without speaking or looking at each other, they moved in flawless precision, back and forth between the kitchen and dining room until every guest had been served.

Frank felt himself staring, for the second time that evening, although the first he'd almost succeeded in blocking from his mind.

"Your eyes are not betraying you," whispered Milo Frederico who sat to his right. "They are identical twins, cousins of Monsignor Santini."

Frank had already pegged Milo Frederico as a quick study, surveying the scene with built-in antennae capable of picking up multiple signals from multiple directions. Like Bruno, Milo seemed ingratiating or aloof, depending on the particular circumstance. Where Milo fit in with this Vatican clique Frank could not determine. Perhaps Bruno's assistant, perhaps his protégée.

The kitchen bickering and the meal progressed through a tuna and potato mousse that equaled any gourmet equivalent. As the novelty of the twins wore off, Frank sorted out his dinner companions and tried to remember their Roman Curio appointments. As did his two Academy peers, Frank listened more than he talked. As with Vatican tradition, the common language was that of Italian.

"There's a rumor circulating about a certain female staffer and a monsignor from the Congregation of the Doctrine."

"If you've heard it, suffice to say it may or may not be true."

"We shall see, only time will tell."

"Time may tell if there is a baby, not who the father is."

"Pity. Raising a child can be such an expense."

"The Vatican has means."

"The Vatican should not pay to cover up the sins of its clergy."

"Then who should pay?"

"The perpetrator, one way or another."

"And what of those who prey on innocent children?"

"Despicable."

"If one cannot find charity within the Vatican, then where?"

"I'm told there may be certain outside funding."

Just then, the twins pushed through the door, bearing a large covered platter. "Ah-h," Monsignor Bono purred. "What have we here, Father Frederico?"

"Pheasant stuffed with rice and wild mushrooms," Milo said.

Bruno removed the cover and sniffed with appreciation. "A Tuscany specialty for special guests, my thanks to all of you."

The twins began circling the table. One of them held the platter of fowl surrounded by an artful display of braised carrots, green beans, and onions glistening with olive oil, while the other filled each plate. After completing their circle which ended with the host, the twins disappeared into the kitchen.

"The wine, Bruno, it is delicious."

"Grazie, it is the finest of Frascati, to honor our Holy Father. And his countryman, of course." Bruno raised his glass in the direction of Stanislaus Zarenski.

"The Pole is an assistant to an assistant of the Holy Father," Milo whispered to Frank.

Along with the others Frank raised his glass, recalling another meal six years earlier with Uncle Mike and Andrew O'Keefe when they enjoyed a bottle of Frascati courtesy of the Bannisters. He and Andrew had been so impatient to begin their vocations. Even then, Andrew thumbed his nose at the art of diplomacy. Someday his mouth would precede his downfall.

A discreet nudge from Milo Federico's foot brought Frank back to the table talk.

"As I was saying, Father Roselli, have you heard anything about a minor uprising from extreme liberals in America?" asked Bishop Martinelli.

Frank recalled the bishop worked in the Congregation for the Doctrine of the Faithful, where the names of rebellious clergy were duly recorded.

The table went silent waiting for Frank's response.

"No, Your Excellency," he said with a straight face.

"That's odd. Evidently, secrets are better kept in America than in the Vatican."

Frank ignored the comment and ensuing murmurs by loading a forkful of green beans into his mouth and chewing until they dissolved into minute particles. He wiped his lips and reached for his glass of Frascati.

Conversation resumed.

"You've heard, of course, about the possible mismanagement of funds in—"

"I'm told they've begun an investigation."

"Pity the auditor who tries to untangle that web."

"Not to change the subject, but what about those two priests who didn't have enough sense to practice discretion?"

"One has been dispatched to a mission church somewhere in a remote part of Asia."

"He'll grow old there," Milo Frederico said in a low voice. "How unfortunate for him."

Chapter 58
Letters

Dear friends of my youth
Who left before your time,
I weep not for your passing,
But for loved ones left behind.
May God's angels ....

> *September 30, 1981*
> *Dear Grandpa Carlo,*
> *Years ago you asked me if I had seen a black man—L'Angelo Nero, you called him—the night of the Illinois Central. At the time I said no because I had no recollection of those horrific minutes following the accident. But now I am beginning to think perhaps this angel and I did meet.*
> *Have you seen him too? What did he say?*
> *Love*
> *Frank*

*****

October 15, 1981
Dear Frank,
About L'Angelo Nero—I knew you must've seen him that night because the emergency crew found you babbling about a black man nobody else saw. I first heard about him from my Louisa when she was dying. And I thought, crazy with fever. Twice when I wanted to let go myself, I witnessed him with my own eyes. He repeated the same words he told Louisa to pass on to me. Good thing I listened. Life has been good, even without Louisa.
I told nobody about L'Angelo Nero. Not your Mama or Jake. Nor your Uncle Mike. But this I tell you now. L'Angelo Nero said God has a plan. To this day I don't know what he was talking about.
Love,
Your Grandpa

Chapter 59
Vatican City, April 1984

For Bishop John Dwyer of Pennsylvania this summons to the Vatican would mark his second in seven years. The first, a candid conversation in the Pope's private residence, had ended with a stern warning for him to cease public criticism of the Holy Mother Church. On his return to America John Dwyer ignored the admonition and continued to inspire an increasing number of disillusioned faithful to embrace his take on Catholicism, one that promised a glimpse of heaven on earth by receiving the power of grace through self-imposed poverty.

"Give your money directly to the poor," he often preached to an audience starved for the undeniable truth. "The Church, in all its glorious wisdom, will find a way to utilize its many resources."

A special messenger had delivered the current Vatican summons, which directed John Dwyer to also bring his noted disciple, Father Andrew O'Keefe. The two men traveled to Rome expecting a private audience with the Holy Father, but at the gate of Vatican City an officer of the Swiss Guard turned them over to a somber underling. Sitting in the rear of a black Fiat, they were driven through the heart of the Holy See, and past the manicured gardens, where official Vatican guides, like hens leading their ducklings, escorted obedient groups of reverent nuns and gawking, camera-laden tourists. At the edge of the walled city their driver parked in front of an obscure building and opened the door for his passengers.

Andrew, who'd recently been hobbled with an unsteady gait,

THE FAMILY ANGEL

insisted on helping his aging bishop navigate the steep stairs. After three flights both men were gasping for air when their escort knocked on a thick, imposing door. He left after introducing them to Octavio Cardinal Lanza, head of the Congregation of the Doctrine of the Faithful, and his stocky assistant, Bishop Tomaso Martinelli. Another priest, younger but also Italian, remained nameless and in the shadows, his only title that of The Recorder. The clerics gathered in a parlor furnished with heavy furniture and dark paintings from an earlier century. Hot tea and plain biscuits from a knee-high table were offered, refused by all, and not offered again.

Cardinal Lanza wore an impressive pectoral cross over his black cassock trimmed with a red sash and row of red buttons down the front. On the back of his head a red zucchetto held in check a thatch of white hair flaring from his stoic face. He delivered the usual perfunctory courtesies in near perfect English and after a discussion of overseas flights and weather comparisons, he nodded to The Recorder, his tapered fingers poised to take notes, as he sat at a gold-trimmed desk in the hushed corner.

"Meetings such as this are always difficult," the Cardinal began, directing his attention to John Dwyer. "Alas, the Church has exhausted its patience and can no longer remain complacent while you continue to incite discord."

The bishop suppressed half a smile. "I speak what I believe to be true, Your Eminence."

Cardinal Lanza shifted to the younger priest. "As I'm sure you must know, Father O'Keefe, many of the changes you extol represent issues the Vatican prefers to address on their individual merit."

"But never seems to resolve," Andrew said. "As I'm sure you must know, the Western Orthodox Catholic Church is garnering a multitude of followers, enough to formally break from Rome."

A slight quiver issued from the cardinal's left nostril. He tapped one forefinger on the arm of his chair. "A schismatic church is by no means remarkable."

"It would be for the twentieth century," countered Andrew.

Tomaso Martinelli filled his lungs with air and ran one hand over a scalp of phantom hair before exhaling through his gritted teeth. "Another minor rebellion, Father O'Keefe, not unlike the petty one in France. The Church has survived worse."

"Unfortunately, minor rebellions have a way of becoming major embarrassments when they go public."

"We are not the enemy, Bishop Dwyer," the Cardinal said. "Encourage your followers to return to the fold, and in return, reap generous benefits for yourself. Perhaps, a privileged post in the Vatican. You could serve on ecclesiastic reviews, have the ears of those closest to the Holy Father."

"Where I'd be buried in a mountain of paperwork, no doubt," John Dwyer replied. "I cannot accept the offer, Your Eminence. My mission must continue."

"Anyone can see you're not well," the Cardinal said, his voice soft and conciliatory. "Why spend your final days mounting a hopeless campaign that only serves to confuse the laity?"

"Patience, Brothers in Christ," Tomaso Martinelli said. "Change will come in time."

"But not in our lifetime," John Dwyer acknowledged with a smile.

"For the Church that began with Christ, the length of time does not matter."

"Excuse me, Your Eminence," said Andrew. "Time does matter. We cannot sit here in silence while the Holy Mother Church ignores the spiritual needs of today's people. You must intervene to the Pope on our behalf. He must hear us out."

One bang of Andrew's scrawny fist to the tea table prompted an uncontrollable cough from John Dwyer's mouth. The Recorder produced a glass of water and two suppressants, which the grateful bishop consumed while his adversaries and Andrew watched.

"The Holy Father has already reviewed your petitions," the Cardinal continued after John Dwyer had regained his composure. "He has given your concerns prayerful consideration."

"Prayerful consideration is not enough, Your Eminence."

"It will have to be, Bishop Dwyer."

"I must speak directly to the Holy Father."

"You spoke to him before. Nothing has changed."

"We will not be silenced," Andrew said, jumping to his feet. "Our message will spread throughout America and beyond—a new Catholicism for the modern world. The Holy Father will regret—"

"Father O'Keefe, please. You are in no position to threaten the Holy See."

Chapter 60
March 29, 1985

A 1969 red Camaro SS picked up the Interstate 55-70 ramp leaving downtown St. Louis and started across the Poplar Street Bridge, a mile-long stretch over the Mississippi River. The Camaro traveled against heavy rush hour traffic inching toward the city and into the glaring sunlight of early morning. The driver adjusted the car's sun visor. Her passenger leaned his head back on the cushioned support and narrowed his red-rimmed eyes to the westbound cars.

"Hang on. We only have another hour or so," Michelle Roselli said. She glanced to her right through tinted aviator sunglasses. "Are you okay?"

"Give me a few minutes," Andrew O'Keefe murmured. "I'm just waiting for my fix to kick in." He closed his crinkled lids over eyes too old for their thirty-five years. From cheekbone to jawbone deep crevices hollowed out the line of his scraggly bearded face. Drab hair hung to bony shoulders that at one time could've challenged those of a football player. Fifty pounds lighter than when he was ordained eleven years earlier, the former meat and potatoes man had foregone the eating of dead flesh and now followed the regimen of an insulin-dependent diabetic. Food measured and controlled along with prescribed drugs provided Andrew sufficient strength to continue his work as the new bishop of WOC, a role he'd accepted after John Dwyer's deadly myocardial infarction which occurred less than twenty-four hours after their disastrous Vatican meeting.

While Andrew dreamed of his latest WOC crusade, a highway sign from the Governor of Illinois welcomed him and Michelle to The Land of Lincoln. For Michelle it meant coming home, again. She followed the elevated interstate, built to circumvent the slums of East St. Louis, and continued east for another ten minutes before exiting onto a two-lane road and heading south.

A clear sky, green grass, and spring blossoms—what better day for traveling, she thought, even the final leg of their journey to St. Gregory. She'd not been home since Christmas before last.

*****

Mary Ann and Tony were in the garden picking red leaf lettuce when they saw the Camaro pull into the long driveway leading to their backyard. Michelle had called the day before, letting them know to expect a guest. A friend of Frank's from the seminary, she'd explained, an exhausted missionary in need of some old-fashioned R & R.

"Can you believe she's still driving that beat-up car," Mary Ann said as they hurried to meet Michelle. "A classic, she calls it."

"Don't get me started," Tony said. "And please hold your tongue. Let's not have any aggravation while she's here. Please, just a nice, peaceful visit."

They caught up with Michelle as she and Andrew were stepping out of the car. "Michelle, you little vixen," Tony said, wrapping her in a bear hug. "Next time don't stay away so long."

"I didn't expect to see you 'til suppertime, Dad."

"What the hell. For you I took the day off."

Turning to Andrew, Tony stuck his hand out. "Welcome, Father Andrew. I believe we met in Rome when you and Frank were ordained."

"Of course, I remember you well," Andrew said, swaying as his hand gripped Tony's.

After mother and daughter exchanged their usual emotional greeting, Mary Ann brushed a light peck on Andrew's cheek. She stepped back and peered into his eyes. "I hardly recognized you, Father Andrew. You look so tired."

"I didn't get much sleep last night." He smiled and shifted his weight to keep from wobbling.

They went into the kitchen and gathered around the table where Mary Ann poured tall glasses of iced tea. After filling Michelle with the latest family gossip, her parents zeroed in on Andrew.

"Michelle tells us you're a Dominican," Tony said.

Andrew hesitated before he replied. "Yes, but currently on leave from my order. You might say I'm on special assignment."

"How mysterious," Mary Ann said. "Still, I suppose the Church isn't above a few covert operations."

Only she and Tony found the comment amusing. He cleared his throat, stifled a yawn, and lifted his arms into a comfortable stretch. "So, Father Andrew, when was the last time you saw Frank?"

"Not since our ordination." Andrew closed his eyes and soothed them with a gentle thumb and forefinger massage. "Please don't think me rude but I'm really quite tired."

A look of concern replaced Mary Ann's smile. "What you need is a nice nap before lunch."

After nodding his thanks, Andrew followed Michelle down the hall to Frank's old room. He was stretched across the bed and drifting into sleep before she closed the door.

Back in the kitchen Mary Ann was hunched over the sink, picking through the lettuce while Tony flipped through the St. Gregory Journal, reviewing news already read and discussed two hours earlier.

"Don't go overboard for lunch," Michelle said. "Andrew doesn't eat much during Lent."

Mary Ann assumed her usual hands-on-hips position. "That's rather obvious. Just what is his problem? Is he on the lam or what?"

"Really, Mom, you watch w-a-y too much TV."

"More to the point: is he on drugs?" asked Tony.

"Well, in a way, but the good kind. He's diabetic and under a ton of pressure. Too much preaching and doing God's work, so little time."

"You of all people, Michelle," Tony said, shaking his head. "How in hell did you hook up with a preacher?"

"Please, Dad. You make Andrew sound like a criminal. He's a priest, just like Frank."

Tony snorted. "He's nothing like Frank."

"The poor man looks as if he escaped from a POW camp," said Mary Ann. She wrapped the washed lettuce in a linen towel and put it in the refrigerator. "If only Frank could see him now."

"Yeah, Frank," replied Michelle, holding back a grin. "Too bad he's stuck in Rome."

When lunch was ready, she checked on Andrew and decided not

to disturb him. She told her parents that if his speech happened to be slurred when he woke up, a quick glass of orange juice would bring him around for the insulin injection.

They sat down to a stack of grilled cheese sandwiches and a bowl of salted lettuce splashed with olive oil and lemon.

After a quick grace, Mary Ann folded her arms and looked at Michelle. "Okay, we know you're holding something back. Out with whatever it is."

Michelle fished a bread and butter pickle from the jar before she addressed the question. "I'm not sure what you mean."

"Cut the crap!" Tony said, slamming his grilled cheese down on the plate. "We're your parents, not some country bumpkins."

"All right, all right. I'll explain what's going on, but only if you promise to back off. Andrew needs all the rest he can get this week. Please, just don't say anything until I've finished." Michelle told them about the underground movement of the Western Orthodox Catholics and Andrew's consecration as bishop after John Dwyer's sudden death. When she paused for a swallow of tea, Mary Ann opened her mouth but stopped short of speaking when Tony shook his head.

Michelle continued. "Before coming here, Andrew and I were in St. Louis, making plans for a powerful demonstration of faith. On Good Friday—one week from today—members of the St. Louis WOC Mission will gather at the foot of the Gateway Arch and reaffirm their commitment to a new Catholicism. Together, we will witness the crucifixion of Andrew O'Keefe."

"Crucifixion," Tony and Mary Ann whispered together.

"Not a real one, of course. After all, St. Andrew the Apostle took four days before he died. Andrew O'Keefe hopes to tolerate his cross for at least an hour—long enough for decent TV and press coverage." She looked from one parent to the other, her cheeks flushed. "Isn't it absolutely incredible?"

"Don't tell me Andrew's going to carry a cross," Tony said.

"Through the park—it's so Filipino and Hispanic, don't you think?" With a wave of her hand she brushed off her father's smirk. "Andrew's faith will give him strength. Personally, I favored his hanging upside down. You know, like St. Peter. Too bad that got vetoed."

"Michelle!" chorused her parents.

"Don't look so shocked. Re-enacted crucifixions are nothing new.

But Western Orthodox Catholicism is. Walter Cronkite will tell the world about WOC on Good Friday's six o'clock news."

"You mean Dan Rather. Cronkite retired four years ago."

"Oh well, you get my drift."

Tony pushed aside his half-eaten sandwich. He scraped back his chair and stood. "No dessert for me. I just remembered some paperwork back at the office." He left Mary Ann at the sink, cleaning the griddle and Michelle digging into the remaining the salad, those precious morsels at the bottom of the bowl she and Frank used to fight over.

*****

The next morning Michelle announced she and Andrew would be driving to Carbondale after breakfast. To explore the possibility of establishing a WOC mission at Southern Illinois University, she told Mary Ann whose only response was to throw up her hands. After waving goodbye from the screened porch, Mary Ann watched the Camaro grow smaller as it rolled down the driveway. When it turned onto the main road, she went inside and placed a long distance call to her brother Michael.

"Michelle's always been a bit radical but this time she's gone over the top," Mary Ann said after telling him about the upcoming Good Friday demonstration. "I swear she's gone daft, Michael. I just don't know what to do."

"Don't do anything," Michael said. "Or tell anyone you called me, especially Michelle or Andrew. Understand? I'll get back to you later."

Chapter 61
Rome, March 30

Two hours later in Rome the afternoon sun streamed into the cramped parlor of Frank's efficiency apartment, its furnishings sparse and nondescript. The mantel clock chimed five times while he paced the worn carpet, exchanging Yiddish dialogue with a Berlitz tape. He kept talking until the sharp trill of his telephone ringing finally broke his concentration. He answered with an abrupt *Pronto*, and hearing the unctuous voice of Milo Frederico, he heaved an inward sigh.

Bypassing his usual inquiry as to Frank's well being, Milo got right to the point. "I apologize for my intrusion but the Bishop would like you to dine with him tonight."

Bishop Santini's again. A last-minute invitation was not unusual, especially if Bruno needed twelve at his table, but dinner on the evening prior to Palm Sunday? Frank recognized the invitation as a command, one he knew better than to ignore. His four years at the Academy were almost over and unlike some of his younger colleagues, thirty-five-year-old Frank had yet to receive his first attaché assignment. At this rate he'd be pushing sixty before he made monsignor, too far from where he planned on finishing his career.

Although he'd attended many social events at the home of Bruno Santini none could match that first evening when he encountered The Black Angel. Had Grandpa Carlo not admitted to seeing him too, Frank would've chalked up his Rome sighting to an empty stomach and bitter Campari. Or, perhaps a case of reoccurring guilt: he still dreamed of his friends, forever teenagers while he grew older and hopefully wiser.

Shortly after that first dinner Monsignor Bruno Santini had been elevated to Bishop Bruno Santini. His guest list continued to be dominated by members of the Vatican Curia but on occasion included a handful of influential Italians. Sometimes prominent Catholics from America—people like Arthur and Claire Bannister, who once trapped Frank in front of Bruno's marble fireplace. Claire brought up their afternoon tea at the Drake, boasting how she'd predicted the ambitious Frank was destined for Rome, and how she'd put in a good word for him with the archbishop. Then Arthur asked where he preferred being stationed after completing his diplomatic training. Frank smiled polite evasiveness to Arthur's persistence until Milo Frederico hurried over with an almost believable apology for having to disengage Frank from his dear friends. To help the bishop resolve some impending crisis, Milo had said, causing Frank to nearly choke on a piece of calamari. What a crock: Bruno Santini needing Frank Roselli.

The one constant Frank anticipated in Bruno Santini's gatherings was Milo Frederico. The sly ferret seemed to know everyone, and probably every shred of scuttlebutt circulating through the Vatican, but rarely did he share those insights, certainly not with Frank. He figured Milo reported every tidbit and innuendo back to Bruno when they were alone. Otherwise they communicated with each other through subtle gestures and piercing eyes.

At seven in the evening Frank arrived for the impromptu dinner and one of the twins answered the door. Either Prima or Seconda, Frank couldn't decide. When they were together, there was no doubt: Prima, the firstborn by three minutes, always dominated her younger sister. Frank paused at the archway of the living room to check out Bruno's guests—a modest three in number given the Lenten season, and that didn't include Milo Frederico, working from a gold-inlaid desk. He looked up, nodded to Frank, and returned to the pages of a leather-bound journal. On one of the sofas perpendicular to the fireplace sat Bishop Tomaso Martinelli and Monsignor Flavio. On the opposite sofa and with their backs to Frank were Bruno and another priest, one Frank immediately recognized by the broad shoulders and dark hair streaked with gray. Frank closed the distance separating them with four long strides. He first greeted Bruno, to have done otherwise would have shown extreme disrespect. Then he acknowledged the other priest.

"Uncle Mike," Frank said, "what a pleasant surprise. I didn't expect to see you here."

After the customary Italian greeting, Bruno poured Campari for Frank, a drink Frank had yet to refuse since his encounter with The Black Angel. Time for business: Bruno positioned himself in front of the fireplace and told Frank to sit next to his uncle.

"I've brought this group together to consider a serious matter," the bishop said. "Not one in Rome but in the United States. Michael, perhaps you should explain."

Uncle Mike. Since when did he get involved in petty power struggles? Frank kept a poker face and resisted the urge to exercise his fingers while he listened to his uncle relay the third-hand account of a proposed Good Friday crucifixion and WOC rally. Damn! The nerve of Andrew: using his years-ago connection with Frank to exploit Michelle and their parents. As for Michelle, nothing surprised him, not even exploiting Andrew to ease her own sorry conscience.

When Uncle Mike finished, he leaned back to puff on his pipe, sending up a smokescreen that told Frank not to jump into the melee feet first. Instead, both of them listened with closed mouths as the three Italians grew red in the face while discussing the latest revolutionary upstart.

"It was no more than a year ago when the Holy See reprimanded Andrew O'Keefe," Bishop Martinelli said. "And his mentor—God rest John Dwyer's tortured soul."

The Italians made the sign of the cross, a sharp contrast to the American priests who only followed suit because Bruno Santini's penetrating gaze indicated they should.

"All the more reason to end this fiasco," bemoaned Monsignor Bono. "Andrew O'Keefe and WOC, indeed a scandalous duo."

"A schism in the making."

"A Dominican begging for excommunication."

"Once a priest, always a priest."

"By the way, Frank, weren't you in the seminary with Andrew O'Keefe?"

"Eleven years ago. I haven't seen him since."

"Perhaps if you were to speak with him."

"Andrew wouldn't listen to me. Andrew never listened to anyone."

THE FAMILY ANGEL

"In that case we'd like you to bring him to Rome."

"To meet with The Holy Father?"

"Or one of his trusted advisors."

"If you persuade Andrew to return, there would, of course, be certain benefits for you, Frank. Twenty long years of snail-paced promotions could be trumped with one plum assignment now, followed by more strategic ones in the future. It is quite possible to achieve Cardinal status by the time you turn fifty."

"Your biological family, Frank, how long since you last saw them?"

"Nearly three years." He raised his brow to Michael. "Maybe you could go with me, Uncle Mike."

Before Michael could answer, Bruno had pursed his thin lips into a negative response. "Another time, Frank, we don't want to alarm Father O'Keefe. And under no circumstances should you tell your family of your impending visit. In fact, tell no one." He motioned his head toward the corner. "Father Frederico will accompany you."

Milo. Frank had forgotten he was in the room. There he sat, at the lighted desk, pen in hand. Pausing from his note taking, Milo looked up and nodded an acknowledgment to Bruno.

*****

Later that evening when Frank returned to his apartment, he couldn't go to bed without making one phone call. Before the first piercing ring had ended, he heard an American *hello* instead of the Italian *pronto;* his uncle's way of saying he expected the call.

"I'm not comfortable with this, Uncle Mike," Frank whispered. "If the Curia needs someone to save Andrew from himself—"

"You mean escort him back to Rome."

"Fat chance of that happening, at least not before Good Friday. In any case, wouldn't the Nunzio or one of his assistants be more appropriate? What about a Dominican?"

"I agree. On the other hand, what better way to prove your diplomatic skills? Consider this your first mission."

"You don't really believe that, do you, Uncle Mike?"

"No, and I regret having involved you. In retrospect and given Bruno's calculated reaction I should've gone to St. Gregory on my own. That said, the assignment is now up to you. When you locate Andrew, don't leave him alone with Milo. Or let him out of your sight. Follow your instincts, Frank. I'll pray for you ... Andrew too."

Chapter 62
Milo Frederico

Three days later Frank departed with Milo Frederico from Rome's Leonardo Da Vinci Airport on Flight 841 to New York. Frank stretched his legs out in seat 2A. In Seat 2B sat Milo. It was Milo who had secured their first class passage, through to St. Louis. And Milo who made the other travel arrangements out of Lambert Airport in St. Louis. All due to the generosity and intervention of one of Bishop Santini's associates, he told Frank. Behind the two priests sat an older couple, returning from their first trip to Italy.

"An incentive earned by selling farm machinery," the man boasted to a pleasant flight attendant, deluxe all the way. And would you believe: we got by without learning one single word of Eye-talian."

"A blessing for all," Milo said in Italian.

When the flight attendant came by with small bottles of wine, Milo picked a fruity Bianco and Frank settled back with a dry vino rosa. He let the wine warm his throat before lowering his voice to speak in the relative privacy of Italian.

"So, Milo, I must confess I'm baffled. Considering Bishop Santini's demanding schedule, why send his most valued assistant to a small town in America's heartland?"

"Ah-h, America has a heart—how interesting. But to answer your question, no one is indispensable. Why did you agree to go?"

Games. Frank could play too. "I had a choice?"

"We all have choices, Frank."

"Not when I'm serving the Vatican, the Holy Father."

"You don't know that, not for sure."

"What about you, Milo? Who are you serving?"

"My father."

"In heaven or in the Vatican?"

"You Americans and your ..." He switched to English. "... your need to connect with the life of a mere acquaintance."

"It's a long flight, Milo. The movie's a futuristic yarn about some boy and his dog."

"In that case," Milo replied, pouring more wine into his glass, "I promise not to bore you. In return you must respect my need for confidentiality."

"In that case I suggest you speak in Italian."

"Indeed." He switched to his native language. "I was born in Florence and still an infant when cancer took my father. My mother managed a small pensione in the Old City. I went to a good school within walking distance from our home. My playground became the *Piazza della Signoria* but unlike the other boys, I never took coins from the Fountain of Neptune."

"Already the makings of a good priest," Frank said although he had his doubts. "Sorry, I didn't mean to interrupt."

"Patience, it is not my intention to bore you. In my thirteenth year I came home from school one day to find my mother sitting in the living room with a priest I'd not seen before. That was how I first met my biological father. The three of us agreed to keep the relationship secret since too many lives would be disrupted, too many innocent people hurt, and for what?"

Frank attempted to stifle a yawn that Milo mistook for another interruption.

"Please, Frank, allow me finish before you speak. During the priest's month-long holiday he and I became inseparable. By the time he returned to his clerical duties, I had settled on a religious vocation. My decision was not difficult nor was it one I ever regretted. Wanting a fresh start, I took my middle name as my first—Milo instead of Santo—and after my ordination, I asked my father to find a place for me at the Vatican. It was, after all, the least Bruno Santini could do for the son he could never acknowledge."

Frank reacted with a knee-jerk that nearly spilled the wine on his tray. He shook the cobwebs from his head and blinked twice. "Bruno?

Dammit, Milo. I can appreciate your wanting to share this with someone but why me?"

"Our mission is about trust, Frank, and loyalty, of course."

"The loyalty I understand, but it doesn't take two of us to bring Andrew back."

"Andrew may be a guest at your parents' home but until you prove otherwise, Bishop Santini still considers your strength to be that of a fundraiser."

"God knows there's never enough money. What about you, Milo? What's your strength?"

"Think of me as a shepherd—one who returns lost sheep to the fold. Or, should it prove necessary, closer to Our Lord."

Chapter 63
St. Gregory, April 3

On Wednesday the early morning sun warmed Carlo's back while he was bent over to strip the meadow of young dandelions. After filling a paper grocery bag, he returned to the duplex he'd shared with Jake for fifty-two years, the last five without Irene. Jake took over the dandelion cleaning at his kitchen sink. He snipped off the roots and passed the tender sprouts through five water baths before pronouncing the greens acceptable for a proper salad. Stored in recycled plastic bags, the dandelions went into the refrigerator and later would be combined with sliced onions and hard-boiled eggs.

"You coming out?" Carlo asked as he headed for the back porch.

Jake dunked the heel of yesterday's cream bread in fresh coffee, held it there to soak up the flavor. "Nah, I ain't read the morning comics yet. They give me maybe one belly laugh every day, which is more than I can say for the guys on TV."

"It ain't about the language," Carlo said. "You gotta be raised American to understand TV humor and that's something you and me can never change."

Jake didn't answer. Maybe his ears were clogged with wax again.

Outside, Carlo leaned back on the steps and reveled in the sweetness of the greening spring. He heard the phone ring and Jake raise his voice to compensate for the hearing problem. The Post Dispatch was still in Jake's hand when he opened the screen door.

"That was Mary Ann. Tony's taking her to St. Louis and they

want us to tag along. And don't ask me why she didn't hitch a ride to the city with Michelle."

"Michelle left at dawn and you know Mary Ann without her morning coffee. She can't juggle it in the car and lecture at the same time. Besides, it's hard telling when Michelle will get home, what with taking care of business for that priest. Not that I care."

"Me either. But I can't say the same for Tony and your daughter. They keep talking with their eyes every time Father Andrew opens his mouth."

Carlo had noticed too, and couldn't abide an entire day of Mary Ann's tirade against their houseguest, or Michelle's usual flightiness. He shifted a bony hip on the worn stairs, and yawned. "Nah, I ain't in the mood for St. Louis. But, if it ain't too much trouble, bring back some salami from The Hill," he said, referring to the Italian section.

When Mary Ann and Tony came by, Carlo stood beside their idling Buick and defended his right to stay home. He only won the argument after delivering an indelicate fart and threatening more if forced to spend hours cooped up in the car. He couldn't help but chuckle as Mary Ann turned beet red and motioned for Tony to take off. They left in a cloud of dust, with Jake grinning from the backseat.

To clear the air Carlo lifted his head and sucked in the scent of lilacs blooming on the south side of the garage. He and Jake had planted the four bushes for Irene after they'd finished building the duplex. She said it would take seven years before they'd enjoy an initial bloom. Carlo grumbled privately to Jake that they could all be dead by then. But in the seventh year the lilacs put on their first show, and repeated it every spring thereafter.

Those lilacs will outlive Jake and me just like they outlived Irene, Carlo thought. *God rest the soul of a damn hard worker and a good woman. If Irene had one fault, it was her worrying. As if worry could ever change what God already planned, like deciding Louisa should make me love her more than life itself, then leaving me a widower with two babies. They're babies no more: St. Michael the Pious, Bossy Mary Ann and her brood—the cream of my flawed legacy. Jake told me coming to America was our greatest blessing; I used to think we were just plain lucky. Now I know better. Maybe it's my age: still going strong at eighty although I haven't connected with Ruby Lee in almost a year. She said she couldn't keep up with me; Ruby Lee always did have a way with words. So did Giulietta.*

Carlo stretched a kink from his leg before starting the short walk across the vineyard to check on Mary Ann's houseguest. The priest usually slept late and seemed half-dazed when awake, which Carlo tolerated out of respect for the collar. For a man with grandiose ambitions Andrew O'Keefe seemed incapable of dragging a heavy cross any distance, let alone endure a mock crucifixion. What the hell did he hope to accomplish, other than a contentious place in the sun?

What about ever-defiant Michelle: aiding and abetting a misguided disciple, however just the cause. At least his granddaughter possessed one crumb of good sense. She'd opened up to him about the Good Friday pretense, and a conversation she'd overheard between her parents regarding a phone call to Mike in Rome. None of this had been shared with Jake, who sometimes talked out of turn, and Carlo didn't want Mary Ann knowing he knew more than he'd let on. And rightly so, she'd been too damn anxious to whisk Jake and him off to St. Louis, which would've meant leaving Father Andrew alone. So maybe the frail man needed an objective ally.

As Carlo approached the grassy area bordering Mary Ann's back yard, he saw a black sedan pull into the driveway. Two men stepped out—more priests, more trouble. The taller one, who'd been driving, stretched his arm into a broad wave. Carlo squinted through his bifocals.

"*Christo.* I don't believe my eyes." He removed his glasses, wiped the lenses, and when he settled the glasses back on his face, a smile crept over his mouth. "Jesus, Mary, and Joseph, look who's here. Mary A-a ...." His voice trailed off as he hurried to meet his grandson.

A triple round of handshakes and hugs occupied Carlo and his grandson while the second priest stood back with dark eyes surveying the scene. Frank's introduction of Milo Frederico as a Florentine prompted a labored dialogue in formal Italian until Carlo finally threw up his hands.

"Forgive me, Father. I ain't so good at proper Italian, not like before. It's either Piemontese or regular American... English, I mean."

They settled on English.

"You should've called, Frank. Your folks ain't home," Carlo said. "They went shopping in St. Louis. Uncle Jake too." He opened the rear door of Frank's rental and climbed inside. "No point hanging around here. Let's go to my place."

Frank shrugged. Milo nodded. They got in, Frank started the engine, and they headed toward Carlo's.

"Nice car," Carlo said as he checked out the interior. Raising his brow, he stuck out his lower lip, and made circles in the air with his hand. Frank's eyes came into play through the rearview mirror. On an occasion such as this, those eyes should've been dancing but were not. Carlo figured they reflected the long air flight, the lousy food. Or worse. He leaned over the front seat and noticed the car phone. "*Mama mia*, your own wire service."

"It came with the car, Grandpa."

"Yes, Mr. Baggio," Milo said as they pulled into the driveway. "One man's luxury is another's necessity."

Another priest pontificating, no wonder Frank looked worn out. After they got out of the car, Carlo led the way to his kitchen. He motioned with one hand for the priests to sit while his other latched onto the basement doorknob.

Frank shook his head, showed his palms. "No wine, Grandpa. It's too early."

"Whadaya mean? It's never too early to welcome my grandson and his sidekick from Italy. Besides, in Rome it's already afternoon." On the way downstairs he yelled for Frank to get out the good glasses. He returned, holding up a trophy bottle. "From the best of our grapes."

"I'm honored, Mr. Baggio."

"Where you from, Father ... before the Vatican, I mean." Carlo held up his forefinger. "Ah, si, I remember, now ... *Firenze*." He sighed. "Well, of course, our Southern Illinois grapes cannot compete with those of *Toscano*."

A stingy smile crossed Milo's lips. "Please, I would very much enjoy some of your wine."

"Spoken like a true paesano, Father." Carlo thought too syrupy, almost like undiluted tamarindo, his laxative of choice. After he poured, they raised their glasses. "Welcome home, Frank. It has been too long."

"*Salute!*"

"Just like old times, when you was a high school hotshot and ...." Carlo winked, a private reminder of earlier times when he and Jake shared their wine and wisdom with him. He exchanged grins with his grandson until Frank remembered the Florentine. "Please excuse our little foray into the past, Milo."

"Every family has its secrets," he replied.

"Some have a way of getting out," Carlo said. "So, Frank, I guess you know about the visiting priest."

"What's to know?"

"He's camping out in your old room, mostly to sleep. We hardly ever see him, or Michelle. She's home too, sassy as ever and driving him around."

"He doesn't drive?" asked Milo.

"I don't ask." Carlo collected the empty glasses and rinsed them in the sink. "Come on; let's show Father Milo the vineyard."

"That's very nice of you, but—"

"Like I said, Father, our grapes don't compare to those in Italy but around here they're considered the best." He opened the back door and motioned the priests out. "Another beautiful day, ain't it. God's precious gift to us."

They strolled through the vineyards, discussing the Tokays and Concords that Carlo pointed out as well as new varieties he and Jake were giving a chance. When Frank drifted toward his parent's house, Carlo grabbed his arm. "Like I said, your folks ain't home. Besides, we'll need some bread, before the good stuff gets picked over."

Before leaving they returned to the duplex because Milo had to relieve himself. As soon as the bathroom door closed behind the Florentine, Carlo nudged Frank, motioning toward the backyard.

"I should wait for Milo," Frank whispered.

"Since when do you and that priest gotta pee together?" He grabbed Frank's elbow and pushed him outside. "You two ain't joined at the hip, are you? Wait a minute. Don't tell me that you and him?"

Frank laughed. "No, that part of me hasn't changed. It's just that Milo ...."

"Don't want you alone with me. I didn't want to say nothing in front of him, but ...."

"But what?"

"The other priest ... he's at your folk's house now. He'll be up by noon if today's anything like yesterday, or the day before. Michelle's in St. Louis too, but not with your folks." He narrowed his eyes to Frank. "But you already know all that, right?"

"I need to talk with Andrew, Grandpa."

"We'll stop by, after the *pané*."

"Of course, the bread ... so where are you buying it nowadays?"

"So where do you think? You know how I feel about that bland supermarket shit."

After Milo came out, they drove across town to St. Gregory's only made-from-scratch bakery. Carlo invited the priests, actually Frank although he included Milo, to follow him into the shop, but both men refused.

"What the hell," Carlo grumbled as he opened the car door. "I just wanted to show off my grandson."

He returned with the last decent loaf of cream bread, and pouted until the Lincoln pulled into Mary Ann's driveway. "You want the suitcases now?" he asked, as they approached the rear entrance.

"There's no need, Mr. Baggio."

"Does that mean you're not staying long?"

"It means we travel light, Grandpa."

"That figures. You go on, Frank. I want to show Father Milo your ma's spring lettuce. She thinks it could be better; I say it's the finest crop we ever had."

*****

After another exchange of priestly glances, Milo followed Carlo to the garden and Frank went into the house of his youth. He made no sound walking into the kitchen. Open casement windows welcomed a fresh breeze while the distant bells of All Saints pealed to announce midday. The Andrew he remembered would've greeted him with a cocky smile and the playful punch of a former athlete. This Andrew sat hunched over the table, barefoot with his back to the door. He wore loose clothing, gray sweatpants and a white T-shirt with the initials WOC arching over the top of an x-shaped cross, a design Frank recognized as the cross of St. Andrew.

"Come in, Frank. I've been expecting you." Gripping the table, Andrew pushed himself up, and then turned to offer a trembling hand. "You've come a long way in a short time."

"We both have," said Frank. Andrew's hand felt clammy but not enough to dampen the greeting. His eyes were rheumy and bloodshot. "You're not feeling well?" Frank asked.

"Judging from the look on your face, not as good as I thought. Don't tell me I'm dying."

"We're dying from the minute we're born. Isn't that what you used to tell me?"

"Enough about death," Andrew said, easing back into his chair.

Frank sat across the table and started rubbing his chin.

"Nervous, Frank? I'd offer you something to drink but you know your mother's kitchen better than I. Speaking of your mother—your father and grandfathers too—I want to say how well they've treated me this past week, in spite of certain concerns regarding my mission. As for Michelle, without her, I wouldn't be here."

Leave it to Michelle. "Just why are you here, Andrew?"

"We all have to be somewhere. Why are you here?"

"To bring you back to Rome."

"I'm not surprised."

"So I noticed. You were expecting me?"

"What better choice. I must commend Vatican intelligence: those conspiratorial elitists, dispatching an ambitious diplomat to thwart a schismatic priest."

"First of all, I'm not a diplomat, at least not yet."

"But when you are, there's bound to be the offering of an attractive post if you can pull this off, right?"

"Look Andrew, let's not talk Vatican politics. I'm here to help you. That is, if you'll let me."

"You've got it wrong, Frank. It's all about politics. We wouldn't be here, having this discussion, if it weren't. All I want is to bring the Church into the twenty-first century bearing the same values it held two thousand years ago."

"For one so humble, why the big splash?"

"How else will I be heard?" He rippled thin fingers through the air. "You tell me: who pays attention to little waves."

While Andrew was talking, Frank debated internally whether to punch him or to hug him. Before he had a chance to do either, the back door opened for Grandpa.

"Good morning, Mr. Baggio," Andrew said in a huskier voice than before.

"*Buon giorno*, Father Andrew," Carlo replied, motioning both men to stay seated. "*Comé sta?*"

"Better, now that you're here." Andrew looked beyond Carlo, to the priest who followed him in. "I should've known the Cardinal wouldn't permit Frank to handle this on his own." He forced himself to stand and extended his hand to Milo. "I believe we've met before, Father. Last year, in that hush-hush meeting at the Vatican, although I didn't catch your name then."

Their hands barely touched in a perfunctory greeting as Milo identified himself.

"Father Milo Frederico performs many duties," Andrew said. "Bishop Dwyer and I first knew him as The Recorder. He helped the bishop contain a coughing spell. Unfortunately, after that the poor man's conditioned kept deteriorating. And now The Recorder wears another hat. Perhaps that of a shepherd, about to escort me to ... God only knows where—perhaps a better place."

Frank did a mental double take. Had he been standing, his knees would've buckled. Milo the Recorder ... Milo, the Gofer ... Milo, of the many hats ... which one did he bring from Rome?

The ticking of his mother's clock took over, its awkward spell broken only when Grandpa ordered everybody to sit. He rubbed his hands together and offered one of his many pearls of wisdom. "When wise men run out of words, they know it's time to eat."

Eat? At a time like this who could eat, Frank wanted to say. But time was running out and for sure Andrew needed some fuel. Frank shoved his chair back. He started to get up, but Grandpa stopped him with a wave of the hand.

"Stay put, Frank. I know your ma's icebox and she never lets it go empty." He brought out Tupperware-encased sliced ham and pre-sliced packets of American cheese. "Sorry, this ain't the lunch Jake or me would give you but it'll do in a pinch." He checked out the breadbox and turned up his nose. "Supermarket rye, no way, I'll get mine from the car. Frank, you get the wine."

"Grandpa, please. We don't need more wine."

"What's the matter with you? Of course we need wine, to wash down the food."

"Mr. Baggio, if you please," said Milo. "I left a package in the car, I believe on the front seat. Would you mind bringing it in?"

Grandpa hurried out to the Lincoln and quickly returned with the bread and a brown paper bag, tall and slender. "You were wise not to leave this in the car any longer," he said, handing it to Milo, "not with that hot sun beating down."

Milo pulled out a bottle of *Classico Chianti*. Frank hadn't seen the bottle before and figured it must've traveled in Milo's briefcase that doubled as an overnight bag.

"Ah-h," Grandpa said, fingertips to lips. "This man's parents taught him well. He brings the best of Toscano. You are gonna let us sample it, ain't you, Father?" He showed his palms. "I know, I know, you don't wanna embarrass me. Our Illinois wine ain't nearly as good as what you brought."

"But your wine is excellent, Mr. Baggio. Frank and I shall have another glass. You and Father Andrew must try the Chianti."

Andrew nodded with his eyes. He broke off a hunk of bread, folded in around some ham, and chomped down. The only one to eat, he chewed and talked at the same time. "Remember that lunch at Pierluigi, Frank? How your Uncle Mike taught us to savor the wine."

"We ate like pigs."

"And argued Church reform until your uncle said, 'Enough.' You backed down, even though—"

"Dammit," Grandpa said. "I ain't seen Michael in years. Too bad he didn't come with you. No offense, Father Milo."

Three sets of priestly eyes settled on Carlo Baggio as he filled a quartet of stemmed glasses: the Illinois wine for Milo and Frank, the Chianti for Andrew and him. Four hands raised their glasses.

"If I may propose a toast," Andrew said, lifted his shaky hand. "To God's plan: may those who follow it, stay the course."

God's plan. Stay the course. Andrew's words slammed into Frank like an unexpected Illinois Central. For a brief moment the clock stopped ticking. He scanned the room, expecting to see the black man. *Dammit, L'Angelo Nero, where are you when I need you. At least give me some kind of signal.* He continued his scan, ending with the table: Milo sipping and observing Andrew from over the rim of his glass; Grandpa, whispering a prayer as he lowered his untouched glass; Andrew holding his to the light, checking out the wine's clarity and color.

"What's the matter, my friend?" Andrew asked Frank. "And you, Mr. Baggio. Not drinking?"

Frank answered for both of them. "About following God's plan, what did you mean?"

"Isn't that the journey that brought us all together?"

Now angel, now ... niente, zero, nothing: just Andrew's eyes locked on his. Frank felt another pair of eyes—Milo's. Frank sensed the aroma of grapes, the pride of his family. Good wine, but probably not as good as Milo's. Milo's wine ... of course: how could Frank have been so stupid. He didn't need any angel leading him by the hand. He reached over and took the glass from Andrew's hand.

Andrew smiled, breaking the spell. With hands braced against the table, once again he strained to stand. "Gentlemen, I'm sorry for being a party-pooper, but I really need a quick nap." He walked to the hallway entrance, stopped without turn around. "Frank, before I conk out, will you hear my confession?"

T'hell with Milo, Frank didn't need his approval. He slipped one hand in his pocket, for the purple stole he always carried, and followed Andrew into the bedroom.

*****

The click of the door as it closed resounded from the hallway, prompting Carlo to clear the table and return the Tupperware to Mary Ann's refrigerator. He picked up his glass of Chianti—untouched since the toast—held it to his nose, and took in the aroma. He hesitated, and then breathed in again. Wrinkling his nostrils in displeasure, Carlo could almost feel the priest's displeasure but for reasons beyond the aroma test.

"Please excuse my poor manners, Father Milo. Perhaps you should taste the Chianti you brought."

The Florentine's ears flushed. Clearing his throat, he took the glass from Carlo. "It is I who must apologize, Mr. Baggio. You were right about my negligence. I should never have allowed the Chianti to be exposed." He carried the glass and wine bottle to the sink and sent the remains of both down the drain. "Now, if you don't mind, I find myself in need of some solitude, perhaps a stroll around the property."

"Take your time, Father. I happen to know Father Andrew prefers long naps."

He watched the priest slide into the Lincoln's front seat and pick up the telephone, his necessary luxury. Maybe he was calling Rome to tattle on Frank. Carlo also made a phone call, his to Abraham Washington, an old friend he once helped by getting him a new start in St. Gregory.

Minutes later, Frank came back, returning the purple stole to his pocket and walking with a lighter step than when he left.

"The Florentine needed some air, to clear his head. And maybe to say his prayers," Carlo said. "You know this man well?"

"Better than I did five days ago. Why do you ask?"

"He pitched the Chianti—blamed its bitterness on the hot sun. But you and I know better, don't we?" Carlo didn't wait for an answer. "I ain't no dummy, Frank. Poisoned wine ... a would-be martyr ... his failed assassin wearing the collar, what's going on?"

"I got blind sighted, Grandpa, but I think I'm back on track." Frank checked his watch. "We don't have much time."

"You're taking Andrew back, you and the Florentine?"

"Not to Rome and not with Milo. But I am leaving with Andrew, as soon as he finishes his penance."

"What the hell, the man's a saint."

"Even saints talk to God." Frank smiled like old times. "Where he acquired this sudden surge of energy beats me. About Milo ...."

"Leave that one to me. You remember Abraham Washington? He's on his way over. Between the two of us, we'll make sure to give the Florentine a proper sendoff."

Carlo grabbed his grandson, kissed both cheeks so he wouldn't forget where he came from. "*L'Angelo Nero*, Frank, did you see him today?"

"Only in Andrew's eyes, Grandpa."

"What'd they say about God's plan?"

"Nothing I didn't already know. Since my diplomatic career just got flushed down the toilet, I might follow Andrew for a while, perhaps raise some financial support for his cause."

"Just don't embarrass the family. Remember, we have our good name to uphold."

Carlo had more to say but Andrew came in, suitcase in hand and a healthy blush to his cheeks. Carlo hugged the priest, surprisingly strong for so little meat on the bones, and whispered in his ear, "I'll be thinking about you on Good Friday, Father. Carry the cross for me too."

He walked outside with Frank and his charge, helped settle them in the car. Neither Frank or Andrew seemed concerned about the missing priest. When the Lincoln pulled away Carlo scanned the landscape until he saw The Florentine walking around the vineyard, checking out the grapes. Milo straightened up and shielded his eyes from the sun as he looked in Carlo's direction and then to the Lincoln as it eased down the driveway, eventually moving to the shoulder to accommodate an arriving pickup truck. Riding shotgun was Abraham Washington, his arm looped around the open window while his son John handled the wheel.

Him and them against one conniving priest, Carlo liked the odds—not that he had any serious concerns, at least not this day. If his grandson hadn't left in such a hurry, Carlo would've told him about the black man who showed up for Andrew's toast. He wore bib overalls and a baseball cap, and stood behind Frank, popping Tokays in his mouth until the four hands lifted in unison.

"To God's plan," Andrew had said. "May those who follow it stay the course."

Everyone understood except The Florentine. He drank first, expecting the rest to follow.

"Not so fast," *L'Angelo Nero* had told Carlo. "That Italian wine isn't fit to drink."

Carlo lowered his glass. "Good thing you said something. I better warn Andrew," he whispered, in a voice so low he only mouthed the words, as if in prayer.

"Andrew can't hear you. And don't bother shouting."

"Then you tell him. Wait a minute … that's why you're here. You came for Andrew, right?"

"That depends on Frank, and whether he chooses to follow God's plan."

"Frank knows right from wrong. He'll pass the test."

"It's only one of many. Frank has a long way to go."

"And what about me, *Angelo nero*? What about me. When will I see my Louisa again?"

"Patience, Carlo. Not today … nor tomorrow, but one day soon."

###

As an added bonus for your reading enjoyment
The opening chapters of
Chicago's Headmistress

CHICAGO'S HEADMISTRESS
A Prequel and Partial Parallel to
THE FAMILY ANGEL

Loretta Giacoletto

Chapter 1
Genoa, Italy 1905

On the morning of her thirteenth birthday Delila Lobianco cracked open one crusty eyelid and surveyed the only home she'd ever known—a cockroach-infested room shared with the whore Editta, a pathetic wretch who often boasted about the title she once held as Genoa's *Puttanesca Numero Uno*. If only Genoa could see its former Numero Uno now, her cleansing routine no better than that of a common alley cat, applying a dollop of spit here, a dollop of spit there. Instead of the usual clothing worn for everyday whoring, Editta, as Delila always thought of her mother, slipped into the only outfit featuring a high neckline and full-length skirt. Editta eased her callused bare feet into scruffy boots that rose midway to meet spindly calves. She propped one foot onto the straight-back chair, leaned forward, and with shaking fingers used a hook to close the buttons on her boot and then repeated the routine on her other foot and boot. Ignoring the cracked mirror hanging lopsided on the wall, Editta plopped her straw hat atop the disheveled pompadour in need of a good shampooing. She opened the rickety door and stepped into the hallway. Delila lowered her eyelid and listened to Editta lock the door. The large key she used would soon weigh down the drawstring bag that held a multitude of useless treasures.

Delila pictured Editta on the same route they'd taken many times, moving quickly from the waterfront, walking uphill, away from the Bay of Genoa and the Old City, through garbage-filled, dark corridors separating row upon row of centuries-old buildings wrought with decay. The tattered hem of her skirt would skim over puddles of open sewage to marry the skirt's older stains with those more recently acquired; brown rats, some as big as cats, boldly scrounging for food and forcing Editta to hasten her once casual pace. Fourteen years in Genoa's hellhole still had not dampened the woman's dreams for the life she kept promising Delila who already towered over her.

And today would be special. Thirteen, Delila's lucky number—no longer a girl, but not yet a woman. She drifted off to sleep again, only to have a loud knock at the door awaken her. One of Editta's drunks demanding the whore should help celebrate his winning at *scopa*.

Editta had taught her well, to never let on she was alone.

"Bravo," Delila called out. "Editta says to come back later. She's busy right now."

The man said he couldn't wait; he needed a woman now, even if it meant taking turns with someone else.

"Later," Delila yelled. "You and Editta: all afternoon."

What little she said didn't matter. When the man's weight pushed against the door to force it open, she hopped out of bed and sought refuge in the obscure shadows.

Delila recognized the lumbering buffoon, the one who always smelled so bad. When he saw her cowering in a corner, he threw back his head and laughed. She tried to run but he grabbed her arm. He swung back and hit her in the mouth, making it bleed.

He said, "You, little bitch, will taste better than your old lady ever did."

Delila stumbled toward the door but he blocked her way. Screaming made no sense. No one would have come. He pinned her arms down. She turned her head from one side to the other. His furry, slobbering tongue found her mouth. She smelled his sweat and fermenting wine, gagged from the dried vomit clinging to his clothes. His sour body leaned into hers. When they fell onto the bed, Delila's soul retreated from her limp body. She willed herself to block out what she could not change, to reserve her energy for when it would count the most. Fortunately, the shit didn't take long to steal the one thing she and Editta valued above all else. He lifted his chest. Howled like an animal.

*****

Editta's journey took her past two crones perched on their second floor balcony. As usual, they were shrouded in the shabbiest of widows black.

"*Buon giorno*, Editta," one of them called out. "Come join us for our morning *latte*."

"*Grazie*, but not today," Editta replied with a wave of her hand. "I'm running an important errand."

And running away from everything the two ancients represented. They'd introduced Editta to life on the streets when they were ready to retire and took a portion of her earnings for the next five years. After Delila was born, Editta sometimes brought her to see the women. They'd seemed old then but must've passed the half century mark a mere year or two ago. In mourning for themselves, the old crones just didn't know it yet and Editta didn't have the heart to tell them. Nor did she want them passing on any of their assorted diseases to her or Delila.

Once plump and pretty, Editta had grown so thin her rheumy eyes had taken on a lackluster quality. A persistent cough gurgled in her throat and on occasion erupted into spasms so intense she couldn't catch her breath. Hollowed cheeks indicated the absence of back teeth, rotted away just like the buildings surrounding her. Black decay marched toward the front of her mouth; racing with the cruelty of time that would soon leave her toothless until God saw fit to take her. But not before she suffered the indignities of purgatory in this world. Like the two diseased ancients, only worse because they seemed oblivious to the living hell they felt no urgency to escape.

Editta turned a sharp corner, bringing her out of the shadows and into the welcoming sunlight that blessed the rest of Genoa. Four more blocks of brisk walking brought her to a busy *panetteria* where she selected a fresh fig and lemon tart, Delila's favorite *dolce*.

Motioning with an exaggerated gesture, she said, "Oh yes, and a dozen amaretto cookies."

The baker's wife responded with a brief nod and filled the order with unusual dispatch, both of the women knowing a wretch such as Editta could turn away respectable business.

After leaving the panetteria, Editta made her way to the street market where she strolled up and down every aisle and stall. No more cheap trinkets for Delila, only the best gold earrings, Editta decided after observing some of Genoa's finest ladies who shunned her very existence.

Just wait, you fancy, clucking hens, she wanted to tell them. Some day my Delila will put all of you to shame.

Editta would've indulged her fantasy longer had it not been for the slight nudge she felt from behind. She held the dolce tightly, her drawstring bag even tighter.

"Whore, where the hell you been?" asked a man whose grin exposed a gaping hole that once housed his left front tooth. At thirty-two, Maurizio Bracca took pride in his contoured face, a pleasant contrast to the occasional flecks of gray streaking his dark, curly hair. His gaunt body bordered on emaciation but the chances of his dying from violence exceeded those from malnutrition.

Editta presented her sallow cheeks to Maurizio, leaving him no choice but a quick brush of the lips while she whispered in his ear. "Today is Delila's birthday. A pair of gold hoop earrings would bring our daughter a lifetime of happiness."

"*Our* daughter, please, must we argue this every year, with twenty-four other johns just as likely as me to have fathered her."

"A wise woman can make the distinction."

"And a wise man is no fool," he said with a wink. "As you may recall, I spent a month in jail around the time of her conception."

"Must you keep reminding me?"

"Must you keep trying to make me into the papa I am not. As for *your* daughter, has she started working the streets?"

"Only as a scavenger but thank you for asking," Editta said. "She is a virgin and will remain so until I find a proper match for her, a wealthy man who will pay handsomely for her to share *la dolce vita,* the sweet life. Have you seen our Delila lately? She is taller than me."

"As if I care ... although ... I do have just the pair of earrings for *your* daughter. Since I keep them in my room perhaps we can make a trade."

Editta checked out the morning sun overhead. "Time is precious. The trade will have to be quick."

"But will it match the value of the earrings?"

"And then some."

Editta followed Maurizio to his room located over a second-hand shop that depended on his stolen goods to increase its inventory. After an hour-long romp evolving into the boredom of repetition, Maurizio pushed her from his bed.

"Out," he said, "before those demons dwelling within your mind and body grab hold of mine."

Having had her fill as well, Editta didn't challenge his remark. "What about Delila's gift?" she asked while buttoning her crumpled blouse.

"The jar on my dresser, give it a shake."

"I earned the earrings?"

He grinned. "And then some."

*****

On returning to her room, Editta found the door unlocked. It's not like Delila to be so careless, she thought while pushing the door open. As soon as she walked in, the packages slipped from her hands. A gasp deep within her throat erupted into a silent scream. There on the bed lay two bloody bodies, locked together and motionless. Editta made a dash for the stiletto she kept wedged between the mattress and headboard. Gone—but where? This pig was sprawled over her beautiful Delila, every inch of his body covering hers. She grabbed his shoulders, and pulling with all her strength, slipped in a pool of blood as his lifeless body rolled to the floor. Only then did she find her stiletto, lodged in the heart of the *bastardo* she recognized as Tito, a Portuguese sailor who came around whenever *The Helena* stopped in Genoa.

Covered with blood but thank god still alive, Delila scrambled from the blood-soaked mattress. She fell into Editta's arms and began flailing the woman's consumptive chest.

"Where were you, Editta? I hate you ... I hate you."

"*Bambina, bambina,* forgive me," Editta wailed through a coughing spell. "If it takes the rest of my life, I will make this up to you. I swear by all that is holy."

"The one time I needed you ... the one time. He came looking for you, not me. But that didn't matter. I had to take your place. He ruined me. Now I'll end up just like you—nothing more than a common whore."

"Shut your mouth and keep your voice down," Editta said, lowering her own. "You won't be the first second-hand virgin. There are ways to make sure your future benefactor will never know the difference. Now take off that filthy nightdress and tell me exactly what happened while I draw some water to clean you up."

Delila told her story while sitting in an all-purpose washtub used for their dirty dishes, their dirty laundry, their dirty floors, and their dirty bodies.

"... Fortunately, the shit did not take long," she continued with a sob. "When he lifted his chest and howled like an animal, I stretched my arm overhead for the stiletto and with all my strength plunged it into his fat chest, just like you showed me. He let out one yell, and then fell on me."

Delila choked back another sob. "I couldn't move, Mama. His heart pumped faster and faster against mine, then slower and slower until it finally stopped. Warm, sticky blood covered me. I couldn't help myself—I threw up right before you came home."

"You were brave, my child. I taught you well."

Having decided to postpone the birthday celebration, Editta covered the trembling Delila with an old blanket and helped her from the tub. Still trembling, Delila curled up in the corner and closed her eyes.

"Rest for now," Editta told her. "Tonight after dark we'll get rid of him. For now, I have to clean up this mess."

Out in the hallway Editta hung this hand-written sign on the broken door.

VACANZA CHIUSO
CLOSED FOR VACATION

Tying the door shut with a rope returned Editta's sense of security, along with the common sense that comes with years on the street. Ever so carefully, she slipped one thumb and forefinger into the pocket of Tito's trousers and eased out a leather pouch, soiled and fat and stuffed with coins. Her bloodshot eyes grew wider with each coin crossing her palm—more money than she'd seen in her entire life.

Quelling the urge to wake up Delila, Editta sat at the table, tapping her fingers while trying to figure out how to remove all traces of Tito. The body was too heavy for Delila and her to move without help. She'd have to pay dearly for strong arms and a poor memory. Considering the day's events, Editta thought it best not to leave Delila alone while she went out to make a deal. Instead, she let the child sleep and allowed herself a nap as well.

*****

Delila stirred with a shudder felt from the nape of her neck down to her toes and everywhere in between. Her body ached in places only she had touched until this day. She sat up, at first not daring to open her eyes but when she did, the room looked just as it did in the nightmare she'd relived in her sleep. Tito's body still lay on the floor, his dark blood sending out a stain that no amount of scrubbing would ever remove. She wrapped her thin arms around long, pony-like legs and let her face seek the comfort of her knees, a moment so brief it counted for *niente*.

"Look, Delila, look."

Delila lifted her head. She brushed strands of straw-colored hair away from her eyes. There stood Editta, holding up a leather pouch as if showing off a prized trophy she'd won at Genoa's annual *carnevale*.

"No wonder the shit wanted to celebrate. What once was his treasury has now become our inheritance."

Our inheritance—if Editta had been working from her room instead of the streets, none of this would've happened. Too late now, they might be able to fool that future benefactor but Delila would carry the memory of this today forever. She forced herself to ask, "How much?"

"Patience, my little heiress, I have not counted our fortune as yet. Just think, for us his passing has resulted in an overdue blessing."

"Today was a blessing?"

"In more ways than that one," Editta said, pointing to the body. "Meet your first benefactor, dead but still giving, a just punishment if ever there was. With this inheritance and the fresh start it will provide, multiple blessings are sure to follow."

"What about him?" Delila wrinkled her nose. "The mess—"

"So awful we can't restore order on our own. I must go out for help."

"And leave me alone with him ... no, no, and no. I'd rather kill myself."

"Then you go. I'll count the money and find a safe hiding place."

Chapter 2
Cleaning Up

After Delila put on her clothes, she followed the same route Editta had taken earlier that day. Unsteady legs strengthened with her every step. Not a minute to waste. No time to stop and catch a breath or wave to the old women calling her name. No time to think about the man she'd killed because he deserved to die. Delila stopped at a dilapidated building housing ground-floor junk shops and entered through a side door once painted green. She climbed one flight of stairs and turned left. Taking a well-deserved gulp of air, she tapped a row of fingers on the door.

No answer.

This time she used her knuckles.

Still no answer but Delila did hear the sound of footsteps inside. In a voice barely above a whisper, she pleaded over and over, "Maurizio ... Maurizio. Please, Editta needs you."

At last the door opened partway to reveal Maurizio wearing nothing more than a pair of wrinkled trousers. "You! How many times must I tell your mama: you and me, we ain't related."

Delila slumped to the hallway floor, her body shaking with each defined sob.

"Ah, this one is also an actress. Do me a favor and save your tears for the gullible *turista.*"

"Please, Maurizio. Keep your voice down. Mama and me, we're in the worst kind of trouble."

"Come in, come in."

She slipped through the narrow opening, stood eye to eye with him until she turned away.

He grabbed her chin, forced her to face him again. His voice softened on asking, "What kind of trouble?"

"I can't tell you here. You must see for yourself. Mama said she would pay."

"Editta pay, since when?"

"Since today, I promise."

He released her chin, spit in one hand, rubbed it with the other. "Where have I heard that before?"

"Never from me, I don't lie ... not to my friends I don't."

"Do not count me among your friends."

She sucked in a deep breath and forced a single tear down her cheek. "Don't make me beg, please."

He glared at her until she produced another tear, a single sob.

"Wait outside while I make myself presentable. And quit that damn whimpering. It's not like you."

*****

Delila brought Maurizio back to the broken door and its pathetic sign.

"Editta on vacation, since when?" he asked with half a chuckle.

"You'll see," Delila whispered before raising her voice one decibel. "Mama, we have company."

The door opened wide enough for Delila and Maurizio to squeeze inside. One glimpse at the room produced his hurried sign of the cross. "Holy Mother and Jesus, dead men I've seen before but never one this bloody."

"Dead is dead," Editta said. "And justice, swift. On the street they say you once killed a man."

"With my bare hands and a garrote ... some lowlife put his hand where it didn't belong. I suppose I could've cut it off but—"

"Please, Maurizio." Editta grabbed his arm. "You I can trust."

"Spare me your trust. Do I look like a common janitor?"

"I have money. Not much, you understand, but enough if you help us get rid of the body."

He brushed her hand away and edged towards the door.

Editta threw herself at his feet. "He tried to rape my baby, but I saved her just in time. She remains as pure as the holy water in San Lorenzo."

"As if you ever stepped foot in the Cathedral."

Editta lifted her head. "It's where I saw you picking more than one pocket."

Delila stepped between Maurizio and the door. "For the love of God, please help us. I killed him, not Mama. The pig was already dead when she came home—after showing some john a good time."

Maurizio pressed his hands to his ears. "*Basta*, enough, I'll help." He pulled Editta up, wagged his finger in her face. "But I expect you to pay me well."

"I wouldn't have it any other way."

"In advance, *capice?*"

Over wine-stained glasses filled with more wine Editta negotiated the fee with Maurizio. Before he had a chance to reconsider her offer, she handed him half of the agreed amount, money already counted out and packaged before Delila had brought him to her.

"Let's get this over with." Maurizio pushed his chair away from the table and stood. He moved to the dead man, bent over, and pulled a knife from one of Tito's boots. "Cut the mattress in pieces," he said, handing the knife to Editta. "And stuff the pieces in pillowcases."

She coughed. "This may take me a while."

"What should I do?" Delila asked.

"Not a damn thing," Maurizio said.

He rolled Tito's body back and forth over the bed sheets, wrapping the corpse so tightly it could've qualified for a burial at sea. Then he helped the ever-wheezing Editta finish her mattress chore. Together they scrubbed the floor until all traces of blood had disappeared and the room looked as it had before, except for the bundles against the wall and the empty bed frame. At that point Maurizio left, promising to return later with more supplies.

*****

Late afternoon found Editta and Delila hunched over their wobbly, paint-chipped table, drinking equal amounts of coffee and latte.

"I don't suppose there's anything to eat," Delila said.

"You suppose wrong." Editta hopped up and got the choice tart she'd bought earlier, the only food they would eat that day. "I did not forget your birthday."

"Neither did I. But this is one day I will never celebrate again."

"Don't be ridiculous. Of course you will."

Chapter 3
Middle of the Night

The dark of night had fallen on Genoa before Maurizio returned, bringing with him three sturdy boards and a strong rope. Assisted by Editta and Delila, he rigged the pillowcases and Tito's wrapped body to the boards and using the rope, fashioned a strong handle.

"Now?" Editta asked.

"Not until the city is more asleep than awake."

Then a heavy rainstorm erupted, sending its vengeance onto the entire city.

"We cannot wait any longer," he said after a while. "Let's go."

After sliding the carrier from the window to the alley below, he crawled through the window, eased down the wall, and waited for Editta and Delila to drop into his arms. With Maurizio at the helm, they began their long trek, dragging the carrier through winding, cobblestone alleys leading down to the bay, all the while Editta and Delila trading off when either needed a rest. The continuing downpour kept the streets deserted and the three abettors drenched. Still, to avoid detection they stayed close to the buildings, grateful for the protective shadows. After Editta finished her second turn, she developed a coughing spell. When she spit up phlegm and putrid pus, Maurizio ordered her back to the room.

"But you need me," Editta wailed.

"Not if you slow us down," he said. "Either you go or I go."

"Pig!"

"Mama, please."

"Dear god, Delila called me mama. I must be dying."

"You're not dying, Editta."

"That's better." Cough … cough. "Now go."

*****

Ten minutes later Delila followed Maurizio into Genoa's *Porto Vecchio*, the Old Harbor. They soon entered an abandoned warehouse where rats scampered underfoot and overhead. Even if the rodents had not been visible, the overwhelming stench defined their presence. Delia tried not to breathe as she helped Maurizio remove the tight wrappings from Tito's corpse, after which they drenched it with decaying garbage, giving special attention to the face and his belly tattoo where a rolling ship had ceased to roll.

"Give the rats and fish plenty to feed on," Maurizio told her. "A chewed-up body with no face makes identification that much harder."

After tying the bed linens around the now empty boards, Maurizio tossed them and Tito's remains into the same waters from which the *Helena* had sailed hours before, minus at least one sailor. Hopefully, her captain would curse the unpredictable Tito for skipping out and vow the no-good would never sail the sea again.

After putting the wharf behind them, Delila and Maurizio retraced their steps to make sure they'd left no incriminating evidence. Any sign of the bloodstains had disappeared, washed away by the continuing rain. As they neared the top of the hill, Delila noticed a pile of rags pushed against an arched doorway. She narrowed her eyes, not wanting to believe what each step forward eventually confirmed.

"Mama!"

Delirious with fever, Editta moaned but did not speak.

Delila knelt beside her mother. She beseeched Maurizio with the soulfulness reserved for the gullible *turisti*, as he referred to her bread and butter. "Please. Because of me we don't have a mattress any more. Could we take Editta to your room until this passes. She'll be good as gold in a day or so."

"Damn, will this never end? She couldn't have the decency to die here in the rain?"

"We can pay." Delila stood and put her hand on his arm.

"Garbage fly, leave me be." After shaking off her hand, he picked up Editta, slung her over his shoulder, and continued their trek but this time on a different course.

*****

As soon as they entered Maurizio's room, he dumped Editta onto the bed they'd share hours before.

"Girl, make some tea for your old lady. Delila ... answer me." He turned, only to find her gone. "Damn!"

Maurizio grabbed his jug and poured wine into a murky glass. When Editta stirred, he poured a second glass, as murky as the first, and lifted it to her parched lips. She took a few swallows, swiveled her head to inspect her surroundings, and released an agonizing scream before a failed attempt to crawl out of bed.

"Basta!" Maurizio's open-handed slap across Editta's face sent her back to the mattress.

The next time Editta awoke was to Delila sitting beside her.

Delila leaned over as if to kiss her but instead whispered in her ear, "Don't worry, Mama. I went back for the money."

Editta squeezed Delila's hand and asked, "All three pouches?"

"*Sì,*" she replied. "The trinity *I* inherited."

Chapter 4
The Covenant

The next day Editta waited until Maurizio left before dragging herself from the comfort of his bed. She stayed up long enough to arrange the bulk of their new fortune around Delila's boyish hips, concealed within the folds of her skirt.

A full week passed before Editta regained her strength. During that time she and Maurizio developed a covenant based on their individual concerns. Editta feared a police investigation would somehow trace Tito's disappearance to her and Delila. Even though the pig deserved what he got, they both agreed Genoa would still like its Old City rid of at least one whore and her bastard urchin. As for Maurizio, he complained his reputation as a shrewd pickpocket had become a liability and was working against him.

"Notoriety breeds recognition," he said with mournful pride. "We need new names, a new city in which to take roots."

After further discussion, they agreed to pool their resources—that portion of the inheritance revealed to Maurizio along with his years of street wisdom—and devise a plan for building new lives in America. They gathered around Maurizio's table, where he opened a bottle of wine and poured three glasses.

"To life," he said, clicking his glass with Editta's and Delila's. After the three took their first sip, Maurizio set his glass down, and said, "According to those who know, the worse will come when the boat docks at Ellis Island."

"You mean the Island of Tears," Delila said.

Editta raised her brow. She stifled a coughing spasm.

"I heard about it, Mama. That's all."

Maurizio nodded. "Si, an unmarried woman with no promise of work and no sponsor to vouch for her could be sent back from where she came. It is the American way, or so I've been told."

"What about a married couple traveling with their daughter?"

Maurizio wagged one forefinger from side to side. "No, no, Editta. There will be no wedding between you and me. But ... if you pay my passage, I will guarantee whatever we need for America to open its doors to all of us. Did I tell you about my cousin in Chicago? For me he will do anything."

"Chicago?" Editta said through a coughing spasm that brought tears to her eyes. "I never heard of such a place."

"I have," Delila said, "from this boy who only stayed one year. In the summer it's hotter than the devil's kitchen and in the winter, rain turns into sheets of ice. People must crawl across the streets because their feet won't let them walk."

"And yet they survive."

"We will need a bathroom," Editta said, "our own toilet and a tub with water that spills from the faucets."

Maurizio showed them the gaping space between his teeth. "In America everything and anything is possible."

"Even in Chicago?"

"Especially in Chicago."

"You know this for sure?" Delila asked.

"Would I lie to you?"

Chapter 5
Crossing Over

True to his word Maurizio did not marry Editta but they did sail from Genoa to Naples as Signore and Signora Maurizio Bracca accompanied by their daughter Delila Bracca. She wore a new pair of gold earrings, a traveling gift from her mother. At Naples Editta insisted they splurge on second-class tickets for the remainder of their trip on the *SS Werra* to New York City. For the extra money the little family could enjoy their own private cabin, however modest, instead of cramming into steerage class where proud men suffered the humiliation of being separated from their frightened women and children.

Two days out of Naples Editta's cough reached an uncontrollable level, as did the blood and pus that returned as quickly as she spit it out. Fevered and chilled, she took to her bunk bed. Once again, as Delila had done many times in Genoa, she climbed into this narrow bed and snuggled into the boney curve of Editta's spine, hoping to stop the shivering that grew worse with each hour.

Annoyed by the inconvenience Maurizio waited until he'd eaten breakfast before contacting the ship's doctor, who waited another two hours before coming to the cabin and examining Editta.

"Pneumonia brought on by consumption," he told Maurizio and Delila. "I suggest you think about altering your original plan for America. This woman will never pass the physical examination when the ship docks in New York."

The status of Editta's immigration would become a concern no one needed to address. On the morning of their fourth day sailing the Atlantic, Delila was holding her mother when she felt the most physical all intimacies—that of another person's death—for the second time in less than two months. The tears she spilled were out of relief as much as for the grief she forced upon herself. Soon after, Maurizio retuned from his stroll around the deck.

"While you were gone, the Angel of Death came and took Mama," Delila said.

The expression on Maurizio's face registered the same relief Delila felt. "This Angel of Death, you saw it ... him?"

"I didn't have to. I felt his presence, felt him suck the life from Mama. Slowly at first, allowing her to resist, then faster, taking her last breath with him when they left together."

"Bah! What does a kid like you know?"

More than you ever will, Delila thought, but held her tongue.

*****

A few hours later four crewman carried Editta's body to the *SS Werra's* lower deck where the captain conducted a brief but moving ceremony evoking more dignity and respect for her death than ever had been accorded her life. Delila stood beside Maurizio and slipped her hand into his. He started to pull away but then squeezed her hand in a way that brought Delila a unexpected measure of comfort. Indeed, as a sharp contrast to the typical Mediterranean display of bereavement, Editta's daughter and the man thought to be her husband showed little emotion. How bravely the poor woman's survivors bear their grief, murmured nearby sympathetic passengers. Delila figured they had attended the service out of curiosity, relieved the deceased belonged to a family other than their own.

"Heavenly Father, accept the earthly remains of ... this woman ..." The captain checked the scrap of paper in his hand. "Editta ..."

"Lobianco," Maurizio whispered.

"Lobianco Bracca," Delila said aloud.

The captain looked from Maurizio to Delila, and when they both nodded, he continued. "The earthly remains of Editta ... Lobianco ... Bracca. Ashes to ashes, dust to dust. Amen."

And with that, Delilah's mother was given to the sea. Just as Tito had been a few weeks before.

End of Excerpt

To find out where to purchase
Chicago's Headmistress
and other works by Loretta Giacoletto,
please visit Loretta Giacoletto's website:
www.lorettagiacoletto.com.

ABOUT THE AUTHOR

Loretta Giacoletto divides her time between the St. Louis Metropolitan area and Missouri's Lake of the Ozarks where she concentrates on writing fiction and essays for Loretta on Life while her husband cruises the waters for bass and crappie. Their five children have left the once chaotic nest but occasionally return for her to-die-for ravioli and roasted peppers topped with garlic-laden *bagna càuda*. An avid traveler, she has visited numerous countries in Europe and Asia but Italy remains her favorite, especially the area from where her family originates: the Piedmont region near the Italian alps.

Made in the USA
Charleston, SC
24 November 2012